D0017020

ROBYN CARR

Runaway

MISTRESS

MIRA®

ISBN 0-7783-2174-6

RUNAWAY MISTRESS

www.MIRABooks.com

Printed in U.S.A.

For Heather Hudson Carr, my favorite.

One

When she walked into the Fort Lauderdale Executive Airport, heads turned. Not just the men's, but the women's, as well. Jennifer was used to this; she did not come by her fabulous looks by accident. Trim, tan, blond, leggy, buxom, with a face that could stop time, she drew the attention of everyone she passed. She went to the counter and recognized the agent, a woman she'd seen several times before. "Hi, Elaine. Jennifer Chaise, here to meet Mr. Noble for the Las Vegas flight."

"He hasn't checked in yet, Ms. Chaise, but you can board if you like."

"Thank you, but I'll wait until he gets here."

"Why don't we go ahead and load your luggage to save time?" she said.

Jennifer gave a nod and a smile, glanced over her shoulder to the skycap who had followed her with her bags, and then went to a leather sofa in the waiting room. From there she could see the terminal entrance.

As she waited for her gentleman friend, Nick, to arrive at the airport, Jennifer reminded herself that not all that long ago she'd been a girl who couldn't afford a bus ticket. Now she was a woman waiting for a private jet. Who would've guessed?

The private jet sent by the MGM Casino Resort would whisk them away to Las Vegas, where they would spend a few days. Nick was what was known as a Whale—a high-stakes gambler. She assumed he lost as well as he won because at least four times a year the MGM would send their Gulfstream to pick him up. But, according to them, gamblers never lost. And, despite the fact that he was married, Jennifer was the woman who accompanied him on these trips.

Jennifer was something of a gambler herself, but she didn't wager money. She put *herself* on the line, betting that she could keep someone like Nick Noble so enchanted by her charms and beauty that he would be a generous suitor. It required quite a lot of skill and confidence. The skill she had acquired over time, but the confidence always threatened to elude her. Sometimes she was required to fake it. All the people who ogled her were completely unaware that beneath the veneer of wealth and glamour beat the heart of an uncertain girl who had come from nothing.

She reached over her knee to smooth her two-thousand-dollar eelskin boots over her shin—they were as soft as butter and were her favorite. There was a time years and years ago, when she was eight or nine years old, that her mother picked through a Dumpster, where she'd seen a pair of discarded shoes just about the right size for Jennifer. That had been an especially bad patch for them. Maybe that was what had fostered her passionate love of footwear. These boots were sage-colored and perfect with the cream skirt and jacket she wore; the skirt was short with a strategic slit up the left side and the jacket buttoned just under her breasts to emphasize her cleavage.

If it were left up to her, she might choose a lower heel, but Nick, for some strange reason, preferred that she look as tall and long-legged as possible. She was a respectable five foot five, but any one of her collection of high heels so exaggerated her height that she appeared five ten. The irony was that Nick was *not* tall. He was a short guy—maybe five-seven—and had a real thing for tall, thin blondes. No short-man complex there. In fact, Nick probably thought he was six-two. His ego was at least that big.

A half hour passed as she waited, and although people couldn't help but stare at her, she didn't fidget. The cabin attendant for their jet came into the terminal twice to speak to Elaine, ostensibly to see if all her passengers had finally arrived. By now the crew would be getting antsy. Nick would never tolerate tardiness in others, but he was rarely on time himself. He could be both aggressive and passive-aggressive, not always a winning combination.

Jennifer pulled her long mane of golden hair over her shoulder and stroked it as if it were a pet. Nick *loved* her hair. So had a few gentlemen before him. She cared for it as if it were an only child.

Elaine came out from behind the counter and approached her. "Ms. Chaise, are you sure you don't want to go ahead and board?" the agent asked her.

She smiled patiently at the young woman. "It won't get him here any faster, Elaine. I'll just wait for Mr. Noble."

"I don't suppose you've heard from him?"

"No."

"Have you, by any chance, called his cell or his car?"

She merely shook her head; there was no point in trying to explain. Nick didn't like being chased down, hounded or prodded, so calling him would only have the opposite effect. He'd just take his time, no matter who was waiting. He said he'd be here, and he would be here. He'd keep everyone waiting, though, in case there was any question as to who was the most important person in this party.

Finally, almost an hour after the scheduled departure time, the doors to the small terminal opened and Nick strode through, rolling up his shirtsleeves as he entered. He was a little powerhouse with broad shoulders and thick, hard thighs. His arms were tanned and very strong, but he had small, gentle hands. He wasn't exactly handsome, but he wasn't bad-looking, either. He had bushy brows, a bald head and twinkling blue eyes. Women found him sexy, but whether that was because of his looks or his power seemed irrelevant.

Nick was the kind of man it was very difficult to say no to; he was flamboyant, exciting, wealthy and had a slightly dangerous edge. Perhaps it was the constant presence of one, two or even three large, quiet men that gave him an aura that was both hard to ignore and impenetrable. Jennifer referred to them as the Butlers, which made Nick laugh, but the more accurate term *goon* came to mind. She tried not to think too hard about them. Nick had quite a collection of men who worked for him, followed him around, traveled with him. Errand boys. Jennifer assumed it made Nick feel important to have them always a few steps behind, ready to do whatever he asked. On this trip it was Jesse and Lou who accompanied them.

The airport agent breathed an audible sigh of relief and Jennifer stood. Nick slipped an arm around her waist, kissed her cheek and said, "Hi, baby. We ready to roll?"

"I think they're all ready," she said. "My luggage is on the plane."

"Good girl. Let's do it. I'm feeling lucky."

Jennifer had met Nick Noble two years before. She had just taken a job in a commercial real estate company where her duties included some secretarial work, as well as property management. It was easy and it paid well. She fielded calls from tenants who needed service such as repairs, collected and deposited rents, and kept track of leases. Her office handled a group of office buildings in Fort Lauderdale and Boca Raton and Jennifer believed she had been hired more for her looks than skills. She was definitely front-office material; the businessmen who leased from them were constantly asking her out.

She hadn't been there long when the owner of the properties they managed stopped by. Nick. He took her to lunch that very day and made it clear he was not particularly interested in her performance as a property manager but, rather, he was romantically interested. Now, Jennifer might look like an easy mark with her swollen lips, full perky breasts and clothes carefully chosen to draw attention to her assets, but she was actually cautious. Nick was made to pursue her for a very long time, during which she learned enough about him to make a practical decision. He was married for the third time, had lots of money, several businesses and an iron-clad prenup. Barbara, he said, was very happy with her club, her jewelry, her big house, and was not likely to make any kind of fuss as long as he dinged her bank account on a weekly basis, and paid off the credit cards.

It turned out that Nick's analysis of Barbara wasn't exactly right. Barbara was extremely jealous and given to tantrums that could be very disturbing. But no one, absolutely no one, told Nick Noble what to do. And although Barbara was unhappy about this liaison, she wasn't unhappy enough to give up the wealth she had married. Barbara Noble, wife number three, had been involved with Nick when he was married to wife number two. Jennifer had absolutely no intention of becoming wife number four, and it might have been that fact more than anything that had kept him intrigued this long.

Nick had gone after Jennifer with gusto. He called, dropped by, had her picked up by a driver and taken to this or that restaurant. There were flowers and weekly gifts. He took her out on his yacht and to his villa in Key West. He worked very hard to woo her. And she worked very hard to be alluring. She played a mean game of hard to get.

In the two years she'd been seeing him she had not quit her job. It was important to her self-esteem that she work at something other than being a mistress. True, she was away quite a lot. When Nick wanted her to travel with him, she did. It wasn't as though her supervisor was going to complain. Nick was a very valued client.

Jennifer relaxed in the luxury of the Gulfstream, a glass of champagne on her side table, a novel in her lap. Nick, however, had been on the phone since takeoff. He frequently stood up, paced, raised his voice or shook his fist at the air. She picked up a few words here and there—"Look, goddammit, that's been the program for years!" and "If it's not delivered on time, you'll pay, and you'll pay big!" Jennifer had nearly perfected the fine art of being oblivious. His business wasn't her business. If she got nosy while he was all riled up, his mood would only get worse. She understood that any man who had the amount of fiscal responsibility that he had might have a short fuse now and then.

After a couple of hours in flight, he'd had enough. Jesse and Lou were sitting in the first two seats on the plane, reclined and sleeping, their backs to Jennifer and Nick. Nick asked the flight attendant for a Chivas on the rocks and came over to where Jennifer sat with her feet up on the ottoman. He sat beside her feet and put a hand on her knee.

"What are you reading, babe?"

She gently closed the book and smiled. "Romance."

His hand moved slowly over her knee and under her skirt, caressing her thigh. "That's a good idea," he said with a smile. He sipped his drink and swirled it in the glass, clinking the cubes against the crystal. And his hand went a little higher.

Jennifer stopped him right there. She pressed the book down, refusing his hand farther passage. The flight attendant had handled a little of everything on this job and would probably know enough to turn discreetly away, get very busy in the galley or something, but Jennifer wasn't having that. "Behave yourself," she told him sternly. "And try to be patient."

Nick chuckled and removed his hand, but he leaned toward her. So she kissed him, a deep and promising kiss. She could taste the Scotch on his lips, in his mouth.

When they parted she said, "You be a good boy and you can get in the hot tub with me tonight." But she knew she would probably be splashing around alone while Nick was preoccupied with poker.

The palm of his hand gently brushed her breast. "Yes, Mommy. Let's see what movies we have." He picked up the remote, turned on the overhead screen and read the directory until he found one he liked. Then he settled back on the leather sofa and shared the ottoman with Jennifer, keeping a proprietary hand on her thigh.

She went back to her book. She knew how to make her gentleman toe the line and that was imperative. It kept them interested. They could be like children sometimes, craving limits. She had very strict standards; she must be treated with respect and dignity. The minute a man made the mistake of treating her as property, she was gone.

Jennifer was a professional girlfriend. A mistress. Not a call girl or prostitute. She was an *excellent* girlfriend. The greater part of her subsistence came from her current gentleman, but she absolutely never asked for a thing. Never. It was always a gift, sometimes with her input, sometimes a surprise. The two diamond rings she wore were surprises, but last year Nick wanted to buy her a car and they went together to pick out her Jag.

Of course, had Nick been less than forthcoming with such gifts, she would have moved on long ago.

How does one get into a profession such as this? In Jennifer's case, quite by accident and in all innocence. She was nineteen when her mother died and there was a little bit of money from the sale of her grandparents' house. Just enough to get her from Ohio to Florida and pay first, last and security on a small efficiency. She longed for the sun to warm her heart, for she had found herself suddenly all alone. She had nothing and no one. She didn't know what to do or where to turn. It seemed she had spent her entire life up to that point keeping an eye on her mother, and when she was gone, exhaustion combined with her grief. She needed a change and a little rest.

She got a job in a fine-dining restaurant in Fort Lauderdale bussing tables on her way to being trained as a waitress; she'd heard the money was good when diners dropped a few hundred on their meals and wines. When one of the slim, young hostesses was a no-show for work, the manager slipped Jennifer into a narrow black dress—the hostess uniform—and she began booking reservations, showing people to their tables and in general making nice with the patrons. She did it well, so they kept her in that job. At nineteen, she was hardly a knockout, but she had a kind of slim elegance, an aloofness, that was underscored by the fact that when she smiled she hardly ever showed her teeth because one front tooth was a little gray and she was embarrassed by it.

Within a couple of weeks she was asked out by an older man named Robert who frequented the restaurant. She shied off, declining. Why would she wish to go out to dinner with a man old enough to be her grandfather? "Because he's richer than God," said one of the other hostesses. "And he's sweet as a kitten. Tell him *I'm* free."

That set her to thinking. She was too alone. She had no family; not even a close girlfriend. She was barely getting by on what little money she made. Her best dress belonged to the restaurant—the little black number she wore for hostessing. And this was a *nice* man, well known around Fort Lauderdale. He was the least-dangerous person alive and very, very chivalrous. He just happened to like young women.

She went to dinner with him in her borrowed dress and, to her absolute amazement, had a lovely time. He was kind and thoughtful and patient, and he wanted her to enjoy herself. They became friends, and so it gave him great pleasure to take her places. It was important that she dress appropriately and so they shopped, outfitting her with more clothing at greater expense than she'd ever had in her life. He didn't think the neighborhood in which she rented her one-room studio was very safe and so he lent her the use of one of his company's corporate apartments, rent free. He had several that were usually used by traveling executives. One more or less made no difference.

And he sent her to a cosmetic dentist. His treat. Her smile, he had said, was stunning, and she should use it often.

Eventually she even enjoyed sleeping with him, but that wasn't really a priority for him. He spent the greater part of his energy on business, a lesser amount in the company of his lovely young mistress, and an even lesser amount with his wife. Jennifer remained his girl-friend for about two years.

Because Jennifer had never been able to trust any-one to take care of her, she was completely prepared for their relationship to be temporary. When it was over, most of the accoutrements would vanish. The apart-ment and leased car would have to be returned, though being rich and a gentleman, he would very likely insist she keep the clothing and jewelry. She was determined to be prepared. So while her gentleman picked up the tab, Jennifer put a little bit of money aside for a rainy day. Growing up hand to mouth had provided her with considerable restraint in spending, and discipline in saving. Jennifer was going to take care of Jennifer, and she realized she had stumbled upon a good way to do it.

The rest, as they say, was history. The first gentle-man came along when she was nineteen, Nick when she was twenty-eight. There'd been a few in between. She had been very fond of Robert and sad when he moved on, and Nick had grown on her in the last couple of years, but the others had been merely business arrangements. The only requirements were that they be rich, civil and derive great pleasure from treating her well.

As Jennifer walked down the wide hall of the MGM Grand Hotel, her extra-short skirt swaying back and forth across her shapely thighs, her high-heeled boots padding softly on the rich and thick carpet, men turned and watched as she passed. Hotel guests and bellhops and maintenance men. Even here in Las Vegas where great beauty abounded, they filled their eyes with her. She walked past a little boy, grasping his mother's hand, who turned and looked up at her. He couldn't be more than four and was fascinated. That's men—so visual. She looked down at him and smiled and winked.

Her shiny platinum hair bounced down her back to her waist. Her eyes, made lavender by the contacts she wore, sparkled under thick lashes, and her lips, full, pouty and glossy, enhanced by collagen, begged to be kissed. To say nothing of her breasts—right up there where they should be thanks to relentless chest presses and a small saline implant under each one, compliments of gentleman number three. If she'd had it this together ten years earlier, she might've tried modeling rather than this current vocation. But this look hadn't come cheap or easy.

She and Nick had been in Las Vegas for three days and tomorrow would be their last day. He was on a real run in high-stakes poker, and every time he wanted to get back to the game he had treated her. One of the gifts was the new tennis bracelet she wore. As well, he gave her a nice crisp stack of Bens—hundred dollar bills—

with instructions to entertain herself. He spent a great deal on her, and she used the money to stay fashionable and desirable, always tucking a little away for that rainy day just around the corner.

She'd had a very good time, though she hadn't spent much of it with Nick. She had shopped, taken in a couple of movies in the screening room, worked out in the private gym, spent some time in the spa being massaged, manicured and pedicured, and she'd caught up on her reading in the cabana by the private pool. Jennifer was tanned, but it wasn't from the sun. She wouldn't subject her skin to that. She was *spray*-tanned. Once a week she would have a facial, massage and a spray tanning that would begin to fade after four days. When she went to the pool or the beach, she lay under an umbrella or cabana. Her skin, she was proud to note, was nearly flawless.

She was with Nick every night, of course. Or make that the wee hours, after many hours of poker. At fifty-four Nick was fit and energetic, sometimes demanding, often relentless when it came to getting what he wanted. And if he wanted her at 4:00 a.m., she was compelled to oblige. Thankfully, it was only on trips such as this that she was on such a schedule. In Florida they kept separate residences and Nick rarely spent the whole night with her.

Sometimes she wondered if Nick wasn't just a little more than she could handle. He was certainly the most virile man she'd been with. Every time she began to consider ending this affair, whether because of Nick's demands or his wife's instability, he'd give her something amazing, reminding her that he was worth every hour of her time. His gift to her last year had been a condo on the beach, and she was weakened by her love for it. Even with her growing savings accounts, it was way out of her league.

However, life could be lonely. Working in a business that catered to Nick, and having a flexible schedule so she could be at his beck and call didn't make the other women in the office particularly friendly. But then, she'd always been a loner. She knew what they said about her, but she was no slut. There had only been a scant few men in her life since she was a teen, and she never dated more than one man at a time. Never.

These were the thoughts that were running through Jennifer's mind as she made her way through the crowds of people in the hotel on her way back to the room. The MGM was putting them up in a suite that was part of a private wing known as the Mansion. Very prestigious surroundings, complete with a crew of chefs, valets and *real* butlers. She'd been there several times with him—he considered her good luck—and true to form, he'd been winning, which made him fun and frisky. It was very easy to get used to living in high style like this, but she didn't take it for granted. She knew how quickly such fortunes could shift—just as she'd had rough times with her mom, she'd had a few high times. They never lasted very long, but she remembered them fondly.

When she reached their suite she quietly opened the door and was instantly taken aback by shouting.

"I don't ask your permission for anything! I'm here

for poker, and if I'd wanted you and all your bitching here, I'd have brought you!"

That was Nick. She peeked in and made eye contact with "butler" number one, Lou. Lou was a mountain of a man. He stood in the foyer, his back to the sitting room, arms crossed over his chest.

"You can't just bring your bimbo to Vegas and toss me to the sharks in Palm Beach while you're here screwing around. They'll eat me alive!"

Uh-oh. That would be Mrs. Nick.

"I'm here for *poker!* I can screw around in *Florida!*"

"Everyone knows you left me at home while you brought that whore to Vegas!"

Jennifer stiffened indignantly. She took exception. At the very least, the pot was speaking of the kettle.

"Why you worrying about what everyone else thinks? You got your big house, your big rings. You don't play second fiddle. You got your *masseuse.*"

"Oh, you have such a dirty mind! Maurice is *gay!*" And with that there was a crash. She was throwing things. It was time to give her some space.

Jennifer backed quietly out of the room, gently pulling the door closed. She went downstairs to a quiet bar, sat at a corner booth and ordered a foamy margarita. She sipped it very slowly, killing time. She'd give Nick and his spouse time to work through this tiff. If she ended up with her own room and a first-class ticket back to Fort Lauderdale, it wouldn't be the first time. It was no big deal.

"Hey, sweetheart." She looked up into the deep brown eyes of a rather handsome and well-dressed man. "Buy you a drink?"

"Thank you, no. I'm waiting for someone. He'll be along soon."

One corner of his mouth lifted in a mocking smile. "Blow him off," he suggested.

She placed both her hands on the table, fingers splayed, roughly sixty thousand dollars' worth of gems glittering on her fingers and wrist. "Oh, I don't think so. I *really* don't think so," she said sweetly with her positively shattering smile. He was dismissed.

She knew better than to flirt or lead men on. For one thing, Nick wouldn't stand for it. More than that, she'd seen plenty of women get themselves in serious trouble biting the hand that fed them. Not to mention the number she'd seen take a dive because they were stupid enough to fall hopelessly in love and believe everything they were told.

Jennifer had never been in love. At least, not since her sophomore year of high school. The combination of watching her mother suffer through frequent broken hearts and having her own trod upon by a stupid high school jock had taught her more than she wanted to know about that emotion. She thought it best to rise above it and live the good life. And her life was *good*.

The fight going on upstairs was upsetting, however. According to Nick, the honeymoon with Barbara was over and they'd gone their separate ways. Jennifer didn't like conflict. She never fought. She was a pleaser. Nick was not similarly disposed; he had a bit of a temper. He was a little scary sometimes. He treated her with kid gloves, but even though she tried to tune him out, she'd heard the way he yelled at people on the phone, threatening them with dire consequences if they didn't get something done to his satisfaction.

That was precisely why she minded her own business and tried not to listen.

She thought two hours away from the suite would be enough, so she gave it another thirty minutes. If the wife had won, she'd be intercepted by one of the guys, like Lou, and escorted discreetly to her own room or suite. If the wife had been successfully sent on her way, she would find Nick, or a note, instructing her to meet him there later. Frankly, she was betting on Nick.

She returned to the suite and quietly unlocked and opened the door, peeking into the foyer. Silence. She stepped inside and listened. Not a sound. Then she heard running water and a man's muffled voice. She plastered that ready smile on her lips and moved toward the sitting room—and was stopped short. A battle had taken place there; a bloody battle. Furniture was tipped over, glass sparkled on the floor and there were actual splatters of blood on the white furniture and carpet.

"Just get rid of her," she heard Nick say.

"Yeah, like *where?*" one of his guys asked.

"Who cares? Don't worry about money, just do it up right. Don't want to draw attention here. And clean up this place—I don't want housekeeping in here asking a lot of questions."

Immobilized by the shock of what she was hearing and seeing, Jennifer stood in the doorway, frozen. Then she saw Nick, shirtsleeves rolled up, splatters of what must have been his wife's blood on his shirt, holding an ice pack to his eye. He walked from the bedroom to the bar. She heard the clink of ice cubes in a glass. He hadn't seen her.

"You seen that bimbo?" Nick yelled into the other room.

"She stuck her head in the door just when Babs started pitching the crystal around the room."

"Shit. Find her. We're gonna have to do something about her, too."

She stepped quietly into the coat closet just inside the foyer, out of sight but not out of earshot. She was just in time. Lou and the other "butler," Jesse, came marching past to leave the suite. "We're gonna need something big and easy to handle."

"Golf bag, maybe."

"Yeah. Or big suitcase on wheels. Y'know, they hold a *lot.*"

And they were gone.

In her entire life, as bad as it had been during some periods, she'd never imagined she'd encounter anything like this. But now, as she stood in the dark closet, a crack of light from the partially opened door streaking across her face, she knew she should have seen it coming. His temper was obvious, even if it hadn't been turned on her. She sensed his businesses were shady, though she had no idea how. But what manner of man needs a couple of big bruisers hanging close at all times?

After a few moments she pushed the door open. She was going to flee, but she heard the shower running. Nick was fastidious. He'd want to wash up if he'd been mussed or stained with blood.

She knew she shouldn't, but she just had to know.

She passed through the chaos of the sitting room and crept toward the bedroom door. The sound of the shower gave her a sense of cover. She looked into the room and there, sprawled facedown on the bed, was Mrs. Nick. Her hand dangled lifelessly off the edge and her hair looked wet in the back. Blood?

God, he'd done it. They'd gotten into it and, whether deliberately or accidentally, in a fit of rage he'd killed her. And now Nick's boys were going to get rid of her body. And then he was going to "do something" about her.

She heard something and craned her neck. He was *singing* in the shower! That's when she knew she'd hit bottom. She had to run. She couldn't take any chances. Any man who could sing in the shower while his wife lay dead a few feet away was no man to trifle with.

She left the suite, left the Mansion and went through the casino. She took a cab to the airport. She had no luggage. Only that little tiny Kate Spade bag, which fortunately had quite a lot of money in it. She didn't know what to do, but she knew what *not* to do. She would not wait around the airport for a flight to Florida so she could be found there. She wouldn't flee to her condo, the first place Nick would look.

But she bought a ticket to Florida on her credit card. Then she bought a pair of sunglasses and a scarf with cash. She covered her platinum hair and her lavender eyes and took another cab, this one to a suburb of Las Vegas. And there, nestled in a little neighborhood inn that did not feature gambling, she cooled her heels and waited for news of a murdered woman. There was a little strip mall and grocery store nearby, a drugstore, a coffee shop, a Goodwill store and army surplus. She only went out after dark, with her bright white-blond hair covered. She purchased a sweat suit and tennis shoes, some cotton underwear, hair dye and a ball cap. Later she picked up some men's clothing at army surplus, hiding her luscious body in the deep folds.

And every day she picked up a newspaper, and every day she stayed glued to the television.

There was no news regarding Barbara Noble. Four days had passed and there was nothing. She called the MGM and asked for Mr. Nick Noble's suite and was told he had checked out. She started to wonder if she had overreacted. Maybe he hadn't meant to get rid of the *body*, but just get the wife out of town. Should she just fly back to Florida, tell him his temper had scared her, apologize for being a flake, get back to work, get on with life? But first, she called the Noble household in Palm Beach and asked for Barbara.

"I'm sorry, Mrs. Noble is not in."

"Can you tell me when it would be a good time to reach her?"

"Mrs. Noble is out of the country and I'm not sure when she plans to return."

Out of the country? The next day there was a small item in the newspaper, but it wasn't about Barbara. It was about Jennifer. The headline read Missing. Her picture was beneath. It was from a photo taken when she was sailing with Nick. Her long blond hair whipped in the wind and her sexy smile was confident and sure; for once the newspaper photo wasn't grainy. The story read:

"Jennifer Chaise, age thirty, of Fort Lauderdale has been missing for five days. She traveled to Las Vegas with friends, who say she disappeared suddenly, without taking any of her belongings with her. Her travel companions report missing a great deal of money and jewelry, and Ms Chaise is believed to be either a witness to a robbery, a victim, or a suspect, and police would like to interview her."

She dropped the paper into her lap in shock. Oh, my God, she thought. And then with a wry smile her thought was, nicely done, Nick. Accuse me of a crime and, when the police find me for you, drop the whole thing. But you'll have *me*.

There was one more sentence. "A generous reward has been offered for information leading to the whereabouts of Ms. Chaise. If you have information, please call…"

She fell back on the bed and thought, *Just when I thought I had everything all figured out. Just when I thought I knew what I was doing, knew what I wanted, knew what it would take to get it. Just when I was thinking about my early retirement.*

She rolled over on her stomach. *Boy, talk about miscalculations.*

Two

The effect of seeing her picture in the paper caused Jennifer to decide she'd better go a little farther afield than a Las Vegas suburb, so she got on a bus. She wasn't sure where it was bound, so she just rode for a half hour through a stretch of desert and got off in the first little town she came to. She walked for about twenty minutes and, after passing several decent places, found a motel that had clearly seen better days. It was a seedy-looking place between a junkyard and a railroad track; there were only twelve rooms. Nick Noble would *never* find it. And if he did find it, he would never expect Jennifer to be there.

She looked at the phone book in room number eight and saw that she was in Boulder City. Good enough, she thought. She'd never even heard of the place. Surely she wouldn't draw much attention here. She could have stayed at one of the casinos off the Strip; the bus had passed several of them, but they were large and their parking lots crowded. Too many people around, increasing the odds of being recognized as the missing girl in the newspaper.

She looked at the map the phone book provided. Boulder City, a small town a mere twenty-five miles from Las Vegas, on the edge of Lake Mead on the way to Hoover Dam. This was the last place Nick would expect to find the classy, bejeweled Jennifer Chaise.

She stood in front of the mirror for a while, not recognizing the woman who stared back at her. Wardrobe by army surplus—very unlike the wardrobe she had left behind. Her face, washed clean of makeup, left her looking very plain and pale. Her expensive artificial tan was fast disappearing. The shock of finding herself on the run likely contributed to her wan look. She flushed the colored contact lenses down the toilet and her eyes went from that sexy lavender to an ordinary brown. Her vision, fortunately, was perfect. She clipped her long acrylic nails and felt briefly crippled.

She had attempted to dye her waist-length golden hair to brown, but had ended up with a rather sickly gray—absolute proof that she'd tried to color it with drugstore supplies. Scissors in hand, she meant to rectify the situation, but a tear gathered in her eye. She'd pampered that sexy mane for how many years? Nick adored her hair; he loved to crunch it up in his fists and bury his face in it. Well, that would never happen again. "And if it does happen," she said aloud, "it would probably be just one last crunch before he crushes my skull." But the hand with the scissors trembled. "Oh, suck it up," she told the reflection. "We'll save a fortune. And it's only temporary—until we figure out what to do and where to go." She stared into her own eyes and, realizing she was talking to a mirror image, said, "Oh, my God, it's hereditary. We have our mother's wackiness."

And then she lopped it off, close to the scalp. She continued this drastic amputation, tears running down her cheeks, until all she was left with was a short, spiky cap of really strange-colored hair. It looked as if someone had colored her hair badly—and then cut it badly. How different could she be? And what could she do to become invisible and utterly unrecognizable?

She thought about it for a moment and then she shaved her head. After brief consideration, the eyebrows that she'd spent a fortune having professionally colored and waxed into a curvaceous arch also went. If she remembered correctly, her original brows were black, bushy, shapeless and met over the bridge of her nose.

Then, despite her determination to be stronger than her circumstances, she cried in a bed with a lumpy mattress and a thin sheet. What had she been thinking, getting involved with a man like Nick? With *any* of the rich older men she'd attracted? It had only served to isolate her from the world. Had she really thought she was so smart, so immune to having her heart broken? This was proof positive that you didn't have to be in love to have your heart broken. She was in a crappy motel in a tiny desert town outside Las Vegas with nothing. With no one. Even worse, now she was in actual peril. Talk about a plan gone awry.

The month was March and she awoke the following morning to chilly air and leaden skies, and the sound of rain. The heater in the room didn't work and everything seemed inevitable.

The morning sky was just painting the dark clouds gray when she couldn't take the cold, dank hotel room another second. She bundled up in a khaki-green windbreaker, her scarf wrapped around her neck and her baseball cap covering her bald head. All her worldly goods were tucked into a canvas backpack. The motel office was still closed; no one there to get the heater going in her room. So she set out to see if there was more to this place than a junkyard and train tracks.

A few blocks away the road forked—the highway went left and she went right. Another few blocks revealed a small town, a street lined with cafés and shops not yet open. She counted three restaurants, all apparently of the no-tablecloth variety. It was an old street with worn sidewalks, but some trendy shops and eateries were peppered amid the older ones, perhaps recent additions to snag the visitors to Hoover Dam, and travelers en route to the Grand Canyon as they passed by the town. The manager of Starbucks was just unlocking the door. A clock in the window of a gift shop read six-thirty. There was a small corner market that looked no bigger than a convenience store, but it displayed a large variety of fresh fruits and vegetables in the window, and a sign that boasted a sale on ground sirloin.

A big white hotel with signs that advertised Underground Dancing and a Dam Museum stood down the street. Across the parking lot was a small brick building painted pink—a dance studio.

She took a left, getting off the main street, and a few blocks later found a park, library, theater and an old residential neighborhood full of tiny, multicolored houses nestled amid tall, full trees. They looked like playhouses, street after street of them. There were obviously no neighborhood-association rules about conformity in this part of the world, as interspersed with well-maintained houses and manicured lawns were battered-looking homes inside cyclone fences that surrounded dirt and weeds. The houses, however, were almost all the same shape. Except one at the end of the street, a square two-story, with a huge peace sign painted on a tall tree stump and flowered sheets covering the windows. It looked like a throwback from the sixties.

Around the corner she saw the post office and wondered if this was the center of town. It didn't even resemble anything close to a desert here in Boulder City; the foliage was thick, and most of the trees had retained their leaves through winter while others showed the promise of new buds on bare branches. Shrubs were dense; grass was green.

She passed a yarn shop, a used-book store and a health-food store. A sign stuck out farther down the street that read Nails. A couple of young women jogged around the park, and farther down the street an elderly man walked his dog. She turned onto a side street, and right between a dry cleaner and dog-grooming salon was a diner with the lights on and a sign in the window that read Open. Above the door in fading red paint was the name of the place—the Tin Can.

This place hadn't seen a renovation in a long time yet was clean and well kept. Since there was a Starbucks on the main street, she supposed this diner was seeing less action than it used to—there was only one customer. With the stools at the counter, booths covered in Naugahyde lining the wall and Formica tabletops, it had the look of a fifties greasy spoon. But a nice, warm one. It reminded her of a place she used to go with her grandpa when she was small.

The bell jingled as she entered. "'Morning," a man called from behind the counter.

She took a stool right in the middle of the completely vacant counter. The man in the booth at the back of the diner had a newspaper spread out in front of him.

"'Morning," she returned. "Coffee?"

He had a cup in front of her in seconds. "Cold and wet out there, ain't it."

"Freezing," she said, pulling her jacket tighter.

"It should be a lot warmer by now. There're buds on the trees and the grass is greening up. Spring's 'bout here. I'll let you warm up a little, then we'll talk about some breakfast," he said. She looked up at him. He squinted at what he could see of her face under the bill of her hat. For a moment she was confused, and then she remembered she had no eyebrows. With a self-conscious laugh, she plucked the cap off her head and exposed her bald head and naked brow. He almost jumped back in surprise. "Whoa. That's a new look now, ain't it?"

"Shocking," she supplied, putting her cap back on.

"Cold, I take it."

"That's for sure."

He was a big man around sixty. Overweight, with a thick, ornery crop of yellow-gray, strawlike hair and square face and rosy cheeks—like a sixty-year-old little boy with big ears. She saw a face she could only describe as accessible. Open. He had friendly blue eyes set in the crinkles of age, a double chin and an engaging smile—one tooth missing to the back of the right side. "I got biscuits and gravy," he said proudly.

"I'm not really hungry," she said. "Just cold."

"You been outside long?"

Oh-oh. He suspected she was homeless. The army surplus fashion, the backpack, the ball cap. "No. Well, maybe a little. I've a room at that roadside place about six blocks from here and I woke up freezing. No heat. And the motel office wasn't open yet."

"Behind that scrap heap and junkyard?"

"That's the one."

"Charlie is not generous with his guests," the man in the booth said with a heavy Spanish accent. "You should say he give you the night free."

"He should," the man behind the counter said. "But he won't. They don't come much tighter than Charlie."

The man in the booth folded his paper, stood up and stretched. Then he took an apron off a hook and put it on. Ah, the cook, she realized. "Um—are you done with that paper?" she asked him.

"Help yourself, *mija*." He proceeded around the counter to the grill and began heating and scraping it. The sounds of breakfast being started filled the diner and soon the smells followed. Jennifer settled herself into the same booth so she could spread the paper out in front of her.

A little while passed, then the owner brought the coffeepot to her. "Have any interest in breakfast yet?" he asked.

"Really, I'm not very hungry."

"You don't mind me saying so—you look a little on the lean side."

"I'm just lucky that way."

"If it's a matter of money—"

She was startled. "I can pay," she said, maybe a little too proudly. Truly, if he had any idea how much money was stuffed inside the Kate Spade bag that was stuffed inside the backpack, he'd be stunned. Not to mention the jewelry. The dawning came slowly. Don't protest too much, she told herself. It was perfectly all right if people thought she was a little down on her luck. And it wasn't as though she didn't know the role—she was intimately acquainted with it. "I might have something in a while. I just want to warm up. And have a look at the paper."

"Sure thing. Just say the word when you're ready. Adolfo has started breakfast."

She drank two more cups of coffee while she combed the paper and found nothing about the Nobles or herself. How long would Nick get away with pretending his wife was out of the country? Surely someone would begin to miss Barbara! Her masseuse, for example.

But who would miss *you*, Jennifer? she asked herself. Would her boss raise an alarm? Ah, her boss actually introduced her to Nick, whom he would probably call. "Nick," he would say. "Jennifer didn't come back to work. Do you have any idea...?" "Oh, Artie, my fault," Nick would say. "I should've called you. She skipped in Las Vegas with most of the cash in my wallet. Met someone with a bigger yacht, I guess. You know these bimbos."

And the women in the office who didn't like her would be just as glad she was gone. She had eschewed the friendships of women to avoid the inevitable jealousy. And, to be free of the commitments friendship brought so she could be available at the whim of her current gentleman friend. Nick, like the others before him, didn't like to plan in advance; he expected her to be ready at a moment's notice. She had kept herself virtually friendless. For the first time in ten years, she regretted that.

Oh, why didn't I go to the police right away! Too afraid. Afraid that, unable to prove anything, they wouldn't believe her. They wouldn't protect her, and before very long she would meet with some unfortunate accident. Or maybe she'd leave the country, like Barbara Noble....

A shadow cast over her newspaper caused her to jump, and there he was again, coffeepot in hand. "Ah, I maybe ought to say I'm sorry. Didn't mean to make light of your—you know—hair. Was it, ah, chemo? Something like that?"

She had a momentary temptation to pretend to have had cancer, but she didn't dare tempt fate that far. Her head bald, her eyes red-rimmed from crying, she probably looked horrible to the old guy. What to tell him? But then, did she have to admit to anything at all? This was a diner, for God's sake. Not a shrink's office or police interrogation.

The look on his face was so sweet. "You just worry about people all the time, don't you?"

"No, I—" He stopped and seemed to gather himself up. "I worry about people," he admitted

"Don't worry about me. I'm not sick and I'm not homeless." I am merely a brainless bimbo on the run from a murderer, she wanted to add.

"Good," he said. He warmed her coffee again before turning away.

The drizzle outside suddenly turned into a relentless splatter against the window. She walked to the front of the diner to look out and was startled to see an elderly woman with a walker and a dog struggling up the curb. The wind and rain lashed at her so hard she almost lost her footing. Jennifer bolted out the door to help her. She hadn't even given the dog a thought, and maybe that was a good thing because she might've hesitated. The dog growled, but not convincingly. Jennifer grasped the woman at the elbow to steady her and told the dog to hush.

The other thing she hadn't thought about was letting the dog in the diner, which she also did. Well, the dog was with the old woman and both were drenched. Adolfo came running with a couple of dish towels and some rapid-fire Spanish, but he wasn't fast enough. The dog, an old and overweight yellow Lab, immediately gave a vigorous shake.

"Aiiee, Alicia," he said. "I'll be mopping all the morning."

"Oh, Alice, you're going to get us kicked out of here for sure. Morning, Buzz."

"Louise," he said. "Don't you have a lick of sense? You shouldn't be out in this weather."

"It's not a hurricane, for God's sake," she grumbled.

"I thought maybe you'd stay home today. It's awful out there. I'll get your tea."

She looked into Jennifer's eyes and said, "That was nice of you. And brave—how did you know Alice wouldn't chew off your arm?"

She continued to lead the woman into the diner and pulled out a chair at one of the few tables. "I'm not brave, but maybe stupid. I didn't even think about the dog till she growled." She gave her a pat. "Alice, is it? How do you do?"

"Well, fortunately, she's sweet as honey—"

"And as old as God," Buzz added, bringing a cup and saucer to the table. He sniffed the air. "Nothing smells quite as bad as that, does it? Wet dog?"

Things in the diner seemed to settle into a routine that everyone but Jennifer was accustomed to. The dog lay under the table at her mistress's feet, Louise pulled her own paper out of the large satchel hidden under her coat, Adolfo muttered in Spanish as he mopped the floor inside the door, and Buzz was putting out coffee cups along the counter. Mopping done, Adolfo was back at the grill, cooking and whistling. Louise seemed to be humming along, albeit off-key.

Jennifer went back to her paper and coffee. It wasn't

very long before he was back again. Buzz. This time he had a plate. Unable to resist the temptation to feed her, he brought scrambled eggs, wheat toast and sausage. He put it down in the middle of her paper. "You a vegetarian?" he asked.

She shook her head. She treated him to a smile. "You're very annoying, you know that?"

"I'll get you some juice. You ought to have juice."

She thought about the last time she had had eggs. It was in the suite with Nick. She'd been wearing a silk peignoir designed by Vera Wang. Eggs Benedict, served under sterling with mimosas and braised potatoes. A beautiful tray of pastries had been sent up with the brunch, but Jennifer never touched sweets. She didn't have her figure by accident.

"Here's your juice."

"Um, would you mind...? Could I have a jelly doughnut please? A big one?"

A genuinely happy smile broke over his face. Buzz liked seeing people eat. He had that doughnut in front of her in no time. "Eat your eggs first," he said.

"Yes, sir."

That was one thing about going undercover, she thought. You don't have to constantly diet. And I'll be damned if I'll ever again work on my looks for a man!

She flipped open the menu that sat behind the napkin dispenser and looked at the prices of what she was eating and drinking. The food was so cheap she almost gasped out loud. How in the world could he make a living, giving food away like that?

Her mind wandered to her classy little condo on the

Fort Lauderdale beach. She often had her breakfast, or at least morning coffee, on the veranda with a spectacular view of the ocean. It was small but elegant, furnished by Henredon, decorated by Nelson Little out of New York. Her carpet and sofas and chairs and ottomans were white accented with ecru, plum and eggplant pillows and throws.

Nick would probably have it up for sale in a week. The homeless of Fort Lauderdale would no doubt be wearing her designer labels within the month.

Buzz's eggs were delicious. Melt-in-your-mouth delicious. Must use a ton of butter.

A few people wandered in while Jennifer ate and all of them knew Buzz and Louise. Adolfo would occasionally peek over the back counter and say, *"Buenos días."* There was a man in his fifties who took a quick cup of coffee on his way to opening up his store, the young housewives she'd seen jogging in the park a while earlier who had been suddenly drenched by the rain stopped in and a woman pulled her car right up to the front door and ran in to have her thermos filled. From the conversation, Jennifer gathered she was a Realtor, one not exactly thrilled about showing houses in such weather.

She noticed the elderly woman, Louise, getting to her feet and shrugging into her coat.

"Hey there, Louise. Let Adolfo give you a lift home. It's still drizzling."

"I won't melt," she said.

"I'm not worried about melting. I'm worried about slipping."

"Watch your step, then," she shot back, clearly knowing full well he was worried about *her* slipping. This made Jennifer laugh and say, "You tell him, Louise."

"You know what I mean...." Buzz said.

"I walk here to walk, not to ride. I'm not worried about a little rain."

Alice lumbered to her feet, stretched almost painfully, and took slow steps toward the door with her mistress taking slow steps behind her, inching along with the walker.

"Louise, I'm pleading here—"

"Get over it, Buzz," she said, reaching the door and pushing it open. Buzz came around the counter to hold the door, but Louise never looked back. He shook his head as he watched her go, then went back behind the counter in defeat.

Jennifer had never taken her jacket off. She slipped her arms through the backpack straps and went to the counter. She pulled six dollars out of her pocket and put it on the counter next to the cash register. "Do you have an umbrella?" she asked him.

"Sure. But I could have Adolfo—"

This guy was too much. A meal service, a taxi service, what next? "If you'll loan me an umbrella I'll go walk along with her, make sure she doesn't fall in a big, deep puddle, and I'll bring it back to you before I'm on my way."

He stared at her for a moment, thinking. Then he said, "Adolfo! Bring that big old umbrella out of the golf bag back there, will you?"

"*Sí. Uno momento.*"

The umbrella was dusty. Obviously Buzz hadn't played much golf lately.

It wasn't difficult to catch up with Louise. Jennifer didn't even have to run. She was just up ahead in the drizzle, inching along. Once Jennifer was alongside, she held the umbrella over Louise and a little over Alice. The dog looked up at her and, if Jennifer wasn't mistaken, smiled. She definitely gave a wag of her tail.

"How about a little company?"

Louise stopped, turned slightly and looked up at the much taller Jennifer. "That's nice of you, young woman. Do you have a name?"

Damn, she hadn't thought of a name! And it couldn't be Jennifer or Chaise or anything similar. "Doris," she said in a pinch, and winced. Where the devil had that come from? Now she was stuck with it for the time being.

"Well, Doris, did you just get out of the army?"

"No," she laughed. "It's just a fashion statement."

"Hmm." Louise looked her up and down but reserved comment. She resumed walking and they went along in silence for a while. Then she stopped, turned to look up at Jennifer and asked, "What brings you to Boulder City?"

Another thing she hadn't rehearsed. She realized she was actually quite bad at this. She'd had the nerve to shave her head and eyebrows, but that's where her imagination had stopped. "I was just leaving Las Vegas and realized I'd never seen the dam or the Grand Canyon. Maybe I ought to."

"Good idea," Louise said, and got back to her walking. It was going to be a very long walk, no matter the distance. She was quite slow and couldn't walk and talk at the same time. If something came to mind she stopped, turned and looked up, spoke, and waited for her answer. "Do you think you'll stay very long?"

"No. Maybe a day or two. Or three." As she said that she looked around. They were passing the park and started up a cracked sidewalk into the quaint neighborhood Jennifer had noticed before. Small town U.S.A. Compared to South Florida it was practically deserted. Much too quiet and ordinary for someone like Nick Noble. This fact recommended it.

"Here we are," Louise finally said, stopping in front of one of the many tiny houses a couple of short blocks from the park. This one and the ones on either side appeared to have freshly painted trim and were well maintained. Louise trudged toward the door of her house. Alice paused only long enough to pee on the grass before they went inside. "Thank you, Doris. I hope you enjoy your time in Boulder City. It's a nice little place." Alice looked over her shoulder at Jennifer; her tail sashayed back and forth a couple of times. They disappeared inside the house.

Jennifer went back the way she had come, spinning the umbrella over her head. When she got to the Tin Can she saw that there were a few more people in there now, and there was a sign in the window that she was quite sure hadn't been there before. Help Wanted.

She took the umbrella to the counter and handed it to Buzz. "She's all set. Stubborn, huh?"

"She likes that walk. Claims it keeps her on her feet.

I think she's around eighty now and she's been getting her breakfast here for thirty years."

"What kind of help are you looking for, exactly?" She surprised herself with the question.

"Little of everything," he said with a shrug. "Place isn't that crowded during the weekday mornings. I can almost handle it myself, but it's better when I have someone steady. Waiting tables, doing dishes, sweeping up. If we go through a busy spell and I have to ask the other waitresses to come in at the crack of dawn, they get all pissy. Not real flexible. You know wo—you know waitresses."

Adolfo popped into view from the grill. "*Sí,* we need help for the help."

"They're precious flowers," Buzz said with a wide grin.

She looked around, and when comfortable that she wouldn't be overheard, she asked, "How fussy are you about references?"

"I'm kind of easy there," he said. "You sound interested."

"I…ah…didn't really think I was looking for work. I haven't waited tables since I was in my teens."

"It hasn't changed much over the years. I pay minimum wage, you bus your own tables, keep your tips, split 'em when you work with the other girls, and can have any meals you show up for, on or off your shift. I could use someone when I open. At 5:00 a.m. Pretty rude hour of the day. Especially for the precious flowers." Grin.

"I like to get up early."

"I guess you don't have ID?"

"I… Ah…" She shook her head. "No."

"You have a name?"

"Doris."

"Well then, Doris. See you at 5:00 a.m. tomorrow?"

She smiled in spite of herself, but mocked herself inside—what the devil are you smiling about? Nick is probably shredding your Vera Wang nightie while you're taking minimum wage in a greasy spoon!

But it was a little honest work and no one would be ogling her. For sure not with her bald head and the masculine clothes. She could stretch the money she had in her backpack a little further and have time to think this through. This diner was safe and clean and warm, the people so far had been decent, and at this stage she wasn't about to take that lightly. Plus, there was no way Nick Noble would end up within twenty miles of a place like this—it was just too common.

It would only be for a little while. She had no idea what would come next, but she was pretty sure it wouldn't be equal to that classy condo with the spectacular ocean view. Those days were pretty much behind her, unless she took a notion to find another rich old boyfriend. And from where she stood, that was about as likely as snow in hell.

"A little tip, Doris. You might try the Sunset Motel over on Carver. It's not too far from here and the owner will give you a cheap weekly rate and heat. It don't look like much, but it's clean and safe. But don't tell Charlie I told you. I consider him a friend, but he's tight as a bull's ass and I don't see any point in my new wait-

ress freezing to death. And you're going to have to get
a scarf or something. You can't wait tables in a ball cap
and I'm afraid that shiny dome on a girl might upset the
tea-and-cookie crowd."

"The...?"

"The little old ladies."

"Oh. Sure. No problem."

"It ain't easy work, but it doesn't pay well."

"Sounds that way," she said, but she said it with a
smile. "Thanks, Buzz. You're a good guy."

"Aw, hell, I'm a tyrant. You'll hate me in no time. Go
get me that sign, will you, girl?"

Hate Buzz? Impossible. He might have been an angel
in disguise. An angel with a few rough edges, maybe,
but angelic just the same.

In keeping with her new appearance, Jennifer had her
left ear pierced and decorated with five silver hoops.
She had to sleep on her right side for a week, but she
didn't resemble the woman who had fled the MGM
Grand less than a week ago.

In the diner she had a little space and time to get back
on her feet, to think about where she'd been and where
she was going—both physically and emotionally. And
she came to realize very soon that Buzz had seen a need
in her and filled it with that Help Wanted sign, which
he kept on the shelf under the cash register. He probably put it out whenever someone he suspected needed
help wandered into his diner.

Buzz was an old bachelor who had run the diner for
forty years. He had a pretty nice house, he told her, but

it was lonely there. He liked to be at work—he was usually there from five in the morning until at least nine at night. He bragged that there was no food in the refrigerator at home, and he paid Adolfo's wife to clean and do laundry for him every couple of weeks.

He was a simple guy and almost everyone who came into the diner was considered a personal friend, except weekend out-of-towners. And what she realized was, if Buzz had brought her into the fold, they all accepted her as part of the family.

"I could use you on Saturday and Sunday mornings, early," he said. "You should take a couple of weekdays to sleep in, but come in for breakfast when you're up."

"You don't have to do that, Buzz," she said.

He took on a mock look of surprise. "You mean you'd eat somewhere *else?*"

She wouldn't dare. At least not yet.

The thing about the diner was, the food wasn't particularly delicious. It was good enough and cheap. And not so much on the greasy side. Everything from chicken fettuccini to meat loaf had a slightly Spanish flair.

"Cheese omelet," a customer would order. "No cilantro."

"I'll try," she would reply.

Jennifer found the Sunset Motel was managed by an elderly woman named Rosemary, who seemed to be expecting her. She cut her a special deal of one-fifty a week if she didn't require housekeeping, and she made it clear it was a favor to Buzz. The accommodations were a definite improvement, but hardly what she was used to. The thread count of the sheets was so low her skin felt rashy, and the bathroom, while clean, had been hard used with the chips and stains to prove it. It was a long slide down from the MGM's Grand, but a damn site safer.

Buzz could easily have handled the work at the diner himself. There were a few people in the morning, mostly regulars she became acquainted with right away. As the morning stretched out to lunch, there weren't many customers.

In the afternoons Jennifer went to the library, where she read newspapers, magazines and used the Internet to research news of Nick and Barbara Noble. So far there had been none. The librarian was a woman just a few years older than Jennifer who wore a plastic name tag that read Mary Clare. After seeing Jennifer there every day for a few days and learning that she worked at the diner for Buzz Wilder, she asked Jennifer if she'd like a library card. To have that, Jennifer adopted the last name of Bailey. Doris Bailey. So after finishing her research, she picked up a novel to take back to the Sunset with her.

She had loved reading since she was a child. It was probably a defense against loneliness; she knew how to plant her eyes on the page and fall headlong into a story, forgetting where she was. She could forget she'd been living in a condo overlooking the ocean at the pleasure of her wealthy gentleman friend, or had lived in an old station wagon parked in an alley. Stories took her out of herself, and she had long regarded the time she spent reading as a little respite from a reality that she had to continually reconstruct. From the time she was a little girl, to being a successful mistress, to being a bald-headed waitress in a greasy spoon, books had been her salvation.

As she was walking back to the Sunset from the library, backpack slung over her shoulder and cap on her head, she saw a black limo driving slowly down the street. The over-dark windows concealed the identity of the passengers, but the license plate read MGM12 and Jennifer knew immediately that it was one of the hotel's cars. She had to tell herself not to pause, not to stare, not to react. It was entirely possible the hotel was taking a guest to view the dam, which she had heard was a magnificent sight to see.

But it was also possible someone she knew all too well was looking for her.

Three

A few days into her new job she was still sweeping up when the afternoon waitress arrived, a high school girl named Hedda. She was a freaky-looking kid with spiked black hair with purple edges, a tongue ring, a little rhinestone nose stud and at least one very large tattoo peeking out at the small of her back over her low-rise jeans. Hedda looked Jennifer up and down intently, and finally a smile broke out over her decidedly beautiful face. "Cool," she said. "Did you do that yourself or have it done?" she asked, indicating the bald head.

"I…ah…I didn't need much help with this," she said, pulling her scarf off her shiny dome. She felt a sudden urge to explain that she was actually very fashionable and had great office skills; that she could do the accounting for a diner this size in her spare time. And she could dance the tango, drive a stick shift and speed read. Not to mention that acquired skill of finding and snagging rich old guys.

"You know what would look really cool? A tattoo. Right on your head. I could tell you the name of a good artist."

"I'll definitely think about that," she said. "But I was actually thinking of trying hair for a change. You know—letting it grow out."

"I wouldn't," Hedda pronounced. "It makes you look like a really cool alien. A pretty alien."

"Wow," Jennifer said. "I haven't had a compliment like that in I don't know when."

"And I mean it, too."

On her first weekend in Boulder City she met Gloria, who usually served the dinner hour and every Saturday morning. Gloria, a woman in her fifties, looked at Jennifer and said, "Holy Mother of God."

"You'll get used to it," Buzz yelled from behind the counter. "Hedda thinks it's cool."

Gloria shook her head. "Why you girls do the things you do is beyond me. Why don't you at least draw on some eyebrows? I could help you with that."

"Thanks," Jennifer said. "I'll keep that in mind."

Gloria had a bedridden husband at home and so she kept very flexible hours, something that Buzz seemed to take in stride. While Gloria worked, a neighbor would look in on her husband, and if Gloria got a call, she dashed off, no matter what she might be in the middle of.

Gloria was best described as a tough old broad. She was a little overweight, but pleasantly so with soft, round curves. She had her short dark hair "done" every week at the beauty shop down the street and it was lacquered into place, not a hair changing from day to day. While her hair was being hammered into place, her acrylic nails were being "filled" and painted bright red, to match her lips. Gloria liked her makeup thick and her eyebrows drawn on in a high arch that made her look perpetually surprised.

"We could do something with makeup," she told Jennifer. "Maybe you wouldn't look so… I don't know… Naked?"

"I thought it would be quite a statement, but maybe I went too far."

"There's no maybe about it, honey."

"Hedda likes it," she added.

"Hedda's the one who should shave her head and start over."

"Hey!" Buzz called. "Don't start trouble. I got enough on my plate with one bald and one with purple hair!"

Hedda took to Jennifer right away, perhaps because they were both odd and had very limited wardrobes because of slim means. She often brought her little brother Joey, to the diner with her. He seemed to be her constant responsibility because of their mother's working hours. She took care of him every night while her mother worked as a cocktail waitress in one of the casinos, and walked him to school in the morning while their mother slept.

Jennifer stumbled on Hedda's home while she was out walking one day. She wasn't far from the Sunset when she came upon a block full of duplexes, four-plexes and tiny bungalows, all of which were run-down and in want of paint and repair. A string of carports stood behind them and the front yards were almost entirely dirt. She saw a German shepherd chained to a tree in front of one house, a truck pulled right up to the front door and a guy working on the engine in front of another, and a little boy playing in the dirt with a toy truck in front of a third. Emerging from the front door of that last bungalow came Hedda, her book bag over her shoulder. The screen door slapped shut behind her and Jennifer felt as though she'd been propelled back in time.

Hedda could have been Jennifer fifteen years ago, except that Hedda obviously took more risks in self-expression than Jennifer had ever dared. She and her mother had lived in a great many dumps like that one, and worse than that, they'd spent time on the streets now and then. There was a four-month period when they'd lived in an Oldsmobile Vista Cruiser station wagon, getting the occasional shower at the Salvation Army.

A woman with stringy hair and wearing a ratty plaid bathrobe opened the door of that same small house and yelled, "Hedda! How many times do I have to *ask?*"

Hedda whirled instantly. "Sorry, Mama," Jennifer heard her say. She dropped the book bag, went back into the house and came out again, this time carrying a trash can. Jennifer was frozen in her spot, watching. Hedda walked around the buildings to the rear where the carports were and emptied the trash into the Dumpster. She dropped off the trash can, picked up the book bag and then, with a pleased smile, spotted Jennifer.

"Hey, Doris," she said. "What are you doing here?"

"Just checking out the neighborhood on my way to the library. I'm at the Sunset, right over there."

"Yeah? We stayed there for a little while. Then the house came open and it has a kitchen. An *old* kitchen, but a kitchen. I'm just on my way to work."

"With your books?"

"It's a little slow in the afternoons. If I get my other stuff done, I do homework," she said. "And hey, if you ever want to get rid of any weekend hours, I'm looking to pick up time."

"I'll keep that in mind."

"I'm thinking of going to the prom," she said, and became instantly shy when she said it.

"Thinking of going?" Jennifer asked as they walked along in the direction of the diner.

"I'm not sure I'm the prom type," Hedda replied, but while she said it she was looking down. "I haven't made up my mind yet."

It didn't take Jennifer long to catch on. It had to do with money. You didn't make much in tips while doing homework. In fact, between breakfast and lunch Jennifer had to look for things to do to stay busy. Before Hedda came in, the diner had been swept, the bathroom was cleaned, the Naugahyde was wiped down and the floor mopped. Adolfo did the cooking and most of the cleanup. Buzz manned the cash register, poured coffee and waited on the counter.

When Hedda arrived at about two-thirty, she did some chores like refilling ketchup bottles as well as the salt, pepper and sugar containers, and then she took the back booth and spread out her books. She might have

a couple of dozen diners in her three-hour shift. Gloria
came on at five, and the dinner traffic from five-thirty
to seven-thirty was steady again with all the usual suspects showing up. Jennifer knew this because she had
stopped in for dinner herself more than a couple of
times. Only on weekend mornings did the place stay
busy. So Hedda would have trouble saving for the prom
on her low wages and meager tips

"Well, you should probably try it once, if you can
find the right dress," Jennifer said.

"That's what I was thinking," Hedda returned.

Jennifer had no idea how long her stash and waitress
job would have to last her, but there was one thing she
did know—she had savings and investments in accounts
that Nick Noble knew nothing about. At least not yet.
She didn't know when or how she'd get back to those
accounts, but unlike Hedda, Jennifer had them.

Her first week at the diner had gone well; no one
seemed particularly shocked to see her and, all in all,
the regulars were friendly. There was Louise every
morning, with Alice, and Jennifer very much looked
forward to seeing them. She loved the old woman's
gruff and direct manner; it was as though being accepted by Louise *meant* something. Then there was
Louise's neighbor—Rose. Slender and elegant, Rose
didn't seem to be big on diner food—she feasted on tea
and toast. Jennifer loved the way the women, so opposite, interacted. Louise was short, stout, with thin white
hair, while Rose was taller, whip thin, with flaming red
hair, though she was over sixty.

One morning during her second week on the job,

Marty, who owned the used-book store, greeted her with "You the bald girl I've been hearing about?"

Well, there you go, she thought. You don't shave your head and go unnoticed. "I guess that would have to be me," she said. "Word sure gets around."

"What else have we got to do around here?" he asked, and grinned so big his dentures slipped around. "Thank God there's a new face now and then."

A couple of Boulder City cops rode their mountain bikes up to the front of the diner, parked them where they could keep them in sight and sauntered into the diner. The sight of them made her instantly nervous and afraid of being recognized, but they seemed more intent on breakfast than anything. Ryan, the pudgier of the two, said, "Well now—what biker gang are you from?"

"Schwinn," she answered, pouring his coffee.

His partner and a couple of other diners laughed, but Ryan just shook his head and said, "Schwinn? I haven't heard of that gang. Schwinn?"

She met Sam the Vet, Judge Mahoney, and the girls from the beauty shop. The joggers were Merrilee and Jeanette, and by their third morning they were calling out "Hey Doris" as they came in the door.

A nice-looking young man came in late one morning and Buzz told her to go introduce herself to Louise's other next door neighbor, Alex.

She took the coffeepot over and said, "Hi, I'm Doris. I see your neighbor Louise in here every morning."

"Hmm," he replied, turning the page on his paper and snapping it open with a sharp shake. She poured him coffee.

"And Alice. We keep dog treats on hand for her." He said nothing. He peered at her from behind the paper, frowning as he took her in. "Bald," she said. "Completely bald. Cream? Sugar?" He merely shook his head and went back to his paper. "Not friendly at all," she reported to Buzz.

"He's the tall, handsome, quiet type," Buzz said.

"Definitely tall. And quiet," she said. "Handsome is as handsome does."

Jennifer was often seen wandering around town in her baggy green-and-tan fatigue pants, an oversize work shirt, a windbreaker tied around her hips, hiking boots and the backpack that was always with her. She went from the diner to the Sunset to the library to the park and back to the diner. And as she went, she was very observant, always on the lookout for that long black limo. But it did not reappear.

The weather was cool and mostly cloudy with occasional showers, so she spent most of her time indoors, passing the time with reading. Four-thirty came very early, which put her to bed by eight or nine, and for this she was very grateful—she had no desire to flop around all night, worrying about a lot of things over which she had little or no control—like being whacked by her ex-beau.

One evening she left the Sunset at bedtime to venture back to the diner. She had a cup of coffee and piece of pie on her mind. There were no customers present. She found Gloria seated on a stool at the counter and Buzz standing opposite her. Adolfo was in his booth at the far rear, newspaper spread out in front of him.

"Well, a person would think you'd had enough of this place for one day," Gloria trumpeted.

"I was remembering that apple pie," Jennifer said. "And the Sunset doesn't have TVs in the rooms."

"I been meaning to get a TV for this place," Buzz said. "But then Gloria would never do a lick of work."

"Probably true. Sit up here, girl. Buzz, get the girl a cuppa."

"You don't ever go home, do you, Buzz?" Jennifer asked as she climbed on the stool.

"There ain't anyone at home," he answered, giving her a cup. He poured coffee into both hers and Gloria's, then he pulled a silver flask out of his pocket and held it over Jennifer's cup. She shook her head no, but Gloria tapped her cup with her spoon.

"Ah," Jennifer said, catching on. "Happy hour."

"Something like that," Gloria said.

"I go to my family at supper," Adolfo informed her from the back of the diner. "My Carmel, she is a better cook than even me. We eat an early meal, then I come back most nights. But Señor Buzz, he can manage if I have need to be home. He doesn't like anyone to know, but he can cook."

"We trade off pretty good," Buzz said. "I like it here. Always liked it here. This old diner is a whole lot friendlier than my house. You want ice cream on that pie?"

"Please," she said. It was kind of nice not to think about the calories for once. This was a big change for her, and she genuinely hoped she wouldn't grow into her baggy pants. Her mouth was watering before she could dig her spoon into the delicious dessert.

She was so busy eating that she never heard the soft knocking at the back door. Adolfo got up to see who was there, and with the door partially open revealing a man in an old and worn coat, he called, "Señor Buzz. Someone here for you."

"Let him in, Adolfo. I got just the thing."

Buzz went back to the kitchen and came out with a steaming bowl and basket of rolls while Adolfo let an old ratty-looking man into the diner. The old guy was in need of a shave, and he shuffled as if his ankles were tied together with a foot-long rope. Without saying a word, the man took the seat at the end of the counter and Buzz put the soup and bread in front of him. He then served the man a cup of coffee and poured plenty of cream in it.

The only person who didn't understand what was going on seemed to be Jennifer, who watched the man out of the corner of her eye while she ate her pie.

Adolfo came out of the pantry in his coat, cap on his head. "I'm away," he said to Buzz. "*Señora, Señorita—hasta mañana.*"

While Buzz was busy with something in the kitchen, Gloria talked about her husband, Harmon, who had had a stroke four years before. She found him on the garage floor, near death. Somehow he pulled through, but with fewer than half his former capabilities. He couldn't communicate very well, but she claimed to do all the communicating for him. He went from bed to wheelchair to bed and could only be left alone for periods of a couple of hours at a time, so when she worked or ran errands, her neighbor looked in on him and called Gloria's cell phone if she was needed. "To tell the truth, I work for a break. You have no idea how hard it is to take care of an invalid. Hard on the heart, too."

The man at the end of the counter stood up and shuffled out the back door without a word, without a thank you or a goodbye.

"Is he homeless?" Jennifer asked.

"Oh my, no. He lives a couple of blocks away. Widower. We don't see too much of him, but Buzz always reminds him that by the end of the day there's usually food that's going to get thrown away, if he's interested. Once in a while, he comes down here and relieves us of the waste." Gloria got up and cleared away the old man's plates. "Not much of a tipper," she laughed. And then, "You're welcome," she yelled toward the door.

The next couple of weeks Jennifer learned that there was much more to the diner than met the eye. More specifically, there was so much more to Buzz. His waitresses needed their jobs—jobs that seemed to be specifically designed for them. And he seemed to have a regular clientele of hungry people who needed a charitable bite to eat. Jennifer even saw Buzz tip his flask over a cup of coffee a transient was having.

"Did I see you just give that man a drink?"

"Appeared he needed one," Buzz said, clearly not interested in discussing it.

And then she realized that Buzz had his own little meals-on-wheels service. He frequently excused himself from the diner for just a few minutes with a take-out carton in a grocery-store sack. Or he'd ask Adolfo or Hedda if they'd drop something by Miss Simms's or

Mr. Haddock's place as they were leaving. It didn't appear to be a scheduled service, unless he had a schedule in his head. Buzz seemed to know when and where to fill a need.

Saturday morning, around nine, found the diner packed to capacity and Hedda was serving up a storm. Jennifer was getting the hang of this waiting business, but she was nothing compared to Hedda in speed and accuracy. "Don't worry about it," Hedda told her. "You're doing great, and I can back you up."

Hedda was picking up orders from the grill and switched the radio station to something with a little more boogy to it. "Oh, Mother Mary," Buzz complained.

A song by Usher blasted into the little diner and Hedda said, "Oh, *yeah!*"

Balancing two complete breakfasts on her arm and a coffeepot in her hand, she two-stepped across the floor in her high-top, rubber-toed athletic shoes to the rhythm of the hip-hop. She put them on the table with a flourish, poured the coffee in spurts that matched the beat, then hopped away from the table on her way back to the counter.

Someone in the diner began to tap on a tabletop to the beat while someone else clinked a utensil against a saucer. Encouraged, Hedda continued to dance around the diner while she picked up plates. It was irresistible to Jennifer, who had always loved to dance. She joined in, moving to the beat as she went from table to booth to table, picking up dishes, then hopped backward and around in a circle just as Hedda had done. They met in the middle, bumped rumps, did a few hops and high-fived each other. There was a bit of laughter and the tapping turned to table banging, which only served as encouragement.

As the waitresses hopped and slid and wriggled around the diner, the patrons kept the beat with enthusiasm. The song was a mere three minutes long, and when it came to an end they took a bow and erupted into laughter. There was a little applause from their tiny gallery. "You're all right, Doris," Hedda said. And she whispered, "Think any of these tightwads will cough up an extra dollar?"

At the end of the shift they pooled their tips and divided them. It had been a good morning; Hedda's face lit up as she pocketed sixty dollars. "Yeah, I think I might go to that prom. My boyfriend, Max, thinks he can borrow his older brother's car for the night."

"Here," Jennifer said, handing her another twenty. "You did twice the work I did."

"No way," she refused. "A deal's a deal. Besides, it was busier than usual. And I think that little hip-hop brought us in a little extra."

"It was a nice break from *la orquesta*," Jennifer laughed.

"Hedda," a woman called sharply.

Both waitresses turned to see Hedda's mother standing in the diner door with her seven-year-old boy by the hand. Jennifer wouldn't have recognized her by the way she looked—her appearance was so much improved from the other day in the doorway of the bungalow. But the sharp tone of her voice was unmistakable. Jennifer was a little startled to see that up close the woman was about her own age, give or take a year. She must have had Hedda as a teenager. She was dressed and made up for work, an old trench coat obviously covering a sexy waitress uniform that included black hose and heels. She was, in fact, an attractive blonde, though a little on the pale side. She would definitely be prettier if she had a smile on her face instead of an expression of sheer annoyance.

"Did you *forget* something?" she asked.

"I was just on my way, Mama. Mama, meet Doris— a new waitress here. Doris, this is my mom, Sylvia."

"Hello," Sylvia said shortly. "Hedda, you're going to make me late by screwing around."

"Sorry, Mama. Just let me get Joey a soda and then I'll take him home." Hedda crouched. "How'd you like that, skipper? Cherry Coke?"

"Yeah!" he said, climbing up on a stool.

"Hedda, I have to talk to you for a minute," Sylvia said. She turned around and headed out the door.

"I'll get that Coke," Jennifer said. "Nice meeting you," she called after the woman.

Sylvia turned and gave a nod, but she was all about business. Late for work, Jennifer decided. She watched through the front window while Hedda and her mom talked for a moment and then Hedda reached into her pocket, withdrew her tip money and peeled off two twenties, handing them to her mom. Then, as Sylvia's hand remained extended, Hedda put out all she had.

Jennifer felt her heart twist. She hoped she would see

Sylvia give her daughter a kiss or hug or some show of affection—at least a smile—but when Sylvia just walked away, Jennifer's twisted heart sank.

Hedda stayed outside awhile after her mother left, staring in the direction of her departure. When she came back inside, she was quieter. To her credit she kept her chin up. And she didn't say a thing about giving her mother money.

There was a coin-operated washer and dryer at the Sunset Motel, so Jennifer put on her sweat suit, the first purchase she had made after fleeing the MGM Grand, and washed her clothing and sheets. Nothing in her life felt more like luxury—even in her Fort Lauderdale condo—than clean sheets. These sheets were a little on the muslin side rather than the nice six-hundred-count at home, but it was the clean smell that counted.

In bed, cozied up to the smell of Downy, ready for a guiltless sleep, she heard the sounds of a neighborhood that was still awake through the thin walls. Someone played a radio too loudly and young peoples' voices could be heard from another block. There were the occasional horns honking, engines revving and the unmistakable sound of a skateboard whizzing past her room.

What am I doing here? she asked herself for the millionth time. Of all the things she had considered for her future, her imagination had never ventured this far. She had thought about a career in real estate, or maybe even a travel agency.

She wasn't missing her sexy clothes, nor did she lament frequent trips to fancy spas or resorts. She hadn't wanted to be the other woman for life and, in fact, the sooner she could leave all that behind, the better. But one thing she had never seen coming was what appeared to be a return to the tough times of her youth.

It had been almost four weeks, and the time had flown by. She appeared to have been left alone by Nick, though he rarely left her thoughts. Every day she expected to see his chauffeured car drive slowly past the diner, but as the time passed she was left to assume he was back in Florida, probably searching for her there, where all her personal belongings were. As for Nevada, had he left the search to the local police?

So she told herself, *easy does it.* Vowing to take it one day at a time until she could figure out how to retrieve her savings and investments so she could truly start over—maybe pursue that real estate or travel agency career—she settled into the sheets.

One of her final thoughts before drifting off was that there were things about this she liked. Getting Louise her breakfast, Alice her biscuit. Dancing around the diner with Hedda. Watching Buzz take care of the neighborhood, in his own way.

She just wasn't crazy about being bald, wearing army surplus or eating Mexican meat loaf....

Four

Jennifer watched as Louise Barstow made her way cautiously down the cracked sidewalk, one bent leg at a time, gripping a cane in each gnarled hand to help hold herself upright. She could see that shocking white hair slowly rise and fall with each step Louise took. Clearly it hurt her to walk, but she had told Jennifer that if she didn't walk as much as possible, bearing the pain of arthritis, she would be bedridden in no time. She rejected the suggestion of a scooter or wheelchair. "I'm degenerating fast enough as it is," she said. "I've seen others my age give in to wheels, and that's it. They quit walking, and the decline is even faster."

She did well for an eighty-year-old with severe arthritis. Right beside her, just about as old and slow, was Alice. At fourteen, she was ancient for her breed. Jennifer was amazed by them both and wondered if she would have that kind of fortitude at that age. She wondered if she'd be fortunate enough to even *see* that age.

Louise was a teacher, a college professor who had driven to Las Vegas and sometimes farther when she was teaching, and Buzz was the only guy in town willing to open at 5:00 a.m. "But I don't teach anymore," she had told Jennifer. "At first it was for the pleasure of company in the morning after my husband, Harry, died, then it was for the exercise and finally it became a matter of survival. But I don't exactly bounce out of bed in the morning anymore."

Jennifer opened the door when Louise finally arrived. "Good morning, Madam Professor," she said. Louise's face brightened immediately and Jennifer knew that she liked being addressed in that way. "Two canes as opposed to the walker—that must mean your arthritis is pretty tame today."

"Hah. You wish. I'm just especially brave."

"Ah, I should have known." She had Alice's bowl of water in her hand and placed it before her on the sidewalk outside the diner while Louise went inside and got settled.

It was one of the high points of the morning for Jennifer when Louise and Alice arrived. The way the older woman expressed herself—a kind of harsh but kindly manner—was a kick. "You're a little rough around the edges, aren't you, Doris?" was one of the first things she'd said to her. And she always asked personal questions that Jennifer skittered around. Direct questions like "Where do you come from and who are your people?"

Jennifer admitted to coming from the Midwest, which was not entirely untrue. Her grandparents lived all their lives in Ohio, even though Jennifer had moved around a lot with her mother. And she said she didn't have any people, unfortunately.

She got Louise's tea right away. "Here you go," she said. "What can we get you for breakfast this morning?"

"I don't know," she answered. "I'm not hungry."

"You will be by the time you start nibbling. Have to keep your strength up."

"Widows tend to skip meals or eat over the sink. Did you know that, Doris? But not Rose, my next door neighbor. She's in so much better shape at seventy, and she fixes a proper supper every night and eats it while seated at the table. But then Rose has never been married, and it makes a difference somehow."

"Why is that?"

"I don't know exactly. It's the *having been* married that does a lot of us in. As if when the old boy goes, there goes the only excuse we have for fixing a good meal. But you didn't see me eating over the sink *before* I was married." She snorted. "Of course, I was married at seven."

"Seven? A little young. Were you one of the Travelers?"

"The what?"

"Those gypsies who marry off their girls before they're out of elementary school. The Travelers."

"You have a very unique education, Doris. For a biker chick."

Jennifer laughed. "I like the news magazine shows— like *60 Minutes*. Now, how about some eggs and fruit?"

"Fine, then. You've been here about a month, haven't you, Doris?"

"Just about. Want some whole wheat toast?"

"No butter. You must like Boulder City a little or you would've moved on. At least to better employment."

"Come on, Dr. Barstow—I couldn't ask for more than this!"

Jennifer loved the way Louise's face brightened whenever she titled her. The first time she did so, Louise told her straight out that it felt rather good to be given that title. After all, she'd come up through the ranks of academia at a time when women were still being admitted with some reluctance.

"Buzz is lucky to have you. You should make him tell you so twice a day."

"He is as free with praise as with pay," she said.

Louise continually surprised her. She was so amazingly observant, for one thing. The first time a couple of Boulder City cops came in and Jennifer found her herself ducking their stares, Louise had said, "If you're going to be so obvious, they're going to know you don't want to be recognized. Look 'em in the eye—that'll fool 'em for sure."

Taken aback, she had replied, "Are you saying they're not all that sharp?"

Louise had shrugged. "We have very little for them to do here in Boulder City, Doris."

Louise had taken to recommending books to Jennifer and every day she went to the library, reading them quickly. In just one month she'd gone through all of Jo-Ann Mapson, Alice Hoffman and Alexander McCall Smith. Louise had speckled some nonfiction in there, as well—*Women and the American Experience,* for starters. That took Jennifer more than one day to get through.

Jennifer took a dog biscuit outside to Alice, gave her some pets, then returned to the diner to wash her hands. She then delivered the fruit and toast to Louise.

"Doris, I see you're letting that hair grow in a little. I wondered what color it was. It's darker than I imagined."

"It's darker than I *remembered*," Jennifer laughed. "I doubt I'll let it get any longer than an inch, tops."

"I just can't imagine what you were thinking. Egad."

"I thought it would be quite a statement. Bold. Different."

Louise lifted her eyebrows questioningly. "Is that a fact?"

"Yes," she said.

"Well, unfortunately it made you look more like a thug. But this is better, this little bit of hair." She reached a gnarled hand out and patted Jennifer's head. "I have to tell you that when you smile, you are transformed. And your smile doesn't really fit with this look—with the piercings and army clothes. But, I've never been very good at fashion." Then Louise abruptly changed the subject. "Is it too late to make it a vegetable omelet? Egg substitute?"

"Not at all. I told you you'd find your appetite once you got started. I'll have it right up," she said, taking the order slip to Adolfo. And then, per her routine, she went back to Louise's table. "I finished *The Seasons Of Women.* Do you have another suggestion? I'll be taking it back to the library this afternoon."

"Hmm. Have you read *Gift from the Sea?*"

"No, I don't think so. I've always enjoyed reading, but I've never been able to do so much. There isn't much else to do here."

"We're a dull lot," she said.

"Oh, I didn't mean it to sound that way. There's no TV where I'm staying and I thought it would be tough, but I like it. It's a nice change."

"Change from what?" Louise ventured.

"Someday I'll tell you all about it, but right now I have to do my chores." She smiled and got away without telling anything. Again.

Jennifer brought Louise more hot water, then went back outside to check on Alice. She liked to linger there, stroke the old girl's head and back. Alice would moan appreciatively, thanking her. Satisfied that there was plenty of water and that it was cool enough in the shade of the diner's awning, she went back inside. As she stood and turned, she caught Louise watching her. Staring at her with a slight frown wrinkling her brow. "I just wanted to be sure Alice was fine. And that she has enough water in the bowl."

"You like Alice, don't you?"

"What's not to like? She's a perfect dog. And I think that besides you, I'm her favorite." She grinned again.

"I've always had dogs. Sometimes more than one. It was difficult when I traveled more, but I love animals. And it's my opinion that people who don't like dogs are coldhearted and impatient. I think that within you beats the heart of a loving woman. Am I right?"

"I hope so, Madam Professor."

"Do you know I've spent my whole life studying women and their issues? I hold a post-graduate degree in women's studies and there is no woman on earth I don't find interesting. And you, Doris, are one of the most intriguing."

"Me? Phooey. If you knew me better, you'd realize I'm very boring. Let me get that omelet for you."

Jennifer went about the business of refilling the sugar and creamers, sweeping up behind the counter and gathering up the ketchup bottles to consolidate them so they were all full. When her breakfast was done, Louise asked Jennifer if she could take a little break. "I'd like to talk to you about something."

"Sure," she said, sitting down across the table from her.

"No. Walk a little way with me. Buzz won't care too much."

"Just give me a minute," she said. She spoke to Buzz, then retrieved her backpack and slipped the straps over her shoulders.

Once outside Louise said, "I don't know what you have in that backpack, but it never leaves your sight."

"Well, not exactly. I just don't leave it behind because… Well, because I travel light, and that means I carry what's important with me."

"Are you planning to stay around awhile, Doris?"

She laughed a little, and with it came a little snort. "How could I think of leaving a fantastic job like mine at the Tin Can?" Then she added, "I didn't think I'd still be here, but I like this little place. I like that there's almost no nightlife."

"Odd that a woman your age would be fascinated by that. But if you are planning to stay, I have a proposition for you. I go to England every spring and come back every fall. My son is there. Rudy. I like to be near him, and I get privileges at Oxford as a professor emeritus. I research cultural issues, women's literature, women's studies. I've been working on a textbook for some time now."

An unusual sound came out of Jennifer. It was a sigh. A sigh of longing. And her tone of voice softened so hopefully. "Please say you want me to go with you and carry your books."

"I'm afraid not. However, my usual house-sitter-slash-dog-sitter has disappointed me. She can't help out this time. You can see that Alice can't be alone, can't be kenneled. In fact, it gets harder and harder to leave her. She's an old woman, is my Alice."

Jennifer was holding her breath and no doubt Louise could tell. She sensed what was coming and began to desperately pray it could happen. After all, the Sunset Motel wasn't a place you'd want to stay for too long.

"I could use a house sitter. For five, maybe six months."

"Me?" she asked tentatively.

"In addition to the house, food, utilities, upkeep and frequent dog walking, I'll pay you a small stipend."

"Stipend?" she asked, a little breathless.

"There's a condition, Doris." She stopped walking. She looked up at the younger woman. "Yes, you look so much better with hair. Mmm," she said, clearing her throat. "I'd like you to tell me what you're hiding."

Jennifer let out her breath in disappointment, shaking her head in defeat before she even realized her actions were as much as admitting there was something major. "I'm not hiding anything," she said.

"Oh, yes, you are. I don't much care what it is, unless you did prison time for ripping off little old ladies." That brought a slight chuckle from her. Very slight. "I'm an expert on women, Doris, and I know how tough the world can be for some. And I'm an excellent secret keeper. It's just that this might be too big a mystery for me. Please understand—I can't leave you with all my worldly goods and my very best friend without knowing why you're hiding out in Boulder City."

Jennifer moved her mouth as though she were literally chewing on the question. She decided quickly it would be okay to be honest. Louise was eighty and not very talkative. If there was anyone in this town who could be trusted, it was probably Louise. "If you tell anyone, it could be very, very bad."

"I have no reason to tell. But I do have a need to know."

"It was a man. He was violent. He—" She took a deep breath. "He threatened to kill me if I left him."

"Do you think there's any chance he could be looking for you?"

"I think there's every chance—but I think this is the last place he'd look."

"And why is that, exactly?"

"Because this is such a quiet place. No gambling, no nightlife, not exciting. It's not what he'd expect of me. He'd think that I'd run off to L.A. or New York City before I'd hunker down in a town full of—" She stopped suddenly.

"Full of little old ladies and their ancient dogs?"

Jennifer bit her lip. "He'd expect me to want more excitement than is found here, Doctor."

"All right, all right, so there is much more to you than meets the eye. I thought as much. Maybe later you'll trust me enough to give me a few more details. I might even be able to help at some point. I do have a lot of experience with this sort of thing. I helped open a facility in Las Vegas that's strictly a women's and girls' shelter. Anyone female can get help there, as long as they're drug free."

"I'm okay here. For now," she said, but there was a tentative tone with it. "But what if something… If I have to leave in a hurry? What about Alice?"

"My neighbors will see after her in an emergency. You aren't using credit cards or making long distance phone calls to friends or family, are you?"

There was a long pause. "No," she finally said. "I really have no one." She couldn't keep the sadness from her voice as she realized that even when she'd had a rich gentleman friend, she had no one. "And I know what I have to do to be invisible."

"Then you'll be very hard to track. So? What do you think, Doris? Can you help me out?"

"Yes," she said, flashing a heartfelt smile. "I could probably do that."

"That's good. Maybe you can come over later and look around. I could show you how to work the computer so you can e-mail me. Rose lives on one side and

Alex on the other and—" Louise stopped as Jennifer's expression changed rather suddenly. "What's the matter, dear?"

"Alex. He looks at me like I'm going to pick his pocket."

"Ignore him—he's not always such a crank. Even Alex warms up after a while. And, Rose... Well, I'm not even going to try to explain Rose. But I leave next week. I need someone to watch over Alice and the two of you get on so nicely. So—that's that. I just can't tell you how much I appreciate this."

"You're sure your neighbors will be okay with this?"

"Absolutely. Thank you for taking it on."

"All right, then," she said, making an effort to keep the relief and excitement from her voice. "I don't have anything else going on."

"Well, isn't this just my lucky day," Louise said. "Oh, and Doris? If anyone comes sniffing around the diner, acting like they might be looking for someone like you, don't smile. That smile of yours is simply unforgettable."

Louise's house was a tiny little brick box that she'd owned for thirty years. It was in a row of identical houses offering up varying colors of brick, siding or paint, just around the corner from the park, theater, post office and library. A few blocks farther was the main street and shops that saw more action from the tourist traffic. She'd had a screened back porch added several years ago so she could work there in nice weather, which in Nevada was most of the time. Garages hadn't come with the houses, but she and her neighbors had added free-standing garages that opened into the alley and gave them easy access to their back doors. Her backyard was small but meticulous, thanks to Alex, who took care of it for her.

Louise sat in the porch at the computer, her reading glasses perched on her nose, a stack of books teetering on the floor next to her chair. She heard the front door open and close. Momentarily Rose stood in the doorway to the porch. "I don't know why I have an extra key," she said. "The door is never locked."

"Neither is yours."

"I'm getting in the habit of locking up when I go to bed at night. I must do it two or three times a week."

Rose was taller than Louise, as was just about everyone, and still straight as a poker. Her face was what she liked to call seasoned, her hair a flaming red; she drove all the way into Las Vegas to have it colored every three weeks. Her hips were slim and her teeth strong, straight and white. She'd taken good care of herself and didn't suffer from any of the degenerative conditions that plagued Louise.

Rose was a perpetual fashion plate. Today she wore a black midi-length skirt and gray snakeskin boots with a slim heel and very pointy toes. A bright orange poncho was draped over her black turtleneck. Amazingly, it did not clash with her teased red hair. Her lips matched the poncho, and gold chains sparkled around her neck and wrists.

Louise lifted her glasses and peered down at Rose's feet. "How do you walk in those things?"

"They look good, that's how. Tell me you didn't go through with it," Rose demanded. "You didn't invite that bald-headed creature to stay in your house."

Louise glanced up over her glasses. "You and Doris will get on very well. It's obvious she could use the support and counsel of an older woman." She pulled off her glasses. "And she's not so bald anymore. She's got a little hair growing in. She's actually quite beautiful…except for that ridiculous mannish costume she wears."

"Phoo," Rose said. "She's going to rob you blind and run off in the night."

"If she runs off in the night, she'll only take what she can fit in the backpack. She doesn't even own a car."

"You have no reason to believe you can trust her."

"She's been working for Buzz for weeks, and as generous as he is, he won't condone any dishonest act. If so much as a quarter were missing, he'd let her go."

"Phoo."

Rose turned and left the porch. She was back a second later with a glass of iced tea—she had helped herself from Louise's refrigerator—then draped herself in the wicker chair opposite Louise's worktable. Although actually only about five foot four, she always wore heels to give her height, and her slender form made it seem she had very long legs and arms. "What did you tell her?"

"That my usual house sitter was unavailable."

"But Alex and I keep Alice when you're gone!"

"Alice will be happier at home. Besides, the girl needs a place for a little while and I'll feel better knowing she's here."

"Utter nonsense. Leave well enough alone."

"She's *obviously* in trouble. And if you dare tell her that I'm doing a good turn, I'll have your hide."

"Alex is going to have a fit," Rose predicted.

"I'll have a word with him," she said. But he should mind his own business sometimes. Although, since he probably wouldn't, Louise figured maybe he could be of help. Louise and Rose had nothing but affection for Alex. He lived on one side of Louise with Rose on the other. Alex was young, thirty-five, and made it his business to look after these little old ladies when he should be spending more energy on beautiful young women. He scolded them for opening the door to strangers, for never locking doors when they left the house, for giving too much information on the phone, for not being more cautious. Rose was right—this was going to bother him. But he'd get over it.

"I was hoping you'd reconsider the trip this year," Rose said.

"Why would I do that? I love my annual sojourn."

"It's getting harder for you, though."

"Tell me about it. Just thinking about that plane ride makes my joints begin to throb. But I like being near Rudy."

"That's just crazy, and at your age," Rose said shortly. Then, softening her tone, she said, "I just thought that might change, is all. As you got older."

"It's a matter of not giving in, dammit. But I admit, it's hard leaving Alice. I always wonder if she'll still be around when I get back."

"I'll watch. But about this girl…"

"She's a good girl. Just odd. She'll be fine."

"I don't like it."

"Well, it's done. I'm going to give her a debit card for groceries and supplies for household upkeep and set her up to receive one hundred dollars a week."

"A hundred dollars? Have you lost your mind?"

"Not enough?" Louise asked, thinning eyebrows arched.

"Too much! Way too much! You're buying her food, paying all the bills, giving her a place rent free…."

"She has to take care of Alice and keep the house in order. It's a job. People get paid for jobs."

"Don't be surprised if you get burned…."

"With you right next door, never giving her a moment's privacy? You're right—she could flee in want of a moment's peace!"

"Ptui," said Rose.

It was just after lunch when Louise knocked at Alex's door. He was pulling on a clean shirt as he answered. "Hey, sweetheart. Why didn't you just call me? I'd have come to you."

"I had to stretch my legs. I stiffen up in four minutes, I think. Can you get that big suitcase from the garage to the bedroom for me? Tomorrow is soon enough if you're going somewhere."

"I'm going to work, but there's no rush," he said, buttoning his shirt. "I'll get it for you before I go."

"And…I have a house sitter. Doris—the young woman who's been waiting tables for Buzz for the last month."

"The girl with the butch haircut and man's pants?" he asked, frowning. He didn't wait for an answer—he knew who she was. And he knew Buzz and his proclivity for giving work to down-on-their-luck transients. "What do you know about her?"

"Let's see. She reads everything I recommend, and quickly. She likes jazz. She's thinking of getting a mountain bike—she used to love hiking. She's very protective and big sisterish toward Hedda, who could use an ally in her life. And—she adores Alice." She leaned both hands heavily on her cane. "Think of her as my houseguest and behave yourself."

He laughed, shoving his shirttail into his pants. "You don't have to worry that I'll come on to her," he said. He went to the breakfast bar to get his wallet and attach his gun to his belt. Alex was a Metro police detective in Las Vegas.

"No, I'm worried that you'll try to investigate her and I just want you to know I would consider that extremely rude."

"I would only do that if I thought there was a reason…."

"As long as you don't think Doris living in my house is a reason. Am I clear?"

He grinned handsomely. "What makes you think you can push me around so much?"

"Old age."

He put an arm around her. "Don't worry—I'll be nice to your house sitter. I'll give her a wide berth. Now, let's get the big suitcase before I leave."

"Don't you usually work days?" she asked.

"My hours have been all over the place lately. We've had a rash of home invasions in the city and I'm going to sit a stakeout with our target team. We think we know who it is, it's just a matter of catching them."

Louise shuddered. "I'm so glad to be living here," she said. "Now, you be very careful, young man."

"Always, my love." He kissed the top of her head.

Jennifer did as much as she could to make herself indispensable to Buzz and Adolfo in the mornings. Then, with most of the chores done by early afternoon, when Hedda came on, the girl had more time to spend on homework.

Buzz and Adolfo had become more like family to her in one month than Nick Noble had in two years, and she was very grateful for them. She cleaned the bathroom, took out the trash, washed up the dishes and pots, swept the walk in front of the diner. She shined the glass, polished the stainless steel, watered the plants and dusted all the old black-and-white photos of Las Vegas celebrities that hung on the walls. This place, the diner and the town, was like a cocoon to her, sheltering her from her past and her future. As long as she was right here, she lived in the moment, and the moment, in all its simplicity, was lovely.

If she weren't so afraid of Nick, she'd almost like to thank him. For the first time in ten years the pressure to be perfect was off. Her constant grip on control was unnecessary—she was loose in this body without all the trimming and constant upkeep. All she had to do was relax into this modest role and enjoy her own feelings for once. There was such amazing freedom in this.

She was beginning to have relationships, shallow though they might be. Still, it was far more than she had indulged in while she was trying to keep some man interested.

From here she could look back over some of her choices. Being the girlfriend of rich older men had seemed like a safe and practical way to spend some time, but suddenly ten years had flown by. She'd gone from nineteen to thirty in a flash, hardly feeling the passage of time. The only way in which she acknowledged aging at all was with the clear realization that she wouldn't be young and beautiful forever, and she would have to plan her next career path with no time to spare.

Now it amazed her that she had fooled herself into believing she could be satisfied with that. Catering to someone else's needs, leaving her own for later, in order to live a material life and avoid the risk of falling in love and having her heart broken? What was that about? Her idea of security was suddenly skewed, for what good were her savings and investments if her life was in danger?

Yet, danger or not, here she was now, a woman alone with simple needs and experiencing entirely new feelings. It verged on happiness. How, she asked herself, had she managed to get to be thirty years old before figuring that out?

While Louise prepared to leave the country, Jennifer went to her house a few times to become familiarized with the place, to get instructions on the upkeep, the bills, the bank, the care of the dog and, most important, the computer. Through that process two things became glaringly obvious. She wondered how Louise, at her age and infirmity, could manage the kind of trip she was undertaking. And second, she realized she would miss her. Jennifer had begun to look forward to her breakfast companion and had come to think of her as a friend, even if they didn't share any personal information.

"I'm taking my laptop," Louise said. "So we can e-mail all the time. I will never be far away with that convenience."

Jennifer's big brown eyes brightened. "It will be almost like having you here."

"Better," she said. "I don't complain about my joints so much in e-mail."

Then the day came for Louise to leave. The cab that would take her to the airport pulled up in front of the diner and Jennifer went out to say goodbye. "Alice is at home, moping. She started acting injured and dejected when she saw the suitcases come out two days ago, and now she's in a full-blown depression. Don't be too concerned if she picks at her food for a couple of days. It's her way of letting us know she has strong opinions about being left behind."

"I'll brush her and take her to the park."

"Try to enjoy this respite, Doris. Make a study of it. Keep a journal or something."

"Sure, Professor. Travel safely."

"I'll see you again soon," Louise said. And Jennifer, without planning to, lunged into the cab and embraced the old woman, shocking her.

"Oh! My!" she exclaimed. And then, recovering

from the surprise, she put her arms around Jennifer and patted her back. "You'll have a good six months. Ignore Alex's pique and take Rose with a grain of salt."

Later that day, as she walked to Louise's little brick house, she strolled down the street at a slow, lazy pace while inside her heart was leaping, and the temptation was strong to break into a run. Right after giving Alice some attention, she was going to take a good, long bath. She'd limited herself to showers at the motel, afraid of what germs might be lurking in the forty-year-old porcelain tub.

She was entering Louise's house now with a whole new set of senses, as if seeing it for the first time. New sight, new smell, new touch. She stuck the key into the front door, but it was unlocked. That would have to change. As she entered, Alice slowly rose from her pallet by the hearth, but she hung her head and put her ears back as if to say, *Do you see this? I've been left again.*

"Hey, girlfriend. Don't worry—she'll be back before you know it."

Alice lay back down, her snoot flush with the floor between her paws, her pathetic eyes glancing upward.

Jennifer lifted the leash off the hook by the door. "Come on, no pouting. Let's take a little walk so you can get an attitude adjustment. Then I'll settle in."

Alice rose slowly to her feet but still hung her head dejectedly as she went to Jennifer.

"Oh, brother," Jennifer said to her. "What a drama queen. Come on, let's go. Enough self-pity."

It took Alice at least a block to get in the mood, after

which she had a rather nice, though brief, twirl around the park. People who obviously knew Louise and Alice greeted them. "Louise gone off to London, has she?" said a man who was walking a terrier. He gave Alice a pat. "I'm Pat from the grocery. Holler if you need anything."

"Thanks," she said. "Doris. From the diner."

"Welcome aboard."

There were three others she passed by—each said hello to Alice, to her, and each one seemed to realize that if someone else was walking the dog, Louise must be gone for the summer.

Just a little exercise and fresh air seemed to do wonders for Alice's mood, but Jennifer was chomping at the bit to get home, *home,* to get settled. And when they did get back, Alice's tail was wagging again and she helped herself to some of her food.

"See? I knew you could adopt a positive attitude if you tried."

The living room embraced Jennifer. The hardwood floor, red brick fireplace, deep sofa and overstuffed chairs with ottomans, worn in just the right places. And books. The wall upon which the hearth stood had built-in shelves on each side, *filled* with books. She went to the shelf to look at the titles and only then did she notice that the dust on the shelf was thick. She ran her fingertips along the shelf and then examined them.

Louise's house was cozy, if a little old-fashioned. And though she had been there a couple of times last week to learn the computer, she hadn't really looked around. The floral sofa and rose-colored chairs were sporting a good bit of dog hair, and now that she thought about it, it was a little on the musty side.

Well, it stood to reason—Louise was eighty. Not only would her eyesight probably be a bit challenged, but she was simply too arthritic for heavy cleaning. Jennifer dug under the kitchen sink and came up with cleaning supplies—dusting rags, scouring powder, glass cleaner. She got busy at once, starting in the living room. There was an old radio on the bookshelf, and as she dusted around it, she turned it on. Frank Sinatra was singing, so she turned the dial—but Frank just kept at it. Apparently the dial was broken, and if she was going to listen to that radio, she was going to hear that kind of music.

She'd rather it was winter, with some cold weather, so she could light the fire and the lamp, grab a book and a soda and never leave. This place felt like a nest for the restless bird. Instead, she opened some windows to clear out the musty smell. She found the vacuum cleaner in the second bedroom closet, and fortunately there were new bags on the shelf.

From just inside the front door, the dining room was to the left, living room to the right, the screened-in porch through the french doors straight ahead. Louise had had the kitchen remodeled, making it the most modern room in the house. And it was used very little, so it wasn't dirty, but Alice's coat seemed to line the floor. The granite countertops needed a good scouring, the cupboard had glass doors that she happily polished, and she brought a high sheen to the stainless-steel appliances. She moved the kitchen table to give the floor a serious scrubbing, and before long she noticed that while she'd been cleaning her heart out, the day had grown long and the sun was beginning to lower in the sky. With the windows open, it was getting cold, and she shivered as she went to close them.

But she was so happy! It felt so wonderful to put a house right—a house she was going to occupy for up to six months. And she didn't have to think about what she could do or wear or say to make a man happy; she only had to think about what would satisfy her.

There was a note on the counter beside the phone with all the numbers she would need and instructions to "take the master bedroom, please." This was all typed; Louise's hands were not agile enough to write legibly with a pen.

She grabbed her backpack and went to the bedroom, where she found a basket on the bed with a note on it. "Pamper yourself," it read. In the basket was shampoo, cream rinse, lotion, soap, shower gel, bubble bath, a new brush and comb, toothbrush and paste, disposable razors and a manicure set. She lifted the shampoo and gave a huff of laughter. She sat down on the bed and saw her face in the dresser mirror. It was the face of Jenny at the age of fourteen—no makeup, lips deflated by the absence of collagen, a dark cap of hair covering her scalp and eyebrows grown out and shapeless from lack of tweezing. With her hair a mere buzz cut, her brown eyes looked large and dark.

Who would have believed the most perfect disguise would be her natural self?

There was one change she'd made since adolescence

that she intended to take to the grave—the veneers on her teeth. If she were really going to go underground, she could probably pop off those veneers and go back to the old mouth.

But no. Enough was enough.

She felt the ache creep into her throat. She had spent so much energy on self-beautification, seeing it as necessary to her lifestyle, and her lifestyle necessary to survival. Yet here she was in her manly pants and shirts, so comfortable but so unattractive. Jennifer, she felt, was gone. As she looked at this new face, even though she remembered it from her youth, she wasn't entirely sure who she was.

Don't cry. You don't have to stay exactly like this. This is only temporary. Until you figure out what to do.

All that was left of her former self, the self she'd worked so hard to create, was the jewelry and money in her backpack. She could have sold the two rings and tennis bracelet, but if Nick was determined to find her, they could be traced, so she simply tucked them into the backpack for safekeeping—for emergencies. She still had some money left, two jobs and very modest needs.

It had been weeks since she'd walked out of the hotel suite. A couple of phone calls from phones with blocked lines revealed that Barbara Noble was said to be living in the Nobles' Caribbean estate. Apparently no one was suspicious of any crime. There had only been that one sighting of an MGM limo—with no evidence it bore Nick or his thugs. Could it be they'd all gone back to Florida and just assumed Jennifer would never dare tell a thing?

Possible, she decided. Only time would tell. And that time she would spend in Louise's comfy house. A very nice place to hide.

She gave the bathroom a quick, efficient scrubbing, then kicked off her shoes, let her khaki pants drop to the floor and stripped off the baggy shirt. While the tub filled with hot, soapy water, she looked at herself in the mirror. Wouldn't people be surprised to know that under the baggy pants and men's shirts was a body like this—high breasts, flat tummy, round butt, long, lean, shapely legs. She preened a bit, one arm over her head, the other stretched behind her back. Then she reversed her pirouette. Something else was growing in—pubic hair. She had endured years of waxing in what was called a Brazilian—total hair removal. Nick had no idea about her natural hair color.

She sank into the tub and sighed audibly. God bless Louise Barstow—this was heaven on earth. Jennifer, who'd flown in private jets to luxury resorts all over the world, who'd been to the finest of spas, who'd worn the most expensive designer labels, was enjoying what felt like the grandest moment of her life in Louise Barstow's bathtub.

Alice walked into the bathroom, sniffed at the bubbles and wagged her tail.

And living with the perfect roommate, she thought. Then she sank out of sight under the water.

Later that evening she sat at the computer. Louise wouldn't be in London yet, but she should have a positive message about Alice waiting for her when she got there. Then a strange thing happened. If Louise had been present, Jennifer wasn't sure she'd even feel like talking. But typing was something else. She had to make an effort to keep it short. There was a long letter inside, wanting to come out.

Dear Louise,
Alice seemed a little depressed when I first got here, but she snapped out of it. I took her to the park. Then her appetite kicked in and she had a little snack. Imagine my surprise when there seemed to be lots of people and dogs who knew her, but then I guess Alice has been around Boulder City for quite a while. You have very friendly neighbors around the park. I had lots of offers of help if I need anything. But I don't, of course.

Are you well? Was the flight interminable? How are your legs? When you have a moment, let me know how you're doing.

Just out of curiosity, why do all the houses in the neighborhood look the same? Was there a builder with a limited imagination?

Breakfast just won't be the same....
Love,
Doris

The next day, Jennifer checked the computer before even lifting the leash off the peg, and to her delight, the computer told her she had mail!

Dear Doris
You should visit the dam and the museum—you'll find it interesting. Boulder City started out as a gov-

ernment town, and all the little houses in my neighborhood—part of the historic district—were built for the managers of the dam project. The workers stayed in dormitories, tent cities and hastily constructed shanties. It was a highly regulated place in 1931, a morally conscious town in the middle of the most liberal, hard-drinking state in the union. The government was afraid if dam workers availed themselves of all the liquor and vice in Las Vegas, they'd blow themselves up with the dynamite they'd be handling. That or die of disease. Much of that enforced morality somehow remains, keeping us a dull lot.

The flight was sheer torture, thank you for asking. And the noise and smog and wet and dark in this, my favorite city, is more than I can take. I'm going to have to admit defeat and sell my flat. Tell Alice that when I come home, I'll be staying.

Thank you for your e-mail, and your conscientious care of my home and friend.
Love,
Louise

She couldn't resist. She shot an e-mail back.

Dear Louise,
A government town—how fascinating. I will go to the museum. Since I'm here, I'll learn what I can.

I know your son will be sorry to hear you're selling your flat. I suppose he'll be visiting you in Boulder City from now on!

A few minutes later, just as she was lifting Alice's leash off the peg, she heard the computer announce her mail. She had obviously caught Louise online.

Doris, my dear,
No, Rudy will never leave England. If you think I'm stubborn—!
Love,
Louise

She sat down at the computer to shoot off another note, but then upon recalling Louise's gnarled fingers, she thought better of it. Besides, it would be something to look forward to later.

Five

Every day, after finishing her work at the diner, Jennifer went to Louise's house, where she began a new routine, quite different from her life before Nevada. First she would take Alice for a twirl around the park. Spring was full on the land, the sun bright and warm, and the trees and bushes were coming alive. Old Alice needed that walk, but she couldn't take too much. Jennifer, however, found the spring irresistible, and after taking Alice home she went out again.

She discovered there was much more to Boulder City than she first encountered. Beyond the historic district that was filled with the tiny homes built by the government for dam workers, there were larger, newer homes. There were also huge homes, apartment and condominium complexes across the highway that led to Hoover Dam, high on the hills above Lake Mead. There were a few fancy golf courses and country clubs scattered around, a Franciscan center, churches both small and large, and more walking and biking trails than she could exhaust in a year. She found an abandoned railroad track that ran through tunnels above the lake—walkers, joggers and bikers were always in evidence. On a hill above the track was a sightseeing helicopter giving twenty-dollar rides.

Then there was the lake, massive and bright blue, busy with boaters and surrounded by parks and camping areas. She felt almost as peaceful walking along the edge of the lake as she did on the Florida beaches. Paths led into the mountains in every direction, and once she got the lay of the land, she thought she would investigate them further.

After walking for miles and sometimes hours, she would return to the house and log onto the computer. She'd ditch the clompy shoes and baggy pants and sit at the computer in her oversize shirt and panties, total comfort, total privacy, totally at home in Louise's cozy little house. This house with the dark, warm colors, the woods and wools, florals and plaids, was so completely different from the sterile condo in Fort Lauderdale. From the beach to the desert. She thought she would grieve for the sound of crashing waves, but each morning when she woke she hugged herself. It was so *calm* here. So quiet. So uncomplicated.

Her life here was so blissfully ordinary. She never would have guessed this kind of simplicity could be so comforting. She felt lucky to wait tables, walk Alice, explore Boulder City and e-mail back and forth with Louise, and it was no longer just because it kept her safe from Nick.

Most of their e-mails were just daily news—Louise would report on the bookstores she visited, historic sights she never tired of, and the weather. Jennifer would mention who came into the diner, pass along hellos from Buzz and the gang and tell her where she'd been walking that day. She lived for those e-mails—it brought her out of herself in a way she couldn't have predicted.

Dear Doris,
I was thinking about you this morning as a whole group of little schoolgirls passed me on the street and I couldn't help but wonder, where is your mother? What kind of childhood did you have? You're so wonderful with Hedda—do you have siblings?
Love,
Louise

Childhood. Being raised by Cherie Chaise was like growing up in a three-ring circus. Manic episodes followed by deep depressions; unstable romantic interests that had them moving all over the country interspersed with running home to Grandma and Grandpa in Ohio. Cherie was whimsical and full of big dreams and the most loving and vulnerable person alive. When that great energy would come upon her, she could take a job and do the work of ten women. Cherie had even been a waitress more than once, and unsurprisingly her tips were huge. But then sometimes it was not a job that soaked up all that manic energy, but perhaps a lover, and she would throw herself into a relationship that Jennifer knew, even when she was very, very young, wouldn't last very long. Or, a great idea would seize her and she would launch into music and acting lessons to become a star, a shopping spree through an office-supply warehouse to start a business. Once they got on a bus with the intention of riding nonstop across the United States from ocean to ocean.

And then she would crash, unable to lift her head, to eat, to wash. And then she would rise! And again they would fly! And laugh and sing and dance! And crash. Time and again Grandma and Grandpa would come to them, fetch them home and beg Cherie not to take Jennifer away again. Jennifer needed stability, they pleaded.

But Cherie needed Jennifer and Jennifer needed to protect her mother.

It was while growing up that Jennifer learned how to take care of herself, how to entertain herself and how to be safe in the most unsafe conditions. She counted seventeen different schools, even though she counted only one school the eight different times she stayed in Ohio. Of course she was a loner; how could she be otherwise? She couldn't have friends—Cherie needed her full attention. And she dared not bring friends from school home, there was no telling what might be going on. The shift in moods could be rapid fire. Cherie might be talking to the walls, hallucinating after days of sleeplessness. Or she could be ensconced in darkness.

Something dawned on her. Perhaps, as an adult, she hadn't eschewed friendship out of necessity because she was always committed to a rich older gentleman. Possibly it had just become a way of life since childhood. A solitary existence.

She had learned to sleep in chaos or stay calm during the black periods. She did not miss the craziness, but she missed her mother so much sometimes. No matter how high or low she happened to be, she was always sweet. Cherie was like a child, so vulnerable and loving.

She had rarely talked about it. She had never told Nick anything personal. He could care less. What he liked about her was her long hair and legs, high perky tits, et cetera.

Now she had someone to tell.

Dear Louise,
Messy. My childhood was a train wreck. My mother, I now realize, was bipolar, but because we were barely scraping by financially she never had a proper diagnosis. She was hospitalized a couple of times and medicated with Thorazine, which had the effect of knocking her out and making her sick—so naturally she feared the doctors. I'm sure it's a good thing I was the only child. I don't think we could have managed more than just the two of us. We had some high old times if the right man or job came along— but it couldn't last long because my mother would sink into a terrible depression and lose her boyfriend or job. Once she got back on her feet, we'd move— a person in a manic state loves nothing so much as a change of scenery and a chance to start over. I went

to over twenty schools. That probably accounts for me being such a loner. After my grandparents died, my poor mother lost the only anchor she had and took her own life. I know she was crazy and sometimes miserable, but the fun times were so fun. And she was a dear. A lovely, kind, sweet but wacky woman. She loved me so. It made her feel so guilty that my life was so dysfunctional. But there were times when life seemed almost normal. You'd have liked her.

I didn't think I wanted ever to talk about that, but thank you for asking.
Love,
Doris

Dear Doris,
You are truly a remarkable young woman. I can't imagine all you must have learned from that experience. What wisdom and tenacity! I'm sorry for the hard times, but so glad you knew your mother loved you.

Now that you don't have to be a caretaker to an ill parent, how do you suppose your life will change?
Louise

Change? Jennifer realized that Louise had the impression her mother had died recently, that Jennifer was poised on the brink of a new life.

Well, maybe she was.

We're friends, Jennifer realized. *Girl*friends. This was something she'd never had. Every time she began

to get close to a friend while growing up, she would be
snatched away again and it would be lost. There were
a couple of women she began to get close to in her
twenties, but she couldn't sustain the friendships because she was too private, too solitary. Women have to
exchange personal items and secrets in barter for friendship and Jennifer hadn't been up to the job. But now…
With her eighty year-old mentor, she was learning.

She depended on the e-mails to sustain her.

After writing to Louise, she would begin her Internet search for any news about Barbara Noble, but there
had been none. She watched the Palm Beach news, sub-
scribed to vital statistics networks, and read online news
sources. Every once in a while Nick's name would pop
up, or he'd have his photo in the paper, which could be
viewed online. He played in a charity golf tournament
in Miami and bought a new yacht. He gave money to
political campaigns and cut the ribbon on yet another
new office building. His wife was never at his side, yet
this didn't seem to raise any alarms.

But…if he was in Miami being a big shot, he was not
in Las Vegas. It was possible he had people looking for
her in his stead, but there was no one she feared recognizing her as much as Nick.

Here's how her life was going to change—she was
going to get this business with Nick Noble behind her
somehow and create an entirely new life for herself. She
made up a new screen name on Louise's Internet account and sent an e-mail to the Las Vegas Metro Police
Department: Nick Noble of Palm Beach, killed his
wife, Barbara Noble, in a Las Vegas hotel and dis-

posed of the body. She hit Send, then deleted the screen name.

She began to tremble. Could that be traced? She thought not. But the PD might connect Nick's name with hers and the fact that she was missing. She thought about repeating the process with the Florida authorities, but couldn't bring herself to do it. She was too afraid of being found out.

Jennifer was taking the trash out of the diner's back door and into the alley when she just about collided with Hedda, who was in a serious lip-lock with her boyfriend. Hedda giggled and separated herself from the boy. "Doris, this is Max," she said.

Jennifer said hi and Max hung his head shyly, looking up cautiously. She assumed he was sixteen, like Hedda. Boys that age came in all shapes and sizes, and this one was about six feet tall, thin as a noodle with size-twelve feet and spiked hair that had been bleached white. And black eyebrows. She almost said, "I was thinking of doing my hair that way," and caught herself.

It was also hard to tell with kids these days whether they looked like they were on welfare, or whether they *were* on welfare. Max wore pants that hung low on his butt, his boxers sticking out, and the hems that dragged over his shoes were frayed. His T-shirt had a couple of holes in it and a ball cap stuck out of one pocket.

"So, what are you two up to? You're early for work."

"I thought we might split a sandwich and do some homework. Then Max goes to work, too, and I'm all yours. I can stay out of your way, or you can go home early."

"Where do you work, Max?"

His voice was so quiet she had to strain to hear. "I wash dogs? Next door at Terry's?" He said it like a question. "Till about six?"

"Wow," she said. "What a fun job."

"They poop in the tub sometimes?"

"So," she said, temporarily at a loss. How do you respond to something like that? "You have to be flexible in this job."

He liked that. He grinned largely and slipped his arm around Hedda's waist. He had straight, white teeth. "Yeah. Gonna be a vet." No question mark that time.

"Good for you. So, let's get that lunch," she said. "You have to keep up your strength. Never know what you're going to find in the bathwater."

"Yeah," he laughed.

She served them up a nice big sandwich along with plenty of chips and pickles. It seemed a good idea to take care of them a little. It was impossible to know if Max was so thin because he was hungry, or because he was sixteen. And she wondered if it would be inappropriate for her to ask Hedda how serious they were. Her mother, Sylvia, was so young, it implied a teen pregnancy. She would hate to see Hedda get caught in the same trap her mother had.

Of course, Jennifer knew how to take care of that little problem.

But no, she cautioned herself. Can't get too personal with someone else's kid. It was just that Hedda was growing on her. It was like looking in an old mirror. And she had long ago developed her habit of trying to keep the vulnerable safe.

There were just a few people left from the lunch crowd when Max went to his job and Hedda found her apron and covered up her multicolored hair. Buzz had disappeared with a couple of bags of takeout for his personal meals-on-wheels program, and now he was back. Even though she was sure he wouldn't mind about the free lunch for Hedda and Max, she felt compelled to tell him.

"You take good care of the girl," he said. "That's never a problem here."

"I swear, I don't know how you make ends meet."

"It's a challenge sometimes, but we always make do. Somehow."

"I'll sweep the sidewalk before I leave. Okay, boss?"

He leaned on the counter. "You're a good girl, Doris, even if you do your hair funny."

"Thanks, boss," she laughed.

The sidewalk didn't need sweeping so much as Jennifer liked to do it. The streets in the afternoon were quiet—very few cars and not many people about. When she got outside she thought about how peaceful this town was, how good life in general seemed to be here. Then she noticed a black sedan with darkened windows parked down the street. Something about it gave her pause.

Then she saw them—a couple of men going in and out of the little shops across from the park. One of them was Lou, she didn't know the other. The one she didn't know seemed to be holding a sheaf of papers. He could be a new "butler," or maybe a police officer? She settled on the new goon—he was about as large as Lou. She hoped he was about as smart.

But there was no question in her mind—they were looking for her.

She felt light-headed. A little dizzy. They walked into the next shop and Jennifer got a grip. Sweep, she told herself. Nick might be in the car. Just sweep and try to act natural. But her mind was racing. Should I run? Had the message to the police through the Internet been traced to Boulder City? If it had, her first contact would come from the police, not these goons, right? Unless the police called Nick and said there'd been a message and then— She stopped herself. She was overthinking it; she had no way of knowing what had transpired behind the scenes, if anything. Sweep. Just sweep. Look down at the sidewalk as though those two lunkheads don't interest you.

Momentarily they came out of the shop and stood talking on the sidewalk. They stopped a man as he passed by and showed him the paper. Ah, she thought. They're showing a picture around town. The man shook his head and kept walking. As he got closer, Jennifer glanced up from beneath lowered eyes and recognized him as someone who came into the diner regularly. And he didn't recognize her from the picture!

This is the moment of truth, she thought. Let them come. Look right at them. Don't blink. And don't *smile!* Look at the picture. If they don't recognize me now and if no one else in town says they've seen the blond woman in the picture, maybe they'll go away and not come back.

Unless Nick was in the car. If Nick saw her, she'd be found out. He wouldn't be fooled so easily.

She swept. It seemed to take years for them to make their way to the Tin Can. She could hear her heartbeat in her ears. She forced herself to remember her long blond hair was gone, her eyes were a different color, her lips were thinner, her eyebrows thicker. Her face had been transformed. Plus, these idiots were probably looking for a blonde in a short skirt and four-inch heels. Sweep and don't think too much.

"'Scuse me," the man said. She looked up. Lou stood back about ten feet, cleaning under his fingernails with a penknife, waiting. She was really short in her flat shoes. Every time she'd been shopping, with Lou carrying her packages, or at the airport, with Lou carrying bags, she'd been considerably taller.

"Yeah?" she said, chewing a nonexistent piece of gum.

"Any chance you've seen this woman around here?"

"No. Why? You lose her?"

"Somethin' like that. You're sure?"

"Buddy, someone like that would stand out. Don'tcha think?"

"Yeah. Don't know what she'd be doing around here, anyway." He looked around and, if Jennifer wasn't mistaken, sniffed the air derisively. "This place doesn't have enough action for our girl."

"That a flyer?" she asked.

"Yeah."

"Gimme a bunch. I'll put 'em up for ya."

"Hey, thanks. Hey, Lou, you want a cup of coffee or something?"

He looked right at Jennifer. Not the slightest question or recognition registered on his face.

"Naw, I'd rather get back. You done here?"

"Yeah. Enough is enough."

They went back to the car and drove slowly down the street. When they were gone, when the sedan had turned the corner and was out of sight, Jennifer started to tremble. She leaned the broom against the diner window and made fast tracks to the bathroom, holding the flyers against her stomach as she went, slamming and locking the door. She tried to slow her breathing, but she was panting.

She had been missing for six weeks. Nick had either returned to Las Vegas sooner than his usual three months, or sent his boys. In either case, she was obviously still a hot item. That Nick hadn't just left this to the police indicated his determination to find her. He must be certain she could do him harm.

She looked in the mirror. She held the picture on the flyers up next to her face. She smiled at herself. Ew, Louise was right—she could hide with this face, so different from before, as long as she didn't smile. But the way her lips parted in a smile was identical to the picture, except that now her lips weren't quite as full. It didn't show in the picture, but her bottom teeth were just a little crooked. But the shape of her smile…

You might know.

Her cheeks were flushed. She splashed them with

cold water. There was a *tap-tap-tap* at the door and Hedda asked, "You okay in there, Doris?"

"Uh, yeah," she said. "Give me a minute, okay?"

"Take your time. Buzz just wanted me to check on you."

She felt weak. She needed to go home. It was almost quitting time, anyway.

She opened her pants and untucked her shirt. She put the flyers against her belly and tucked in her shirt and cinched her belt. She bloused her shirt loosely and left the bathroom.

Her eyes glassy and her cheeks pink, she approached Buzz. He took one look at her and said, "Oh-oh. That hit you kind of sudden."

"I'll be all right. But I think I better head out, if that's okay with you."

"You bet. I'll call and check on you later."

"No," she said, a hand on her stomach. "In case I lie down for a while. All right?"

"Sure, Doris. Gosh, I hope it wasn't..." He turned suddenly and spoke over the counter to the grill. "Adolfo? Check the expiration date on the eggs."

"I'll see you tomorrow," she said weakly.

"You want a lift?" he asked as she was heading out the door.

She just shook her head without turning around and lifted her hand to wave goodbye.

The way she held the flyers against her waist might look as if she had a precarious control on nausea, but she was only trying to keep them from slipping down the baggy leg of her trousers.

She took a deep breath, the cleansing breath of a bright, crisp, fragrant spring. It was so clean in Boulder City. So quiet she could hear the birds sing. And twenty-five miles away was the glittering gem of Las Vegas, where, very possibly, Nick Noble played poker while his thugs combed the outlying towns for Jennifer.

But they hadn't found her! They would go back to the city and tell Nick about the little town they had visited, about how the fanciest restaurant in town was just a café. Well, that wasn't entirely true—there were some ritzy places associated with country clubs, but they were membership-only clubs and Jennifer hadn't been anywhere near them. If Nick's boys had gone to those places, no one would have reported seeing her. If Nick was going to send his boys to all the little towns in Nevada looking for her, they'd be very busy. And they had *already been* to Boulder City!

There was absolutely nothing to link her to this place. Nothing! They had asked around about her and no one had seen her. They had looked right at her face and not known her. They had no reason to come back.

By the time she got home she was smiling. Her cheeks were still a bit flushed, but now it was from relief. Happiness. Alice lay on the cold stone hearth, her favorite spot. Jennifer rushed to her, fell to her knees and took her big Lab head in her hands and kissed the top. "Al, baby, I did it! They looked right at me, didn't know me, and *left!*" Alice's tail thumped on the floor twice. "I think we're going to be okay!"

Jennifer turned on the old radio. Frank Sinatra sang

out of the box as usual. She turned up the volume and started dancing around the living room. She let her pants drop and kicked them aside. Flyers fell to the floor and she gave a loud whoop of laughter, giving the pages a kick. Next went the shirt, which she twirled over her head before letting it fly, stripper fashion. In bra and panties she danced and sang, "I've got the world on a string, I'm sitting on a rainbow... Got the string around my finger..."

Alice sat up and watched this crazy display, cocking her head right, then left. Jennifer did a little cha-cha, a little twisting, a little Charleston and knee-slapping. She twirled around in a couple of circles, coming to stop as she faced the doors to the screened porch where, just on the other side of the screen with a hedge clipper in his hand, stood a man, looking in at her, mesmerized by her underwear dance. *Alex.*

She screamed, tried to cover herself and ran to the bedroom.

Poor Alice didn't get her walk. Once Alex was gone, she had to make do with the backyard. And Jennifer didn't get her walk, either, because she was just too mortified to show her face outside of the house. She opted for an amazingly long soak in the tub with extra-high bubbles. Still, she could not wash away the stunned look on Alex's face every time she closed her eyes.

Well, it was slightly better than what she'd gotten from him in the diner the past few weeks. If he looked at her at all, his expression seemed disapproving.

When Louise said Alex looked after the yard, it never

occurred to Jennifer that he'd be lurking back there while she wasn't home. She hadn't thought about it much, but she would have expected him to knock on the door and say, "I'll be doing a little clipping and trimming in the yard now."

He wasn't much older than her—a few years. Passable in the looks department. Maybe a little more than passable. And she'd only seen him in a polo shirt or sweatshirt in the diner. The shoulders and chest that strained against the fitted T-shirt were muscled. All that yard work…

After her bath, she lay on the bed in the darkened bedroom, staring at the ceiling. Great way to not draw attention to yourself.

The doorbell rang and she sat up with a start. She turned to look at the clock. Five-thirty. She could see that the sun was making its downward slant into evening. The doorbell rang again, insistent. Oh, God, she thought, if he's coming to apologize or laugh at me I'll kill myself.

She rummaged around in Louise's closet for something to cover herself with. Louise had moved almost all her clothes to the second bedroom to give Jennifer plenty of room for her scant belongings, but she'd left behind a few blouses, jackets and a wonderful old chenille robe. She slipped into it and realized it smelled like her. Talc and violets and soap. She went to the living room where Alice was already at the door, her nose right in the crack where it opened, her tail swishing back and forth.

"Who is it?" she asked the door.

"It's Rose."

"Oh. Um. It's not a really good time, Rose."

"Oh, phoo. Be a good sport, Doris. What could you possibly be doing? Not fixing your hair…"

Jennifer made a face. Grain of salt, she remembered. "Well, just a minute, then."

"Hurry up. I have my hands full."

Jennifer looked around the little living room and porch. Tidy. The flyers were in the trash can under the sink. On the off chance Rose made herself that familiar with the house and saw them, she plucked them out and stashed them in the bedroom, under the pillow. Then back to the front door, where she asked, "Are you alone?"

"Well, of course. Who in the world would I bring with me?" Jennifer cracked the door and there stood Rose in all her splendor. She wore turquoise capri pants and a blouse that looked more like several flowing, multicolored silk scarves than a shirt. Heeled sandals adorned her long, slim feet. Then there was jewelry…plenty of it. And in her hands, a bottle of wine, a corkscrew, two wineglasses and a plate of canapes. "Louise asked me to look in on you from time to time. I thought it was high time we got to know each other. We can toast your summer with Alice." She bent at the waist and got nose to nose with the dog. "Hello, dear." She came inside, gently pushing Jennifer out of the way.

Rose seemed to fill the small room with her beauty, her erect posture, her sheer flamboyance. She placed the tray of canapes on the coffee table that sat between the sofa and two overstuffed chairs and went about the business of opening the wine. Jennifer took note of her graceful fingers, manicured nails in a color that not only matched her toes and lips, but her blouse as well, a cheery mauve that blended perfectly and somehow did not do battle with her red hair.

"Did you notice that Louise has no wineglasses here? She broke the last one about the time the doctor suggested that alcohol and arthritis medicine probably didn't mix. After that it was only the rare drink for her, and if I didn't bring the glasses we had to drink out of jam jars." She twisted and twisted and popped. "Ah," she said, pouring. She handed a glass to Jennifer and then, pausing to sniff the air, said, "Oh—someone's been primping."

"Louise left me a basket of bubble bath and smelly soap. And lotion and things. It was very sweet."

Rose wrinkled her brow. "I admit I've only seen you at the diner, but I didn't think you were the bubble bath type. I guess I was wrong. Well," she said, lifting the glass toward Jennifer. "To a pleasant summer in a small town."

"Oh, yes," she agreed. "Thank you."

Then Rose draped herself gracefully on the couch, more reclining than sitting. What had Louise said? That Rose was seventy? She didn't look it. Or perhaps it was that she looked as if she *could* be seventy, but she was such an excellent seventy it was hard to believe—her skin was luscious. She'd probably had a little work done. And another thing, she was incredibly fashionable, from her clothes and hair to her makeup, which was flawless. Many women had the awful tendency not to change their hairstyle after the age of forty, which resulted in all these seventy-year-old women wearing thirty-year-old hairstyles. Their makeup was usually the same stuff that worked for them when they were in their thirties and forties. And with failing eyesight, the lining of lips and eyelids tended to be a tad sloppy, not to mention what happened to the rouge on cheeks.

But not Rose. Rose clearly paid attention to details. She was very beautiful. Very with it. She was, Jennifer realized, what she thought *she* would become. Before she shaved her head, of course.

"So," Rose said, sipping a bit of her wine, "No husband? Boyfriend? Family?"

"I'm afraid not. I just broke up with someone and I'm a little… Well, let's just say it would be ideal for me to be alone for a while. I'm not interested in another relationship."

"Parents? Brothers and sisters?"

"No. Unfortunately."

"Can you really be that alone?" she asked bluntly.

Jennifer bit her lip, looked away and found that her eyes began to fill. Oh, please don't let me cry, she thought in panic. Please.

"Oh, phoo, I'm so damn outspoken. Don't answer that. At least, don't answer that yet. Later, when we're better friends. Tell me what you think of the wine. It's a very good Bordeaux. Hmm?"

Jennifer got hold of herself and sipped. She had learned quite a lot about wine, thanks to Martin, a gentleman friend who had preceded Nick and had a great love of fine wines. She swirled the dark red liquid in the glass and observed the silky coating it left on the crystal. She let the bouquet rise to her nostrils and then took a small sip. "Very nice," she said. Not cheap, she found herself thinking. "This is very thoughtful of you."

"Not at all. Now, besides serving chili and eggs, what do you plan to do with your summer here?"

"Hiding out" wouldn't be an appropriate answer. Truth to tell, she hadn't thought about it. She was living one day at a time, and today was the first day she'd really felt there was a good chance she could exist here without being found out. Ohio had crossed her mind— she wondered if she could go back there and reconnect with her past, her childhood. There had been some happy times there, when Cherie and Grandma and Gramps had enjoyed a small measure of control. There might even be someone there who would remember her. But that was in the future, long after the summer. "I guess for starters, I'll discover Boulder City."

"That shouldn't take long," Rose laughed. "Fifteen thousand people and a great big lake." But as Rose talked on, she revealed so much more than that—free concerts in the park, community theater, art shows, farmers' markets every week. Fifteen thousand people who enjoyed culture and small-town values, but used the upscale community of Lake Las Vegas and the city for their high-end entertainment and dining, keeping this little mountain town quiet and very family oriented.

Jennifer pulled her knees up and encircled them with her arms, sipping her wine and listening to Rose talk about her life in the town, starting with moving into this neighborhood at about the same time Louise did. Although they were as different as two women could be, they hit it off at once. Louise was widowed and had to adjust to life without her longtime husband, Harry. But Rose had never married, she said somewhat defiantly. Or proudly. Whatever, the statement came with a lift of her chin that made Jennifer smile.

They had a second glass and Jennifer's cheeks began to glow with the warmth of good wine and conversation. What had Louise said? Take her with a grain of salt? Why, Rose was wonderful. Sitting here in Louise's chenille robe, her hair less than an inch long and her eyebrows growing in all funky, Rose would have no idea how alike they were. If she had met Rose two months ago, they might've gone shopping together. Or to one of the fancy Las Vegas spas.

Eventually Rose's eyes fell to Jennifer's toes, sticking out from under the robe. Her toes were bright red. She hadn't thought anyone would notice. She found the polish under Louise's sink and it was *old*.

"Nice color," Rose said. "I believe it's called Matador."

Jennifer shrugged. "I was just playing around."

"There's more to you than meets the eye."

"Well…probably not."

"Hmm. Well, is there anything you would like to ask me? About the house, the town, whatever?"

"Yes. Would it be helpful if I took care of Louise's yard? Since I'm here?"

"It might be," she said. "But Alex is used to doing it and might take offense."

"Well, then, when does he come?"

"I'm afraid it's just whenever he has the time or the inclination. Why? You don't want to be surprised again?" Jennifer blushed. "Oh, phoo, get over it. If I blushed for every time a man saw me in my underwear, I'd have high blood pressure."

"I can't believe he told you!"

"He was… What should I say? Maybe as surprised as you."

"What did he say?"

"He said you shouldn't quit your day job."

Jennifer couldn't wait to e-mail Louise after Rose's visit. She was at the computer that night before going to bed.

Dear Louise,
Well, I finally spent some time with her—Rose. She brought over a bottle of wine to toast my summer with Alice. So thoughtful. And she is funny. A little outrageous. She told me that you two hit it off instantly, even though you were very different. But she seems to be the kind of person you can't help but like—she's so direct and honest.
Tell me, Louise—how is your son, Rudy?
Love,
Doris

The very next morning:

My Dear Doris,
So, she descended on you. Well, it took her much

longer than I thought it might. I wasn't sure she'd give you a whole day much less a week to yourself. Try to imagine us thirty years ago. I was a fifty-year-old academic working ferociously on the Equal Rights Amendment while Rose, at forty, was hiring showgirls for casinos after years of being a dancer herself. I don't think she wore much while she danced, if anything. Single, many men, flamboyant, exploitive. We were at opposite ends of the female spectrum.

But Rose might know more about women—having worked with them, hired them, managed them—than I, with my Ph.D. in women's studies. We joined forces in getting that shelter in the city up and running—we both saw the need for a place for sheltered women in need even if they weren't wives. Even if they were, for example, girlfriends or showgirls or even prostitutes.

But look out for that wine trick. She'll get you drunk and make you talk.

Love,
Louise

Jennifer took closer notice of her neighbors. Rose drove a yellow Mustang convertible, usually with the top down and her flaming red hair wrapped in a long silk scarf. Alex drove an SUV—but she saw him leaving and returning so seldom that she couldn't figure out his schedule, nor did she have a clue what work he did. She planned to ask Rose the next time they got together.

She saw Rose being picked up for what looked sus-

piciously like dates by two different men on two separate evenings. One was silver-haired, one was balding,
but both were pretty classy-looking and came for her
in nice cars. Alex, on the other hand, was never seen
with a female. But that was no indication there wasn't
one in his life; he could be going to her house. *Their*
houses.

Rose left her house one afternoon, returning with a
few grocery bags and a bunch of fresh flowers. Alex left
and returned with peat moss for the yard. Since Louise
had been gone, Rose had not been seen in the diner.
Alex, on the other hand, had been showing up more
often.

She was a long way from having them figured out.
But she envied the normal look of their lives.

When she was slipping off to sleep she found herself
thinking about them, creating rich fantasies in which she
was just like them—one of the ordinary neighbors. A
real person. Someone with a good uncomplicated life.

She was awakened one night by a fierce pounding
on the door, accompanied by the doorbell and Alice's
bark. Jennifer's heart was thumping and terror gripped
her. Her first thought was that they had found her. The
bedside alarm clock announced 2:22. She wrapped the
chenille robe around her and, without turning on any
lights, went to the door.

"Who is it?" she called.

"Me. Hedda."

She opened the door immediately. Hedda held Joey,
her arms crossed under his bum, his long, skinny legs

dangling. His head rested on her left shoulder, her backpack on her right. She was looking down, then slowly raised her eyes.

"Do you have room on the couch, Doris?" she asked.

The shock of seeing these kids here, like this, had paralyzed her tongue. "Ah, yes! Of course!" She held the door open.

Alice stepped back also, wagging her tail. Hedda entered, head down, and dropped her backpack just inside the door. She moved toward the couch, carrying her heavy load. He was sound asleep—she must have carried him all the way from her house. Blocks and blocks. Alone. At two in the morning.

"No, Hedda. Let's put him in my bed. I have to get up pretty soon for work, so I'll take the couch."

"I can't do that to you," she said.

"Come on," Jennifer said, leading the way.

Left without a choice, she followed. She laid Joey gently on the white sheets. "I'll get a cloth and wash his feet," she said softly.

"No, don't bother with that—you might wake him." She grabbed her hand and pulled her out of the bedroom. "What's going on?"

"Um… My mom has company," she said, eyes downcast.

"Does she know where you are?"

She looked up. Clearly she was so embarrassed. But of all the people she could have gone to, she came here. Jennifer wasn't even sure how she knew which house was Louise's.

"She won't even know we left. When she wakes up,

she'll think we went to school." She shrugged. "So, no biggie."

"Oh, Hedda," she said.

"Don't tell anyone. Okay?"

Aside from a whispered "thank you" the next day at the diner, nothing more was said about the incident. Jennifer wanted to tell her she understood that kind of instability, but the right moment seemed to elude her.

The one thing she was able to do was tell Hedda, "It's okay to come over. No matter what time of day or night."

And Hedda said, "Thanks. It doesn't happen that often."

But Jennifer suspected it did.

Six

As if it had happened in a split second, Jennifer became aware of a town full of roses in full bloom cast against the emerald-green of the grass and trees. The rains of winter had given way and the bright spring sun brought out the color. Everywhere she looked, thorny sprigs had exploded into velvety roses in every imaginable color, while in the Midwest and northeast the ground was still covered with snow.

"I've never seen anything like it," she said to Buzz. "I'm from the Midwest, where roses are tough and hard to keep going. Neighbor women were out in their hats and gloves every single day, coaxing them to stay alive and bloom." She remembered it was the bane of her grandmother's existence. She called her roses finicky and stubborn and cranky. She worked relentlessly to keep those rose bushes going, year after year, through snow and frost and bunny rabbits; it was like a part-time job. And hers were only red and pink. Around Boulder City there were yellow, white, lavender, even black, not to mention the two-toned petals and varying crossbreeds.

"Because the rose is a desert plant," he said. "They like the fall and winter, but they love the spring. Summer's the only season they're not wild about. The heat's a little tough on them—they lay fallow."

"Someday I show you a real garden," Adolfo promised. "My Carmel, she is the queen of roses."

"I'd love that," she said, surprising herself. Was she accepting an invitation to someone's home? Jennifer was getting very brazen. It was perhaps surviving an evening and bottle of wine with Rose that made her so. That, and being overlooked by Nick's henchmen.

She wanted to know more about these new friends but never seemed to find the right moment to ask them for the more personal details of their lives. But there was someone she could ask. Someone who'd been having breakfast at the diner for thirty years.

Dear Louise,
I find I'm growing very attached to my new friends, yet I don't know very much about them. I'm getting to know Rose better, little by little, but Buzz is such a sweet mystery. He seems committed to helping people in small but significant ways—I can't help but wonder why he didn't marry and have a family. And Adolfo, what a gem he is. Has he been with Buzz for a long time? Sometimes they seem like a little old married couple. And my Hedda, my dear Hedda—I might be getting too attached to her. It appears her life is just about as unstable as mine was at that age,

but for entirely different reasons. Just the other night she came pounding at the door in the dead of night with her little brother hoisted over her shoulder—looking for an empty couch for the night because her mother had "company." Now I find myself sleeping with one eye open in case she should need me.
Love,
Doris

My dear girl,
I asked Buzz that same question once—why hadn't he married. He shrugged his shoulders and said he asked someone once, but she had someone else in mind. I didn't have the nerve to pry, but I've always wondered if it could have been Gloria. They're awfully tight. He'd do anything for her. As for Adolfo, you describe his relationship with Buzz perfectly. Even though they sometimes squabble, even though I'm sure Adolfo could find more profitable employment—they will never part company. When you do have a chance to meet his family, don't pass it by. They are an amazing group and will embrace you as though you're one of them.

And little Hedda—I'm so glad she has found you. None of us knows much about her, but having seen her mother just a few times, I see problems. She's an angry young woman who seems to feel unjustly burdened by her children. You can't possibly be too attached—the two of you will make a formidable team.
Love,
Louise

* * *

After work, and after walking Alice around the park so she could visit with other dogs, Jennifer was again at the library. She was there at least twice a week but had not noticed the small stack of flyers with her face on them. They sat at the very end of the checkout desk along with other flyers advertising classes, programs and local entertainment. She wished she could ask how long they'd been there, but that would be too telling. Had Lou left them a couple of weeks ago? Had he been back? She had no way of knowing since she had never paid attention to any of the handouts.

She went into the stacks, selected her books, making sure one was at least as large as the flyer. She went through the process of borrowing from Mary Clare, who always had a comment. "You're going to love this one, Doris. It's great."

"I noticed a lot of titles by this author."

"You can get through at least spring on her stuff, if you like it. How's Alice?"

"She's great. She gets a little more exercise with me than she could with Louise, and I think I've loosened up those stiff old joints. She's moving around a little better." She gathered her books. "Thanks, Mary Clare."

Jennifer went to the end of the counter and took her time looking through all the flyers and leaflets. She slowly read through a bright orange advertisement of the community theater group's new program, perused the local garden club's meeting dates, gathered up sheets on Pilates, yoga and tai chi in the park. She put her books right on top of the flyers with her face on it and when she picked them up again, all the missing-person flyers came away with her.

Rather than panicked, she felt very serene about this move. That girl didn't look like her. If Nick's goons could look right at her and not see her, her disguise, hiding in plain sight, was working fine. She wouldn't pass muster that easily with Nick, but Nick was very likely to hire this hunt, not participate personally. He was more interested in poker. Still, the flyers had to go.

A wry smile rose to her lips as she tried to imagine Lou even thinking to go into the library to leave them. She had always considered him too dense to connect her love of reading to the library. Was he smarter than she realized or had Nick made the suggestion? Nick was very conscious of her always having a book going. She was never without one.

She had a sudden and crystal-clear memory of her youth—in one of the schools she attended when she was fifteen or sixteen. She had tested well and her English teacher and counselor said, "You're college material, Jennifer."

"Funny, ha-ha," she returned. "I don't think anyone in my family could manage—"

"Your scores are incredibly high. You could get a good scholarship. You should think about this. Tell your mother."

But she couldn't tell her mother something like that. Cherie was too fragile. If she was manic, it could send her into a whirlwind of applications, visiting universities, and who knew what else. If she was depressed, feelings of inadequacy might send her to bed for weeks.

In either case, she could never leave her. And her grand-parents were teetering on the edge of poverty. Her grandfather had been a bus mechanic before retiring, and every bit of his savings plus most of the equity in their little house had been spent getting Cherie out of this or that jam. College was a notion no one in her family could even entertain.

But she had nurtured a secret dream that she could somehow further her education, collect some big fancy degree and feel, every single day, that she was making some kind of significant contribution. It wouldn't hurt to pick up a nice paycheck at the end of the day. Like Louise—smart and independent and doing something that mattered. How about going off to a foreign country for months at a time to study and write? It was a rich fantasy, but short.

That was a long time ago.

She thought about the flyers clutched under her books. To be on the safe side, she went to the post office to buy a book of stamps and look around, but she didn't see any reflections of her former self there.

Not only did she not look like that woman anymore, with every passing day she felt less and less like her. At first she had been so shocked by how plain she was underneath all the hair and makeup, but she was growing so comfortable in this new skin. She had even thrown caution to the wind and bought a pair of khakis that, while not tight, were not as loose as the men's pants she had worn for a month. Khakis and a polo for work now. And at home she shrugged into a pair of jeans for her daily hike, right after she destroyed the flyers.

There was a small park across the freeway from which you could see the huge beauty of Lake Mead. She had spied it the week before and thought that in warm weather it would be the ideal place to lean up against a tree and read for an afternoon. It sat at the base of a small mountain and in front of a complex of condos and town homes. The landscape sloped down toward the lake, and there was nothing to obstruct the view. Since there were also swings, two tennis courts and a baseball diamond, she assumed it had been built for those condo tenants, but it was not fenced and didn't appear to be private. Today seemed like a perfect day to relax under that tree.

She read for a while, but her eyes and her mind wandered, drawn by the massive blue beauty of the lake at the base of the hill. She thought about the flyers, thought about what she would study if she could go back to that day the counselor had told her she was college material, and even thought about what wine she might buy to return the favor to Rose. She thought about how good it felt—having come so far despite the tough times. And now, who could argue that sitting here, under this tree, wasn't the perfect life? She had a sense that nothing could go wrong, nothing could hurt her.

She nodded off and began to dream of wearing gardening gloves and a wide-brimmed hat, tending roses that grew along a fence from which she could see the ocean. Behind her was a house; an old country house with a peaked roof, dormer windows and a porch.

In this dream she became two people—herself and her grandmother. As she clipped the flowers, swept the porch, sat in a rocker with a bowl of snap beans in her lap, her grandfather sat in the opposite chair with his newspaper in his. They had never lived in such a house; theirs had been a brick rambler in a Columbus suburb on a fairly busy street. But this old house seemed familiar somehow. She could hear the ocean, the mighty waves, and feel the sea breeze on her face.

Her grandfather spoke her name. "Doris. Just don't move."

She heard the hissing of the water and told her grandfather she would be still. She smiled at him—why not move? she wondered.

"Doris," he whispered.

Why did he call her that? That wasn't really her—

She opened her eyes and for a moment she was not sure she was awake. She was surrounded by many beasts—four-legged, hairy beasts with incredible horns.

"Shh…" someone said.

She turned her head and there was Alex. He knelt beside her at the base of the tree. He reached for her hand and gently pulled, getting her up on her knees. "Slowly now," he whispered, and quietly directed her behind the tree. Then he placed himself behind her, edging her knees apart so that he knelt between them, putting her between the tree and himself. "Just in case there's any butting," he whispered into her ear. "Just don't move." Kneeling there within feet of all these snorting, grunting, chewing animals, it no longer seemed much of an issue that recently this man had been staring gape-mouthed at her as she danced around in her underwear. In fact, feeling the front of his body against her back, she felt she knew him very well. His arms were around her, gripping the tree, pressing her close to it for safety. He had been less than friendly in the diner. Apparently he'd gotten over it.

"What are they?" she whispered back.

"Bighorn sheep. Ewes. Rams. They come down to this park to graze. We'll be fine—be very still."

She couldn't take her eyes off their matted hair, their giant hooves and those *horns*. The rams' were curled back around their heads and looked monstrously strong, while the ewes' were straight, slanting backward. Smaller than horses but larger than goats, they grazed all around her. Some of them—males—were so large they might've weighed two hundred pounds. What she had thought was the ocean in her dream had been the convergence of these animals, perhaps thirty of them, grazing contentedly on the park's grass.

Fifty yards to her left, where a street fronted the condos, she saw there was a bus with the label Vegas Fantasy Tours on its silver side. People had disembarked and were standing around taking pictures of the herd. On the other side of the park at a gratefully safe distance two rams suddenly butted heads, scraping their big hooves in the dust.

"If it were mating season, or if the lambs were here, this would be a very dicey spot," Alex whispered. "We'd be in trouble. But the ewes are pregnant. Judging by their shapes, it won't be long."

"Really? When?" she asked, her voice filled with childlike wonder.

"Soon. When they come, we'll look from a safer distance."

A sense of anxiety suddenly came over her and she

realized it was simply because he'd made a reference to something they'd do in the future. She'd always been very sensitive to any statement indicating future plans. Since childhood that had been a big issue. Promises of something to come usually meant disappointment. Or it could hold an ominous warning. No wonder she'd stuck to rich old men and had never put down any real relationship roots! She was afraid to depend on any person or event that might exist in the future.

"Do they scare you?" he asked in a whisper.

"No. No, not at all."

He rubbed her upper arms with his hands. "It seemed like you got tense there for a second."

She took a deep breath and blew it out slowly. "No, I love them. Maybe I was just a little excited."

The herd continued to graze without seeming to pay any attention to the humans behind the tree, or the ones at the roadside snapping pictures, but they did seem to be moving away from Jennifer and Alex. The ewes were heavy with their pregnancies and the rams seemed to prefer bachelor groups rather than staying with their mates.

She breathed slowly and quietly, enjoying the incredible experience of being amid these creatures she couldn't remember ever seeing before, even in a zoo.

"They don't smell all that great, do they?" she whispered.

She felt his body shake in silent laughter.

It was a long while—a good thirty minutes—when one large matted male sauntered out of the park toward the road. A second followed and a third. It was as though he had called "time" and all the animals were to leave. They formed a perfect thin line of rams and ewes as they walked down the road a few blocks to the mountain. She noticed a trail snake its way up the hillside to the very top. She watched in fascination as they made their way slowly toward home.

Her legs were getting stiff and sore, and her knees were numb, but she didn't want this to end. She wanted to stay in this little pocket forever. Alex seemed in no hurry to move, either.

When the animals had left the park and the air cleared somewhat, she realized that Alex wore a very alluring cologne. She lay her cheek against the tree and closed her eyes, inhaling the attractive scent.

He could have gotten up and moved away. There was no danger from the sheep—if there ever had been—as they were starting up the hill. It wasn't until they could hear the engine of the bus start up that Alex scooted back and stood up, as did she. He grinned a very handsome grin. "Have you ever seen anything like that in your life?"

"Never," she said, a little breathless. "I'm still seeing it," she said, looking around the tree at the sight of the sheep moving up the mountain to the top. "I thought I was having a dream about the ocean—it was their hooves all around me, I bet."

"Probably."

"How did you find me?"

"I didn't. They've been grazing in this park for years. I was on my bike and I like to see them come down. There you were," he said with a shrug.

He turned toward the condos and waved. There were several people sitting on their front patios just to watch the sheep, and probably more were looking from inside.

"The sheep don't mind people being here?"

"I don't think they really noticed you. They're used to a human scent around here, it being a park and all. And you were asleep," he said, bending to pick up her forgotten book. "If there had been people using the park, they'd have gone back over the hill. I don't think they'd attack unless threatened or provoked. But during mating season, they're pretty oblivious to everything but getting their girl, and you don't want to get in the middle of that. Believe me."

"And there will be babies soon," she said dreamily.

"You might want to give them a little space when they have the lambs. You just never know."

"Oh, sure," she said, leaning back against the tree. "I'm nothing if not polite."

"Did you walk here?"

"I like to think I hiked," she said, and forgetting herself completely, she smiled. "There are the greatest trails and parks around here."

"Want a ride home?"

"On your bike?"

"I'm afraid that's the only option I have."

"That's okay. I'll go ahead and walk."

"You sure? When was the last time somebody bucked you home?" He grinned boyishly, full of trouble. This was a whole new Alex.

"Bucked?" she asked with a laugh.

"Isn't that what you called it as a kid? That's what I called it. You jump up on the handlebars and I do all the work...."

"We used to do it the other way—one sitting on the bicycle seat and the other one standing to pedal."

"Girl stuff. We did it the *dangerous* way. Come on," he said, taking her hand. "You don't weigh hardly anything. But those legs..." He looked down the length of them. "Spoke material. You'll have to keep them out of the way."

"I don't think this is a good idea...."

"What the hell, Doris. From what little I know of you, I thought you were the fun-loving type." She blushed despite herself. How was it, she wondered, with her level of experience with men, that this simple guy on a bike could make her *blush?* He dropped her book in a leather pouch fastened on the back of the bike. "Come on—live a little dangerously."

Little did he know... "I'm heavier than I look."

"You're actually pretty skinny. But another month of eating Adolfo's food should get you right. Come on. Jump on."

"Really. There's a hill and everything—"

"Nothing I can't handle," he said, puffing up a little. At least he didn't flex his muscles.

She struggled onto the handlebars, gripping the bars on each side and tucking her feet back out of the way. "This is so nuts," she said.

His voice was that of an excited kid. "I haven't done this in *years.*" He pushed down on one pedal and the bike went a little off balance. Jennifer flipped right off the handlebars and tumbled onto the dust. She rolled over and looked up at him from a sitting position on the ground. "Whoops," he said.

"Whoops?"

"That was a bad start. I've got it now."

"Oh, *puleese*," she returned. But she got up and situated herself on the handlebars again, giving him a second chance. This time when he put his weight on the pedal he kept the bike from going off balance, but it did twist and turn and cause her to laugh and scream and giggle until he got it under way.

After a little while he was in balance and she was comfortable. But there was a hill to climb and she could hear him start to breathe hard. She said, "You're right, this is very nice."

"Yeah," he said breathlessly. "Great."

"Want me to get off and walk a bit, until you're up the hill?"

"No. I...got...it."

"You sure? I know I'm heavy."

"Got...it..."

"So, how long have you been going to the park to watch the sheep? And by the way, when do you work?"

"Talk...later..."

She smiled. She knew that. It was just a little of the devil in her. After all, he'd seen her in her underwear, she'd like to see him at least struggling up the hill.

But damned if he didn't make it, impressing her, knowing it was a difficult thing to do. Once he was on flat ground he sat back on the seat and began to whistle. She didn't know the song at first, then she recognized, "I've got the world on a string, sitting on a rainbow," and she squealed with laughter wilder and louder than she'd indulged in for ages.

"I knew it—you're a cad!"

He began to sing the song. Before long she was singing along. This somehow caused him to swing wide in an *S* pattern down the middle of the street. She had to grip extra hard in the turns. Down the road they went, laughing and singing and almost toppling at each turn, looking more like teenagers than their actual ages. Then they got to Louise's house.

She jumped off. "Thanks, Alex. That was actually fun."

"You are heavier than you look," he agreed.

"You're stronger than you look," she said, but she said it with a very big smile. She grabbed her book out of his bike pouch. "See you around, pardner," she said, jogging toward her front door. She turned once she got there and added, "Oh, by the way. Would you mind letting me know when you're going to be doing the yard? Just a knock on the door would help."

"Awww…"

"Now, be mature. Although I know it's hard for you."

"All right."

"And…you know…thanks."

"Anytime."

She went inside, gave Alice some love and a trip out back, and got right on the computer.

Dear Louise,
I had the most magical afternoon of my life. I had decided on a park for an afternoon of reading and…

* * *

Alex put away his bike and closed the garage door. He opened the window over the kitchen sink and heard, from the house next door, the soft strains of "I've Got the World on a String…" He smiled to himself. He went to the desk in the bedroom he used as an office, opened the drawer and looked at the face on the flyer.

He had been coming out of the barber shop a couple of weeks ago when he ran into a man who was showing the flyers to passersby. Alex asked if he could have one. On first glance, the resemblance wasn't obvious, but a couple more breakfasts at the diner assured him. It was her. It didn't take him long to decide what he'd do—he was very good at playing his cards close to his chest. He'd watch her, maybe check her out, but no way was he going to tip someone off about her whereabouts. If she was in hiding, there was probably a good reason.

"Jeez, Doris—it must have been pretty scary to drive you to such lengths…."

And then he gently closed the drawer on her face.

The way she behaved around him, especially today, he suspected she didn't yet know what he did for a living. Louise must not have told her. The old girl was pretty good at keeping her hand to herself, as well.

But it was going to come out pretty soon.

At the end of Jennifer's shift, as she was getting ready to leave, Buzz looked up at her from where he sat at the counter, his checkbook, calculator, canceled checks and bank statement spread out in front of him.

The expression on his face indicated he faced sheer chaos.

"Doris," he said, frustration drawing out the name. "I have to figure this out. Do me a favor? On your way home, drop off a take-out order? It's for Mrs. Van Der Haff. It's only a block out of your way."

"Sure, boss."

"Adolfo's getting it ready." He grabbed a napkin out of the dispenser and wrote the address on it. "Just go left instead of right at the corner."

"Do I know her? Has she been in here to eat?"

"No. She doesn't get out."

Very soon she realized she had been by this house before, on one of her many walks. It was one of those that seemed to be falling apart. The front porch, obviously added on many years earlier, sagged dangerously. A cyclone fence bordered the yard, which was nothing but dirt and dead weeds, and there was an old red metal sign on the gate that read Beware of Dog. The windows were too grimy to allow even the faintest light within.

"Yoo-hoo," she called into the yard. Nothing. She had never seen a dog in the yard that she remembered. At least not a scary one. Surely Buzz would have mentioned if there were something to be concerned about. She looked around for a sign—anyone who let a yard go to such ruin was obviously ill-disposed to pick up droppings.

Still, she entered cautiously. She tested each step onto the porch and tried to step lightly; it looked as if it might give way. Once she was on the porch, she found it was firm enough. It didn't even squeak—it just listed.

She knocked on the screen door and waited. And

waited. And waited. She couldn't find a doorbell. She pressed her ear to the door, knocking again, and finally she heard some stirring inside. Very, very slowly.

"Who is it?" came the feeble female voice from within.

"Doris. From the diner. I have your takeout."

The door creaked open and there stood the tiniest woman with very sparse, kinky white hair on her head. She wore a flowered cotton dress that hung on her bony frame and it had a couple of tassels on the zipper pull. "Takeout?" she asked faintly.

"Buzz asked me to bring it by." Jennifer smiled at the woman.

"You're not Buzz," she said.

"No. I'm Doris. I'm one of the waitresses."

"Oh," she said, making no effort to open the door.

"Can I bring it in?" she finally asked.

"Oh. I suppose." She moved away from the door very slowly.

When Doris got inside she found the place was barely furnished, but full of newspapers, magazines and books, stacked on the floor, in corners, filling the hallway. There were a couple of trash bags, full of either trash or something else. In the little living room there was but one chair, a recliner that seemed to be losing its stuffing and its will to live, and an ancient metal TV tray, bent and rusted at the kinks. There wasn't another chair or sofa in sight. The whole place was musty, dirty, cluttered and falling apart.

"Why don't you sit down and let me put it out for you. I can set it on the tray here."

"Oh," she said. Head down, she shuffled back to her chair, which took her some time, and finally began to lower herself. After just a short trip downward, she let herself drop with an *oomph.* "All right," she said. Then she looked up at Jennifer with sad, rheumy eyes and smiled, showing slippery dentures.

Jennifer put the bag on the tray. "Now, let's see what we have. " She pulled out the napkin, shook it out with a flourish and draped it across Mrs. Van Der Haff's lap. She pulled the cardboard container out of the bag and opened it up. "Ah, the house special, I see. Meat loaf, mashed potatoes, lima beans. Mmm. It looks like you're going to need some utensils. In the kitchen?" she asked.

"I suppose," the old woman said.

The kitchen was in a pretty bleak state. There was a kettle on the stove, a cup with an old, wilted tea bag in it, dishes in the sink, an open cracker box on the counter. Even though she knew it would be intrusive, she opened the refrigerator. There was a brown banana, a small carton of milk, an opened can of green beans and, staring out at her, several cardboard containers from the diner. She closed it gently, so as not to be heard.

There was a can opener lying on the counter and Jennifer opened the cupboard door above it, afraid she was going to see cat food. She sighed in relief to see four cans of tuna, thank goodness!

In the drawer she found a few utensils, and she chose a spoon and fork, then returned to the living room. "Now, I think you're set. Would you like me to take the food out of the carton and put it on a plate for you?"

"No. No, don't do that," she said, grabbing the box

in both hands as though it might be snatched away from her. "That would make a dirty dish."

"You're right. We have to be practical. By the way, where's the dog?"

She kind of ducked her head and said, in nearly a whisper, "There hasn't been a dog in years. Keeps the burglars away."

"Certainly," Jennifer said. As if there was anything to steal. She looked around uncomfortably. She wondered what Buzz did after putting out the food.

Mrs. Van Der Haff began to slowly pick at the food, one delicate bite at a time, chewing carefully. Jennifer watched this for five minutes or so, the woman not looking up from her lunch even once, when she said, "Well, I believe I'll get going, unless there's something more I can get you."

Fork in hand, she waved Jennifer away without looking up.

Once outside, she felt her heart threaten to collapse in sadness. This is what happens when you're old and left entirely alone with no one to look in on you, no one to help out. And clearly the woman lived in abject poverty.

This could happen to a person like me, she thought. If I don't plan carefully and make some sort of arrangements for myself in old age. Because I have no one.

She went back to the diner instead of going home. "Mission accomplished," she told Buzz. "Anytime you need me to deliver, it's fine."

"Makes you feel kind of spoiled and lucky, don't it?" he asked.

She nodded and thought, even me. Even me.

"Has she no one at all?"

"There's a son somewhere, but I don't think he comes around. I drop by and check on her from time to time."

"Someone should take out the trash," Jennifer said. "I guess I could've done that while I was—"

"Trash? She has trash to go out?"

"Well, there were several big bags, tied off. I just assumed…"

"That's not trash," he said, looking back at his mess of calculations. "That's stuff she can't stand to part with."

"Stuff? Like what kind of stuff?"

"I've never had the guts to ask."

Jennifer's brief visit with Mrs. Van Der Haff stirred deep thoughts about the future, and not entirely pleasant ones. But then she thought about Rose, unmarried and independent and not in any way pathetic. In fact, she was empowering as a role model.

There was a wine shop in town. New, according to Buzz. Jennifer decided to take a bottle of wine to Rose's house to return the favor, but more to have her company for a little while. She had messages to pass on from Louise, questions to ask about Alex, and just being with Rose gave her a lift, a feeling of optimism.

As the door to Rose's house opened, Jennifer presented the bottle as a maître d' might. "I know you have the glasses."

"Perfect," Rose said. "Absolutely perfect." She held the door open.

Jennifer stepped inside and instantly felt she was intruding; Rose had her dining table very richly appointed with china, crystal and tall tapers, not yet lit. "Oh, I'm so sorry. I should have asked. You're having company."

"No, I'm not," Rose said, taking the bottle from her.

"But your table…"

"I'll set another place. I won't be having dinner for another hour. We can have a leisurely glass and then I'll split my Cornish game hen with you. I never eat more than half. You'll love it, especially after weeks of that diner food."

As Rose went into the kitchen with the wine, Jennifer looked around. Rose's small house, the floor plan identical to Louise's, was coordinated in perfect country French, right down to the lace runner that lay down the length of her light oak table. Her wallpaper was a pattern of dark green and terra-cotta flowers, and the plates on her table were rimmed in the same dark green. There was an oak buffet that matched the table upon which sat a silk flower arrangement that matched the wallpaper.

Louise's house was comfortable and serviceable, but this was absolutely stunning in its perfection. Like Rose.

She came back first with the opened bottle and two glasses. "Have a seat in the living room and pour for us, will you?" She went again to the kitchen and came out with a place mat, dishes, flatware and a linen napkin. She made a place for Jennifer at the opposite end of the table.

Jennifer looked down at her sweatshirt and jeans and

felt she should have dressed so much better than this to come to Rose's house. But then, she didn't actually have anything better. "Are you sure you aren't expecting company?"

"I hardly ever have company. I go out, but I don't have men in—it gives them ideas. I have a few friends over for cards now and then. Retired dancers and floor managers, you know. But otherwise it's Louise and Alex and the occasional out-of-towner—the out-of-towners less often every year."

"But your table—"

"I'm very good to myself, Doris. It's a very important custom." She plucked a glass gracefully off the table and glided down into a sitting position. "Every night that I eat at home I set a proper table and make a civilized meal. Single women—especially old ones—tend to skip meals or eat out of opened cans. Louise is especially guilty of this."

"Oh, that reminds me. My reason for coming over. I had an e-mail from Louise today and she specifically asked me to tell you that she spent the day in Piccadilly and saw female impersonators whom you would have loved."

Rose made a face. "Phoo! That witch! She did that on purpose. Trying to make me envious. She always tries to get me to go with her and I can't."

"Can't?"

She leaned forward. "That would involve an airplane. I don't *believe* in airplanes."

Jennifer laughed in spite of herself. "Fortunately, they believe in you."

"Don't be pert."

"Is it the claustrophobia?"

"No. It's being hurtled through space in a tube going hundreds of miles per hour."

"It's very convenient," Jennifer pointed out.

"Ptui."

"I'm amazed. You seem so fearless. So...*brazen.*"

She smiled broadly, showing her beautiful teeth. Clearly she was flattered by the remark. "Thank you, dear. You know, I've been thinking about you lately." Rose leaned forward and studied Jennifer closely, the slightest frown wrinkling her brow.

"Have you?"

"Yes, actually. I think we need to find someone who can shape up that haircut of yours. Take the 'go navy' look out and put the chic in."

"Oh, Rose," she laughed. She rubbed a hand over her hair, which had grown in quite a bit in the several weeks since she'd shaved it. "You're too much."

"Honestly, Doris, do you have any *real* objection to looking like a woman?"

"I'm not very prissy, Rose."

"Of course not, but we can work with this," she said, reaching across the short distance that separated them and grasping Jennifer's chin. She turned her head left, then right. "This shorter-than-short look has potential. Not many women have the cheekbones for it." She held Jennifer's chin still and stared deeply into her eyes. "Although you try to hide it in the most horrible clothes, you're very beautiful. With just the smallest effort, you could present a stunning look." She leaned back again. "I saw you on his handlebars, laughing your ass off."

She colored a little in spite of herself. These people all seemed to have a gift for catching her unawares and leaving her slightly embarrassed. This flush had nothing to do with being caught with a man, as Jennifer was more than experienced in that arena. It was being caught at anything that drew attention to herself. She should be keeping a lower profile, just to be safe. "Guilty," she finally said.

"You *must* be feeling guilty, blushing like a schoolgirl. Don't be embarrassed. A woman could hardly do better than Alex."

"Now, Rose, I don't intend to *do* Alex."

Rose roared with laughter, loving that. "Well, I won't tell him. It might break his heart."

"By the way," Jennifer asked. "Does he work?"

"Oh, my, yes, he works. He's a police detective."

Jennifer tried to keep her expression steady. Bland. "Really?" she responded flatly.

But clearly she hadn't succeeded. Rose lifted one eyebrow and peered at her. And, uncharacteristically, remained very quiet for a long moment. At last she said, "I think that air of mystery may work for you, Doris. You're excellent at it."

Seven

Jennifer lay on the living room floor, resting her head on Alice's side. Alice was not only a very good pillow, she was also a good listener. "Police detective?" she asked Alice. "Could this get any worse?"

Jennifer wasn't quite sure who she should be more worried about—Nick or the police. They were both frightening prospects. If the police recognized her, wouldn't they arrest her for that missing money and jewelry Nick claimed she had stolen? A search of her belongings would produce it—and then it would become her word against Nick's. At the very least, wouldn't they contact Nick and tell him his missing person—and money and jewelry—had been located?

She played it out another way in her mind. What if she went to the police and told them everything? What she heard, what she saw, why she ran. Wouldn't they be compelled to search for Barbara Noble's body? How long could Nick keep them at bay by pretending she was out of the country?

But…if they looked for Barbara and found she was *indeed* missing? That her *body* was missing? Wouldn't they then do whatever they could to keep Jennifer safe? Safe…so she could *testify* against Nick? Oh, God, that was even more daunting.

She rolled over, buried her face in Alice's soft fur and moaned. Alice yawned loudly and rolled onto her back to have her belly scratched.

"No matter how I play this thing out in my mind, it just keeps getting worse."

She sat up and absently stroked Alice's stomach for a while, deep in thought. Alice slowly got to a sitting position, leaned forward and gave Jennifer a tender lick on the cheek, making her laugh. "Did I leave a little Cornish game hén on my cheek?"

She hugged the dog. "I might be a little nervous about how this is going to come out, but I'm not complaining," she said to Alice. "I pretty much have it made. And you are truly the best roommate I've ever had." She hugged the dog and resolved to try to just go with the flow. One day at a time. "Come on, girlfriend. Off to bed with us. Four-thirty comes pretty early."

When Jennifer opened the door to the diner right at 5:00 a.m., she was greeted by the sounds of sniveling, arguing, lecturing and grousing in Spanish. Behind the counter in the grill area Hedda's mother, Sylvia, sat on a stool. She was swearing and complaining very angrily, but it was muffled as her face was obscured by an ice pack held to her nose. She wore her short black cock-tail-waitress uniform and black mesh stockings, but one leg was torn, exposing a bloodied knee. She was all high heels and cleavage, but her hair looked as though she'd taken a roll down a hill.

"What's going on?"

"Oh, God, does *she* have to be in on it?" Sylvia griped.

"For God's sake, Sylvia, you want me to ask her to wait outside while you make excuses for some useless son of a bitch you brought home from the bar? For about the hundredth time?" Buzz demanded.

She wailed, "It's none of her goddamn business!"

Jennifer crept closer. "He *hit* you? In the face?"

Sylvia pulled away the ice pack and Jennifer gasped. Her nose might be broken and both eyes were going to be black. And there was the unmistakable odor of alcohol. Plenty of it. "It wasn't his fault," she said with a hiccup.

"You hit *yourself* in the face?" Jennifer asked.

"Very funny."

Jennifer went to get her apron. "I wasn't trying to be funny. Where are the kids?"

"I haven't even been home yet," she said. "They don't know about this."

"Thank God," she said. "You can't put them in danger like this. Jesus."

"Mind your own business!"

"She's right. I should call a cop," Buzz said.

"You do that and you know how bad it can get for my kids. Believe me, I never let that loser anywhere near them."

"Well, that's something," Jennifer said, imagining another nocturnal visit from Hedda while Sylvia "entertained."

"I hit him first," she said.

"Es probable verdad. Estúpido."

"What?" Jennifer asked.

"Is probably truth," Adolfo said. "Stupid people. No respect."

"Are you going to let him talk about me like that?" Sylvia asked Buzz.

"I *agree* with him! Stupid people. No respect!"

From the alley behind the diner a man yelled, "Sylvia! Sylvia!"

"Ho Dios. Aqui hay problemas." He looked at Jennifer. "Big trouble."

Sylvia yelled, "Go away, Roger! Someone's going to call the cops!"

But he was undeterred, pounding at the door. "Let me in! Wait till you see what she did to *me!*"

And that's when it started. A melee. Roger somehow got into the diner through the back door, which probably hadn't been locked in the first place. He was shouting about the scratches on his face and neck, which were admittedly gruesome, while Sylvia was shouting about her nose, which might be broken. Buzz was shouting at both of them, saying that they were no better than scrappy trash the way they fought, and her raising two kids in that kind of chaos, she should be ashamed. All the while Adolfo was yelling about *Estupido, bastardos* and *no respeto.*

Roger advanced on Sylvia, shouting, calling her vile

names. Sylvia advanced on Roger doing the same. And Buzz tried to put himself between them. Adolfo was yelling about the *policía* while Jennifer backed up against the pantry door. Roger shoved Sylvia into Buzz, but Sylvia, though small, seemed possessed of a wiry strength and wound up to sock Roger right in the chops when she seemed to twist her ankle in those three-inch heels. Her swing went awry and found Jennifer's jaw. Jennifer felt her head explode and then the lights went out.

She wasn't unconscious long, but when she came to, everything about that wild morning had changed. She was cradled in Adolfo's arms while Buzz held a cold cloth to her jaw, cheek and eye. She struggled to sit up and heard a siren in the distance.

"Easy, *mija*," Adolfo said. "You went out like the light."

"Jesus, did anyone get the license plate number?" she asked. She looked around. "Where are they?"

"Are you kidding?" Buzz asked. "Gone, like the cowards they are. Don't worry, Doris. I'll take care of you. I called the paramedics, and if you have to go to the hospital—"

She grabbed his hand and looked into his eyes. "Buzz. I *can't* go to the hospital."

"It's all right, Doris," he said, patting her hand. "Don't worry about money right now. I'm more than ready to—"

"No. I can't. Please, I'm fine."

Adolfo began to gently massage her shoulders. *"Ella tiene miedo."*

"Oh?" Buzz asked. "Doris, you don't have to be afraid of anything."

"I'm not afraid," she said, getting to her feet. Once standing, she was very woozy and not too steady, but she got her balance quickly. Although her jaw pounded and she was light-headed and her eyes were glassy, she forced a smile. "Besides, I'm fine. You check on Sylvia. At least check on the kids. I'll be fine."

"I'm not so sure. Why don't you let them just look at you—"

The sirens came closer. "Because I can't, Buzz. I can't. If they think something is wrong and want to take me in and I refuse... Look, just tell them the person you called about is gone and refused to be seen by any paramedics. Or send them to Sylvia's house—that would serve her right." While talking, she was making her way toward the bathroom. Then she stopped, retraced her steps and grabbed the cold pack. She shook it at them both. "I'm gone. Remember." And she ran for the bathroom.

"Why is every woman I'm within ten feet of a nutcase?" Buzz asked rhetorically.

"*A lo mesor tu eres loco.*"

"Is that so? I'm crazy? You don't think I'm so crazy when I pay you a little extra."

"*Sí. Muy chicuito.*"

"Oh, bite me, as Hedda would say."

Jennifer listened at the door while Buzz tried to explain that the waitress who was accidentally punched in the side of the head decided she was fine and just wanted to go home. It took a while, as the paramedics were reluctant to be called out at such an unholy hour only to have it be a false alarm. Maybe in some of the busier neighborhoods of Las Vegas the paramedics would be up all night, ready for the next call, but as one paramedic pointed out, "This is Boulder City, man. I was just getting to the good part of the dream!"

All the while Jennifer wondered if she was making the right decision. She felt a little empty-headed, like maybe her brains had been good and rattled. Finally, the place was quiet enough that she thought it safe to leave the bathroom. All she could hear were the soft murmurings of Buzz and Adolfo.

Not Buzz and Adolfo. There stood Alex.

He fairly scowled as he looked at her.

"Hey," she said.

He took her chin between his thumb and forefinger and turned her face this way and that to examine the injury. Frowning, he said, "Hey."

"You're up early," she observed, at the same time noticing that he wore an extremely wrinkled pair of chinos, a ratty sweatshirt and no socks—hastily dressed. Of course he was unshaven. They had *called* him. And he must have raced to the diner; she hadn't been in the bathroom all that long. She tried not to stare at his bristly chin, his mussy hair. She tried not to think about the fact that this must be what he looked like when just waking up. Ruggedly handsome.

"Buzz said you had a little trouble here."

"*Grande,*" said Adolfo.

"Well, Doris didn't have the trouble. I mean, she accidentally got socked in the jaw when Sylvia and some horse's ass got into it right in my grill, duking it out. She got sideswiped. And she don't want any medical attention, but you can see she can't work. So I thought, you being right next door…"

He let go of her chin. "You couldn't wake Rose. You'd never hear the end."

"Tell me about it."

"Come on, Doris. I'll take you home."

"Thanks, Alex, but really, I'm fine."

"You're not fine," all three men said.

"Well, I will be. Just let me have a couple of aspirin and give me a minute."

Alex grabbed her hand and pulled her toward the door. "Come on. Let's not be stupid. Or stupider."

She pulled her hand out of his. "Hey. I was an innocent bystander here. Don't act like I just got into a rumble." And then she swayed again.

"*Suavemente.* Gently. Is not the señorita's doing, *Alejandro.*"

"I know. You're right. I'm a little cranky in the morning."

"Well, settle down. I'm the one who got punched." She walked past him, grabbed her hoodie off the hook by the door and said, "Are you walking me home, or what?"

He was cranky, she was huffy, but about a block down the street, the sun just barely coming up over the mountains, she took a deep breath and slowed her pace a little. The fresh morning air did wonders for her head.

"What, exactly, happened?" Alex asked her.

"Just what Buzz said. Sylvia was having a fistfight

with some guy named Roger and I think she slipped. I saw her fist miss Roger's head by a mile and that's the last thing I saw."

"Talk about being in the wrong place at the wrong time."

I seem to have a penchant for it, she thought. "No kidding."

"That's why Buzz looks out for Hedda. Sylvia's a little unstable."

"That's an understatement."

"You must think this is the craziest place you've ever been."

"Hah. I might if I were a normal person, but if you knew how I grew up… Well, forget it. It was like a flash from the past."

"I'm sorry to hear that."

"I'm sorry I lived that. But hey—I'm fine now, right? Except my reaction time sucks."

"Yeah. You need to practice ducking."

"Gotcha."

About halfway home, he reached for her hand. She stopped dead in her tracks and looked up at him, shocked. "I'm a sucker for a beat-up woman," he said, and, pulling her along, held her hand the rest of the way home.

Jennifer couldn't remember the last time anyone had held her hand. High school? Oh, she'd had plenty of men, some lusty men, but walking her home and holding her hand? Long ago and far away. There had been that one time, that one boy in high school to whom she'd given her heart, and when he broke it she swore off love. From that point on she'd been in charge of the relationships she had. She might have been physically and mentally in tune to the men in her life, but she was emotionally unavailable, and she knew it. It had been quite deliberate.

As she held his hand, she remembered what it was like to feel innocence and love. To have the feeling come to you and be completely vulnerable to it. At least she hoped she was just remembering it and not actually feeling it.

Once home, Alex went inside with her. He directed her to the couch, where he propped a couple of pillows at one end, instructing her to keep her head elevated. He fixed up a new ice pack and brought her two aspirin. Alice immediately came to her, laying her head on Jennifer's belly to offer both comfort and support.

Alex sat on the coffee table, elbows on knees, and looked into her eyes. "You must be really afraid of something to refuse to let the paramedics even check you over."

She stared back at him. He was so earnest. So kind. "I'll be fine. Buzz shouldn't have called them."

"He should have called the police."

He had a very small scar that cut through one eyebrow. He had a cleft in his chin, just a little one, tucked there under the bristles. He probably knew how handsome he was. He probably broke hearts all over the place. She was very grateful to be immune. "He did."

"I mean the Boulder police. Those two would have gone straight to jail. There isn't any need for one or the other to press charges. If there's battery, there's an arrest. Or two. Might do her good to spend the night in jail. But Buzz is afraid Children's Services would haul off Hedda and her little brother.... Still..."

Jennifer felt tears threaten. "It's all right," she said, but she said it in such a soft whisper that he could barely hear her.

"So." He touched her cheek on the side that wasn't injured. "You know I'm a police officer."

Her lips moved over the name "Rose."

"Ah. Sure. The girls are very proud of that, that they have their very own cop taking out their trash and trimming up their yards. But Louise didn't tell you before you moved in?"

She shook her head. "Frankly, it took me by surprise. I wonder why she didn't tell me."

"Well, I've asked them not to brag about it—I don't like to bring my work home." He shrugged. "She might've thought you'd bolt if you knew."

"Should I? Bolt?"

"There's absolutely no reason to."

He smiled at her. Oh, damn, there was a dimple. She had managed to forget about that for a while. She tried to sniff back a tear, but it escaped and she made a sound that was half hiccup and half sob. He'd think she was crying about being afraid of the police or something, but she was crying because he held her hand and had a dimple. And immunity was slipping out of her reach. Her control, her greatest asset, was going bye-bye.

"Is there any way I can help you, Doris?"

She just shook her head and tried to get a grip.

"Are you on the run?"

She took a deep breath and willed her voice not to tremble. "Just from an abusive ex-boyfriend who said he'd kill me, and I believed him." She shrugged. "I just want a little time to get my life together."

"What's his name?"

She pursed her lips and closed her eyes, causing a large well of tears to overflow and run down her cheeks, then shook her head. No way.

"Do you trust me?" he asked.

She shook her head again. Why should she? One ride on a guy's handlebars didn't make them soul mates. She opened her eyes and said, "Hey. I trusted *him*."

"I want to ask you a question. Just one. Please don't lie to me. Have you broken any laws?"

She sat up straighter, dropped the cold pack into her lap and said, "I swear to God, Alex! I've never in my life broken any laws!" He stared at her hard. "I swear to *God!*"

"Okay," he finally said, giving her hand a squeeze. "Don't worry about anything, then." He stood up. "That aspirin will kick in, but keep the cold pack on, okay? I'll take Alice for a little walk around the park. Get some rest. Relax."

He lifted the leash off the peg by the door, which brought Alice immediately to him. "Fair-weather dog," Jennifer accused.

"We'll be right back."

"Thanks," she said.

"And when you're ready, you tell me how I can help you."

She didn't say anything and he left. But she thought,

wouldn't that be nice? To ask someone for help and have it delivered, free of obligation. Just like good friends. Friends who trust each other. Wouldn't that be nice? Wouldn't that be rare?

She slept, and when she woke, Alice was back, lying faithfully beside her. A throw was placed over her and on the coffee table beside her was a sandwich covered with plastic wrap along with a glass of water.

Alex believed her. Not just because he wanted to, but because his gut instinct had kicked in. He had looked a lot of criminals in the eyes while he asked them questions and they very seldom fooled him. They very seldom told the truth, too. They'd lie about their name, where they got the car, who they were with, where they were going, whether they had any warrants. Most of the time, just an honest answer would cut them a break.

Her eyes were honest and earnest. She was hiding from someone, very likely the abusive ex like she said, and she hadn't broken any laws. It certainly was not against the law for an adult to be missing.

He hadn't particularly liked the looks of the man who'd handed him the flyers outside the barber shop, however.

He went to work a little early that afternoon and began a search of both Jennifer Chaise and Doris Bailey. He had a couple of hours before his shift and a real need to know.

There were lots of winners, lots of outstanding warrants, but luckily for Jennifer she didn't fit any of the descriptions. There was one match—Jennifer Chaise of

Fort Lauderdale, missing. No wants or warrants. If Jennifer was hiding now, it appeared to be for the first time. She had a Florida residence, two previous residences, Florida driver's license, social, no priors, and a good job with a commercial real estate firm. Clean as a whistle. So far. The next thing he'd do is check out her place of employment and see if she could afford her address and car on her income.

Then he did a search on the man who had reported her missing. Nick Noble. He ran an out-of-state check—bingo! The guy had an arrest record about ten miles long—fraud, conspiracy, trafficking. And *no* convictions. He was not currently wanted or indicted, and could go to the police fearlessly.

"Whatcha doing?"

He looked over his shoulder at his partner, Paula. He lifted the flyers with Jennifer's picture on it. "Someone was handing out these flyers all over Boulder City, so I was checking her out. Actually, she checks out just fine, but the guy who reported her missing doesn't check that well. He's had quite a few brushes with the law."

She studied it. "Have you seen her?"

He hated that, when she could nail it like that. She was just about as good at detecting a lie as he was, so he tried to avoid telling one. "I was curious about why someone would be looking for her in Boulder City. She's from Florida and disappeared from the MGM Grand, according to the report."

"Maybe whoever put out the flyers left them in a lot of small towns around Las Vegas."

"Maybe," he said.

"What's your interest in her, Alex? Really?"

"I think maybe she's missing on purpose. And I think it's possible the guy has accused her of stealing to get the police to help him find her. And I think he might know where she's been hiding out. Now what I'd like to know is why he wants her so bad."

"Well. She's very beautiful," Paula said, looking at the flyer.

"There's that." Hmm, he thought, she still is beautiful and doesn't look very much like that anymore. But there was no denying she was sexy, alluring and unconventional.

Paula picked up the report filed when Noble notified the police of the theft. "We have bigger fish to fry than this," she said. "She was his squeeze. She took a few souvenirs with her when she left him. He's been in lots of trouble with the Florida police—he's probably a sleazeball."

"Right," Alex said, gathering up the papers he'd printed out and putting them in a file, which went right into his desk drawer. "But if she took souvenirs, it's the first time on her record. I'm just saying."

"Uh-huh. And we have a string of home invasions in Northeast. Are we going to work?"

"Yeah, yeah. We have a target team to sit surveillance with us. Let's go."

Paula began to whistle. The tune was *Alex has a girl-friend, Alex has a girlfriend.*

"Drop it," he said, his voice threatening.

She continued to whistle until it became difficult to whistle and smile at the same time.

* * *

Dear Louise,

Every day here gets more interesting than the one before. Did you know that Buzz delivers meals to people he knows are hungry? I haven't been able to figure out if he has a set schedule, but yesterday I took lunch to a little old lady just a couple of blocks from here, and she lives in abject poverty. Someone should be taking care of her. Someone should do something about that house. And another thing that happened—I got right in the middle of a knock-down fight between Sylvia and some guy she picked up and I was decked. Poor Hedda!

Oh, and here's one for you. I just found out that Alex is a cop. You might've warned me.
Love,
Doris

Dear Doris,

Buzz has been doing that for years. He's very careful. He does exactly the right amount because he doesn't want to hurt anyone's pride. He knows that even those destitute little old people are fiercely independent and don't want to give up their homes, however humble, to be caged up in some kind of government-run facility. Yet, there comes a time when it's necessary.

That Sylvia. Poor Hedda indeed. Watch out for her.

As for Alex—I had hoped you'd begin to like him

before you found out. I don't think you have anything
to fear from him.
Love,
Louise

Jennifer was rested and ready to go back to work just
twenty-four hours later. She had only a slight discolor-
ation along her jawline and, remarkably, no headache
at all. The only thing that threatened to give her one was
the way Buzz kept apologizing, as if it was his fault. Apparently he'd felt such guilt about the incident, he'd
talked about it the whole day while she was home nap-
ping off the assault, but in deference to Hedda, he
played it up as an accident. He said Sylvia came in for
a cup of coffee, slipped and her flying arm accidentally
made contact with Doris's jaw, but Jennifer's regulars
had a comment or two.

"Heard you got decked," said Marty, the used-book-
store owner.

"I knew I shouldn't have stayed home," she answered. "It's nothing."

"You get one off or just go down?" asked Terry from
the dog-grooming shop.

"Hey, it was just an accident," Jennifer insisted.

"I bet Sylvia was wasted," Terry said.

Jennifer slid into Terry's booth. "Do you know Sylvia?"

"I've seen her a time or two, that's all. But Hedda's
boyfriend works for me. Max. He isn't too crazy about
his girlfriend's mom."

Hedda could have complained to Max, but somehow

Jennifer doubted it. Max probably knew more than he let on to Hedda. He probably complained to Terry.

A little while later Ryan rode his mountain bike up to the diner. Judging by the pudgy looks of him, the policeman had been spending a little too much time in there. He was a sweet guy, and maybe not the sharpest tool in the shed, but he seemed to do a decent job of helping to keep peace in a peaceable town. She recalled how nervous his police uniform had made her at first, but she got used to seeing the town's officers at the diner, especially Ryan, who was there at least once, sometimes several, times a day. None of the local cops looked at her as if anything was out of the ordinary.

"Hey, Doris," he weighed in. "I heard you took a punch." He stared at her face, looking for damage, but it was very slight. He squinted. "Doesn't look too bad."

"It was an accident, Ryan. Nothing to get excited about. You want coffee? Eggs? The usual?" she asked, changing the subject.

"Thanks, Doris," he said, and found a table of guys he knew. He was just that easy to turn off the path. Jennifer hoped he never had to look for any real criminals.

After work she went to the computer before even taking Alice for her afternoon walk. She wrote a long e-mail to Louise, giving her an update. She told how everyone in the diner seemed to know what had happened and asked if she was all right. She confessed that Alex had taken good care of her. It was the first time in her memory that so many people seemed to be involved in her life—and at a time she was wishing to be invisible.

She hit Send and leashed Alice up to take her to the

park. They had a nice long walk and sat for a while under a tree. When they got home she turned on the computer to do her usual Internet search for any new mentions of herself or the Nobles. The computer told her she had mail. Louise had answered right away.

Dear Doris,
It sounds like you may have found a home. A family, however oddly gathered. Think about trusting. It might be the way to go. You've held your breath just about long enough. I think you're safe. At any rate, I can vouch for them.
Love,
Louise.

The next morning after the breakfast rush, while Jennifer was taking a break with Adolfo's morning newspaper, she looked up to see Sylvia standing in the doorway of the diner. She just stood there, looking uncertain. She should have had a contrite look on her face, but she didn't. Not even under these circumstances.

"Come on in, Sylvia. I'll buy you a cup of coffee," Jennifer said.

Once invited, she stomped into the diner quickly, sliding into Jennifer's booth. She had attempted to cover her blackened eyes, but it didn't take a very close inspection to see the purple lurking there.

"You okay?" Jennifer asked.

"Fine. You didn't say anything to Hedda, did you?"

She shrugged. "Everyone here played it off as an accident—"

"It *was* an accident!"

"In the middle of a brawl." Jennifer hadn't thought about any of this in advance. In fact, she never expected to see Sylvia. But once the confrontation was here, she wasn't going to play dumb. Sylvia should be apologizing rather than defending herself.

"Just so you didn't say anything."

"She's pretty smart, your Hedda."

"I don't need her giving me that look, like I've been a bad girl. I'm the mother."

I would beg to differ, came instantly to Jennifer's mind, but she held her tongue for Hedda's sake.

"Does it hurt? Your nose?"

"Yes, if you must know."

"It doesn't look broken. But your eyes—"

"I'm okay. I'm, you know… That sort of thing doesn't happen to me very often. Bad judgment."

"Sure."

"I mean it!"

"I'm not arguing! Jesus!" Jennifer took a breath. "Do you have some makeup in your purse?" Jennifer asked.

"Yeah."

"Come here," she said, sliding out of the booth and heading for the bathroom. "Let me see what you have."

Sylvia followed, but slowly.

"Come on—let's see what you have for makeup. Maybe I can help?"

"You?"

"Yes, funny as it sounds. Come on now, don't play shy."

Sylvia cautiously pulled out a makeup bag, making sure Jennifer couldn't see any of the other contents of her purse. Jennifer poked through the makeup for a moment. She was pretty well stocked with eraser, base, powder, shadow, liner. "We'd be in better shape if Gloria were here—she has a veritable cosmetic counter in her purse. But I can work with this."

She moistened a paper towel and dabbed gently at Sylvia's bruises so she could start from scratch. She dotted the area with white eraser, covered that with flesh-colored concealer, topped it with base, repeated that process again, and then finished it off with powder. Then, to put the focus elsewhere on the woman's face, she lined her eyes and lips and applied liberal shadow, mascara and lipstick. In just a few moments, the black eyes were barely visible.

"Yeah. Better. I wondered how I was going to explain this at work."

"You can always go with the accident story."

Not only was Sylvia apparently not big on apologies, she was also not given to thanks. She nodded and said, "I'd better get going. I'll be late."

"Sure. Take it easy."

Sylvia left the bathroom, head down, and was out of the diner in seconds.

Phew, Jennifer thought. She must be a dream to live with.

When her shift was over, Jennifer went to the supermarket at the far edge of town, a place she'd only been once before. She preferred the small corner market where everything seemed to be fresh and there was no waiting. But, for what she had in mind, she needed a larger store. She bought several magazines—all spring editions for teenage girls.

High school had changed a lot in the past couple of decades. It used to be 8:00 a.m. to three, no matter what. Now there were split shifts, releases, early outs and all kinds of different schedules in the same school. Hedda went to school from 7:00 a.m. till 1:00 p.m., took six straight classes without a lunch break, then went to her job at the diner.

When Jennifer got to the diner at three in the afternoon, Buzz had gone on an errand. Adolfo was at the grill, Hedda was behind the counter and there were three girls in a booth, drinking Cokes, sharing a large order of fries and laughing. Jennifer hadn't even noticed that Hedda was grimacing. "Hey," Jennifer said, fanning out the magazines. "I brought us something fun."

"What's that?"

"I thought we could look through them, get some ideas for prom dresses."

The diner grew suddenly quiet.

Hedda grabbed the magazines quickly and said, "Shh." She took the stack to the far booth, the one that Adolfo favored when he wasn't at the grill and where Jennifer liked to read her morning paper. She slid in, her back to the counter, so she could keep an eye on the only customers in the diner.

Jennifer slid in across from her. "Is it a secret?" she asked in a whisper.

"From them," she whispered back.

"Why?"

Hedda leaned across the table. "Those would be the mean girls."

Jennifer straightened sharply, then looked over her shoulder cautiously. Though they all had different hairstyles, they still seemed to have more in common than unique traits. One had short, spiky blond hair, one had long, straight blond hair and the third had her medium-length blond hair pulled up and clipped on the top of her head.

Why are the mean girls *always* beautiful blondes? Jennifer found herself wondering.

And then she wondered if the fact that the most popular girls in high school always seemed to have that enviable mane of golden hair had anything to do with her choice to color her hair that way for so long. "I was blond for years," she confessed. "Are they mean to you?"

"Me and everyone," she said with a shrug. "Well... Not everyone."

"Why are they mean to you?"

"It's not personal," she said. "It's about always being the new kid. You know—you have to *earn* your entrée." She took one magazine off the stack and opened it on the tabletop. "But I don't think I want into that little group."

No sooner did she say that than there was a series of noises—the clink of dishes, a gasp, a splash, giggles. A Coke was tipped and spilled off the tabletop and onto the floor. Hedda sprang out of her booth and went for a rag to clean it up.

The girls in the booth sat idle, a snicker here and there. Usually when there was a spill at a table, people would scramble to grab napkins and start mopping up themselves before the waitress could even get there, but not these girls. Clearly the Coke had been spilled on purpose and they were getting some kind of perverse pleasure out of watching Hedda clean up.

"So, Cinderella, you going to the prom?" one of them asked while the other two covered their snotty smiles with their hands.

Hedda just cleaned up; she didn't answer.

"Hedda," the girl demanded. "Are you going to the prom? I asked!"

Hedda looked up from where she crouched to wipe the floor. "I haven't decided."

"Sure," one of them said.

"Yeah, right," said another.

It took everything Jennifer had not to get up and intervene in both the cleanup and the snide remarks. By the time she thought her willpower was almost spent, Hedda had already schlepped her wet rags back behind the counter, and the girls were left to whisper among themselves. Thankfully, inaudibly.

Always being the new kid, Hedda had said. They must move around a lot. And they'd been in the motel until their little house came up for rent.

Jennifer had not had girlfriends for much the same reason. She was always new at the school, plus Cherie, being crazy as a loon, wasn't someone Jennifer wanted people to know. And she had to stay pretty close to home to look after Cherie, because who knew what state she was in? She never let anyone get very close. When she was teased because her clothing was shabby, or she was in want of a shower, she closed her ears. Since she couldn't change anything, she made herself impenetrable.

She remembered herself as a shy and morose kid, but Hedda, for all she went through, was cheerful and open. She didn't play up to these girls with her happy spirit, but among people who were nice to her, she was every bit the extrovert.

As Hedda was coming around the counter, the girls got out of the booth and sauntered toward the door. In confusion, Jennifer watched them leave. They didn't stop at the cash register and Hedda didn't stop them. Instead, Hedda simply cleaned up their dishes and put them in the kitchen.

At that moment Buzz returned, holding the front door open for the girls.

"Hedda, they didn't pay. And they sure didn't leave a tip."

"It was only a couple of Cokes," she said. "I can cover it. Don't say anything."

"Why not? If Buzz knew what they were up to, they wouldn't be allowed in here. He has that sign. We reserve the right to refuse service to anyone."

"Oh, that would make school so much nicer for me," she said.

"I see," she said. She was seeing far more than she liked.

Jennifer touched Hedda's cheek. "You know, you don't have to be that tough. It's okay to get a little help sometimes."

"It's okay."

"How long have you been here, Hedda? In Boulder City?"

"Six months," she said, turning the page of a magazine. "But we just came from Henderson. We've been around here a long time. Lots of waitress jobs in the casinos, where the tips are good. We've been on our own about a year. Since my mom's last boyfriend moved on."

"Gosh, I'm so sorry."

"Me, too. I'm pretty sure it was my fault."

She reached for Hedda's hand, grabbing it. "Hedda, it *can't* be your fault."

"No biggie," she said, pulling her hand away. "There's more where he came from."

A familiar hurt crept into Jennifer's breast and she wanted to promise never to leave Hedda. But she couldn't promise anything.

"I want to say something to you," Jennifer said. Hedda looked up from her magazine. "I know you have a lot to put up with—and that some parts of your life aren't easy. You work hard, you have a lot of responsibility and, like me, you're not rolling in dough. A lot of people would let that make them mean-spirited and sulky, but you see the bright side of everything. You let the tough stuff just roll off while you get on with your life. And you have the absolute best personality."

"Yeah?" she said, smiling somewhat shyly.

"Yeah. And I'm just damn proud of you for that. You're the bomb."

Eight

Alex worked in the detached garage with the door up. He had put new tires on a secondhand bike, polished it up a little, replaced the seat and put some reflector tape on the rear bumper. It was a shiny red mountain bike and looked damn good even if it did have some miles on it.

It was that time of day—early afternoon. She finally came walking past after her shift at the diner. "Hey," he called.

"Hey," she returned. "New bike?"

"Sort of." He wondered if she had any idea how much she had changed. She'd been in town just over six weeks, in the house next door for just a couple, but her transformation was amazing. The first time he'd seen that shocking bald head and pale face he'd figured she was sickly or homeless or addicted to something or other. But Buzz usually just fed high-risk transients, he didn't employ them. And Buzz had good instincts. Over the weeks not only had her hair grown out, giving her a very sexy cap of thick, dark hair, but all that dog-walking and hiking and heavy food at the diner had rendered her tanned, freckled and filled out in just the right places. Her face was no longer so thin, her eyes no longer had that appearance of being sunken under a browless forehead. Rosy cheeks glowed under sparkling brown eyes under shapely dark brows. Those eyes would not sparkle unless she was happy.

The picture on the flyers showed a model-quality blonde. The girl in his driveway was a wholesome-looking country girl. From artificial and flawless to natural and squeezable. She had that scrubbed look of a pure beauty—literally, the girl next door. Of course, it didn't hurt that she'd finally, very recently, traded in the men's baggy fatigue pants for some stylish khakis that fit. Fit that cute, round little bum.

"Come and take a look," he invited.

"Was there something wrong with your bike?"

"Yeah. I was bucking someone home and the whole frame got bent up."

"Oh, Alex! Oh, God, did I do that?" She stepped aside to grab the handlebars on his blue mountain bike, examining it closely. "If I hurt anything, I could…" She twisted it left and right, rolled it back and forth, frowning in confusion. Then finally she looked at him and saw his grin.

"Gotcha."

"You have a mean streak, don't you?"

"I stopped by the bike shop and the guy had a really good deal on this secondhand number. Doesn't look too bad, does it?"

"No. Doesn't really look secondhand."

"Go put on some shorts. Let's take 'em out for a spin."

She looked so surprised. Hadn't she known he got the bike for her? "Are you kidding?"

"'Course not. I mean, Doris—I wouldn't call you overweight, but I don't want to spend all summer with you on the handlebars." He shrugged. "Even if the view isn't half bad…"

"Oh, my God, Alex," she said, bending over to roll up her pant legs.

"You'd be better off in shorts," he said. And he thought, I'd be better off if you wore shorts, that's for sure.

"I don't have shorts," she said.

"How can you not have shorts?"

"Not everyone is as well decked out as you, Alex." She grabbed the bike right out of his hands and mounted it. "I don't know how long it's been since I've ridden a bike. Too long, that's for sure." She applied foot to pedal, went down the drive with a "Whooo-hooo" and yelled, "Can we go see the bighorns?"

"Sure. Let me get my keys."

"You'd better hurry. I can't hold myself back."

She rode the bike in a couple of wide circles in the street in front of his house, trying to rein in her enthusiasm, but he took her at her word and hurried. The next thing he knew he was struggling to keep up with her. When he did catch up, they rode side by side, but they didn't talk. Jennifer was completely absorbed in the bike, the ride, the bright sunny day, the wind whipping around her. He loved the look of satisfaction on her face. She sat straight and tall on the bike, and peddled fast and hard. Every now and then she would look over at him and smile. Her smile could get her into trouble; it was dazzling, stunning and unforgettable.

He was in trouble and he knew it.

They got to the park before the bighorns visited their favorite grazing spot, so she just kept going, around a couple of blocks and back to the park. She did this again and again, and finally the first of the sheep could be seen coming over the hill. She found a little patch of grass across the street from the park in front of one of the condos and plunked herself down. She patted the ground beside her.

"I guess you don't like the bike," he joked.

She gave him a brief little grin, then looked back toward the hill to watch the sheep come over and down the steep, curved path. They were the most amazing herd, lumbering down trails that humans would have trouble traversing, yet slowly and steadily and gracefully, they approached.

Then she thought about something Alex would probably never understand—she'd been given some mighty flashy things in the past several years. Jewelry, cars, clothes, a condo on the beach. Recently, these gifts had been from Nick, but before Nick there was Gregory, a gentleman in his sixties whose wife preferred to live in France while her husband, the president of a successful accounting firm, worked in Florida. Before Gregory there was Martin, whose full-time job was managing his money, and before Martin was Robert. All of them rich, all of them sophisticated and very civil. Well, until she got to Nick, who was sophisticated and civil at first, and always with her, but she caught on very quickly that he was a tough with a temper. It served her purpose to ignore that as long as he treated her decently. And generously.

The material things she'd acquired before, in that other life, the life of Jennifer, meant nothing compared to the bike.

She reached for his hand and held it while they watched the sheep. Neither of them spoke. The ewes were heavy with their lambs and the rams watchful, but again, they stayed in their bachelor groups. Some people came out of their condos and sat on their front patios to watch, a couple of cars pulled to the side of the road and stopped. Time flowed like a river while she held his hand and lived in the moment.

She hated for it to end, but when the sheep began the steep climb to go over the mountain, she turned to Alex and kissed his cheek. She had tears in her eyes.

"It's a little overwhelming, isn't it? The bighorns," he said.

"It is," she agreed. "Thank you for letting me ride the bike, Alex."

"You can keep it at Louise's if you like. So you can ride it anytime you want."

She had long ago developed the fine art of accepting outrageous gifts graciously, but this was so different. So much more personal and touching. She shook her head and a big tear slid down her freckled cheek. "I think that's the nicest thing anyone's ever done for me."

"Gee, Doris—you've been deprived."

She laughed. "Yes, and no."

He tilted his head and waited for her to explain.

"My mom and I were poor on and off while I was growing up. You know how fortunes can shift. We seemed to struggle all the time, with brief periods of relief. We had to rely on my grandparents to rescue us a lot, and there were food-stamp days. But later, after school, when I wasn't poor, I'm beginning to see that in many ways I was even poorer. If that makes any sense."

"I don't get it," he admitted.

"You can have material wealth and be emotionally bankrupt."

"And you had wealth?"

"No," she laughed. "But I had no trouble paying my bills, and always had plenty to eat. Now I realize there was some important stuff missing."

He touched the tear stain. "Do you realize that when you first got to town, you didn't have all these freckles?"

"I was always very careful with the sun. The sun really brings out my freckles."

"You look like a fourteen-year-old girl. I could be arrested for what I'm thinking."

"Alex, you don't want to get mixed up with me. I know I'm not your kind of girl."

"And how would you know that?"

"Instincts. Anyway, why are you thirty-five and single?"

"Like that's a disease of some kind?" he countered.

"Ah. Gay. I understand," she teased.

He didn't waste a second thinking about it, but pushed her to the ground and kissed her. Kissed her very, very well, leaving absolutely no doubt as to his sexual preference. He expertly moved over her lips with precision and desire and urgency. When she didn't part her lips automatically, he parted them for her with his tongue, but then he used the caution of a practiced kisser and didn't invade the velvety cavern of her mouth. He teased. Hard, persistent lips, curious tongue. And held her so close.

Then he let her go.

She caught her breath. "Oh," she said. "*Not* gay. Well, life holds many surprises."

"I've been divorced about ten years. I'm not currently involved with anyone."

"And you don't want to get into anything with me. Trust me."

"Here's a surprise I don't want to get caught in. I don't want to be the rebound guy, even though the guy was a bum. You have to take at least six months, maybe a year before you'll be able to make an intelligent decision about—"

"Rebound?"

"Yeah. You said you left a guy. An abusive guy."

"This is true. But Alex, I didn't love him. I was just with him. That's why I'm pretty sure I'm not your kind of girl. You don't strike me as the kind of guy who likes girls who can be with guys without loving them."

He laughed at her. "Doris, you're a kick. I don't give a rat's ass about what you felt for the last guy. Or the last ten. But you're a little bit right. I don't like girls who are just with *me*. So think about it. The ball is actually in *your* court, not mine."

She lay on her back, and as he leaned over her, she looked at his handsome face and thought, you are not going to trap me and hurt me. I'm going to stay at least one emotion ahead of this. But she said, "There weren't ten."

"Well, that's something. I guess."

Alex was screwed and he knew it. He liked Jennifer a lot. Over the past ten years he'd had a quiver or two, but no big huge vibrations. There had been lots of fix-ups, something he attributed to the fact that he'd had so many female partners, and as everyone knew—women can't stand the sight of a bachelor. But aside from some dates, some laughs, some nights on the town, he hadn't been caught.

It was so ironic, the way she'd changed from a classy blonde to a down-home brunette with the most desirable freckles he'd ever seen. He'd married one of those sexy blondes ten years ago. She was so damn gorgeous that whenever he'd thought of her back then he'd just about burst into flames. He hated to leave her, couldn't wait to get home to her. Then one night he found her in bed with one of his buddies.

He came home early from his job as a cop. With a gun on his belt, he had somehow managed not to shoot them both. To this day he wasn't sure how he had pulled that off, because the pain of her faithlessness had seared through him with such ferocity he could still call it up and relive it.

Later, after she'd gone, he had found out that that wasn't the first time. Of course. Someone who will take that kind of chance has taken it before and will take it again. In fact, she'd been through quite a few men since then, in marriage and otherwise.

The pain of the breakup had been fierce, but by now the only thing he still felt plenty bad about was how stupid he'd been. There is nothing more pathetic than idiots in love. He'd run into them on the job every once in a while. A woman would call the police department and say the ex-boyfriend or -husband wouldn't leave. Sometimes it was dangerous, but often it would be some fool sitting on the curb in front of her house, crying. A miserable clod suffering through the pain of being dumped. He'd pull him away, saying, "Buddy, in a couple of years when you're sane again, you're going to remember this night and be so freaking embarrassed."

Needless to say, his feelings for Jennifer scared him a little. After all, she'd been with a guy she didn't love—a guy the law had looked at closely many times. So what was to say she couldn't be *with* Alex for a couple of years and then *with* someone else on the side? Déjà vu?

But there had been something about the way she measured out the details of what she had told him. She seemed to be playing it very safe—almost afraid. And when she did let a little piece of information go, it was clearly the truth, even if it wasn't particularly flattering. She didn't have to tell him that she hadn't loved the last guy she was with.

Then there was that underwear dance, and it wasn't just the underwear, although that was dynamite. It was that there was joy in her. Joy that didn't come out to play very often.

It boiled down to this: She let freckles grow on her nose, danced in her underwear when she thought no one could see, sang off-key very, very loudly when something moved her, let herself gain ten pounds, cried at the sight of the bighorns grazing close by and took very jealous care of Alice. She was a good person and somehow he knew this absolutely.

Jennifer had gone straight home to the computer, but she didn't do her usual Internet search. She just couldn't wait to write to Louise.

Dear Louise,
I know your advice is good. My new friends are kind, honest people and I must learn to let down my guard a little. Growing up with my crazy mom was both awful and wonderful, but I never knew what to expect. It was like growing up in a minefield. It could be a happy day filled with rewards like ice cream for dinner, or it could be a bad day when all the blinds are drawn and any sound at all would be either weeping or yelling. I learned to walk very gingerly till I knew. I trained myself not to have expectations. I was scared a lot as a kid and I had to find a way to give that up before I became crazy, too. The way I managed was to maintain control. Oh, my goodness, I had so much control. Do you know how hard it is to give up? You can't imagine.

I rode bikes with Alex to see the bighorns today.
He kissed me.
Love,
Doris

Alex would have much rather stayed in the grazing park for another few hours, kissing and talking,
but he had had to go to work. As he listened to the
briefing for his shift, his mind was all tied up in how
grateful Jennifer had been for the bike. He was happy
about that and was planning for tomorrow's assault on
the girl next door. While one of the robbery detectives
was outlining a plan for surveillance of suspects
who'd been very successful in ripping off quiet little
neighborhood bars, Alex was taking some notes, but
he was thinking about freckles. He glanced over at
Paula to make sure she was paying closer attention
than he was.

When the briefing was done, his sergeant asked him
to come into his office. Paula said she had some things
to look up on the computer and told Alex to take his time
with the boss.

"You ran a check on an out-of-state the other day,"
the sergeant said. "It flagged the FBI and the bureau
would like to talk to you."

"Who was it?" Alex asked.

"Hell if I know. Don't you know who you ran?"

"Can't recall," Alex said. In fact, it could have been
anyone. He was a robbery detective and any suspects
would be checked for out-of-state warrants. In Las
Vegas, where there were three hundred thousand visitors

a day, there were a lot of nonresidents. The way the system worked was that if you ran a check on someone the feds were watching, it would flag them and then they'd get in touch to see what the locals had. If, for example, he did a computer check on the president, the Secret Service would be knocking on the door within the hour.

In Alex's case, he'd run a great number of people in the past couple of months.

"Is this urgent?" Alex asked.

"I'm not sure. Here," he said, handing Alex a phone message slip. "Call the guy and ask him when he wants to see you."

"Jesus, I hope these guys don't screw up a perfectly good investigation," he groused, reaching for the office phone. It happened all the time. They'd be working on a case, have someone pinned down for a crime, start writing the warrants for search and seizure, get a team ready to go in and get the suspects, and the feds would step in and say, "S'cuse me—but we're looking at them for federal crimes. Dibs."

"Dobbs," said the voice that answered the phone, and Alex was momentarily thrown. *Dibs. Dobbs.*

"Ah, Detective Nichols here," he said. "Metro. Robbery. You wanted a call about an interstate search?"

"Yeah. Let's grab a cup. Starbucks on Charleston. Don't bring your partner."

Right away Alex hated this guy. "Is this *about* my partner?" he asked.

"No," Dobbs said in a patronizing tone. "This is

about *you*. And you might not want to have your partner in on this."

If she were an idiot, maybe that would be true, but Paula was a good partner and smart as the devil. Not only would he not chance her thinking he didn't trust her, he wouldn't sacrifice the brain power she could add to any situation. "When?" he said.

"I'm leaving now," Dobbs said. "Don't keep me waiting."

Alex hung up the phone. Although it hadn't been intentional, now he was glad he had used a Metro phone. The caller ID on the Fibbie's phone would have revealed Alex's cell phone number, and he already knew that Dobbs wasn't someone he wanted to hear from on a regular basis.

Dobbs. He kept rolling the name over in his mind. He knew a lot of FBI guys. He worked with them regularly and, for the most part, had a good relationship with them. But occasionally some Fibbie would come to town from out of state with some big ax to grind and a real hard-on for some suspect, and the whole process of trying to make an arrest would be a huge, complicated pain in the ass.

He grabbed Paula and said, "Come on, we're going for coffee with some fed who wants to talk to me about someone I ran through an interstate search. I guess I flagged them."

"Who?"

"His name is Dobbs, but he can't be from Vegas because I've never heard of him."

"No, stupid," she laughed. "Who'd you run?"

"Hell if I know. I ran a million people last month alone. How about Wollach? He had warrants all over the country."

"You have absolutely no idea?"

He stopped walking. "Did you run someone that lit up the board?"

"I don't think so. Why?"

"Dobbs told me not to bring my partner."

"Then why are you bringing me?"

"Because you're my partner. I don't take orders from the FBI."

She just looked at him for a long minute. She was little. Kind of cute. Only thirty and married six months. No one would think she could do much good in a fight but, oh man, if Paula's job was to back you up, *game on,* as they liked to say. It was a high compliment if the guys liked working with a particular woman cop, and Paula was one of them.

She smiled at him. "I never give you enough credit."

"Then you better start," he said.

They didn't bother to hash over all the suspects who'd come across their desks in the past month. The Fibbie would tell them who he was looking at, and they'd either work out a way to bring him in, or one or the other of them would let go of the case. Probably Metro would give it up. But then probably the feds would need Metro's help....

"God," Paula said when they arrived at Starbucks. "Do you think he could be more obvious?"

On the patio, as far away from the coffee-drinking crowd as possible, sat a man in a suit and a black trench coat. He was large, heavy, hair cut in a buzz that left him nearly bald, and he wore telltale thick-soled black shoes, white shirt and thin tie. The local FBI tended to fit in much better, actually looking as if they might be regular citizens. This guy looked as though he wanted to guard the president. In 1965.

Alex and Paula were not trying to hide their professions. They wore plainclothes — jeans and khakis with badges, guns and handcuffs on their belts. So as they approached the trench-coated man, he looked up and all parties recognized one another. It was seventy degrees outside and Alex desperately wanted to ask Dobbs if he was warm enough in that trench coat.

"Dobbs?" Alex stuck out his hand. "Alex Nichols. My partner, Paula Aiken."

Dobbs had small blue eyes that slowly moved from Paula to Alex to Paula. "Have a seat," he said. "Unless you want to get some coffee?"

"No, thanks," Paula said. "It'll keep me up."

"Let's get to it," Alex said.

"Nick Noble," Dobbs said.

Where do I know that name? Alex asked himself.

Paula elbowed him. "That missing person."

"Oh, yeah. He reported a woman missing. A friend of the family, he said."

"Not exactly. She was his mistress."

"Was?" Alex asked.

"She's *missing,*" Dobbs said tiredly. He sighed. It was obvious he disliked having to work with the local idiots. "You *ran* him. Why?"

"Oh, that. I found the missing-person flyers in my

neighborhood. *My* neighborhood. I checked the case file. I ran the girl, too—in case I run into her. I took a look at the arrest record for Noble and decided she's better off missing. What's your heartburn?"

"We want the girl."

"Oh, really? You want her for…?"

"Questioning."

"Should we be beefing up our search for any reason? Has she done anything?"

"Noble says she stole money and jewelry from him."

Alex laughed. "That's why I *ran* her. Her record is clean. Totally clean. But his isn't. Seems pretty obvious to me that he accused her of stealing to get a little professional help in getting her back."

Dobbs was getting impatient. He was clenching and unclenching his fist on the tabletop. "We'd really like to talk to her."

Alex tried to keep from rolling his eyes. The royal "we." "Do you want a little help in finding her?" Alex asked as patiently as he could. "Is that why you invited me here today?"

"No, I don't need help! Do you know where she is? Did you have a personal reason for running her and Nick Noble?"

"Oh, for God's sake," Paula huffed. "What the hell's the matter with you? We're not working missing persons. He was just checking the status of the stupid flyer. You want something or what?"

"You were there?"

"There? You mean at the office while he was doing his search? Right there. We share a computer, as a matter of fact. I saw enough of the results to see we have way bigger fish to fry. We don't need this missing person for anything."

"Dobbs," Alex said. "We could have done this on the phone."

"I *need* this woman. She may be able to help us. Noble is guilty of multiple felonies ranging from conspiracy and trafficking, to fraud and money-laundering. He has dozens of businesses he runs drug money through. If she was his mistress for two years, she knows things."

"According to his record, no one's been able to make anything stick. He's not wanted," Alex said.

"He's slippery."

"Slippery isn't illegal."

"We're going to get him. It's a matter of time. Maybe you could help. Huh?"

"Is the DEA in on this?"

"Noble washes up money for drug dealers, but his trafficking is primarily in high-ticket stolen goods, so the DEA is just getting in my way. I was hoping you could take me to this woman."

Alex sat back. "That was a stretch, Dobbs. I was just running a check. It's what I do a hundred times a month."

"Fuck."

"Hey, don't be upset. I'll keep my eyes open. You have a card?" Dobbs fished one out of his pocket and thrust it at Alex. "Are you working out of this field office?" Alex asked.

"I'll hang around a couple of days and see what they have, then head back to Florida. This guy. He's dirty."

Alex studied the card. "Dangerous?"

"Probably," Dobbs said, standing. "And a regular guest here. Your casinos fly him in to gamble. He loves to gamble. Why they want crooks at their tables is beyond me."

"Hey, I *ran* him, Dobbs. He has zero convictions. He's a model citizen. Apparently with a ton of money."

Dobbs inhaled sharply, his cheeks puffing out a bit. "Details."

Alex remained seated. This guy was rough around the edges and there was no indication he was clever or canny or sensitive. Even if he didn't know Jennifer, no way would he like turning her over to Dobbs. This was a guy who looked as if he couldn't wait to just put her on a hook at the end of a line and use her for bait.

"Call me if anything comes up," Dobbs said.

"You bet."

He didn't say goodbye. He left Alex and Paula at the table.

The patio sat right on a busy street. Birds picked at crumbs on the ground, cars drove by, people talked. Alex studied the card. There was a sudden splat of bird dropping on the table; it missed the card by millimeters.

"Where is she?" Paula asked.

"Where is who?"

"Alex…"

"Are you asking me in an official capacity?"

She leaned forward. "I'm a police officer. Everything I ask is official—eventually."

Yeah, there was this little rule about withholding. But there was another small factor, and that was that police officers had *discretion*. The woman had not committed any crimes. Arresting her or turning her over was not an imperative.

"She's obviously hiding," he said. "And it sounds like she has good reason."

"You've seen her," she said.

He swallowed. "I have not met anyone who identifies herself as Jennifer Chaise, missing person."

Paula waited a second and then said, "Shit."

My dear Doris,
I'm completely unsentimental, so the fact that you've been kissed means as much to me as your seeing the bighorns. One thing, however, is very important to me, and that is Alex. He might appear to be tough and even cynical, but beneath that he carries a very tender heart. Be gentle with him. And for advice about men, see Rose.
Love,
Louise

There was a knock at Jennifer's door in the evening. It wasn't very late, but it was already dark and she had been yawning her way through a pretty good book. The old-fashioned house in an old and remarkably safe neighborhood meant there was no peephole. Alice went directly to the door, sniffed at the crack and wagged.

It was Hedda and her little brother, Joey. Just the sight of them scared Jennifer a little. Sylvia at her worst came instantly to mind, and she assumed they needed rescuing again. She tried to stay even, not show any alarm. "Hey," she said. "What's up?"

"I'm sorry to bother you," she said, tears in her voice.

"I told you—anytime. Tell me."

"I need help."

Jennifer swung the door wide. "Come in, come in. What is it, kiddo?"

"Advanced algebra," she said. "I thought by now I'd get it, but I'm lost."

Jennifer's expression registered her panic, even if she was relieved to know Hedda wasn't trying to escape some crisis at home. But advanced algebra? With all the drama that had surrounded her life lately, algebra should be good news. "I'm not sure you came to the right place. I don't even remember having algebra, much less advanced. What about your boyfriend?"

"Max? Forget it," she said. "He's a great guy, but I don't like his chances at veterinary college."

"That bad, huh?"

"Up till now, I've been helping him."

"Alice!" Joey announced, yanking out of Hedda's grip and rushing toward the dog. He flopped down on the floor and began gently stroking her head, which she answered with grateful licks.

"Well, that takes care of him," Jennifer said. "Let's get a Coke and take a look at the book," she invited. "I'll see what I can do, but I warn you, it looks bleak."

Joey rolled around on the floor with Alice while Jennifer and Hedda sat at the dining room table. They started out with Hedda explaining the parts she did understand, but the only reaction Jennifer had was "This isn't even about *numbers!*" Indeed, it was about trains leaving their stations and moving toward each other at varying speeds and when would they meet. Three apples and two oranges is six dollars, one apple and two oranges is four dollars, how much is an apple? "Oh, my God," Jennifer moaned. "I'd just pay the freaking six dollars!"

Then there were triangles and rectangles. "I get that," Hedda said. "But these trains, barges and buildings are killing me."

Within about thirty minutes, Jennifer was starting to catch on, but it was clearly going to take all night for her to learn the basics, and she'd probably never be of any help. She went to the list of names and numbers Louise had left her and placed a call to Alex, her best bet. But of course he wasn't home. That would be too easy. So she left him a message asking if he could help with algebra. Then she called Rose, and though Rose didn't have the first idea, she came straight over to see what the challenge was.

"Ptui," she said. "This can't be a good way to train a young woman's mind. It looks like gibberish to me."

"Here's what I get so far," Hedda began again, deciphering the problem so far, assigning letters to the unknown numbers.

Jennifer went to the living room, where she lifted a sleepy Joey onto the couch, told him to go ahead and close his eyes, and covered him with a throw. Just as she was returning to the table, there was a knock at the door. Alex.

"Any chance you know algebra?" she asked.

"Well, I *used* to," he said.

"Advanced?"

"Now, there you're getting into murky territory. But I'll have a look."

It turned out his memory of algebra wasn't exactly fresh, but his resourcefulness was greatly improved since his algebra days. He went to Louise's computer, looked up www.algebra.com. In one short hour he had not only gotten Hedda through her problems, but had a very good start on getting Rose and Jennifer on board.

It was after ten when Hedda pronounced herself up to speed. Jennifer's head was on the table, eyes closed. She was not only tired, her brain was taxed.

"I say we celebrate," Alex suggested. "I'll go next door and get my tub of rocky road ice cream and then I'll drive you home."

"It's okay," Hedda said. "I can walk. It's not that far."

He stood and went to the door. "It's too far for tonight. Poke Doris—wake her up and tell her to find bowls." He was back in what seemed like seconds.

Poor Joey slept through the ice cream and he also slept straight through all the laughter.

Among them they were aged seven, sixteen, thirty, thirty-five and seventy. And, Jennifer realized, this was as close as she'd come to "family" since her mother and grandparents were alive. It felt very, very good.

Nine

Jennifer bought four pair of shorts, three sleeveless Ts, a tube top that left her shoulders bare and a basket for the bike. She didn't think Alex would mind about the basket at all. Then she bought a flat of seedlings. Flowers and vegetables. Pansies, snapdragons, daisies, tomatoes and zucchini. She'd have bought more if she could have gotten them home on the bike, but as it was she had to balance the awkward flat on the handlebars.

Minimum wage plus tips was below poverty level unless you had virtually no expenses. She had her breakfast and lunch at the diner and Alfonso usually forced something on her as she was leaving work—roasted chicken, a thick slice of meat loaf or an enchilada, taking care of her dinner. She paid no rent or utilities, bought very little food, and she was managing to buy only the most essential clothing. With Louise's monthly stipend as well, Jennifer was actually getting ahead. Not to mention that little stash she had of cash and jewelry.

As much as she might have resented it at the time, Jennifer had learned how to manage on a shoestring early in life. There had been so many times when her mother had been on a mental bender and they'd had practically nothing, or they'd be waiting for help from Grandma and Gramps. If Jennifer couldn't hold it together there was the threat of a visit from Children and Family Services or the equivalent, depending on the state. There was always a risk of being removed from Cherie's custody. Jennifer might have been better off had she been taken from her mother, but not so for Cherie. Cherie couldn't make it without her, and Jennifer had known that since she was in first grade.

Later, after Cherie was gone, attaining a certain amount of personal wealth had become important to Jennifer—as important as security. After just a little while of being a successful mistress she'd amassed a comfortable nest egg. She now imagined the mail piling up in her Fort Lauderdale condo—bank statements, portfolio updates, checks—stuff she couldn't touch without giving away her current location. Money she'd be willing to walk away from if it meant risking life and limb.

Nick had a key to that condo, of course. She supposed if he was criminal enough to kill his wife, he was certainly not above opening her mail.

In the past few weeks, Jennifer had given a lot of thought to what security really was, and it seemed to have little to do with money or material wealth. It was more about having people in your life you could trust and depend upon. It was about connectedness, comfort, safety.

She could start from scratch if she had to. Jennifer was nothing if not resilient. And now that she had a better idea of what she needed in her life to be happy, truly happy, she felt it was all within reach. All she had to do was finish with that business in Florida so she could put it all behind her.

She thought about Hedda, whose life was completely different from her own yet so much the same, and she hoped beyond hope that the girl wouldn't have to manage in similar ways as an adult. For all of Hedda's hard work and optimism, she should at least get a crack at an education, a career.

As she unloaded her flat of flowers—twelve dollars' worth—Jennifer thought about what she used to spend on waxing, facials, hair, nails and spray tanning alone, not to mention makeup and clothes, and it blew her away. This life was indeed the simple life, and it was this kind of simplicity that allowed her to thoroughly enjoy a flat of flowers. She didn't even realize how much she had missed that. She'd been longing for it without even knowing. She had become exhausted by the work involved in sheer upkeep.

This was a spring like nothing in her memory! Fort Lauderdale could hint at spring, but the ocean didn't burst into bloom, and the palm trees did little more than grow dates and dump them, sticky and messy, all over roads and sidewalks.

Boulder City was an oasis in the desert, alive with deep shades of green and blossoms everywhere. The birds had grown loud with their lust and joy, and the sun was now greeting her soon after her rising time of four-thirty. She could remember a spring or two in Ohio when she and Cherie had been at Gram and Gramps's—bright, glowing springs that filled you up inside and made you want to burst into a run or a song. But with Cherie's instability always hanging close over their heads, even the joy of spring was subdued. There had been nothing like this.

Jennifer found some old gardening gloves and tools in the garage. Clearly they hadn't been used in many a year, perhaps decades. The gloves practically disintegrated on touch. Jennifer didn't need them, really. She wasn't trying to protect her manicure; she kept her nails short and scrubbed clean. It felt good to dig them into the soft earth.

She planted daisies and pansies along the front of the house. In the backyard she cleared a spot in the corner that would get morning sun and afternoon shade. She rode her bike back to the nursery and loaded up the basket with mulch and potting soil and pedaled back. The weight of the load made riding hard work; she thought of her health club membership with an amused laugh. Hah! She should have discovered biking, gardening and waiting tables years ago!

She created a safe little harbor in the backyard for her tomato plants. Among them she scattered some marigold seeds to keep the bugs away.

Alice sauntered outside through the opened door and flopped down beside Jennifer. "What do you think?" she asked the dog.

"I think it looks good, for a beginner."

She looked to her right and saw Alex peering over

the wall that divided their backyards. He had his fore-arms on the top of the wall, his chin resting on them. He would have to be standing on a box or something—the wall was easily six feet high.

"Who are you calling a beginner?"

"Well. You. But that's okay. You need any tips, you know where I am."

"Yeah—hanging over the wall, spying. What if I'd been a topless gardener?"

His face cracked a roguish grin. "Be still my heart," he said. "Adolfo asked me to come and get you. Change into something festive. You're going out with Rose and me."

"Festive? Me?" She stood up and brushed her hands together to get rid of the dirt. "The most festive thing I have is a pair of jeans. What's going on?"

"You don't know what day it is, do you? Haven't you noticed decorations around town?"

There had been some lanterns strung up around the park; a few plastic flower arrangements here and there. She shrugged.

"What did you think it was?" he asked.

"I don't know. Spring?"

"Spring is almost over. It's Cinco de Mayo. The day the Mexicans ran the French and Spanish out of Puebla. Adolfo's having one of his parties."

"Oh," she said. "Gee. Look, I have to get up pretty early and—"

"Don't even start, Doris. If you don't go, you'll be in serious trouble. Go get ready."

"Hey, Alex, it's not like he invited me or anything. I didn't have a chance to RSVP. I can't just—"

"He wouldn't have thought of it," Alex said. "It's Adolfo and his family and friends. He knows we all know there's going to be a celebration—it's not a formal thing. Music, food, drink, dancing. Trust me, you don't want to miss this."

She put her hands on her hips. "Look. We sort of talked about this before, without really talking about it, but I—"

"I know. You're in deep cover. But this is different, Doris. It's not public. It's Adolfo's friends and family—mostly Mexicans from around Boulder City and Henderson. Absolutely no chance anyone you're avoiding would be there. A million to one chance, anyway. And I'll protect you." He smiled. "So, let's go."

"But I don't have party clothes," she said in frustration.

Alex sighed. "Okay. Alex to the rescue." And he disappeared.

Jennifer looked at Alice. "How do you put up with him? He's so annoying."

Alice had no advice.

Jennifer picked up the empty plastic flats the plants came in, the empty bags from the mulch and potting soil, threw away her trash and went inside to wash her hands. Cinco de Mayo? Who'd have guessed.

There were a quick few taps at the door and it opened to reveal Rose. Or was that Carmen Miranda? She had a multicolored, layered skirt, peasant blouse pulled down off her shoulders, and on her head was a very elaborate fruit bowl. Over one arm she had draped clothes, and in her hand dangled at least three pairs of sandals. "Take these into the bedroom and see if anything will work. Go, go, go. And put on some lipstick or something. This is a *party.*"

"But…"

"Oh, don't be difficult. We're going. We always go to Adolfo's on Cinco de Mayo. Believe me, you'll be glad in the end."

Jennifer showed her hands. "I need a shower."

"That shouldn't take long. It's not as though you have to curl your hair. But please, a little mascara?"

Reluctantly, Jennifer accepted the clothing and went off to her shower. She grumbled as she ran the water and disrobed. She'd clean up, act agreeable, but then she'd have to come up with an excuse of some kind. A sudden bout of flu? Food poisoning? Heat prostration from the gardening? She wasn't in a partying mood. It had taken a while to get used to the crowds that came into the diner for breakfast on weekends; she had barely become comfortable with the idea that so many people around town seemed to know her already. A party was out of the question.

But she shaved her legs with cream rinse. It was a little trick she'd learned from a stripper years ago—it left your legs so much softer and nicer than with shaving cream or soap. And after she dried off, she lotioned up—the desert, in any season, was hard on the skin. Then, just to appear cooperative, she looked at the clothes.

Hmm. A skirt and blouse, a strappy sundress, a pair of dressy capris and a peasant blouse. These were obviously Rose's, but they sure weren't the kind of clothes you'd expect a seventy-year-old woman to be wearing. She donned the sundress. Something snagged at her heart—it was lovely. Sexy and feminine. The straps crossed in the back, which was low. She couldn't wear a bra, but with her girls right up there on her chest, it worked great without one. Peeking out from the front was an old friend she hadn't let out in a while, her cleavage.

She leaned toward the mirror. With the sun on her cheeks and shoulders, she looked pretty good. She put on some eyeliner and mascara—no shadow or foundation, but a little darkening on the lids and lashes. She lined her lips with a pale peach liner—something quite old from under Louise's bathroom sink, and then added some of the lip gloss from the little Kate Spade bag she kept hidden in the backpack.

Look at that, she thought. Not bad. She didn't look anything like the blond bombshell Jennifer Chaise, but she didn't exactly hurt the eyes. In fact, she looked years younger than Jennifer Chaise. She had grown to like the freckles and the ordinary-size lips. What had made her think she needed those bee-stung lips, anyway?

She tried on the sandals. They were about a size smaller than her own, but when she tried a pair of backless mules with a small heel, they worked.

When she went into her living room she found Rose sitting on the chair and Alex standing, a hand braced on the fireplace mantel. She stood before them, all thoughts of bailing on this outing gone from her mind.

Rose smiled a crooked conspirator's smile, as if to

say, I *knew* it! "Look at you," she finally said. "At last, a real girl!"

But Alex was speechless. He stared, his lips parted in an *O*. He closed his mouth, shook his head and held out a hand. "You'll thank me for this someday, Doris. You won't find a better party than the one at Adolfo's."

She put her hand in his and with the other, gave Alice a pat. "I won't be late," she said to the dog.

"She'll be late," Alex corrected. "I've already watered the dog and locked the back door, so let's do it."

Alex drove them out of the historic district to a neighborhood where the houses were bigger than the tiny boxes that had been originally built by the government, but like in the historic district, individual taste was an option. They passed a big to-do in the park and Jennifer learned that there were celebrations all over town, but the one at Adolfo's house would be the most authentic and intimate. *Intimate* turned out to be a relative term; as they drove down Adolfo's street they found it lined with trucks and cars, the sound of music and laughter ringing out from blocks away.

She would have known Adolfo's house without being told. There were two huge trees in the front yard and they were decorated with something akin to Christmas lights, lanterns strung across the eaves and carport, luminaires lining the drive and sidewalk. The sun was just barely lowering in the sky, and Alex had to toot the horn at a bunch of young men kicking a soccer ball around the street in front of his car.

"Intimate?" Jennifer heard herself ask.

"Everyone here has known Adolfo and his family for

a long time. Carmel and Adolfo have many wonderful celebrations here—the Day of the Dead is something you don't want to miss."

"Day of the—"

"All Saints Day," Alex clarified. "And Christmas for this family goes on for literally months. They're very religious. Very respectful of the saints and their days. And—"

"And very good partiers," Rose interrupted. "I knew parking would be a problem."

Alex dropped the women in front of Adolfo's house and drove off to find parking. Rose was off like a shot down the driveway with a large platter of sweets for the party, and Jennifer was left to slowly follow. Rose darted around the corner and into the house while Jennifer just got to the edge of the backyard and stood self-consciously by herself, taking it all in—there were people everywhere. A huge crowd. Young men stood around a keg of beer while others tended a barbecue; old women sat in lawn chairs under a big tree; children ran about; women of all ages totted food and drink to several large picnic tables that were lined up end to end across the yard. There was a gazebo at the far end of the driveway and under the roof was a small band—guitarists and mariachis. A couple in brightly colored clothes danced in front of them, and when the music ended the man lifted his partner high in the air and everyone applauded.

"Doris!" Adolfo cried. "Carmelita!" he called to his wife. A very beautiful, very full and round Latina woman came up behind him. She wore a colorful apron and held a dish towel in her hands.

Adolfo grabbed Jennifer and gave her a welcoming hug, muttering something very approving in Spanish as he looked at her in the dress and pronounced her *muy bueno*. Then he introduced her to Carmel who, likewise, had very positive things to say in Spanish—Jennifer nodded, wishing she had some idea what they were. Then followed a long line of people whom Adolfo presented. Maria, Andreas, Stefano, Juan, Eduardo, Lydia, Jesus, Jose, Madeira, Theresa, and on and on he went until Jennifer was long past remembering anyone but Carmel. To further confuse things, his introductions were half in English and half in Spanish.

She saw that in addition to the keg and a cooler filled with soft drinks, there seemed to be a bar set up near the house where electricity for the blender was available. A large bowl of limes sat atop the bar, and leaning against it was, surprisingly, Buzz, and beside him, Gloria. He nodded toward Jennifer and lifted a glass.

"Adolfo, who's minding the diner?"

"It's closed. Señor Buzz put up a sign. *Ido de pesca.* Gone fishing." He grinned. "Buzz would not miss a celebration at the Garcia homestead."

Still more people lined up behind Adolfo, and one by one he introduced them. His brother, his nephew, his neighbor, his old friend, his wife's sister, a friend from their country, which she learned did not mean Mexico but rather a region of Mexico. Another neighbor, a son-in-law, and a wee tot whom he lifted into his sturdy arms as he said, "Juanito, the newest bambino. My grandson."

Caught off guard by the beauty of the little boy, Jennifer forgot her nerves for a second and put out a hand, a finger, which Juanito happily grabbed. "Oh, Adolfo, he's precious. How old is he?"

"*Dos*. Two and then some. But he thinks he's as big as all the others and chases them from morning till night. Oh, Señorita Doris, when Alex told me he was going to bring you, it made me so happy. I am proud to have you in my home, with my family."

"He told you—? But Alex made it seem as though you expected me."

"*Sí*, I expected you if Alex could find a way to persuade you. And now you can see the flowers and plants that Carmel tends. She has the gift of the thumb *verde*."

Someone was at her side, passing her a drink in a plastic cup. She turned to see it was Alex, not looking in any way remorseful. "Maybe you'd better have one of these," he said.

"*El perdón*, you are in good hands," Adolfo said, leaving them to play host to what Jennifer feared were hundreds of people.

She took a sip of the margarita. It was delicious, and strong. "You tricked me," she said to Alex.

"Well, let's just hope I tricked you into having some fun."

"You shouldn't have done that. It just pays to be honest."

"You wouldn't have come if I'd been completely honest. Besides, I only stretched the truth a little bit. You heard him—he wanted you here very much." Alex gestured to the gathering. "And as you can see, you couldn't be safer. If you're going to enjoy only a few outings, this is one to take in."

"Hmm. Well, now I probably won't trust you again," she sagely advised him. But rather than being chagrined by that, he laughed outright. And loudly enough to turn a couple of heads.

He leaned close to her ear and whispered. "Hell, Doris, you don't trust me, anyway, so who cares? Huh?" He clinked her plastic glass with his and said, "Welcome to the neighborhood just the same."

A few more people from the gathering approached them, and to her surprise and extreme pleasure, Alex continued with the introductions. "This is Jesus, who works with Adolfo's son, Manuel, and Rosa is his wife. Here is Selena, who lives down the street and is always here for the holidays, unless she goes home to her country in Mexico, and this is Roberto, who lives on the other side over there—he helped Adolfo and his sons build the gazebo and barbecue." This went on and on until a woman—clearly not Latina—approached. "Hey!" Alex said, pulling her in for a hug. "I wondered if you'd make it. You bring John?"

"He's in the house getting the piñata ready for later. Stuffing it." She looked at Jennifer, stuck out her hand and said, "Hi, I'm Paula. I work with Alex."

"Hello," she said. She took another bolstering sip and was finally grateful to Alex for having produced the drink.

"Here's how it works, Doris," Alex was saying. "Last year I brought Paula and her fiancé, John, and now Adolfo would feel someone from his family was missing if they weren't here. You have to die or leave the country to get out of it."

"Who'd want to get out of it?" Paula said. "Believe me, you are never going to eat better in your life. They have *carne asada* on the grill, barbecue chicken, tacos, quesadillas, and when you taste the corn you're going to faint. They cook the corn on the cob in the husks smothered in mayonnaise, cheese and chili. To *die* for. Nice to meet you—I'm going to get a beer."

When Paula left, Jennifer asked, "She works with you how?"

"She's my partner. Excellent cop. Good person. John is a firefighter. Cops and the FD seem to hang together. They marry one another a lot."

"She's awfully small to be a police officer."

"Dynamite comes in a small wrapper, too. Not to worry."

Jennifer took another drink and said, "Um, Alex? I've been gardening and riding the bike back and forth to the nursery all afternoon. I didn't exactly eat anything. And this drink is *muy* potent."

"Doris. You're bilingual," he laughed.

"I'm going to be before long the way Adolfo mixes up his Spanish and English at the diner. I'm also going to be drunk."

"Never fear, Alex is here. Rosa! Could we have a little something to take the bite out of this margarita?"

"*Sí, amigo. Ven aquí.* We have chips and salsa and guacamole here. Beans and tortillas coming up with *salada*. And we do have lemonade and Pepsi for the weak."

"Hah! We can hold our own! We just need a taco bed for the tequila!"

* * *

As the sun slowly lowered in the sky and the lanterns and lights came up, Alex was tempted to hover near Jennifer, but the men kept drawing him away. He managed to make sure her plate and glass were always replenished, but he wasn't able to stay at her side. Still, he couldn't draw his eyes away from her.

Over the course of the next couple of hours he watched as she held a variety of babies and small children. She visited with Rose, then Paula, then Gloria. As Alex watched, a very elderly Hispanic woman sat beside her and he could see Jennifer draw her eyebrows together as she concentrated on understanding her. Carmel and Adolfo, though constantly busy, kept close watch. Young men paused before her and made her laugh, young women brought her food to taste. They made a big deal over this darling young woman in the sundress and called her Alejandro's *la amiga*. Alex's girlfriend.

"It's nice to see you here with someone under seventy," Paula said into his ear. He looked at his partner with a small smile but said nothing. "She's not what I expected."

"What did you expect?"

"Well… The picture…"

"Shh," he warned.

"No one heard," she said. "I'm surprised you heard," she added.

The music grew louder and the laughter reverberated throughout the neighborhood. A group of strong young men rousted everyone from the picnic tables and moved them to the edges of the yard so that the piñata could be hung. Dancing began in earnest on the cement of the carport. As Paula stood beside Alex, watching, Adolfo and Carmel swirled onto the cement driveway and, to the shouts of their family and friends, danced their celebratory dance. Others began to join them. Rose appeared in the arms of one of Adolfo's neighbors, a man young enough to be her grandson, and although he was a talented dancer, she was clearly his equal. Gloria and Buzz twirled around clumsily but happily. Someone grabbed Jennifer's hand and tried to pull her from the picnic table. She shook her head and resisted, but was no match for the Latino's insistence. They stood at the edge of the dance floor while he tried to explain to her what he was going to do and she listened carefully, nodding. Then they began to dance, stilted at first, then burst into the *maringá*. Though she was slow at first, there was no question she knew what she was doing. As the music changed, and so did the dance, it became apparent that Jennifer could salsa with the best of them.

Alex watched in both fascination and appreciation as her dress swirled around her thighs. As the young Mexican man twirled her expertly, she threw her head back and laughed. Alex could tell it was happening to her again—she had forgotten to be wary, and the joy that was natural to her was sneaking out. It made him grin like a kid. Hands plunged into his pockets, he rocked back on his heels.

"Alex!" Paula shouted. He turned sharply to look at her. "For God's sake, what planet are you on?"

"What?" he asked.

"I've been talking and elbowing you! You haven't heard a word, have you?"

Well, what the hell did she expect when Jennifer was doing the *maringá* with the handsome young Latino? "Sorry," he said. "What did you say?"

"I said, after the piñata, John and I will drop Rose at her house. You can stay on with the beautiful *Doris,*" she said, sarcasm drawing out the name.

"Thanks," Alex said.

The dance ended and shouts and applause filled the air. Adolfo rushed to Jennifer, clapping and exclaiming, *"¡Mi Dios! ¡Qué talento!"*

Alex grabbed another bottle of beer. Paula was helping John and some others string up the piñata while the kids were swarming the backyard, anxious to crack it open. Meanwhile, Jennifer was being passed from hand to hand in the dance. Even Buzz turned her around a couple of times. Alex thought he should get his chance before she was exhausted, but she was so much fun to watch and he was having such pleasure doing so. Every now and then she would catch his eye, smile and wave just as she was spun off by yet another new partner.

When the music changed again, Alex put his beer down on a picnic table and went to claim her. "You've been holding out. You're a dancer," he said.

"Not really," she protested, her cheeks flushed. "I admit I love to dance, but I'm a good follower, that's all."

"Oh-ho, I doubt that," he laughed.

As if by magic, the next song was a slower pace and he pulled her into his arms. If either of them had looked closer, they would have seen their host instructing the guitarists to slow it down.

"Thank goodness," she sighed, leaning against him gratefully. "I'm nearly worn out. I don't think I could jig around this carport one more time."

"Good," he said.

She curved against him and proved she was, actually, a very good follower. But he didn't plan on going far or fancy, he just wanted to hold her. And on the excuse of exhaustion, she lay her head against his shoulder and sighed. Her shoulder, tanned and freckled and glistening with the perspiration of dance, was right there at his lips; her arm circled his shoulders with comfortable possessiveness. His hand on her waist pulled her tighter, and as the music played, he felt himself moving her from the middle of the dance floor to the edge, farther from the crowd.

Jennifer felt at home, safe in his arms. She lay her head down, pulled him tighter and prayed he wouldn't release her. Around them was the noise of partyers yelling, laughing, singing, clapping—but they began to seem farther and farther away. She had the vague sense of being alone with him and blamed exhaustion and the alcohol, then she blessed them both, for the stirring within her felt real and very welcome, and she didn't want to fight it.

The music changed and changed again, but they continued to rock back and forth in a slow sway as if they were alone. His lips touched her shoulder and she brushed hers against his cheek. She found he had moved them into a corner of the carport and under the canopy of a drooping California pepper tree. It was there that he stopped moving his feet, pulled back slightly, lifted her chin with his index finger and moved his mouth over hers.

The thrill of his kiss shot through her and her arms went around his neck, her fingers digging into his hair to keep him close. She opened her lips under his and welcomed him; she moved her body against him so that he would have absolutely no doubt she wanted him. And want him she did, in a way so primal and natural, she was shocked by it.

The loud crack of the piñata bat suddenly rent the air, followed by screams and laughter as penny candy scattered, being chased by little ones. The noise broke apart a delicious kiss and they turned their heads to look, but Alex used a gentle hand to direct her eyes back to his. "Let's get out of here," he said.

"Rose," she whispered.

"Rose is taken care of. Paula and John. They may have left already. Come with me?"

She nodded.

Jennifer laid her head back against the cool leather of Alex's front seat. She closed her eyes while he drove; he placed a hand on her knee.

Think about it, she told herself. A waitress and dog-sitter falls in love with the nice man next door. A handsome, tender, strong, honest man. After a life so disjointed and fraught with worry, could I just this once luck out and stumble upon a stable and trustworthy man who cares for me? She saw a picture of it in her mind—a small Boulder City house, a couple of puppies, a garden, bicycles. She wouldn't change a thing. After beachfront condos, private jets and Jaguars, could she be happy like that? Only for fifty or sixty years.

But when he learned all there was to know about her, would he feel the same way?

Alex pulled his car into his garage. He killed the engine and they sat in the still, quiet dark. He reached for her, kissed her again, long and lingeringly, and asked, "Your house or mine?"

"I want to be near Alice," she said. "She's so...you know."

"Good enough," he said.

They held hands as they walked across the lawn. She opened the door with her key and Alice greeted them. "See, I told you I wouldn't be late," she said.

Before she could get any more involved with the dog, she found herself pulled into Alex's embrace yet again. He turned her and pushed her back against the closed front door. Alone now with no intruding laughter, music or partygoers, Alex pressed himself against the length of her and applied himself to the task of seducing her with bold and serious intention.

She found him totally irresistible. *Totally.* The feeling *rocked* her. There was no distorting the fact that while she'd had quite a few men in her day, she hadn't ever felt helpless or vulnerable to the emotions that drove simple-headed women into the arms of conquesting men. But this guy was working his magic on her and she was melting. Literally. She felt him firm up against her while she became damp and pliant and ready.

She wanted him. She wanted to give herself to him. But it came to her suddenly that to do so while there was still so much deception on her part would be wrong. If it wasn't enough that he didn't even know her name, he would have to know about her history with men before they could become intimate. For the first time, it would be more than sex for her. It would be the whole of it— giving and taking.

"Alex?" she whispered against his parted lips.

"Hmm?" he returned while his hands roved down to her buttocks and pulled her hard against him.

"I don't want you to go, but I might…might need more time before…"

Alex groaned.

"I want to be sure," she said, but what she meant was that they *both* should be sure. He should know what he was getting into so he didn't have any regrets.

His lips left hers and his head dropped slightly, banging the door over her shoulder. "Okay," he finally said. "Perfectly understandable." He kissed her again. "Perfectly impossible."

Ten

Alex stayed the night, just in case Jennifer changed her mind. They went to bed, but in most of their clothes. She in her dress; he removed his shoes, belt and shirt. He curled around her back at first, kissing her neck, whispering that the moment she was ready, all she had to do was nudge him and he would take very good care of her. But thanks to beer, margaritas and dancing, his promises soon turned into soft snores. Very soon he rolled over and she was left to spoon his back.

Snuggling was something she never did. She hadn't had a relationship that lent itself to closeness. Sex, yes. Intimacy, no.

He never stirred when she got up at four-thirty to go to work, or when she ran the shower and let Alice out in the yard. She scribbled him a little note and headed for the diner at sunrise.

Buzz was in the grill and there was no sign of Adolfo. "Our cook isn't coming in today?" she asked.

"He'll make it sooner or later, but there's no hurry. So. You and Alex? Huh?"

"Just friends, Buzz. He's right next door is all."

Buzz chuckled and his belly jiggled. "Good thing my neighbors don't kiss me like that. I live next door to old man Roberts. Bristly chin, very few teeth."

Jennifer put on her apron. "But what a great party, huh? Adolfo has such a wonderful family. So many fantastic friends." She tried to keep the sigh from her voice. "I can't imagine."

"Tell me about it," Buzz concurred. "But we shouldn't complain, Doris. We have to play the cards we're dealt."

She leaned her elbows on the counter. "You ever feel ready for a new deck?"

He seemed to think about that for a moment, then shook his head. "Naw. I don't think I could be any luckier. Nor happier."

"What are you happiest about?" she asked.

"Well, in case you hadn't noticed, I have a lot of fun. I have good friends and I make the absolute most out of what I got. This is just a little diner, and it keeps a lot of people happy and well fed. I don't know what more I could ask for."

"I was thinking about family...."

"I think of all of you as my family." Then he smiled broadly, nodding his head so sharply that the haylike thatch of hair flopped on his forehead. "I keep you irritated enough, don't you think?"

Elbow on the counter, she leaned on her hand. "You never married."

"Never found anyone who would have me." He chuckled. "Except Adolfo."

"You two are like an old married couple. You've been together a long time, haven't you?"

"Over twenty-five years. He's good people."

"The whole family is wonderful. How do you do that? Create a family like that?"

"They stick together, the Garcias. They work together, help each other. And, they never give up."

"You know, Buzz, I don't think I've told you this, but you gave me a great opportunity here, with this job."

"This crummy job?"

"It's good work. I needed something like this. Needed to slow down and take a long look at my life. It was time for a change."

"Well," he said, wiping the counter in front of her. "We aim to please."

Because she couldn't shake the memory of leaving Alex in her bed, the morning dragged by. Adolfo finally showed up at a little after nine, looking a little worse for wear but pleased with himself. Hedda showed up early, a bunch of pictures torn from the magazines in her notebook for Jennifer to ooh and aah over. And then finally it was time to go home. Even after a long introspective morning, she still didn't know what she was going to say to Alex.

She was saved from that challenge. At the bottom of her note he had written, "I had a great time, too. Had to go in to work, but hopefully that means I'll be home a little earlier. I'll give you a call. And my cell number is 555-7678." It sounded as though Alex was moving into a relationship.

Louise had said, For advice about men, ask Rose.

After Alice's constitutional, she tapped on Rose's door. "Are you busy, Rose?"

"I was going to go shopping, but it can wait if you need something."

She took a deep breath. "Can you tell me about Alex?"

Rose's eyes took on a special light and she smiled. "Come in, Doris. Let's have a Coke."

Alex, Rose told her, bought the little house on the other side of Louise about twelve years ago. He was a brand-new, twenty-three-year-old police officer in the city, single and pleasant to be around. Then a couple of years later a beautiful young woman appeared—the new wife.

"We weren't close friends at that time," Rose said. "So we didn't know that Alex was engaged and we weren't invited to the wedding. When Patsy showed up, I swear the whole street brightened. She was so effervescent, so alive. It was easy to tell that Alex had never been so happy. We saw a lot more of him in those early days. I imagine it was because he wanted to be home with his pretty young wife whenever he could."

"What happened to her?" Jennifer asked, quite sure she was going to hear the tragic story of a love gone wrong, leaving Alex devastated.

"One day we noticed the young woman was gone and Alex's house seemed to be shut up tighter than a tick. If it hadn't been for seeing him go to and from work now and then, we'd have thought he moved."

"What happened?"

"She left him. Or he threw her out." They sat at the kitchen table with their sodas on ice and Rose leaned closer. "Alex was a very junior police officer at the time—a uniformed officer. He didn't have much seniority so he worked nights and weekends. But his wife was not alone and lonely—when she wasn't out until late at night, she had company in. She always seemed to make it home before Alex showed up, and her company would always leave before he got home. I was the one that pointed it out to Louise, and you know what she said?"

"I can't imagine," Jennifer said.

"She said I had a dirty mind. Phoo."

Jennifer thought about that for a while. "Poor Alex," she said softly.

"There hasn't been a woman in that house since. I'm not saying he hasn't dated—I wouldn't know about that. But if he's brought anyone home with him, he snuck them right past Louise and me. Now, Louise might mind her own business most of the time, but I'm on the neighborhood watch. And I mean *watch*."

Then undoubtedly Rose knew where Alex had spent the night last night, she thought.

"Has he ever told you what happened? With his wife?"

"I've never asked," Rose said. "It was clear that whatever it was, it was very painful. He was a long time in coming around. It was a couple of years later when he was cutting his front lawn—he just kept going until he'd cut all three lawns. It's not as though they're very big. Then one day he trimmed all three front hedges. Then some spring flowers appeared around our doors, so Louise and I had him to dinner. The help with the lawns was never negotiated—it seemed to coincide perfectly with our lawn boy going off to college."

"But you're very close now...."

"We're friends, Doris. But he doesn't confide in me." She smiled a little wistfully. "We actually have a good time together, Alex and I. I'm very careful, you see—I don't want him spending all his time with old women."

"But he seems to have a wonderful life!" Jennifer protested. "I've met his partner and her husband. He personally introduced me to half of Adolfo's family and every one in the neighborhood—he knows everyone. He may not be married or dating, but he has a very full life. You can't deny it."

Rose lifted just one finely arched brow. "Is he dating now?" she asked.

Jennifer didn't answer right away because she was deep in thought. How was it possible this attractive and sensitive and funny man hadn't had a significant woman in his life in at least eight years and now, suddenly, a couple of months after meeting her he was ready to take a chance again? On her? What would he say if he knew what her life had really been like? "I don't know," she said softly.

"He seems a little preoccupied with you," Rose said.

"I don't know," she said again.

"Save all that coyness for someone else, darling. I can see right through you." She stood up from the table. "We should have a little wine now. Loosen your tongue." She went to her wine rack and turned bottles until she found one she liked.

"Louise warned me about you. She said you'd get me drunk and make me talk."

"How is the old girl?"

"She's having a high old time. There's one thing that's so crazy, Rose. I always ask about Rudy, but all Louise will ever say is that he's just the same."

Rose was in the process of pulling out the cork and her hand froze. She turned to look at Jennifer, a most peculiar expression on her face. "Oh, my dear," she said finally. "We really do need that wine."

"Why? What is it? This whole thing is so strange. She did say she was going to see her son, Rudy, didn't she?"

Rose poured two glasses of wine and took her seat again. "I think what she said was, she was going to be near Rudy. You see, Doris, Rudy is dead."

"Louise's history is fascinating. And tragic. She married a California engineer in the forties. Harry was his name. They had only one child, Rudy, born just a year after they married. Louise was first a teacher and then, after going back to college for her Ph.D. with a baby in a stroller beside her during most of her classes, an academic. They were true intellectuals, bohemians. Harry and Louise lived as equal partners before that was fashionable. But it wasn't easy to get an education and pursue a career while also a wife and mother. I suppose that's why she went in the direction of women's studies and women's literature.

"They did a great deal of traveling back then, and spent several years in Europe, mostly London. Harry worked for the Department of Defense as a consultant, which took him all over the globe, and Louise was welcomed at international universities in her studies."

"She must have been a formidable academic," Jennifer said.

Rose smiled. "Sometimes, Doris, you remind me of her. Your choice of words. Brings you quite a bit above what one would expect from a waitress in a diner."

"Well, I read a lot."

"Hmm. Well, Louise's son, Rudy, loved London. He went to boarding school there in his teens, and although he went to UCLA, he also did two years at Oxford. It was always his plan to finish postgraduate studies in England and perhaps live there at least a few months of every year. Louise was crazy about that idea.

"But then there was a rift. Vietnam. Harry had served in World War Two, did government work for many years and was, at least in that regard, a conservative. When your number comes up, you go. Not so Rudy, who protested the war. He burned his draft card. They had bitter arguments, but in the end Rudy left the country for England and denounced the U.S."

"He was a draft dodger," Jennifer said, fascinated.

"That's right. Now, Louise wrote to him daily and she signed the letters Mom and Dad, but Harry was not getting over it. He didn't write to Rudy and he rarely read the letters Louise received. After being away only four months, Rudy was killed in London as he stepped in front of a cab. Among his personal effects were instructions to bury him in England.

"Louise went to England alone to bury her son because Harry was determined to bring Rudy back to the States. Harry had this thoroughly irrational belief that Rudy might have been safer in Vietnam. Here she was—stuck in the middle even after Rudy was dead. It was the darkest time in her life—her only son gone and her beloved husband still furious with him.

"Needless to say, this wasn't good for their marriage. Louise hated that Harry couldn't bend a little, and Harry hated that Louise could so easily forgive their son's disloyal politics.

"By then Harry was nearly sixty, ten years older than Louise, when he took an engineering job in Boulder City. It was the early seventies and he didn't expect to be there for long, so Louise stayed in Southern California at UCLA and Harry went back and forth. Their marriage was strained, their grief was deep, and life for them was hard. Harry's angry heart soon gave out and he died suddenly in his sleep. In his personal effects were the instructions to bury him in Boulder City. It was like retaliation."

"My God, she must have been devastated!"

"Devastated and suddenly alone, with her son buried in England and Harry buried in Boulder City. So Louise sold her California house at a very tidy profit and moved. She was only fifty then and healthy as a horse—a very sad horse. But she was a much sought-after academic in the field of women's studies, which was just blossoming. She bought a house in Boulder City and a flat in London, where she spent anywhere from three to six months a year."

"She divides her time between Harry and Rudy?" Jennifer asked, wiping a tear away. "Even though they're both dead?"

"I know," Rose nodded. "Makes her sound like a flake, doesn't it? But somehow it gives her comfort. Not that she's caught hanging around cemeteries too often. The thing to understand about Lou is that she needs so little. Give her a good big dog, a library, a pad of paper and pen, and she can entertain herself for decades. I know she adored Harry and Rudy, but I'm pretty sure she didn't plan her life around them. She traveled, studied, wrote. She was an independent woman with a family."

Jennifer blew her nose. "I wish I had known all that. I wouldn't have kept asking about her son."

Rose laughed. "That's funny. Her saying he's just the same."

"It's awful."

"Well, you should give her hell. Shame on her. Acting like she's visiting her son when he's been dead thirty years. That woman. She can be so *out there*." She sighed. "But then I probably seem a little over the top, too. Not too many women of my generation go to such lengths to remain single."

"Weren't you ever tempted?"

"Of course, darling. But I knew myself too well. I couldn't be tied down."

Rose poured more wine and began on her story. As a young woman, Rose was determined to be discovered as a great dancer. There was but one small problem. She wasn't.

She was a fairly *good* dancer, though. She shook the dust of Nebraska off her heels when she was eighteen and headed for New York City. She could hold her own in a chorus line and she had the impossible delusion that she was going to be a star. It didn't take long for her to come to her senses. The only jobs she could hold in New York were backup dancer or chorus-line member on short runs, and she couldn't afford to live in the city. She borrowed some money and made her way to Los Angeles, where anyone could be a star.

Anyone but Rose, it would seem.

At the ripe old age of twenty-three she took a trip to Las Vegas, which at the time was just a little oasis in the desert with a few nightclubs and casinos. Most of the town and virtually all of the gambling was being run by the mob. Rose had become frustrated with New York and Los Angeles, but it had never occurred to her to relocate until she saw an ad for a hostess at the Sands Hotel. She checked it out and learned that all that was required of her was that she dress in glittery clothing and greet people. She took the job.

Jennifer said nothing—but she was stunned to hear that their beginnings were so similar. They were hostesses.

Over the next several years Rose did a variety of things in Las Vegas, from dancing to managing young dancers. She found that the less she wore, the more money she made.

"Rose, you were a stripper!"

"Well, from time to time. But we did a much better job of it then. We never got completely naked. And if a man so much as suggested that I sit on his lap, he'd be removed from the club. It's quite a bit different now."

She met a lot of celebrities and dated rich men who were fond of throwing their winnings around. It was customary to give the woman at your side, who brought you luck at the tables, a nice cash tip. Rose was far from famous, but she was definitely living the high life.

Of all the men she kept company with when she was in her twenties, only one really captured her heart. He was an air force pilot stationed at Nellis Air Force Base at the edge of the city. He was sweet and handsome and asked her to marry him. He wanted to go home to Wisconsin to the family farm, settle in the same small town he'd grown up in, surrounded by aunts, uncles and cousins, and breed up a flock of kids.

"I still think about him sometimes," Rose confessed to Jennifer.

"You said no?"

"I did. I said no."

"But you loved him!"

"Yes, but I didn't think I could live the life he was describing. I was a kid during the Depression. I grew up in a house with squabbling parents who had nothing, never could seem to scrape together enough money for even a decent pair of shoes, and I was bound and determined to live better than that."

"Maybe he was a rich farmer," Jennifer suggested.

Rose's eyes glanced upward as if remembering. "I was young, but for the first time in my life I was wearing fine, fancy clothing, going to parties with rich people and celebrities. I bought a car—a convertible—and rented a house with a swimming pool. I just couldn't imagine wearing overalls and going out to the chicken coop to gather up eggs for our breakfast."

Jennifer bit her lip and said nothing.

"I couldn't convince him to give up the idea of that simple life and stay with me in Las Vegas, a booming town. He hated it here. And although I cried when he left, it wasn't long before I had another man in my life—a rich and generous one. I was respected, well paid, never lonely. I moved to Boulder City when I was only forty, though I continued to work in the city. I might not have a pension, but I have a nice little nest egg. I did well for myself."

"Do you ever regret your decision?"

"Do I ever! Do you know what that rat bastard did? He spent about six months on the farm and then got a job with United Airlines. Do you know how much money airline pilots make? Especially the older ones who started flying way back when? I might've lived with the many of my dreams, not on a farm but in high style, and had six children to boot!"

Children.

"Did you want children?"

"Doris, I think every woman wants a child, even if that want is stored in the back of her mind. And a child with the right man? Well, no use crying over spilled milk. I had a lot of nice suitors over the years, but that rat bastard was the only one I would have ever considered marrying."

Rose's lips curved in a knowing smile. "I recognize

that look," she said to Jennifer. "The shocked and stricken look on your face. You haven't even allowed for the possibility of living happily ever after. Of finding true love and having a family. Have you, Doris?"

"I... Ah..."

"You're almost thirty, Doris. What have you been doing up till now?"

"Well... Let's just say that the two of us have more in common than you might think."

"There is one major difference," Rose said. "I can't go back to being thirty. You still have time for a course correction."

When Jennifer got home, she went directly to the computer. It was her intention to e-mail Louise about the story Rose had told her, but while she was trying to think of what she might say, she went through her routine of checking the Internet for any news of the Nobles.

In the Living section of the *West Palm Beach News,* along with the anniversary and charity-event announcements, was a small item with a picture. Mr. and Mrs. Nicholas Noble off on a three-week cruise. There they were, waving from the deck of the ship, all smiles. Everything would seem to be in order except for one small thing. It was a newspaper file photo. Jennifer had seen it many times before. It was years old, perhaps a honeymoon photo.

He was getting away with it, she thought in sheer dread.

Alex was tied up on a case but called her four times to tell her he would be coming by after work, if that was all right. She hoped he couldn't hear the trepidation in her voice. It was there because she was thinking she might have to give in and tell him about Nick. About what she was running from.

Normally she would have fallen asleep before ten, but the tension of mulling this over and waiting for Alex was keeping her alert. When there was a knock at the door a few minutes after ten, she jumped up and threw the door open without even asking who was there.

There stood Hedda, Joey over one shoulder and her backpack over the other. "I'm sorry," she said.

"Don't be," Jennifer said. "I'm happy to see you. Go put Joey in the bed and let's have a diet cola before you turn in."

"Okay." She dropped the backpack and started through the living room. She turned back and said, "Doris, I don't know what I'd do without you."

While she was tucking in her little brother, Jennifer made a couple of colas on ice and brought them to the living room. She put them on the coffee table and curled up on one end of the couch. Hedda came back and claimed the other end of the couch.

"I've tried not to pry, but maybe you'd better tell me what's going on at your house."

Hedda shrugged, grabbed her drink and took a sip. "We're in the way. Again."

"What do you mean? Exactly," Jennifer pushed. Even as she did so, she remembered how impossible it would have been to get her to talk about her mother when she was a teenager. And how much it might have helped if she had.

"My mom has had pretty rotten luck with men," she said. "My dad left her before I was a year old. My first stepdad didn't hang around long, either. And Joey's dad… A couple of years."

"What about Roger?"

"Roger?" she asked with a short laugh. "Who's Roger?"

So maybe the kids didn't know about that night. Or early morning.

"Does she have a lot of boyfriends?"

"I wouldn't say a lot. But sometimes she drinks a little too much. She says she just wants to enjoy life a little, it's tough enough. But sometimes she enjoys life a little too much, you know? She's usually real good. I mean, too tired from work to drink too much. She might have a couple when she gets home, which is really late, but… But sometimes she might stop at a bar with some of her waitress friends. Sometimes she might have too much."

"And tonight was one of those nights?"

"Yeah. So Joey and I took the pullout couch, except we didn't really. I just stuffed some school clothes in the backpack for him and we were good to go."

"Hedda, did it ever occur to you that maybe you and Joey should be in a foster home?"

"Oh, man, we tried that once," she said, shaking her head. "We weren't together and both of us were in awful places. My foster father could drink my mother under the table. No, I just have to make it one more year."

"And?"

"And I'll take care of Joey and Sylvia can do whatever she wants."

"You ever think maybe she should consider something like AA?"

"She went once," she shrugged. "She said she just didn't have the problem those people had. I mean, she can sometimes drink a little too much, but it's not like every day."

"Every week?"

"Not even."

"But pretty often. Too often."

"Sometimes it's too often. But, Doris? Except for the times she brings someone home, which isn't all that often really, I like her a lot better when she's had a couple of cocktails. At least she's not so frickin' *mad*."

It was awful to think there was absolutely nothing she could do to help. Jennifer couldn't be a foster parent. She wasn't even sure she'd be in Boulder City in another six months. And here was this sixteen-year-old holding it together for her little brother.

But holding it together really well, as a matter of fact.

"Joey's dad is about ten times as screwed up as my mom, but he has really nice grandparents in Tucson. They try to see him, when my mom will let them. They even try to make me feel like I can come anytime, but I've tried that and it's not too cool. While they fuss over Joey, I am completely invisible. I'm better off with Sylvia for now.

"It's not the greatest—but we're going to get past this. You know?" Hedda asked.

"I know," Jennifer said. "My mom heard voices sometimes."

"She did?"

"Totally mentally ill," she said. "I didn't bring friends around because she might be having a conversation with a couch pillow."

"Wow."

"So, I do know how you feel."

There was a soft knock at the door and Jennifer said, "Alex. He said he was going to stop by after work." She went to the door, opened it enough so that Alex could see Hedda sitting on the couch. "Hi," she said. "I can't play. I'm having a sleepover."

Jennifer wished she hadn't seen the picture of the Nobles waving from the deck of the ship. She was haunted by the knowledge that Nick was successfully creating little scenarios of Barbara being away, traveling, vacationing, when in fact she was dead. It was just like reliving that day at the MGM.

She'd have to go to Alex. Of all the people she was growing to trust, he was the only one she could think of who might actually be able to help her. After a quick walk around the park with Alice, she saw Alex's car was in his open garage. It was nearly dark when she knocked at his door.

"Hey!" he said happily when he saw her. "Was the sleepover a success?"

"Raging. I was just getting back from a walk," she said. She heard the nervousness in her own voice. She was feeling both desperate and afraid. "Alex, did you ever wish you could turn back the clock?"

He held the door open for her to come inside with Alice. "Did I do something I shouldn't have?"

"I didn't mean about the other night. I meant... I mean in general. Wish you could go back in time and do things differently?"

He put his arms out to her, pulling her against him gently. Comfortingly. She lay her head against his chest and let him just hold her for a minute. "Everyone wishes that at some point in their lives," he said. "Everyone."

"Alex, I am such a screwup."

"Naw, I don't believe that."

"Oh, believe it. And you're the unlucky doofus who drew the short straw because I can't think of anyone else to dump this on."

His smile was tender. He lifted her chin with a finger, placed a sweet kiss on her lips and said, "Go ahead. Tell me Jennifer's life story."

She jumped back a foot, out of his arms. Alice skittered at the surprise movement. Jennifer wore a look of shock on her face that actually brought a half smile to his lips. "You *knew?*"

"Hey, I'm trained to know these things."

"How many other people know?" she asked, still backing away.

He shrugged. "No one around here, as far as I know."

"Around *here?*"

"I was forced to tell Paula. But believe me—it's better that she knows what I know than to have her guessing. Now, why don't we just..."

"Wait! Wait!" She shook her head in disbelief. How long had he known? Since the first time they saw the bighorns? Had he just been playing her, trying to trick her into trusting him enough to spill her guts? "I have to think about this." She turned away from him to leave.

"Hey, Jennifer—don't overthink this," he said. He reached out and grabbed her wrist, but she snatched it away. "I just want to help."

"You lied to me!"

"I didn't lie—"

"You lied! Every time you called me Doris, it was a lie. You knew who I was and what I was hiding from!"

"Actually, no. I'm still not sure what you're so scared of. But if you tell me, I'll—"

"I don't think so, Alex. I think I've lost my nerve. At least right now."

"Don't walk away like this," he said. "You have some kind of heavy load and I only want to share it. Jennifer, it's my *job.*"

"I don't want to be your *job!*"

"That's not what I meant and you know it. It's my job to help when someone's in trouble or afraid of trouble."

"I…ah…I need a little time to think. Okay? Just give me a little time to think this through."

"Why? You wanted to tell me about it. You wanted my help. Let's do it. Let's talk about it now."

"That was when I thought I'd have to explain everything. That was before I found out you already know all about me, pretending not to." She opened the door and stepped out. She looked over her shoulder. "You should have been straight with me from the beginning."

"I didn't want to push you. Scare you off."

She gave a huff of laughter. "Well, in fact…" She

backed away and Alice went with her. "Now you're going to have to be patient."

She jogged across their front lawns and let herself into Louise's house. She leaned back against the closed and locked front door and said, "Dammit, Alex."

This put a new face on things. She thought he was falling for her, falling for a waitress named Doris. It was possible he could care less; he could be undercover, watching her movements. He could be just about ready to investigate her for stealing from Nick. And if he searched her belongings he would find two diamond rings and a tennis bracelet given to her by Nick and a nice stack of hundreds that she'd come away with from the MGM Grand.

Alice, tired, wandered over to the cool tile floor near the cold hearth and flopped down. Jennifer sat on the edge of the sofa, thinking. The house grew dark around her. All these people she had borrowed from Louise's life were retreating in her mind. What she thought was Alex's genuine affection was probably him doing his job as a cop, checking her out. When she turned out not to be Doris, would everyone change their feelings toward her?

And would Alex tell someone at the police department, who would get the word to Nick?

At about 9:00 p.m. she made up her mind that she would have to leave Boulder City. The only light she turned on in the house was in the master bath. In the shadows she packed her backpack. She took as much as she could by way of clothing, but much would have to be left behind. She draped over the sofa the clothes that Rose had loaned her for the Cinco de Mayo party. She filled Alice's dish, knowing she wouldn't touch it until morning. And poor Hedda—but what good would she be to Hedda if Nick *"took care of her."*

She struggled with a note. It was in her heart to explain, but in the end all she could write was, *I'm sorry if I let anyone down.*

She put the backpack by the front door and lay down on the floor by Alice, her head on Alice's back. She hummed a few lullabies and wiped impatiently at tears that slid down her cheeks. When the hour was sufficiently late and the sky reliably black, she kissed her old friend on the head. "I love you, old girl. I'll call Rose in the morning—she'll take good care of you."

She tucked the key under the front mat and began walking. She headed toward the dam where she hoped to hitch a ride to the Arizona side. If she could get to Flagstaff or Laughlin, she could get a bus ride to Ohio. Maybe if she could go back in time, back to where she had some childhood memories that didn't hurt, maybe she could rebuild her life. For sure there wouldn't be any posters with her face on them.

She passed the park—she would so miss the park. She wouldn't get to see the lambs. There would be no more celebrations at the Garcia homestead.

And Alex...the brush with romance that wasn't would fade from her memory fast.

"I can't believe you would leave Alice," he said.

He was sitting on top of a picnic table in the park, partially hidden in the shadows. His feet were on the bench and he leaned his elbows on his knees. She was frozen.

"I didn't want to. I had to."

"You didn't *have* to," he said, anger edging his words. "You could have just told me the truth, let me help."

"You could have told the truth, too."

He stood up abruptly and came toward her, causing her to back away a little. "Hey, enough of this crap. I didn't betray you. I haven't sold you out. All I know is that you're scared of someone—and I think I know who, but I don't know why. All I'm guilty of is keeping my mouth shut while you learned to trust me!"

"You don't under*stand!*"

"You're right—I don't! And you're not making it any easier!"

"Alex, he killed his wife! I saw him!"

Well, that did it—shut him right up. In fact, if she wasn't mistaken, it kind of knocked the wind out of him.

"Well, holy shit, Doris."

"See? You just don't know the half of this mess. And I don't feel like being your *project*. It's enough that I'm Buzz's and Rose's project. But—"

Something about that seemed to rile him up, because he took three long strides toward her, pulled her into his arms, kissed her so hard it nearly knocked her out of her shoes and, when he was finally done, said, "Jennifer, if you can't tell my feelings for you are real, I am way rustier at this than I thought. Now, dammit, let me help you with this mess so we can get on with our lives."

"Our lives?"

"Yeah, ours. Jesus, you are so pigheaded you make me tired."

"How do you know you're still going to want to know me after you know everything about me?"

"For God's sake—I've been a cop for twelve years. Do you honestly think you can come up with something I haven't seen before?"

"Seeing it on the street and having it right in your…" She stopped.

He sensed she was having trouble, so he gave her a little squeeze and tried to finish for her. "In your arms? So—look at your options. You can run and never know, or you can stay and see if this thing between us works. Either way, if you don't get this trouble behind you, you're going to have to deal with it forever."

That was true. Also true was, that of the entire police force, Alex might be the only one she was willing to take a chance on. "I wasn't going to abandon Alice. I was going to call Rose in the morning. If she didn't answer, I had your cell phone number. And the key is under the mat."

"I know. I watched all that."

"You were spying on me?"

"I was afraid you might bolt. You were pretty pissed that I knew your name."

"How long have you known?"

"Since the flyers were put out. About the time you moved in next door. Now, come on, let's go home. Tell Alice everything is going to be all right. Then you can give me the whole story and we'll get you taken care of."

"Okay, then," she said. As they began to walk back toward the house she slipped her arm around his waist. "I really hated leaving before the lambs."

"There are lambs every year, sweetheart," he said.

She began to cry. She leaned on him and cried into his shirt. "It isn't just the lambs. It's Rose and Hedda and Buzz. It's the Garcias. It's *you*. Alex, I don't want to go."

"Good," he said, comforting her, stroking her back. "We don't want to lose you."

Eleven

When Jennifer unlocked the door and flipped on the light, Alice didn't come to her. She raised herself on her front legs, but her back legs stayed grounded. There was a dark stain not very far from the dog. "What in the—?"

Jennifer looked at the stain; an accident clearly tinged with blood. She knelt in front of Alice, who whimpered in either pain or confusion. "Come on, girl… Tell me what's wrong."

Alex tried to hoist Alice's hindquarters up, but she had no control of her legs and couldn't hold her own weight. She was paralyzed at least from the hips down. "Jennifer, we've got to get her to the vet."

"Louise wrote the name down for me," she said, rising. "There's an after-hours emergency vet…."

"I know where we're going. Just grab a towel for the car." He hefted all seventy-five pounds of Alice into his arms and headed for his car. "Get in the back with her," he told Jennifer.

As they drove, Alex dialed his cell phone. "Sam," he said. "I know, I know—but it's Alice. She can't move her hind legs and she left a mess on the floor not far from herself—like maybe she dragged herself away from it. No, no, she'd only been alone a half hour or so." To Jennifer he asked, "Any other symptoms earlier in the day? Has she been eating, drinking, et cetera?"

"Perfectly normal. A little slow and achy—but that's to be expected."

Jennifer cradled Alice's head on her lap in the back seat, gently stroking her. All thoughts of her own predicament were suddenly gone. She lay her head atop the dog's and prayed that they could have a little more time together. She couldn't believe she'd almost left her! She might've died...*alone.*

They didn't drive very far before Alex stopped the car in front of a yellow house converted into an animal hospital. He turned around and spoke over the seat. "I know about the emergency vet in Henderson—but Sam and Alice go way back, so I took a chance and called him. He's coming over to meet us."

But she wondered if what was happening to Alice was beyond the skill of even the best vet.

It was only a couple of minutes before Sam Gunterson pulled his Jeep into the parking space in front of the office. He'd been in the diner a few times, but Jennifer had never been happier to see him. While he unlocked the door, Alex carried the patient. "There are very few women I'd get up in the middle of the night for, my dear," he said to the dog, giving her a fond pat. "Hey, Doris, how you doing?"

"Not so great at the moment," she said quietly.

"Try not to worry too much, Doris. Alex, I'm going to have you put her in the surgery for me. Then I won't have to move her to do an exam, take blood, X ray or any other procedures. And you two can wait out front."

Jennifer stood in the small, deserted waiting room until Alex returned. The expression of worry on his face made her realize that he felt at least as attached to Alice as she did. "If I'd been successful in running away, we wouldn't have found Alice. At least not to-night."

He just put his hands in his pockets, watched her face and waited.

"I came to Las Vegas with a guy named Nick Noble," she said. "I've been his…his mistress for just under two years. We'd been in town for three days when I came back to our room and found he was in a brutal argument with his wife, Barbara. She was throwing things and they were both yelling. One of his guys saw me peek into the room and then quietly duck out. I went to a bar in the casino for a couple of hours, and when I came back it looked like a bomb had gone off in the suite. Barbara was facedown on the bed and I heard Nick tell his guys to get rid of her. And, he said, 'Find that bimbo I brought with me—we're going to have to do something about her, too.'"

"And you left," Alex supplied.

"I just went to another hotel for a few days and watched the news and newspapers. I don't know what I expected— but I sure wasn't prepared to see a picture of me as miss-ing, along with the accusation that I had stolen from him."

"You have jewelry and money?" he asked.

"Two rings that were given to me quite a while ago and a tennis bracelet I got on this trip. Then there was the cash. Nick was in the habit of giving me shopping money to keep me occupied while he played poker. When I saw the picture of me that was published, all that long blond hair that Nick loved so much—well, you know what I did."

"Your life must have been very complicated."

"No, Alex. It's complicated now. My life was very simple before—mainly because I operated in an emotional vacuum. All I had to do was be pleasant and beautiful and low maintenance. Nick took care of everything. It was pretty easy to primp and dress well and be available for dates."

"Dates with this married guy you didn't even love?" he asked, but he didn't ask it in an incredulous manner, as though she must be crazy.

"Exactly, Alex. This married guy was on his third wife—and I had no intention of ever being the fourth. The most I could do for him was make it look like he had attracted a hot young chick."

"How'd you get together?"

"I worked for a property management company. I was a secretary-slash-agent. I managed a few office buildings—rented space, wrote leases, collected rent and occasionally called a plumber or electrician if something was broken. The buildings were an investment of Nick's. He came in to the management company to meet with my boss and he asked me out." She took a breath. "I didn't go out with him right away."

"Why didn't you go to the police immediately?"

"I don't know. I've been thinking about that a lot. How would this be different if I'd gone to the front desk and said, 'There's a dead woman in Nick Noble's room.' But I wasn't sure the hotel wouldn't cover it up. You have no idea what lengths they went to to keep him happy and coming back. They sent their private jet for him four times a year and put him up in the most luxurious suite imaginable. Even if they wouldn't have broken the law for him, I thought they might worry more about his safety than mine. After all, I was just his bimbo.

"Then there was something about the way I found her—and him. When his guys left the room, I heard the shower running. I tiptoed into the suite, poked my head into the bedroom, saw Barbara's lifeless body and heard him singing in the shower. Singing. All of a sudden everything I knew about him, but had denied to myself, came rushing into my mind. He's cold. Dangerous. Powerful. Unremorseful. I ran. Alex, I had no one to run to. No family, no friends, no one who would've helped me. I just got away from there. I covered my tracks by going to the airport and buying a ticket in all my long-legged blondness and then, covering my head with a scarf, took a cab to a neighborhood hotel off the Strip.

"By the time I thought maybe I had made a mistake and would have been better off telling someone, Nick and his thugs had had time to get rid of her and clean up the evidence." She shrugged. "Then I saw he reported *me* missing. I thought I was cooked."

"You don't watch much crime drama on TV, do you?" Alex asked. "We can still go into that suite and find evidence."

"Am I going to be in trouble for leaving?" she asked him.

"Let's not get ahead of ourselves. I don't know that we can even be sure about what you saw."

"Her body, Alex. I saw her body. The hair on the back of her head was matted and wet with blood."

"A lot of red, was there?"

"Not a lot, really. Splatters around the suite."

"Okay, I'm going to look into it. And you're going to be Doris for a while longer while I do. But this time, you don't run again."

No, she thought. No more. She shook her head. She wasn't going to run from any of it anymore. "I'm a little scared," she said.

"I don't blame you. I'll do everything I can to keep you safe."

Suddenly it wasn't Nick she was most afraid of. It was Alex. What if, after she revealed the whole truth about herself, her gentlemen friends over the years and how she'd lived on their generosity, Alex lost all respect for her? But all she said was "I appreciate that. Thank you."

Alice had a tumor that was pressing against her spine, causing temporary paralysis. Sam Gunterson operated on her first thing the next morning. There was a higher than usual risk, given Alice's age, but she had a strong spirit and pulled through. She had to stay in the veterinary hospital for a couple of days, so that was where Jennifer would spend the afternoons until Alice could come home.

Dear Louise,
I'll start off by saying that everything is going to be all right. Alice gave me quite a scare last night—she couldn't get up. Alex and I rushed her to the vet— Sam came in just for her. It turned out she had a tumor on her spine, which he successfully removed. She's going to be a little weak and wimpy for a while, but Sam is convinced she will make a full recovery. I swear, she took ten years off my life.
Love,
Doris

My dear Doris,
Thank God you were there! I can't even bear to think of how frightened poor Alice must have been—and how much she must have appreciated you taking such good care of her! Thank Alex for me, too.
Bless you!
Louise

Jennifer was wiping off a couple of the tabletops just prior to retiring her apron, anxious to get over to Sam's to see how Alice was doing, when Hedda came into the diner to relieve her. The girl seemed to be in a nasty little mood, a very unusual circumstance. Even with all she had to put up with daily, she never failed to have a cordial smile and greeting. Today she didn't say hello, didn't look up as she entered and seemed to stow her purse under the counter with a pretty rough thrust.

"Nice to see you, too," Jennifer teased.

"Sorry," she said. "I have a lot on my mind."

"I'm sure. With prom getting so close."

"Yeah."

"Have you been shopping for your dress yet?" Jennifer asked, ducking a little to get under Hedda's downcast eyes.

"No. Not yet."

"What's up, kid? Something wrong?"

"Finals. It's almost time for finals."

Jennifer grabbed her wrist and dragged her past the grill toward the back door and bathroom. "Hey," Hedda protested.

"Hey, nothing. I have to get going—Alice is under the weather. But I can't leave my precious little diner in the hands of such a crab apple. What's your deal?"

"Nothing, I said. Just got a lot on my—"

"Last week you couldn't shut up about the dress you were going to get for the prom. Now you have finals on your mind?"

Tears gathered in the girl's eyes. "I'm not going."

"What?"

"You heard me. Now, let's drop it." She pushed Jennifer aside and stepped inside the bathroom, locking the door.

Memories flooded back to her. Jennifer had never gone to a prom or homecoming. Hell, she'd never gone to *anything!* She'd never been around a school long enough to be asked. And if she had been asked, chances were she'd never be able to float the whole dress issue. But she'd known her fair share of guys in high school, and she knew what they were capable of. In fact, all the heartache surrounding these events was way more crystal clear to Jennifer than any of the glitter and fun of it.

"Come on, Hedda," she said to the door. She leaned her ear against it. Just barely, muffled in there, was sniffling.

Jennifer went to the cash register and got the key to the bathroom. She unlocked the door and let herself in. "Hey!" Hedda protested from behind the fluffy white toilet tissue that soaked up her tears.

"Look, Hedda, I spent my entire high school career crying by myself in bathrooms. I'm not going to let you start doing it. It's a terrible habit to get into. Now, what happened?"

"Nothing."

"Did Max change his mind about taking you?"

"No. I just can't go is all."

"Since when?"

She sighed heavily and impatiently, but the tears rolled down her cheeks despite her attempt to appear annoyed. "Since my mom needed the money for the car insurance and we had to make some choices. Okay?" And she blew her nose heartily.

This was also something with which Jennifer had a great deal of experience. Single mom, a kid or two, no money... The specifics didn't matter—they just didn't have much. They lived paycheck to paycheck with very little left over. And Sylvia had to have *her* evenings out now and then....

"Oh, is that all?" Jennifer heard herself ask.

That brought a stunned look from behind the tissue. "Is that *all?*"

"So we're just talking about a dress?"

"*Just* a dress," Hedda said with sarcasm. "My mom talked about looking around for a used one. My luck, it would probably end up being one of the mean girls' hand-me-downs. Wouldn't that be cool."

Jennifer reached out to her, using her thumb to wipe away a tear. "That might be easier to work around than you think. I might be able to come up with something."

"*You?* You're even less prom-appropriate than I am! I mean, no offense."

She pursed her lips together and huffed. "While this is true, I also have a fairy godmother right next door. And a couple of saved-up bucks."

"Swell, but I doubt I could ever repay you."

"That's the beauty of it—you wouldn't necessarily have to. We could come up with a plan—you could help me out with taking care of Alice or something. The details aren't important—you know?" She broke into a wide grin. "Friends are there for each other."

"I don't know," Hedda said, blowing her nose a final time. "It seems like you're always there for me, but there isn't much I can do for you."

"We'll see about that. Are you free tonight after work?"

"Yes and no. I have to baby-sit at six so my mom can go to work."

"Oh, not to worry—we can take care of little brother."

She winked at Hedda. "Don't give up yet. We'll get this handled."

Hedda just looked at Jennifer, unbelieving. "Sure," she said.

The minute Alex got to work, before the briefing even started, he told his partner everything Jennifer had told him, bringing her up to speed.

"We're going to be forced to talk to Dobbs," Paula said to Alex. "There's no getting around it."

Alex knew it. In his efforts to locate Barbara Noble he was coming up empty. There was no indication she was dead, but no indication she was alive, either. In trying to trace her movements, he'd discovered she had gone from one vacation home to another, from a spa to a cruise—all out of the country. A couple of phone calls revealed people who claimed to have seen her—but what if that wasn't really her? Anyone could be a stand-in.

"I just hate to draw Dobbs's attention back to Jennifer. I'd like to know what he wants from her first."

"We have to call him before he calls us," she said.

"You do it," Alex said. "At least make it look like it's a police thing, not a neighborhood thing or a romance thing."

Paula peered at him. "So—it is a romance thing?"

"Well, I'm *trying!* There have been one or two little things clogging up the works! Like a possible murder!"

Paula put the business card from Dobbs on her knee and dialed her cell phone. "You have to admit, if that's what happened, she has good reason to be scared." She listened for a second. "Yeah, Dobbs, this is Detective

Aiken from Las Vegas Metro. I want to run something by you, might be information you need. We have a C.I. who says he has it on good authority that Nick Noble killed his wife, Barbara." She listened for a moment. "Well, how we got it was the C.I. claims it happened here in Vegas, at the hotel where he was staying. It's pretty murky since we can't get any confirmation from the hotel that the wife was in town, and we haven't been able to confirm our efforts to locate her." Again, she listened. "Well, I was told by the concierge of a spa in Costa Rica that she had been there, but she hadn't been to that spa before, so they weren't familiar with her. Coulda been anyone, huh? Huh? Oh, yeah? Oh, yeah? No, sorry—I can't give that up. But I don't think this has anything to do with Noble—our C.I. was trying to trade us anything under the sun for a walk and I just thought I'd give you a call. Better to be safe than sorry, huh?"

She clicked off and looked at Alex. "Barbara Noble is not dead."

That seemed to knock him back in his chair. He waited for more.

"I doubt Dobbs believes we have a confidential informant, but since he knows we know they're watching Noble, he was able to verify that Barbara Noble is alive and kicking. But here's the thing that's a little strange—he didn't ask me for any details of the alleged 'death.' Why do you suppose that is?"

"Because he knows all about it. Because he knows everyone who was there."

"You're going to have to tell Jennifer. And between

the two of you, see if you can figure out why she'd be a threat to Noble, since we know she didn't witness a crime. More important, let's see if we can figure out what the FBI wants."

Jennifer would have enlisted the assistance of Rose on the shopping trip in any case, but the issue of needing a car clinched the matter. Besides, the only shops Jennifer knew about were on the strip—Chanel, Armani, Brighten—and she couldn't help quite *that* much, even if she had once frequented those shops. Jennifer needed some direction for shopping for prom dresses she could afford. And Rose had a black belt in shopping.

"Do you think she's going to let you buy her a prom dress?" Rose asked.

"I think she'll show sufficient resistance," Jennifer said. "She's really proud. So, worst-case scenario, we do a little shopping, a little trying on, see what's good, and then go back for the dress later."

"Ah," Rose said. "Then we knock her over the head on prom night and pour her into it?"

"Whatever it takes," she said.

"This is a strange thing you're doing," Rose pointed out, unable to resist letting her eyes rove over Jennifer's attire.

"I know. I hate proms. What they do to girls is offensive to me. Everybody in that age group gets all overwrought at this time of year, panicked at the thought of going or not going. It isn't really all that important, is it? Which is why, at the age of thirty, I am still thinking about the effect that proms had on me. And why I don't want Hedda, who has a chance to put on a pretty dress and go, to miss it over a car insurance payment."

Rose smiled at this. "You don't want her to regret missing it at thirty."

"Let's just try to make this sort of fun. Okay?"

Jennifer phoned Alex at work to tell him what she was doing and to ask if he'd have time to drop by later. He promised to be waiting at her house when she finished the shopping trip. Then she and Rose gathered up Hedda and her little brother, Joey, and headed down the hill to the Henderson Mall. At seven years old, Joey wasn't very excited about shopping, but it turned out that he was very easily bribed with a promise of ice cream at the end of the evening.

It was only a twenty-minute drive, but it was twenty long minutes as Hedda kept any trace of enthusiasm from her expression. She sat quiet and serious in the back seat next to her brother, her arms crossed over her chest, her eyes downcast. "Did you bring any of the pictures of your favorites along?" Jennifer asked her. She shook her head. "Do you have anything in mind?" she tried. Again, Hedda shook her head. "Are you going to speak tonight, or just shake your head?" Hedda raised her eyes and shrugged.

As they were entering the mall, Hedda dragging behind, Jennifer whispered to Rose, "This is more what you'd expect from a girl in Hedda's circumstance. Ornery. Surly."

"She usually copes so well."

"Too well, I suddenly realize," Jennifer said.

The mood prevailed even as Jennifer and Rose gath-

ered up dresses for Hedda to try on. Hedda went
through the motions of fitting and rejecting them one
at a time. Jennifer thought it was probably her pride—
not wanting to take charity from anyone. Or possibly
she feared her mother wouldn't allow it in the end. And
it started to look as though Hedda could get out of this
arrangement by failing to find a suitable dress.

But then it happened, as it so frequently did—she
was captivated and turned upside down by a slim pink
sheath with feather straps. The moment Hedda slipped
into it, pulling the straps up over her shoulders, she
began to glow.

"Oh, my," Rose said.

The dress was narrowly fitted and sank into a low V-
shaped neckline with a very low back, also in a V, all
lined in the same soft pink feathers.

"It reminds me of my boa," Rose said.

Hedda's tattoo peeked out from her lower back, just
above the dress, and she smiled as she looked over her
shoulder to spy it. There was a slit in the skirt on the
left side, baring a shapely leg to the thigh. With just the
right pair of high-heeled sandals, she'd be the dancing
queen.

The color, with her creamy skin and coal-black hair,
was stunning. Her burgundy highlights, which Jennifer
sincerely hoped she would get rid of for the prom, even
complemented the dress. And the feather straps were so
unique—the dress didn't even need jewelry. But Jennifer was already thinking about a small necklace and
maybe a thin, sparkling bracelet.

Finding the dress was almost as painful for Hedda

as it was exciting. Tears gathered in her eyes and Rose sprang at her with a tissue. "Don't!" the older woman commanded. "It might water-spot!"

"I can't do this," Hedda said. "I just can't."

"Don't be so silly!" Rose said. "Can't you see it's more fun for us than for you?"

"It is, Hedda!" Jennifer said.

"My mom probably won't let this happen," she said with a giant sniff. "She's all pissed off about it, anyway. She thinks it is so selfish of me to want to do this. I didn't even have the guts to tell her about this shopping trip. I said we were going to watch a movie at your... I mean *Louise's* house."

Joey was busy making faces at himself in the floor-length mirror. "Won't someone tell?" Jennifer asked Hedda, glancing at Joey.

"Maybe. Maybe not. It's not like they *talk*."

"Hmm, I feel some ice cream coming on while you two finish up business," Rose said. "I'll meet you down at Stone Cold. Take your time."

Jennifer didn't even think about the strange fact that Rose had left the shopping to her, someone she didn't think had an ounce of taste. Rose took Joey away.

"Why wouldn't your mom let you go?"

"Because she's mad about everything. She's jealous and pissed off all the time. And she hates me."

"Hedda, mothers don't hate their daughters. It just isn't—"

"Believe me—if I weren't the baby-sitter, I don't think she'd keep me around."

Jennifer stroked her upper arm. "Sweetheart, your

mom is probably just in a constant bad mood because she has to work so hard all the time. It's not your fault, after all."

"Yeah, that's what you think," she said, slipping the dress down over her shoulders and reaching for her baggy T-shirt.

Jennifer remembered seeing Hedda hand over her earnings to her mom and never even get a thank you, much less a hug. She remembered the woman's errant fist all too well. And then there was that issue about drinking a little too much and bringing home "company."

"Well, I'm sure you're wrong," she said in spite of all that. "But no matter what's going on with your mom, we can work around it—this isn't about her. This is about you. But one thing at a time. Let's get the dress, find some shoes, and then we'll work out the details."

"It might be a waste of money," Hedda said.

"Look, if it doesn't work out, we can always return the dress. But I like to think positive."

"I'd like to, too," she said. "But I have more experience in this than you do."

"I know, kiddo." Jennifer looked over Hedda's shoulder and met her eyes in the mirror. "When I was your age, I didn't trust my crazy mom a bit," she said, knowing Hedda couldn't possibly know how wacked out her life was. "It's hard, being a teenager. I know you don't believe this now, but even the luckiest teenagers feel like they're underprivileged. Sometimes, just feeling like the world is against you all the time, you just don't take advantage of the opportunities that actually do come along. I know I didn't. I just accepted the idea that I was alone and no one could help me. Hedda, this is an opportunity. You're not as alone as you think. It's a pretty dress. We can keep it at Louise's house. If you think you need to, you can get dressed for the evening there."

"Behind her back?" she asked.

She shrugged. "I hate lying. But I hate for you to miss your only chance to go to the prom even more."

"Isn't that kind of devious?" Hedda asked.

"It is. I'm a very bad influence." Plus, it made her very angry to think that Sylvia would actually deny Hedda something so special, especially if it didn't put her out at all.

"I don't know…"

"Decide later, then. Right now—we need some shoes."

Later, when they were walking with their packages to the ice cream shop, Hedda asked, "What opportunities would you have taken advantage of?"

She thought for a minute. "I would have tried to get an education. I had a couple of teachers tell me I was smart enough to go to college and I didn't believe them. When believing them was tempting, I thought I'd never, in a million years, be able to afford it."

"Could you have afforded it?"

"No," she said with a smile. "I should have let someone help me."

After Hedda and Joey were dropped off at home, Jennifer carried the dress and shoes back to Louise's house. There were some lights on; her heart picked up a little speed as she realized Alex would be waiting for her.

"Hey!" she said when she entered, and saw that he had brought Alice home from the veterinary hospital. She draped the dress over a handy dining room chair, left the shoes on the table and went immediately to Alice. The Lab stood and wagged, but only took a couple of delicate steps in Jennifer's direction, so Jennifer knelt on the floor in front of her. "Easy does it, girl-friend," she told the dog. "Don't want to overdo it." To Alex she said, "How's she doing?"

"She's making great progress. Sam thought she'd do better here with you than in the kennel. Don't get her excited…."

"Like I could," she laughed.

"We went outside for a little while." He nodded in the direction of the dress. "I guess that means you had success."

"She looks absolutely beautiful."

For a moment neither of them spoke, and very slowly Jennifer became aware that something hung in the air between them. Something perhaps ominous.

"I have some good news and some bad news," Alex finally said.

Twelve

"What could the FBI possibly want with me?" she asked, a sense of panic dropping into her gut.

"They won't say. You're not in any trouble, I know that. It was when I tried to look into Nick Noble's background that the red flag went up and an agent contacted me wanting to know what I was looking for. They do that—flag the computer file to see if any other police agencies are interested in their suspect. It might give them more evidence to bring him in. Noble wouldn't know that—unless he has an informant in the bureau." He shrugged. "I told the agent I'd seen the missing-person flyers in my neighborhood and wanted to check it out."

"But that was a while ago…" she said.

"Yeah, it was. But I had to go back to the fed to find out about Barbara. Paula made the actual call. She told the agent we had a confidential informant who claimed Mrs. Noble had been murdered by Mr. Noble at the

MGM Grand. The fed said he could guarantee that didn't happen. They've been watching Noble for a long time—they know his wife."

"Then what did I hear? What did I see? She was dead, Alex. I just know it."

"How long were you gone from the room?"

"A couple of hours. Maybe a little more. But—"

"Come here," he said, patting the sofa beside him. She went to him and he held her hands as he said, "A lot could have happened in that time," he told her. "Barbara could have been drunk. Passed out."

"But I saw blood."

He shrugged. "A little? A lot? Splatters? The kind of splatters that could come from a bloody nose caused by a slap?"

She turned that over in her mind. "Nick had an ice pack on his face. Maybe it was his blood. But she was lying facedown and it looked to me like the back of her head was all wet and kind of matted."

"If she hit him in the face hard enough to hurt him and draw blood, it is possible one of his assistants could have hit her in the head with something like a bottle or a vase…? Something that contained water? Is it possible that in two hours of fighting with her husband she started drinking heavily and passed out? And maybe someone tried to revive her by throwing water on her? Or how about this—the wetting of the hair was something that happened in the argument—he threw a drink at her. Two hours later she was asleep, thanks to some booze, some Xanax?"

She pulled her legs under her and sat on them. "I

guess anything's possible. So, why would he be looking for me?"

"Jennifer, he's into you. You're his squeeze."

"He called me a bimbo. He wanted 'something done' about me."

Alex tried to keep his smile to himself. He pinched her cute chin between his thumb and forefinger. The way she looked now, she just didn't qualify. "He likes bimbos. Maybe he just wanted to make sure you got an explanation before you said anything that would get him in trouble. Maybe he wanted to be sure of your silence."

"It didn't sound like that, Alex."

"In the moment, it didn't. But the feds are watching him, and in watching him they're very sure who Barbara is. If they say she's alive, she is."

In the way a person's life can flash before their eyes, Jennifer quickly reconsidered everything. Was it possible Nick had been singing in the shower because he had a tune on his mind rather than because he was wicked and unremorseful? And had he sent his guys looking for her after her disappearance because he wanted her back?

"You know," Alex said, "he might have been worried that something happened to you. Or maybe it occurred to him that if you'd had an accident or been the victim of a crime, he might be blamed."

"Does this mean I'm not in danger?" she asked very softly, very cautiously.

"To tell you the truth, Jennifer, I'm not sure where we're at. I think the big X factor here is what does the FBI think you can tell them?"

She curled herself up a bit smaller and leaned against Alex. Reflexively, his arms went around her. She chewed on one of her short nails, thinking, shaking her head.

"You were with him a couple of years," Alex said.

"I know this isn't easy to grasp, but we had an arrangement. Like an arranged marriage without the marriage. We never talked about it. I knew what my role was—it wasn't complicated. I worked on being pretty and being absolutely no trouble. In exchange for making him look good, he was very generous. Believe me— he had money to throw away. Nick is the kind of guy that if you asked him why he has eight yachts, he'd answer that he just sold one."

"Unbelievable. I can't even relate."

"Believe me, after the way I grew up, hand to mouth, it's very easy to get used to that lifestyle. But the thing that made it work for me was that I made sure I was emotionally unavailable. I was remote—that's probably why he wanted me so much. And I ignored the fact that he had these goons with him all the time. I never listened to his conversations. I learned how to close my ears and concentrate on filing a nail or reading a book. I had no expectations. I was as low maintenance as a statue."

"Where was your security?" he asked.

The thing that she'd been most proud of suddenly seemed shameful. But she was committed to telling him the truth. There was a lot more truth to tell him, but she'd take one thing at a time. "He was extremely generous. I was headed for an early retirement, but I'm sure it never occurred to him I was saving in order to stop being his mistress."

"So—can you think of anything about Nick that would interest the FBI? He's been arrested before, you know. Fraud, trafficking, money laundering."

"The minute I saw what I thought was Barbara's dead body it came to me that I'd been in serious denial—that clearly Nick was a thug himself. Maybe a mobster. But honestly, I can't give you any specifics. I never saw anything illegal. From time to time I'd meet business associates of his—nice people, to the last one."

"What about his investment properties? Anything there that didn't gel?"

"It was perfectly legitimate. I'm sure I was hired because I looked good and could deal with people, especially businessmen."

"Is it possible it was a setup to run money through a legitimate corporation? Did you actually see the buildings, the offices and the tenants?"

"I did," she said. "They were very real."

"There's an easy way to get to the bottom of this," he said. "We can set up a meeting with the feds and they can ask their questions."

She chewed her lip for a moment before saying, "Do I have to talk to them?"

"No. But it's always better to be cooperative."

"Can we stop the clock for just a little while?"

"It wouldn't be good to wait very long. They could find you before you have a chance to go to them."

"Could you get into trouble for not telling them where I am?"

"Yes. But not the worst trouble imaginable. Don't worry about me."

"Could we wait till the prom is over? Till the lambs come?"

He pulled her closer. "I don't know if we have that kind of time."

Jennifer sat down at the computer after Alex left. Although it took hours, Jennifer wrote Louise the entire story of how she came to be a bald-headed waitress in Boulder City. She stayed up till the wee hours in order to get it all down. She even gave the details about her part-time job as a girlfriend to the rich old gents. And what at the time seemed the harrowing witnessing of a murder, and how she had finally braved bringing Alex into her camp and asking for his help.

...So you see, Louise, I am not what you thought I was. I didn't tell you a tenth of the truth about me. I apologize, I was afraid. But I fully intend to see this through, to talk to the FBI, to try to get my life back. Not that life, but one that makes more sense. The life I'm living right now, as Doris the dog-sitter/waitress, makes a lot of sense.

Your friends will take care of Alice very well, should anything go wrong.

Thank you, and again, I'm sorry for the deceit.
Love,
Jennifer

She forgot to turn off the computer when she went to bed. In the morning when she woke, there was a message from Louise.

My dear girl—Jennifer,
Never question my judgment! You are exactly what I thought—honest, decent, wise and fearless! You've been through quite a lot and have proved you have the stuff great women are made of. I couldn't be more proud of you. And I am profoundly proud to be your friend.
Love,
Louise

The next day as Jennifer waited tables for the breakfast crowd, visited the library, walked around the park—without Alice for the time being—there was a new spring in her step and her smile was a little quicker. She greeted people a bit more enthusiastically than she had. The message from Louise lifted her heart and made her feel fifty pounds lighter, despite the fact that she still had much to deal with.

She realized that in just around three months, she had created a kind of lifestyle that she had always craved and had never before been able to envision. She had *friends*. She felt she belonged. She wasn't working at keeping up some pretense that would keep her image intact.

There was a vast difference between having a career and living one. In her old life, the life of Jennifer, there was no difference between her vocation and her personal life.

The news that Barbara Noble was alive and well changed a few things, also. Despite the fact that the authorities wanted to talk to her, she now had no more reason to fear Nick Noble than she did the day she got onto the MGM Gulfstream with him. She didn't know what condition her condo and car were in—it was possible that in anger over her disappearance Nick had appropriated them. But she still had bank and investment accounts. She was no longer destitute.

That early retirement she had been saving for was going to come much earlier than she anticipated. She wasn't going back to that other life, and although she couldn't deny strong feelings for Alex, it had nothing to do with him.

Over the next week Alice began to get around better, nearly ready for her return to the park. Her appetite was improved and Jennifer was hopeful that she would greet Louise happily in the fall. Alex had taken on the habit of having his breakfast almost daily at the diner, not to mention frequent visits next door in the evenings, but he had not yet been invited to spend the whole night.

She did a little shopping, had her short cap of dark hair trimmed, plucked some of her new eyebrows into an attractive shape and bought a little makeup. Nothing fancy, just some liner, gloss and blush—not that she needed it. The sun on her cheeks gave her a glow, as did her relief. The patrons of the diner didn't know what caused the new effervescence, but they noticed.

Ryan rode his police vehicle, the mountain bike, up onto the sidewalk while she was sweeping and said,

"Doris, I've been thinking. Maybe we should catch a movie on your day off."

She almost dropped the broom. The shock on her face made her look stricken and she was speechless. He had barely ever spoken to her, and he had never flirted.

"Or, maybe we should get a bite to eat somewhere."

"Ryan," she finally mustered, "did you just ask me on a date?"

"Yeah," he said. "I'd pay, too."

Don't laugh, don't laugh, don't laugh, she instructed herself. "How nice of you. But Ryan, I don't have any days off."

"None?"

"Not with Alice recovering from surgery."

"Well, jeez—when are we going to go out, then?"

"We'll just have to talk about this later," she said. She hoped that "later" she might be able to tell him she was seeing someone. But until Alex knew everything about her, she wouldn't dare presume. And then there was the FBI. What an odd triangle.

"Okay. How's Alice doing?"

"Pretty good. How about a cup of coffee? Or a Coke?"

"Sure," he said, parking his bike and sauntering into the diner. Once inside, he found a couple of guys he knew. He never specified the coffee or the Coke.

Jennifer went behind the counter, fixed a cup of coffee and said to Buzz, "You'll never believe what just happened. Ryan asked me out on a date."

"Ryan must be the only guy around the diner who doesn't know you're already dating someone."

"Did you ever get the idea he wanted to *date* me?" she asked, still a little stunned. Hedda came in the back door for work, stashed her purse in the pantry, grabbed her apron off the hook and joined Jennifer behind the counter. "Ryan just asked me out on a *date*," she said to Hedda.

"Get outta town!"

"Seriously," she said, and carried the cup of coffee over to his table. He was in a conversation with the guys and seemed to have already forgotten about Jennifer.

When Jennifer was once again behind the counter, Hedda asked, "What did you say?"

"I said, 'Would you like a cup of coffee or a Coke?'" She shook her head in bemusement.

"If you're in no hurry to leave, I have a couple of quick errands," Buzz said.

"We'll be fine," she assured him. She watched in satisfaction as he served up a meal into a take-out carton. "Mrs. Van Der Haff?" she asked.

"Yeah." He grinned. "She asked me if that girl is ever coming back. I told her one of these days."

"Today?" she asked.

"Actually, I have a couple of stops. Next time."

It wasn't long before the diner was empty again. When Jennifer was stacking some dirty dishes, she asked Hedda if she could manage alone. "Sure," the girl said. "Adolfo is here if anything challenging comes up."

Jennifer went to the little bungalow near the Sunset Motel in which Sylvia and the kids lived. There was a small window of opportunity to see Sylvia alone—

while Hedda was at the diner. And before Sylvia went to work. She thought she'd just get the lay of the land and, if it seemed prudent, speak to the woman about encouraging Hedda to go to the dance and have a good time.

Joey was running back and forth around the trees with a couple of neighbor kids, churning up the hot dust of the grassless yard. The windows were open, though it was already in the high eighties. A rusty air-conditioning unit hung from a window; Jennifer suspected it didn't work. Spring had given way to summer, and by the height of the afternoon it would be nearly one hundred degrees in the Las Vegas valley, a few degrees cooler in Boulder City.

She listened at the screen door but heard nothing from inside. She rapped on the screen door and called, "Yooo-hooo."

She heard a groan. Then, "Who is it?"

"Doris. From the diner."

It was a while before Sylvia came to the door, tucking her wrinkled blouse into her jeans. Her hair was stringy and there were dark circles under her eyes. "Hedda in trouble?" was her first question.

Jennifer laughed. "Hedda? When's Hedda ever been in trouble? She's a dream come true."

"That so?"

She turned around and walked back into the living room without inviting Jennifer in. So, she opened the door and invited herself. "I hope I'm not intruding," she said with a decided lack of sincerity.

"I'm just waking up," she said. She sat on the couch

and lit a cigarette; the couch seemed to list to the starboard. "I was on my feet till after two."

It was nearly four. Jennifer looked around the room and saw that there was no other place to sit. The kitchen, though tiny, had room enough for a little table and two aluminum chairs, so she pulled one into the living room.

"That's a tough job," Jennifer said. "And in those shoes!"

"Yeah, it is." She took a draw on her cigarette and tapped it into an overflowing ashtray. "What can I do for you?" she asked with the exhalation. The tone of voice and unpleasant look on her face suggested that Sylvia felt cheated. Robbed. Shat upon.

"Oh. I heard a couple of the high school girls talk about the prom. Coming up real soon," she said.

"So?"

"I was wondering if Hedda was going."

She sucked on the cigarette again. "Why didn't you just ask her?"

"I thought it might be safer just to ask you—in case that boyfriend of hers hasn't asked, or there's some other problem."

"Problem? You mean like the fact that a kid like Hedda can't afford things like proms." She tucked her hair behind her ear and looked at her watch. It was a couple of hours before she had to go to work, but with the way she looked right now, some major reconstruction would be necessary to make her look decent.

"Well, here's the deal. I know it seems unlikely, but I happen to have a dress. Very adorable. It was a bridesmaid's dress, but it doesn't look like one. The bride didn't make us get dresses uglier than toads and—"

"She won't take it," she said, stamping out her cigarette.

"Sure she would, if she doesn't already have a dress. Did you get her one?" she asked, as if she couldn't see the raveling carpet, listing couch, disheveled house that baked in the sweltering heat of the un-air-conditioned room. This was where Hedda and Joey slept, in this room, and that was *not* a fold-out sofa bed. There were exactly three small rooms and a bath—living room, bedroom, kitchen. The kitchen was hardly bigger than a closet. It reminded her of the apartment on the *Honeymooners*.

"I don't know if you've noticed, but coming up with a prom dress would be a little tough for someone like me."

"Well, then, I guess it's lucky I have this dress. Here I am, thirty, and still thinking about the fact that I never went to a prom. Did you?"

The minute she asked the question, she regretted it. She knew the answer before Sylvia gave it. She lit another cigarette before saying, "I had Hedda when I was fifteen. No, I never went to the prom. Hedda's better off saving her money for something useful."

"Are you angry with me?" Jennifer asked.

"I don't have time for this," she said.

Jennifer leaned toward her. "What can I do to help, so that you have time to talk about Hedda?"

She sucked on the cigarette. "You can mind your own business."

"Hmm," Jennifer said, standing up. She put the chair

back at the kitchen table, and as she did so, she noticed the empty Jim Beam bottle in the trash. Well, Sylvia was over twenty-one—she was entitled to a drink after a hard night. "Okay, then. I just thought—"

"You know, coming in here like this and making me feel like trash isn't going to help anything."

"I didn't mean to—"

Sylvia stood up. "It isn't easy, you know. I do the best I can."

"I'm sure you do. Really, I didn't—"

"You think this is what I had in mind for my life?" She took another angry drag from her cigarette, stubbed it out in the full ashtray and glared at Jennifer. "This is *not* what I planned on."

She wondered if she should suggest that life had a strange way of giving you gifts you couldn't plan—like Hedda. Or maybe she could tell Sylvia that she hadn't had much more growing up and understood the frustration. But instead she just said, "I'm sorry, Sylvia." And then turned to go.

It was very likely Hedda was right, Jennifer thought. Sylvia might indeed hate her and blame her for almost everything that was wrong with her life.

Alex was called to his sergeant's office, where he found Dobbs sitting in front of Sergeant Monroe's desk at an angle. It wasn't a big office and Dobbs was a big guy who seemed to fill the entire space on his own. He wasn't wearing the black trench coat, but he was apparently committed to the thin tie. When Alex entered, Monroe stood up. Not so Dobbs.

"How you doing?" Alex said politely, extending a hand.

"Not good," Dobbs said, eschewing the handshake. "You screwed with me."

"What are you talking about?" Alex asked.

"Okay, okay," Monroe said. "Have a seat. Let's see where we are."

"I think we know where we are," Dobbs said. "I asked him to turn over this woman if he found her and he said he would. Now he's found her and he's hiding her."

"For God's sake," Alex said. "I don't think you have your facts quite right."

Dobbs leaned forward, elbows on his knees. "Do you or do you not know where Jennifer Chaise is?"

"I do. I don't know her as Jennifer Chaise, however. She hasn't told me her real name."

"And didn't you promise to bring her to me if you found her?"

"I did not."

Dobbs sat back in his chair, stunned. "All right, this is bullshit. I want this guy turned over to your Internal Affairs Bureau. He's a liar and a—"

"Boss, Aiken was there during this interview. She's right in the briefing room."

"Call her."

Alex used his Nextel radio to send a twittering noise to Paula. "Aiken? Come to the spanking room." Monroe frowned and Alex grinned. The detectives all used cubicles and the sergeant was the only one with an office and a door that closed. If you were called to the office, chances were even you were going to be reprimanded for something—thus it was referred to as the spanking room. He hoped it appeared obvious to all present that he wasn't concerned about this issue. It was only a few moments until she opened the door.

"Yes, sir," she said.

"Aiken, were you present during a discussion between Alex and Agent Dobbs?"

"Yes, sir. At the Starbucks on Charleston. I don't remember the exact day, but I could go look it—"

"We don't care about the day!" Dobbs snapped. "Did you hear this guy tell me that if he found Jennifer Chaise, he'd turn her over to me?"

"God, no," she said with a laugh, as though Dobbs couldn't possibly be more absurd.

"Aw, Jesus Christ—these two have their story cooked!"

Alex looked up at Paula from his chair, made a face and shrugged in helplessness.

Sergeant Monroe folded his hands on his desktop. "Maybe if you'd let me ask the questions, we can find out what's going on. Aiken, tell me what went on between these two at that meeting."

"Sure," she said, leaning a hand on the back of Alex's chair. "Agent Dobbs told us, on the downlow I presume, that they'd been watching a guy by the name of Noble. A Nick Noble." To Dobbs's nod, she went on. "They suspect him of multiple federal crimes and therefore would like to talk to his ex-girlfriend, who has been missing. Alex asked him if he needed help finding her and he said no. In fact, he yelled no. Dobbs asked if we knew where she was and I can't remember

Alex's exact words, but I think it was something like, 'Why didn't you just ask me this on the phone?'"

"Why didn't you just tell Agent Dobbs where the girl was?" Monroe asked Alex.

"Couple of reasons. One, she isn't wanted. There's no warrant for her arrest. Two, she's been keeping a low profile because she has this idea her ex-boyfriend could be dangerous. Could want to hurt her. From what she told me about him, that seems a pretty safe bet. Three, she says she knows absolutely nothing about any of Noble's businesses. And four—I've been dating her."

"You're *involved* with her?" Dobbs shouted.

"Yes. By the way, I gave her your number and she plans to call you, to see what it is you want. But she's house-sitting for my eighty-year-old neighbor, taking care of her dog while she's away, and the dog had emergency surgery. Plus, like I said, she can't think of a single thing—"

"I'm serious, I want these two turned over to IAB!" Dobbs said.

"Take it easy, Agent Dobbs," Paula said. "You know the law—she doesn't even have to talk to you if she doesn't want to. Alex could have told you exactly where to find her and she could have slammed the door in your face. Now, if you'd have had a warrant…"

"See what I'm talking about?" Dobbs asked Monroe. He looked back at Alex. "You want a warrant? I can have a warrant in five minutes."

Alex leaned forward, pulled a slip of paper off the sergeant's scratch pad and wrote on it. "Don't bother," he said. "Here's the address and phone number. Go talk to her. I'm sure she'll do her best to help you. She's a very nice person—try not to scare her."

He didn't take the slip of paper. "We already know where she is. Someone's picking her up now."

"Then what's this about?" Alex asked.

"This is about knowing which asses to kiss, Nichols." Dobbs stood. "You're getting yourself mixed up with some wrong people. This chick? She's a whore."

Alex flinched and looked as if he might spring to his feet, but Paula put her hand on his shoulder. While she couldn't possibly hold him down with one small hand, it served as a reminder to keep his cool.

"This Noble is not her first, but he might be the youngest. It's how she makes her living, boinking old rich guys and collecting the fees. She's not who you think she is. She lives in a condo on the beach, drives a Jag and has a big-ass bank account."

"She lives next door to me, which is how I met her. And she has no arrest record."

"Of course not. Because she's canny. She doesn't charge. She accepts donations. That's still a whore in my book."

He opened the door to leave and said to Monroe, "Thanks for nothing." He did not close the door softly.

"What a fucker," Monroe said. "Jeez." He looked at Alex, Paula, then back to Alex. "You two. That was stupid."

"Not totally stupid, boss," Paula said. "We didn't exactly have a plan—but missing isn't against the law. She's an adult. She hasn't done anything wrong. Both Alex and I had doubts about Dobbs's character. It wasn't just Alex—I didn't want to turn her over to Dobbs, either. We both had the idea Dobbs might want to use her for bait to reel this Noble guy in—and if he's dangerous, that's not such a great thing."

"I did tell her, you know. I told her the FBI wanted to talk to her and she's nervous about it, but she's not uncooperative. And that other stuff Dobbs said about her. That's probably bullshit. He's a real asshole."

Jennifer was just getting ready for the lunch crowd when the yellow Monte Carlo pulled up to the front of the diner. Two men got out, came inside, flashed their credentials and said, "Jennifer Chaise? FBI. Will you please come with us for a conversation."

She looked over her shoulder to a gape-mouthed Buzz and began to remove her apron. "Buzz, please ask Rose or Hedda or anyone to check on Alice and make sure she has water and gets let out."

"What did they call you? What?"

"I'll explain later, Buzz. Please?" She pulled her house key from her pocket. "Rose has a key, but if she's not around today and you have to see about Alice…"

"You want me to get you a lawyer or anything?"

"No," she said. "I haven't done anything wrong. Apparently I know some people who have."

Then she went with the men to their office in Las Vegas, where she sat for seven long hours. Some big bulldog named Dobbs yelled and hollered and threatened, but he was quickly replaced by a civil young man named Jeff, to whom she bared her soul. She told him everything he wanted to know, but she didn't see how any of her information would in any way incriminate Nick.

"Is Barbara really alive?"

"Oh, yes. Very much. Spending his money like mad."

"Well, good. I guess. Listen, I'm very tired," she finally said. "I have a sick old dog at home."

"That would be Alice?"

She looked surprised. "You don't have the place bugged, do you?"

"No. We would have to think you guilty of some crime, get a judge to sign a warrant, et cetera. And frankly, we don't know what it would get us."

"It won't get you Nick Noble. I hope never to see him again." She sighed. "Really, are you just about done?"

"Sure," he said, turning off his tape recorder and folding his notebook closed. "If we think of anything else, can we give you a call?"

"Why not? I don't seem to have any secrets anymore. Oh, by the way—you wouldn't happen to know anything about my condo? My car? My belongings?"

"We haven't seen any moving take place over there, but if it's in his name, he could have sold it all by now."

"And my things?"

"That's something you'll have to check out for yourself."

"By now I bet he's pretty pissed off."

The man shrugged. "He seems to be a man with a temper."

"At least he didn't kill his wife," she said. "At least he's not a murderer."

"We're not looking at him for that, no."

It was nine o'clock before she got home, and she was exhausted to the bone. The famous Las Vegas wind was whipping through the trees ferociously, bending them over. As the car pulled up to the front of her house, she saw Alex sitting on the front step. The agent who drove the car asked, "Would you like me to see you in?"

"No, thanks. That's my next-door neighbor, waiting up for me."

"You sure you're okay?"

"Oh, absolutely."

It had been a long afternoon for Alex. Jennifer had never called him to tell him about the FBI, though she could have. She wasn't a suspect, there would have been no reason to deny her the use of a phone.

Maybe it was the tension of waiting that had worked on Alex. He was exhausted and feeling angry, but he hadn't thought he was angry with her. Yet the moment she came into view, something rose up in him. Something he hadn't felt in years. It might have been fierce jealousy, it might've been that he felt stupid for trusting her so much. Or it might have just been that even though he thought what Dobbs said about her was probably bullshit, it still ate at him.

She came toward him with her arms out. "Oh, Alex," she said, leaning into him. "What a day!"

"Come on," he said, pulling her toward the house. He opened her door and let her precede him inside. The sound of the wind whistling through the eaves and rattling the windows reminded him how old their houses were. It brought to mind a condo on the beach. A Jag.

She went first to Alice, as she always did, stooping and kissing the top of her head. "Hey, girlfriend," she said. But she was so kind, he found himself thinking. She had such a sweet and sensitive nature. These things didn't add up.

He stood just inside the closed door. "How was it?" he asked.

She whirled around and flopped on the couch, putting her feet up on the coffee table. "It was very long. For the most part it was just tedious, but there was this one big guy who was horrible. Rude, insulting, horrific. They must have been watching through that mirror thing because all I had to do was say I wouldn't talk to them if he was going to treat me so badly and he was taken out and a very nice gentleman replaced him. Someone named Jeff."

"You answered all their questions?"

"Every last one. I'm not sure what it is they think Nick has done, but I don't think I was of any use at all. Did you tell them where to find me?"

"No," he said. "In fact, I got my ass chewed for not giving you up."

"Oh, God, I was afraid of that. Was it just an ass-chewing? It wasn't worse than that, was it?"

"It was just a slap on the wrist." He took a breath. "You didn't tell me what you did for a living. Dated rich old dudes."

She stiffened. "I might've described it differently, but I guess that's not incorrect."

"Why don't you describe it for me," he said. He heard the sarcasm in his voice and wanted to pull his words back in, soften them, scrub them up a little, but it was too late. He was pissed. He didn't know at who or really why. Maybe because Dobbs knew something about her that he didn't know—and he had held her and kissed her and begged to make love to her. Dobbs hadn't.

She sat forward on the sofa, putting her feet on the ground. "Okay, here's how it was. When I was just a kid and my mom and grandparents had recently died, a very kind gentleman named Robert, who was as old as my grandfather, dated me. I had nothing. I had less than nothing. I had a job as a hostess in a restaurant, rented one room, had a mouth full of bad teeth, and if I was slender it was probably because most of the time I didn't get enough to eat. I quit high school, couldn't get a good job, and this nice, generous man wanted to help me out. I guess you could call him my sugar daddy."

"The first of many." He couldn't believe how little control he had over his tone, his choice of words. It humiliated him to be so mean, yet it seemed beyond his control. "Were you going to tell me?"

"Absolutely," she said, straightening her spine. "Look, I can understand you being a little put out, but I didn't do anything wrong. After Robert moved on in a very mutual and cordial parting of the ways, the next man I dated was very much like him—he was in his sixties, very wealthy, and though married, his wife lived in France and they hadn't seen each other in years. He was also very generous. But I want to make it clear, I never asked for anything. I always worked. Kept a full-time job. I got my GED and even took a couple of classes at the community college."

"How many, altogether?"

She stood up. "Alex, what is this? I had four relationships that were sort of long term—two or three years. In between I dated quite a few men—they did not become serious. Have you seen any women in those years since your divorce?"

"Yes," he said resolutely. "I have even given them a trinket or two. Not, however, a Jag."

"Well, I admit, I was very fortunate."

"Fortunate? Shit! Yachts, private jets, limos?"

She was aghast at his anger, but thought—good. Let's get it out. Let's put this behind us once and for all. This is the moment of truth. "Yes. All that. And diamond rings, trips all over the world, plastic surgery. One man even gave me a racehorse."

He nodded at her chest. "Which one gave you the tits?"

She lifted her chin proudly. It's not as though she'd had to be talked into them. She'd been as flat as an ironing board, and loved the idea of finally having breasts. She appreciated it as much as her new smile. "That would have been Martin."

The wind seemed to escalate outside and there was a clap of thunder. A summer storm was approaching.

"Did they love being played by you?"

"I don't think you get it, Alex," she said, stepping toward him. "I wasn't playing. I was absolutely sincere. Although I was never in love with any of them, I was as devoted as I could be. I never cheated, I never threw over one man for another, I never lied."

"But you told them you loved them," he accused.

"No. That was completely unnecessary," she scoffed. "Why are you so angry with me? Were you under the impression I was a virgin? I told you about the arrangement I had with Nick and you weren't nearly this judgmental."

"I thought he was the only one."

"There haven't been dozens, for God's sake."

"Did it ever occur to you that there wasn't much difference between what you did and what a high-priced whore does?"

She took another step toward him. She wanted to scream and slap his face, but she kept control. "There is no comparison. There is, however, a very close comparison to what happens in an arranged marriage."

"You slept with rich old men for gifts! Big gifts, like trips to Europe and diamonds and furs."

"I slept with them far less often than you might think. Mostly I accompanied them. You would be amazed at how important that is to some men."

"Then why the hell are you flirting with me? I don't measure up to this standard! I will probably never do better than a secondhand *bike!*"

She tried being gentle and cajoling, sensing there was some jealous pain associated with this. Outside, the lightning flashes came more often, as did the loud rumble of thunder. If she hadn't been in the grip of a good fight, she might've run to the window to watch the rain come.

"Look, coming out of the kind of childhood I had, it

was easy for me to be seduced by these material things. And I had no complaints about my life—it's not hard to get used to luxury. I didn't realize until this event with Nick sent me fleeing into Boulder City how friendless I was. It's really caused me to rethink my priorities. I wish you could know how much that bike meant. That bike meant more than a diamond ring. I had been with men who wouldn't break a sweat buying a plane—yet not one of them ever made a sacrifice for me."

"They just made you rich."

"I've saved a couple of bucks. But Alex…"

"Are you saying you're going to reform? Play it straight now?"

"Play it straight? Alex, I didn't do anything wrong. I never lied to anyone, I never took anything that wasn't freely given. I never cheated on anyone. I have nothing to reform. All I have to do is live my life true to myself. I like this life—this real life. I'm much happier here, living like this, than I was before."

"That's what you say now. A year from now, when you're tired of clipping coupons or pinching pennies, when it gets tough making the car payment or whatever, you know what to do, don't you? You just find yourself a rich old guy with bulging pockets and—"

"All right! That's it!" she yelled. "This conversation is over!"

"I think we're just beginning!"

"No! You're leaving. I could call the cops! And now that my cover is blown, believe me, I won't hesitate!"

"You could call the *who?*" he asked, bending at the waist and pushing his face in hers.

She stared at him for a moment, then turned to the phone on the kitchen counter. "Don't bother!" he said. "I'm outta here."

The moment he left, Jennifer felt like the wind had been knocked out of her. She looked askance at Alice, who was lying flat on her belly, snout on the floor, and she almost appeared to be covering her ears with her paws. "Whoa," she said to the dog.

It had been a long day and she was overwrought herself. But she had this insane idea she would come home to Alex, fall into his arms and be comforted by him. What had happened instead was too crazy for words. But the bottom line seemed to be that he couldn't cope with the kind of life she'd lived before. This was something she thought she had prepared herself for—but apparently she'd been in denial, because his anger hit her like a brick in the gut.

Perhaps there was something indecent about it, because she hadn't loved those men. They hadn't loved her, either, but that wasn't the point. She wasn't pure because she hadn't been driven by pure intentions. She had been looking for a way to keep from getting hurt and to keep her head above water.

However, her intentions were pure now. She wanted to help Hedda if she could, she wanted to work with Buzz on feeding some of the town, she wanted to be best friends with Louise and Rose, and she wanted to love Alex.

She had wanted to. Maybe not anymore.

She began to cry. It was amazing how she had held

tears at bay for so many years and now it seemed every time she turned around, she was whimpering.

This was considerably more than a whimper. She was gasping. "God, Alice," she wailed. "I thought if I could just tell the truth… I pretty much fell for him even though he's the biggest pain in the ass…. I wouldn't have told him that way, but… And I don't know if it matters that I only told him all that because I *wanted* to…. When you love someone you have to…"

She heard the rain begin to pelt the windows even as the wind howled. She got up, blew her nose on a tissue and looked out the front window. There, pacing back and forth like a lunatic in the pouring rain, his head down, his strides long and angry, was Alex.

He had absolutely no idea why he'd said those horrible things. He didn't know if Dobbs had goaded him into it or if somewhere, deep down, he didn't want to get involved with a woman who could do that—be with someone she didn't love just because she'd get nice things.

Oh, hell—women fall for men in uniform all the time. Cops and firefighters walk into bars and can just about have their pick. Shamefully, Alex admitted to himself that he'd taken advantage of that a time or two. Where was the difference?

The rain came, and he thought, figures. Now that you've said all the things that cannot be unsaid, you have completely ruined any chance of ever going forward with her. Now it's raining on your stupid head. Lightning should strike you and put you out of your misery.

Oh, said his alter ego, Now you want to go forward. Nice going, dumb ass.

I always wanted to go forward, it just set me back on my heels to hear that she'd been a—I knew she'd had another life—but I didn't know it was that kind of life.

She hadn't been a whore. Those were Dobbs's words. You heard her—she'd had relationships with these guys, and it made sense to her at the time. She must have been scared and desperate at first. What else did she have going for her?

Well, you're too stupid to live. Now, just when you could have had her, you've lost her forever. No way she can forgive the way you talked to her.

As if to prove himself wrong, he ran up the two steps to the door. He banged on the door just as thunder roared. She opened the door, tissue to her nose, eyes moist with the tears that he had caused. He had to yell to be heard above the wind and flapping of tree branches.

"I'm an idiot! I love you!"

She stared at him for a moment. He felt the rain drip off his thatch of thick brown hair. She pushed open the screen and said, "Okay, then. Come to me."

Thirteen

She pulled him inside and put her arms around him, pulled him soaking wet against her. She lay her cheek against his shoulder and let herself cry. His arms went around her. "I have no idea what happened to me," he said. "Multiple-personality disorder, probably."

She looked up at him. "Did you get everything off your chest?"

"Jennifer, I said things I didn't even know were in me. Honest to God, I don't know what made me so mean. I'm so sorry. I don't think I even meant some of those things."

"You were pretty convincing. Pretty angry."

"Yes. But at what, I'm not sure. So stupid. Besides being an idiot, I must have been scared."

"Of?"

He wiped a tear off her cheek with a knuckle. "Of losing you. I know your life isn't here. Whether it involves men or not, I know your life is somewhere else. Where you have a home, a job, roots."

She shook her head. "In three months I've had more here than I had in Florida in eleven years. Without even meaning to I put down some serious roots." She laughed through her tears. "For someone who was trying to be invisible…"

"I should have waited for you to tell me," he said.

She began unbuttoning his wet shirt. Between kisses she said, "When things started to get heavy the other night, I couldn't let you go any further until you knew everything about me. I was going to tell you right away—but so many things happened in the meantime. Hedda, Alice…"

She slipped her hands inside his shirt and spread them across his chest. The shirt fell from his shoulders and he pulled her against him, kissing her deeply.

"You should have no regrets," she said.

"Neither should you." He slipped a hand under her shirt and found a breast, then undid her bra and found it better. Her breath caught. "I can't give you all those things," he reminded her.

"I want you for yourself," she said, raising her arms so that he might pull off her shirt and bra. She pressed herself against him. "Things don't mean as much as you think."

"If we ever go anywhere, we'll be flying coach." He bent to kiss a shoulder and worked his way back up her neck to her lips.

"The only place I want to go now is to bed," she whispered against his mouth. "And the sooner the better."

He lifted her in his arms and carried her the very

short distance to the bedroom, blessing the smallness of these houses as he did. He fell with her onto the bed. They kicked off their shoes without breaking their embrace. Tongues played and probed, hands went to belts and waistbands, lightning lit the room in brief flashes, illuminating them as they shed their clothes.

Her hand closed around him and she sighed. "Oh, Alex," she said approvingly. His response was a deep moan. He ran a line of kisses from her neck, over her chest, lightly sucking an erect nipple, down over her flat belly, pausing only briefly before moving over the soft mound to lick, not gently, her moist insides. She rose against his mouth. "Oh, Alex!" she cried softly.

Her hand tightening around him, he was a doomed man. And she was drowning him, so there appeared no reason to wait. Rising again, she must have had the very same thoughts, for she gently guided him into her. He pressed in slowly, as slowly as he was able, and her legs instantly wrapped around him to keep him there. They rocked, and rocking quickly became a bucking. He pulled upward, grabbing her buttocks in both hands so the friction would bring her quick results, locking his mouth over hers. As her tongue entered his mouth, he sucked it gently. In a spasm, he felt her insides grab him, vibrate around him, torture him at length. She held her breath, held his shoulders, and he pumped. And let himself go.

They fell onto the sheets in relief but couldn't let go of each other. "Oh, my," she said breathlessly.

He touched her back, her arm, her lower spine, her breast. He took a moment to catch his breath, then said, "Now that that's behind us, we can take our time."

"Oh, my," she said again.

"Then you approve?" he asked.

She answered with her lips. Even though they were spent, they lay kissing and touching, entwined, toes caressing toes, knees knocking knees, until within her Alex began to grow anew. This time, though passion stirred as hot, the urgency would not hinder them. This time would be for the sheer pleasure of waiting and enjoying. He turned her on her belly, pulled her on his lap, rolled over and let her be on top. Still, in the pulsing end she proved her vocabulary was limited. "Oh, my," she said.

He braced an elbow on the bed and looked down at her. "Jennifer, I'm in love with you. I'm sorry for the way I behaved earlier."

"Let it go, Alex. I have."

"There's still a lot we have to learn about each other, about where we came from and who we are, but I give you my word, I will never raise my voice to you in anger again. Never."

She put a palm against his cheek. "I love you, too, Alex. And what you have offered me is more than I could ever have imagined."

He grinned devilishly. "It appeared you were nicely satisfied."

"Very nicely," she said, smiling back.

"Did I forget anything?" he asked, giving her butt a squeeze.

"Well, we might have considered a condom."

He was frozen. Speechless. Hopeful idiot that he was, he'd even had one in his pants pocket—not that one would have gotten them through the night.

"Rats," he finally said.

* * *

Deep in the night, Alice began to howl. It was a deep and mournful sound. Jennifer bolted out of bed, not even entirely sure it was Alice—she'd never heard a sound like that before. She grabbed the chenille robe and raced to her, leaving Alex to fumble for his pants in the darkness.

She found Alice sitting up in the arch of the French doors that led to the porch, her snout raised as she howled. The sky was dark, but the rain had stopped. When Jennifer reached her, she gave a final howl, a couple of barks; then lay down on the floor with her snout between her paws.

Jennifer dropped beside her. "What *is* it?" she asked the dog.

Alice merely gave a whimper.

The lights were still off. "Prowler, maybe?" Alex suggested.

"Oh, Alex, what if Hedda came and we didn't hear her?"

"I'll check around," he said.

"Be careful!" she ordered him. Then she turned her attention back to Alice, petting her.

She made Alice get up and walk around a little to be sure she wasn't in some kind of terrible pain, and the dog seemed to be able to move around all right. But she wanted to lie in the doorway to the porch. Every so often she would emit a whimper. A little cry.

Jennifer curled herself around her and lay with her on the floor.

Alex came back to report there was no one around

the house and the doors were all locked. "If anyone had knocked or rung the bell, I'd have heard," he said. "I'm a light sleeper."

"She's still very upset, but she doesn't seem to be in pain. She can move around all right."

He looked down at the two of them on the floor, then sighed in resignation. He went to the bedroom, retrieved pillows and blankets, and cozied up with them on the floor. And that was how they spent the night.

"Doris, I can't seem to find anything wrong with Alice," Sam said.

"She whined all night," Jennifer explained to the vet. "This morning she wouldn't eat and all she does is lie with her nose pointed at the porch. Louise's office. Sam, that's a new spot for her. She usually likes it by the hearth where the uncarpeted floor is nice and cool."

"Maybe she's just missing Louise. I'll do a blood draw to check a few things, and give her a vitamin supplement. But this might just be old age taking its toll."

"I can't let anything happen to her!"

"Doris, there are some things we just can't control. Louise and I have talked about this. She and Alice are both ready, when the time comes."

"Well *I'm* not!"

"See if you can get her to take a walk around the park. I'll call you with the test results later."

"Okay. Come on, girlfriend."

But Alice wasn't interested in the park. She'd take a few steps and lie down. Jennifer didn't want to tug on her too hard, but it took quite a bit of coaxing to get her

to take even a few more steps. In resignation she decided she'd better speak to Buzz and take the rest of the
morning off. Tugging and coaxing and pleading, she got
Alice pointed in the direction of the diner, and then
suddenly the dog perked up and took off, pulling at the
lead.

When they got to the diner, Alice became animated.
She was usually content to lie outside in the shade, but
today she whimpered at the door and wanted to go in.
Jennifer looked around, saw that there were only a couple of people, friends of Alice's, so she let her come inside. But that wasn't enough—Alice pulled the lead
right out of Jennifer's hand and began sniffing all over
the diner, from the front door to the back. She went from
booth to booth, table to table, then tried to get behind
the counter. Jennifer had never seen her so excited.

"Buzz," Jennifer said, "I'm going to have to take the
morning off. Something's wrong with Alice."

Buzz leaned over the counter. Alice was panting, her
tongue hanging out and her eyes bright and sparkling.
"She looks pretty good to me."

"She's acting very strange. She was up last night
howling, barking, whining. This morning I could hardly
get her to cross the park to Doc Gunterson's—and then
I couldn't drag her back, but the minute the diner came
into view, she bolted over here. Look at her—she's all
wound up. Think she's looking for Louise?"

Buzz went to the dog biscuit jar and pulled out a nice
big one for Alice. He offered it to her and she flopped
down on her belly, snout flat to the floor.

"That would be a 'no thank you.'"

"No kidding. Okay, I can cover you. Let me know how she is."

"Sure."

"And about that other thing. The guys who came for you yesterday? If you don't want me to ask…"

"I'll tell you all about it once it gets straightened out. Okay? Right now I have to concentrate on my girl here."

"Just so you know—if you need anything."

That was the thing about Buzz, about most of them— offering help even though he couldn't be sure that Jennifer was a law-abiding person. And it was from the heart. Buzz trusted his instincts, and his instincts told him she was okay, and he went with that. She wondered how often he got burned.

"Thanks," she said. "Come on, old girl. Let's go home."

Going home took a while; Alice's heart just wasn't in it. By the time they made it home and she took up her place on the floor facing the porch, half the morning was gone. Jennifer called Rose to tell her what was going on, just to keep her in the loop. Five minutes later, Rose was at the door. She had something draped over her arm.

"You have tennis shoes, right?"

"Yes. Why?"

"You can't do anything right now. Alice is just going to lie there. Come to aerobics with me." She held out an exercise ensemble.

"Oh. I don't think so," she said, backing away. "I took the morning off to be with Alice."

"What are you going to do? Sit here and stare at her? Come with me."

"I don't know," she said. But she wanted to. She missed her workouts, her gym.

"Don't be shy, Doris. You can keep up with a few little old ladies, can't you?"

"I'm not sure I can," she said. But her hands were reaching for the clothes. And a slow smile was beginning to appear on Rose's face. "How long is the class?"

"Just an hour. It looks like all Alice is going to do is lie there and wait."

"I just feel so sorry for her."

Rose went to Alice, crouched and gave her a pat. "I know. But remember, she's a bit melodramatic. She always puts on a show when Louise leaves."

"This is a little worse," she said. "But you're right, I can't do anything. And I don't think she's in danger." Jennifer held up the shorts and tank top. And smiled. "Sure, I'll go with you."

Jennifer had to laugh at the way they drove in Rose's convertible, top down, to the little dance studio a few blocks away. Everything in this town was just a few blocks away! "You'll thank me for the ride home when the class is over," she said.

One thing that Jennifer hadn't counted on—Rose was a liar. There were not a few little old ladies in this class, even if it sometimes seemed to be a town full of them. Rose was far and away the oldest one there, and one of the most fit. A couple of the trim young mothers who jogged in the park and then went to the diner for sticky sweet bear claws and coffee were there, stretching out, and when they saw Jennifer they called to her and waved.

The instructor, a woman in her thirties and hard as a rock, was clapping her hands. "Come on, girls! Stretch out and get your steps! I see we have a newcomer. Stay up here close to me so I can help you with the steps if you need me. Let's go, let's go, let's go!"

"Oh-oh," Jennifer said. "I have a feeling this is going to hurt."

"It'll hurt good," Rose said, grinning.

And before she knew it, the music was on and they were away. They started off slow, but the pace picked up instantly. There wasn't a single step she didn't know, even if the routine was slightly different. Jennifer had been doing aerobics for years and she caught on quickly. Plus, it was true what she said—she was a good follower. Too good, it had become clear. It was time to stop following and begin making her own life.

It felt good to move her body, to jump around, to skip and hop and sweat. She clapped her hands with the group and even let out the occasional whoop. She looked around the room when she could manage—there were about twenty women ranging in age from twenty-five to Rose's seventy. There were only a couple of women around sixty or more, and they moved a lot more slowly and cautiously than Rose.

Rose was obviously still a dancer. She was agile, strong and very coordinated. She had great rhythm and style, and abounded with energy. Luckily for her she didn't suffer any of the debilitating conditions some women her age had to endure. Rose was flying through the class, barely breaking a sweat.

Time flew by and before she knew it, they were done. The young women she knew from the diner rushed over to her. "Doris, you're great!"

"This is nothing new for you—you didn't have any trouble keeping up!"

"Does this mean you're going to come regularly?"

"I don't know if I can. But this was fun, thanks."

"All right, ladies, enough chatter. Get a mat and let's stretch out!"

The tempo of the music calmed as they went through the motions of stretching and doing some floor exercises. It was during this phase that Jennifer's mind wandered to last night and her most amazing lovemaking with Alex. He was completely there for her, putting her needs and desires ahead of his own. His touch was thrilling, his technique creative and satisfying, his character loving. She had never felt like this before.

And he was there with her when she woke up in the morning. He was there for *her.*

This was an entirely new experience. Even as a child, she had been conscious that the needs of someone else superceded her own. Although her mother loved her very much, she couldn't really take care of her. Jennifer had to look out for Cherie.

"Now, doesn't that feel better?" Rose asked her as they were leaving the class.

"Much," she replied quietly. It was just beginning to occur to her that she could bring elements of her old life to her new. She didn't have to choose between being an overpaid mistress or an underpaid waitress. She didn't have to choose between being a caretaker or being taken care of. There was a vast and interesting area in between. "But I have a lot of things to straighten out," she said.

"What?"

"Oh. Sorry, Rose. My mind was wandering. Listen, thanks so much. I'll wash these things and get them back to you right away. After a quick shower, I'm going to write to Louise and tell her Alice is a little—I don't know—under the weather."

"Oh, phoo. Neurotic, that's what she is," Rose said.

Jennifer found that her roommate was the same—morose and without appetite. She sat on the floor beside her and tried to hand-feed her a morsel, but Alice wasn't interested. She wrote a long e-mail to Louise and mentioned Alice but didn't want to alarm her. Jennifer promised that she was watching her closely.

It was the end of May; Jennifer had been in Boulder City for three months and her life was completely changed. She was dead in love with Alex and had no idea what to do next. She had never dared believe life had happy endings for girls like her—poor girls from disjointed and dysfunctional families. But before she could address that, she had to find a way to straighten out that mess in Florida.

Doc Gunterson called to say Alice's blood work was fine, and aside from being a little overweight, she appeared to be in the best of health.

It was five o'clock when there was a knock at the door. With a lift in her chest, hoping it would be Alex home from work, she rushed to open it. But it was a man in a suit. With a briefcase. "Doris Bailey?"

She felt a jab of fear. "Yes?"

"My name is Wendell Phillips. I'm an associate with the Johnson McGee law firm. I'm afraid I have some bad news. Mrs. Louise Barstow passed away yesterday in her London flat. She was found by her charwoman."

Jennifer's hand went to her mouth and tears welled up in her eyes. "Oh, she can't be gone," she said.

"The word I was given was that it was a peaceful departure. She was sitting in her favorite chair with a morning cup of tea and a newspaper. I'm very sorry for your loss. I've been asked to notify Mrs. Gillespie and Mr. Nichols, as well."

"It's Miss Gillespie. Rose has never married," she said with a sniff. "Alex Nichols is not at home. He's a Las Vegas police detective. Should I call him at work?"

"That would probably be best. And Miss Gillespie?"

"Let me go with you," she said. "Oh, God, poor Rose. Louise was her very best friend."

Rose took the news stoically. She was relieved that Louise had slipped away painlessly, as though just going to sleep. "But I hate that she was so far away. I wish she'd been next door."

"She left instructions to be cremated," Mr. Phillips informed them. "What shall I tell them is to be done with the remains?"

"Oh, get a gaudy urn of some kind and ship her home," Rose said with a flourish of one hand, turning away. Jennifer heard a sniff. "We'll take care of her. We know what to do."

"Let me get something for you, Rose. A cup of coffee or glass of wine?"

"Thanks, but if you wouldn't be hurt..." She turned back and there was a little glistening in her eyes, and for the very first time since Jennifer had known Rose, she looked drawn. As though she'd aged suddenly. Her face, usually taut and smooth, seemed lined. Her eyes were very sad. "If you wouldn't be terribly hurt, I'd like to be alone for just a bit."

"Sure," Jennifer said. "Of course. I'll go home and call Alex."

"Do. He'll have a hard time with this. He adored Louise. Comfort him, and I'll be along after a while."

She wants to have a good cry, Jennifer thought. And she wants to do it alone.

"We have a little paperwork," Mr. Phillips said. "But I believe everyone involved in Mrs. Barstow's estate is clear on what she intended."

"Yes," Rose said. "There's plenty of time for all that. I'll be glad to call you."

As they walked back to Louise's house, Jennifer said, "Mr. Phillips, I'm simply house-sitting for Louise. I'm taking care of her dog. Is there something I should be doing? Should I turn Alice over to someone else and move out?"

"I'm sure there's no hurry on that, Ms. Bailey. For the next couple of weeks, at any rate. Sit tight and I'll be in touch."

"Poor Alice. Mr. Phillips, she's very, very old. She can't change roommates too many times. She's having a rough time right—" She suddenly stopped both talking and walking. Wendell Phillips paused and turned to look at her. "What time did you say Louise died?"

"Sometime yesterday morning. Her charwoman went to the flat around 9:00 a.m. and, according to the surgeon, she hadn't been gone long."

"And the time difference is—?"

"It's seven hours later in London."

"I see," she said, continuing on to the house. When she got to the door she turned and extended her hand. "I'll call Alex now."

He pulled a business card out of his shirt pocket and handed it to her as she was going inside. "We'll be in touch."

Alice was still lying on the floor, looking into Louis's office. Jennifer went to her, kneeled down and, with gentle hands, lifted her head. "She's gone, Alice," she said. "It was gentle and now she has no pain when she walks. And she'll be waiting for you. It's going to be okay now." She kissed Alice's head and stroked her for a moment.

Alice looked up at her and then slowly got to her feet. She walked over to her food dish, looking back at Jennifer once, and then began to eat.

After calling Alex, Jennifer hooked Alice up and walked her to the diner. It was the most efficient way she could think of to get the word out that Louise was gone. This time Alice behaved as usual—slipping under the bench at the front of the building and waiting patiently for her water and biscuit. It seemed she was done looking for Louise.

Jennifer got there just as the changing of the guard between Hedda and Gloria was taking place, and everyone present accepted the news with sadness and loss. She gave Hedda a hug and told her to go home, get all her homework done and get some beauty sleep. Just a few days till the prom, and not a time for a sixteen-year-old to be sad.

"Should I come over tonight?" Hedda asked in a whisper.

"I want to be sure Rose is all right, and she might not feel like visiting. But of course if you need a place..."

"Thanks," she said.

"Are you all right?"

"Sure," she said somberly.

Jennifer hopped up on a stool at the counter. "I just don't want to go home yet. I can't stand to think there won't be an e-mail from Louise." And there was another small matter—her house-sitting job was likely to come to an end very soon. Where was she to go? She wasn't ready to even think about returning to Florida.

Gloria delivered a couple of plates of the house special—meat loaf with a decidedly Spanish flair—then sat down beside Jennifer. "Buzz, I think our girl here could use a little bump."

"What say, Doris?" he asked, already pulling the flask out of his pocket.

"Thanks, but not in the coffee, okay?"

Buzz grabbed a coffee cup from the rack under the counter. He poured the amber liquid neat into the cup and then fixed her an ice water chaser.

She took a tiny, tentative sip. It made a nice warm

path down her throat, a calming river of, to her surprise, delicious brandy. "Buzz, that's wonderful," she said appreciatively.

"You thought it was some old rotgut, didn't you?" he grinned. "You oughta know I take better care of my people than that."

She took another sip. "That's a very expensive brandy, Buzz."

His eyebrows under his floppy hair lifted and he didn't say anything for a minute. Then he said, "Why am I not surprised that a little bald girl in army dungarees would know something like that?"

"Oh," she said, surprised. "I tended bar once or twice. You know."

"Hmm," Gloria said. "I'll have a shot of coffee, Buzz." She took an appreciative sip of her own and said, "I'm going to miss that old girl, but I'm sure not going to miss watching her struggle for every step. At least I'll sleep easy knowing her joints don't pain her anymore."

"Amen," Buzz said.

"I wish old Harmon could slip off like that. Poor old guy—I know he's miserable half the time. I can see it in his eyes. I even thought about saving up drugs—but the problem is I don't have any really good ones. The kind that'll kill you."

"Gloria!"

"It's no kind of life, is all," she said. "But that old Louise, for all her struggling down the sidewalk every morning, I think she had a good time. Don't you, Buzz?"

"I do," he said with a nod.

"Imagine that old woman dividing her time between two cemeteries!" They both had a good laugh over that and Buzz got himself out a cup and tipped his flask three times.

"If Doris here is going to start drinking with us, I'm going to have to buy a bigger flask," he said, and again they laughed until they had tears in their eyes.

But not Jennifer. She just stared at them. "Did you two get an early start today or something?" she asked.

"No, honey. This is a little on the early side. I say we drink to Louise. May she find peaceful rest."

They lifted their coffee cups, clinked and put them back on the counter. The two diners got up from their booth, wandered over to the counter to pay Buzz, and left. Gloria went to bus their table.

"Does Louise have any family anywhere?" Jennifer asked Buzz.

"I don't believe so. In thirty years, I'd have heard."

"Not even a great-great niece or nephew?"

He shrugged. "I think you're looking at her family right now. And, of course, her best friends, Rose and Alex and Alice."

"I'm a little worried about something," she said. "The lawyer who came with the news said I should just stay put for the time being, and of course I can't even think of leaving Alice, but I want to do what's right. Should I be clearing out?"

Gloria came up behind her with her arms full of dishes. "It's like you say, girl. You can't leave Alice. You just stay put till someone says otherwise."

"Hmm," she said, taking another sip. She had investment and bank accounts, not to mention personal items in Florida. The way she had felt yesterday, she could put off getting that all sorted out for months to come. But in this case, it might be necessary to get that mess in Florida handled soon; it might be the only way she could get on with her life, afford the rent and expenses that would no doubt come due. She was no expert in legal affairs, but it seemed to her that if someone died, their accounts were closed.

"I'd better get going," she said. "Thank you for the nip, Buzz. I don't think it cleared my head, but it might've calmed my nerves."

"Doris, I know I don't have to tell you this, but it's real important you remember that Alice isn't going to be far behind Louise."

"I know," she said, and she said it very, very softly.

"You're fond of that old dog, it's very plain to see."

"I am. But I'm a big girl. And I think she wants to be with Louise."

"Oh, I'm sure. Reckon they have pooper-scoopers in heaven?"

Jennifer hadn't been home long when Alex came to the door. She threw herself into his arms and that's when the tears came. "I know we shouldn't be so surprised," she cried. "But you just don't know how much I depended on Louise. We e-mailed every day. Sometimes they were so brief. Sometimes just a couple of lines. But there were times I sat writing for what seemed hours." She sniffed back tears and looked into his sad eyes. "I told her everything before she died. Everything."

"And let me guess—she accepted you completely."

"Completely."

"It was a lucky day for all of us that you ran into Louise and made friends."

"You can't know how much I owe her."

"Rose isn't answering her phone or door," he said.

"I'm not surprised. She asked to be left alone for a little bit. I think she wanted to have a good cry. You know how proud Rose is—appearances are everything to her."

"I'll let her be for a while," he said. "I'll try again later."

"Alex, Louise died at about two in the morning. Nine o'clock in the morning in London." She could see that he wasn't making any connection. "I think maybe she swung by and said goodbye to Alice."

He frowned, thinking about that. And as he remembered the howling from the night before, a smile grew on his lips. "Wouldn't that be just like her. How's Alice doing now?"

"All calmed down. I really think she got riled up and wanted to go with Louise."

Alice was back in her usual spot, and he went over there to give her a pat. "You'll be going with her soon enough, old girl. You stay with us for a while, okay?"

Alice rolled over on her back, acquiescing.

Jennifer came up behind him and put her arms around him. "Will you be all right if you don't have Louise to look after?"

He rubbed the arms that circled him. "As long as I have you."

"You have me."

She asked him to stay with her. She had never before asked a man to stay the night. But for probably the first time in years this solitary person who'd survived quite well without friends just didn't want to be alone. In fact, loneliness was a new feeling for her, and she welcomed it. It meant there were people in her life she craved.

They turned on the TV and nestled into the couch cushions, their bare feet on the coffee table and Alice lying peacefully in the space between the sofa and table, under their raised legs. Alex found some basketball game but turned the volume down low. By nine o'clock he was sleeping, every once in a while emitting a snore or soft grumble. She thought about just pulling the throw at the end of the sofa over the two of them, and then remembered Rose.

There were soft lights behind the blinds in Rose's living room, so Jennifer knocked. Rose didn't answer, so she rang the bell. Still nothing, so she pounded on the door. Since that didn't bring any answer, either, she became worried. Her fleeting and hysterical thought was, *I can't lose both of them in one day!* She turned the knob and, of course, the door opened right up. No one bothered with locks around here except police officers and women who were hiding out.

There were candles lit in the small living room and Rose sat in the corner in her chair. She wore a pale pink dressing gown and held a box of tissues in her lap. "Louise was right," she said. "We really should start locking our doors."

"I'm sorry, Rose. I couldn't help it—you scared me by not answering."

"Now you see I'm fine, you can go."

"Alex is also worried," she said.

Rose didn't say anything.

Jennifer went closer and knelt on the floor before Rose. She reached for her and lay her head in Rose's lap. Almost reluctantly, Rose began to pat the soft cap of dark hair that covered her head.

"Where did you come from, little Doris? How is it you've come into our lives and taken Louise's place?"

She lifted her head in surprise. "I can't have done that, Rose. I miss her, too. We were becoming good friends through our e-mails every day."

"You know I don't have a computer," Rose said.

"We'll get you one."

"I don't want one. I think it's devil-inspired. I'm saying, I never e-mailed her."

"I know…"

"But I talked to her every day."

Jennifer's eyes were wide with shock. "You never—"

Rose was shaking her head. "I never said." She swallowed. "She was my oldest friend. Even though there were others I knew longer, Louise was my oldest and dearest friend."

"You talked every day? She wasn't sick, was she? Was it like they said—that she just went to sleep?"

Rose nodded. "I told her all about you. About you and Alex, about the party at Adolfo's house. About Hedda and the prom. She was proud of you. She said, 'See Rose, I told you she was quite a girl.' And I said, phoo. She's no girl. She's thirty already and hasn't begun to settle down."

Jennifer felt the tears wet her cheeks.

"I wasn't able to tell her about Alice acting up. There was no answer at her flat. She may have already been gone."

"Yes."

"I scolded her for not telling you about Rudy and she said it wasn't that important. She said she wasn't going back and forth for quite the same reasons anymore. It was more or less habit. She was an odd old duck. But so good. And she was more than ready. She complained much more often about the pain of her joints. It was, at times, unbearable. But do you know the worst for me? To know she was alone. I didn't want her to be alone when she died."

"I don't think she even realized…"

"I guess what I mean to say is that I don't want to be alone. But what can we do about that? I never had a family. And so—"

"You won't be alone, Rose. I promise," she said. "You have family now."

Fourteen

The prom was a welcome distraction and Hedda could barely contain her excitement. She planned to work her schedule as usual, Saturday afternoon and Sunday morning. She needed a little extra help on Saturday night, she told Jennifer nervously. "My…ah…my mom can't get off work Saturday night, and that's where she makes her biggest tips, so I need a baby-sitter for Joey."

"You know that's no problem."

But Jennifer knew there was more to the story. Sylvia was not going to allow this special event. Hedda was a sharp cookie—she wasn't going to draw Jennifer into her conspiracy.

"Okay," Jennifer said. "Tomorrow, as soon as you get off work, grab Joey, come over and let's work on your hair and makeup."

"Great," she said, beaming.

Alex spent most of Saturday morning working on all three lawns. He mowed, trimmed, repaired sprinklers, edged along the sidewalk and weeded out planter boxes. While he was in constant evidence outside, Rose and Jennifer were assembling things inside.

"Do you think he could be more obvious?" Jennifer asked Rose.

"Phoo. He can't admit he's as interested in this night as we are."

"Should we invite him to play? Or should we make him beg?"

Rose pulled the curtain on the front window to one side and looked out. "Too late. Here's our girl on the fly."

Hedda was walking at nearly a run, pulling Joey along. She wore a tank top, overlong shorts and her high-top rubber-toed tennis shoes. Over her shoulder she carried a plastic bag. Jennifer looked at her watch. It was five-thirty. Max would be coming for her in about an hour and a half.

She lifted Alice's lead from the hook on the wall and the old girl got lazily to her feet. She was on the front step with the dog just as Hedda came flying up the walk. "Joey, how would you like to take Alice for a little walk with Alex?"

Alex looked over the hedge at Jennifer. He smirked. "Hey, Hedda. Big date tonight?" he asked.

"Very funny, Alex. Joey, will you be nice? Go with Alex?"

"Come on, sport," Alex said, laying down his hedge trimmers. "Let's go get a couple of beers, watch some sports, pick up chicks."

"'Kay," he agreed, taking the lead from Jennifer.

With Alex and Joey gone, the transformation commenced. Hedda was shuffled into the shower where towels, soap, shampoo and a robe were waiting for her. The women paced outside the door impatiently while she got cleaned up. When the door to the bathroom finally opened, they literally pulled her from the room.

A chair was brought from the dining room into the bedroom. Rose insisted she be the one to help with Hedda's hair on the grounds that all *Doris* knew about hair had been awfully drastic. So while Rose employed the blow dryer and curling iron, Jennifer worked on Hedda's nails. There wasn't much to them, given her line of work, but they shaped up nicely and looked much improved with some clear polish.

There was a bit of a tussle over the hairstyle. Rose was fond of big hair, back-combing and the like. Hedda was more than willing to alter her usual spiky coif for something a little more formal, but every time Rose teased it up, Hedda would pat it down.

The makeup was much easier—there was very little disagreement. Since Hedda didn't usually wear makeup, they went easy. A little base, a little eyeliner, soft lip liner and gloss.

They heard Alex and Joey come back but wouldn't let them into the bedroom, where all the really serious work was taking place. When it was almost time to get the dress out of its protective bag, Jennifer pulled some tissue paper out of a dresser drawer.

"I don't know if this is still traditional for a prom, but I thought you might like to have this," she said, peeling back the tissue.

"A garter," Hedda said. It was the same soft pink as the dress with little pearls in the shape of a heart. She looked at Jennifer with tears in her eyes. "I was going to skip it," she said.

"We're not going to skip anything. And here's a little something else," she said, producing some very sheer pink panties, fancier and more expensive than anything Hedda had ever had.

"Oh, God, how *gorgeous!*"

"You may show Max the garter, not the panties," Rose said. She grabbed Hedda's shoulders, turned her in the direction of the bathroom and said, "Put on your lacies and let's get this show on the road."

Moments later, Hedda stood before them in all her pink glory. Rose produced a sheer shiny white shoulder wrap and Jennifer went back to that same dresser drawer and brought out a slim, glittery bracelet. As she put it on Hedda's wrist, the girl gasped. "Is this *real?*"

"Don't worry. It has a safety latch."

"Doris, I *can't.* It's too much."

"It's perfect. Isn't it, Rose?"

Rose looked at her strangely. She crossed her arms over her chest. "Perfect," she agreed, but in her eyes there were a thousand questions.

The doorbell rang.

"Show time," Rose said, handing Hedda a small satin clutch. "You have a house key for this house, lip gloss, tissue and a couple of twenties in case you need a cab home."

"I won't need a cab," she laughed.

Rose left the bedroom to get a look at Max. Hedda

would have followed when Jennifer pulled her back. Whispering, she said, "Just a minute. Two things to remember. No drinking and driving, and remember how old your mom was when you were born?"

Hedda nodded.

"I'm taking a big chance here. I've known all along I'm going against your mother's wishes."

"Doris, no one has ever been this great to me. You rock."

"Well, rock on back here at a decent hour. If you scare me at all, I'll shave your head."

Jennifer wasn't sure what she was expecting from Max—maybe some tux pants that were hanging off his bum, exposing his boxer shorts. She had found herself hoping that the older brother's car he was planning to use wouldn't be too big a wreck; she'd hate to see that adorable dress get ripped, snagged or smeared with dirt.

Waiting just inside the living room door with a plastic corsage box was Max, his hair looking a little like an unmade bed but actually better than usual. And he wore a very nicely fitted tux—white. And he said, "Wow!" when he saw Hedda.

And Jennifer said, "Max! Wow yourself!"

"Thanks," he said, smiling shyly. He handed Hedda the plastic box. "We have to drive over to my folks?" he said uncomfortably, his voice rising in habitual question. "Pictures?"

"That's cool," she said. Because clearly Hedda was feeling very much like having her picture taken.

"We have to take some pictures, too," Alex said, and

Jennifer noticed for the first time a camera sitting on the coffee table. "Let's get some outside. Under the tree."

That was the first time they saw the car. A Lexus.

"Max, is that your brother's car?" Jennifer asked.

"Naw. He's got a Honda? It's a real nice Honda, though. This is my mom's? She says if I so much as scratch the paint, she's going to—well, actually, you don't want to know what she said she'd do, but it's very painful." No question in his voice now. This, Jennifer realized, was how you knew Max was making a statement that brooked no doubt.

It took just a little while for them to snap some pictures and be on their way with Hedda yelling for Joey to be good. Alex draped his arms around Jennifer's and Rose's shoulders as they watched the young couple drive off.

"You took pictures," Jennifer whispered sentimentally. "That is so sweet."

"Wanna go spy on them?" he asked her.

"Can we?"

He nodded. "We can spy, then we can go park somewhere and make out. If Rose will babysit. I have just the enticement. I have ice cream and a DVD of *Shrek*."

The high school held their prom in a ballroom at the magical Ritz Carlton at Lake Las Vegas. The night was unseasonably cool and the breeze refreshing. Surrounded by mountains, the resort community was like a glittering gem in the middle of the desert.

Alex and Jennifer were there before most of the teenagers so they walked around, hand in hand, looking for a prime viewing spot. They bought icy Frappuccinos and found a bench inside the Ritz, not very far from the entrance the kids would use for valet parking.

It wasn't long before they began to arrive. They came in colorful pairs and in groups. Jennifer was delighted to see Max and Hedda come in with another couple. And Hedda, having such a good time, didn't even notice that Alex and Jennifer were sitting nearby.

"You did a good thing here, Jennifer," he told her. "She's going to remember this for the rest of her life."

"There are lots of similarities between the way I grew up and Hedda's life. But what about you, Alex? How'd you grow up?"

"Lucky. Nice, Midwestern folks, two brothers, both in law enforcement up north. My dad was a cop and now he has his own locksmith shop. I have to say, I never really struggled. My only struggle was that I was the youngest and the smallest. I didn't think I would ever hit puberty."

"Well, you hit it and passed," she laughed.

He put an arm around her and they leaned back against the wall, enjoying the sight of the young people, formal and so happy, going in and out of the Ritz.

"I know you were married once," she said. "But what has kept you free for so long?"

"Nothing clicked," he said with a shrug. "It's not like I was avoiding women or relationships. Between Paula and my last few female partners, I've been fixed up a dozen times. And I'm a real good sport. I've always been open to the idea that it could happen again." He gave her a squeeze. "I figured this time I'd know what I was doing."

"It shouldn't have happened this way. I shouldn't be so lucky," she said. "You should be married with three cute kids who play lots of sports and drive you crazy."

A woman in a cocktail waitress outfit stomped past them just as Alex was saying, "That's pretty much what I expected. What my brothers have. But I—"

Jennifer's eyes were following the woman. "No!" she shouted suddenly, and leapt to her feet. She ran after the woman to stop her. Alex was right on her heels. Jennifer touched Sylvia's arm, turning her about. "No," she said more softly. "Don't do this."

Sylvia's face was twisted with anger. "She doesn't have *permission!*"

"What do you care?" she asked pleadingly. "It's one night, it's not putting you out, it didn't cost you anything."

"She's supposed to be baby-sitting!"

"You're here—that means you've already found out that Joey is with Rose, watching a movie. He couldn't be happier."

"I told you to mind your own business."

"All right," Alex cut in. "We're not doing this here. Come on, let's take it over there, out of the traffic."

He pulled gently on Sylvia's elbow and she snatched herself out of his grasp. "Don't you *touch* me. I'm going to get my—"

Jennifer was gripped in sudden panic. "Sylvia, don't! Come on, let me buy you a drink. Let's just talk about this over a drink!" Even as she offered, she knew this was like throwing gasoline on a fire. But it was the only thing she knew would work to get her out of here before Hedda was humiliated.

Her expression changed. "Where?"

"Someplace quiet. My treat."

She glared at Jennifer for a moment, then nodded and walked out ahead of them.

Jennifer whispered to Alex to find them a quiet bar nearby and leave the women alone to talk this out. And, she added with a cringe, "I don't have any money."

"Don't worry about it," he said.

Lake Las Vegas was not only too regal and sophisticated for what they had in mind, it was also too crowded. Alex shepherded the women into his car, declaring they'd come back for Sylvia's car later, though in his mind he must have known they wouldn't. He drove them to Henderson, a quick twenty-minute trip, to a little neighborhood bar close to the interstate.

The only thing Sylvia said from her place in the back seat was "You shouldn't have interfered."

"We'll talk about it over a drink," Jennifer replied.

The women took a booth in the back while Alex sat at the bar. Sylvia ordered a boilermaker and Jennifer watched as the angry look began immediately to melt off her face. Then Sylvia began to talk.

She talked about the tough childhood she had had, the abusive parents, bad times in school, becoming pregnant at fourteen, delivering at fifteen. She'd been in and out of foster homes, her parents unstable. She'd moved many times, starting in Albuquerque. She'd been married three times and all the bums had run through whatever they could get out of her and left her high and dry. She complained about her job, which she probably had lost from walking out tonight. She hated Boulder

City and wouldn't be there except that the last guy she lived with worked at the dam. She hated Nevada, for that matter, but there was no denying there were good waitress jobs there in the casinos. She went on and on and on about how rotten her life was, how two kids didn't make it any easier.

She had six boilermakers and an unknown number of cigarettes and was still in the first volume of her life story, but she hadn't said a word about Hedda and Joey, except to complain that motherhood was hard. It was all about Sylvia. But Jennifer had been able to get a few details.

When Sylvia raised her hand to the waitress one more time, Jennifer said, "That's got to be it for tonight," she said. "But maybe we can do this again sometime."

"You sure?"

"Sure. Let's get going. Tell you what—we'll drop you off, and if you give me your keys, Alex and I can ferry your car home for you tomorrow morning. You'll have to sleep in to get ready for work tomorrow night."

"Awww," she said, reaching across the short distance that separated them to run her fingertips along Jennifer's jawline. "That's so sweet."

She was considerably more talkative on the way home than she had been before, much to the annoyance of her hosts. Fortunately it wasn't a long drive. It was just after ten when they got to the little house and Sylvia was well on her way to being plowed. "Sure you won't come in for another drink?" she invited.

"No, thanks." Jennifer faked a yawn. "I'm bushed."

There was a long silence as they left Sylvia in front of her house. Finally Alex said, "Well?"

"Damn, Alex, I found out way more about Sylvia than I ever wanted to know."

"I'll bet."

"Her life is more of a train wreck than mine—but here are the two things I know that I consider valuable information. One, Joey's father may be a loser, but apparently he has grandparents who are good-enough people to have pestered Sylvia to see the boy. Hedda seems to have only Sylvia and Sylvia's dysfunctional parents, who, fortunately, have no interest in her. And two— she's an alcoholic."

"You think?" he asked facetiously.

"Maybe someone should contact Joey's grandparents," she said.

The opportunity to bring up the subject of Joey's grandparents came sooner than Jennifer expected. She had not imagined what the onset of summer would bring—the temperatures rose to one hundred degrees daily and the nights were often rent with violent desert storms known as the monsoons. School was out, there was no air-conditioning in the house in which Hedda lived, and the intensity of the heat and the boredom of the days made it difficult to keep Joey occupied, and therefore not easy for Sylvia to sleep. Hedda came in for her shift at one, Joey in hand. There was an angry red welt marking her cheek and her eyes showed the anguish of crying.

Jennifer wanted to storm over to that nasty little shack and knock Sylvia into the middle of next week, but she kept her cool. "Here's what I want you to do," she told the girl. "When you get up in the morning, go straight over to my house. Er, Louise's house. I don't know how much longer I'm going to be able to stay there, but when that business is all settled, I'll have to go somewhere."

"Are you sure it's okay?"

"I'm sure. But one more thing, Hedda. I know you think you can do everything, but I think you should give yourself a break and consider contacting Joey's grandma and grandpa." The girl instantly dropped her gaze. Jennifer lifted her chin. "What's the problem?"

"They live in Arizona."

"So?"

"They would take him away," she said, her eyes watering.

"Arizona isn't so far away. Look, you don't have to make a decision right away, but Hedda, you're almost seventeen. You have to think of Joey, too. Could he have a better childhood in Arizona?"

"Probably," she said. "But my mom won't give him up."

Jennifer almost said, I don't see why. But she held her tongue.

"You just think about it." She touched the girl's reddened cheek. "Meanwhile, just go to my house."

"You don't understand," she said. "She needs me. As long as she has me and Joey, she manages to hold it together."

"I do understand," Jennifer said. "I've been there. But in case you hadn't noticed, she's not holding it together very well these days."

She shook her head. "She'll get a grip. She always does."

It was with Hedda on her mind that Jennifer brought up the subject of the house with Alex. "I wonder if I should be looking for a place to live that will take Alice," she said.

An expression crossed his face that was almost a wince. "Listen, I didn't mean to keep anything from you, but the house is to be mine. Louise told me a few years ago that if she didn't have to liquidate her property to go into a nursing home, she would leave me the house as long as I would watch over Alice."

"Why didn't you just tell me?"

"I don't know. Because I didn't want to change anything."

"But you have to know that things are changing," she said. "Not the least of which is that Doris is leaving and Jennifer is emerging. I have some explaining to do."

"There's plenty of time," he said, reaching for her.

Alex had a hard time focusing, now that he'd had sex. He appeared to be insatiable, and every second they were alone he was pulling her into his arms, tugging at her clothes. She could keep him under control, but the problem was that every time he touched her, she couldn't think, either.

"I wish we'd get enough," she said. "So we could deal with some of these practical matters."

"There isn't enough," he answered. "I've been thinking of taking a leave of absence from work."

Fifteen

Jennifer took the bike out at first light. The sun was coming up earlier with the lengthening of the days. Although she'd ridden back to the park several times, braving the increasing afternoon heat, she hadn't seen the bighorns. But as she got to the park at dawn, she saw the first glimpses of them coming over the mountain and down the trail. It hadn't occurred to her that they would change their grazing habits as the weather changed, but here they were in the cool morning light instead of the midday heat.

She got a spot on the grass, lying the bike beside her, and watched as they approached. She wished she'd thought to bring Alex, but it seemed so unfair to wake him at dawn when he didn't have to go to work until later in the morning. As for work, Buzz wouldn't get excited if she didn't show at five on the dime.

The night before had held the kind of magic she wasn't sure she was entitled to. In all the fantasies of her deprived youth, her Prince Charming had owned a Jag and a yacht, had a mansion in the Azores and his own jet. And when he swept her onto the dance floor, she was always wearing a long white chiffon gown.

But in reality the man to whom she had given her heart wore chinos and loafers, a cotton polo shirt and a Timex. He was far from rich, except in kindness and humor.

They had been right in this spot last night, in his car, necking like high school kids do. With each touch of his lips, she melted further into his arms. The moon had been high and full and reflected on the lake below, and Jennifer knew her most impossible dreams had come to life.

Just when she found herself begging Alex to take her home and to bed, he had other ideas. They went to the Boulder Hotel, where there was underground dancing in the basement underneath. "This is for the younger set," he said with a laugh, meaning for folks in their thirties and forties.

"I love to dance," she said.

"I know. I love to watch you dance."

On that particular night, swing was the dance of the evening. And Alex, who always seemed one surprise ahead of her, twirled her around very expertly and nearly wore her out. Then home, where Louise's old bed was made to creak and rock until the wee hours of the morning. Alex was still there, snoring, when Jennifer got up for a quick ride before work and was now, miraculously, watching the sheep descend.

As they neared, she realized with a leap in her breast

that the lambs had come. There were three. No, four. No, *eight* little ones trailing along with their mothers. And just as Alex had predicted, the rams were not separating in the same distant manner; they were sticking pretty close to the ewes and lambs.

It was so hard to just sit there and watch. She felt like part of the family and she wanted to get closer, to pet them. But these were not sweet little white lambs like the one that followed Mary to school. These were brown, rather dusty and their new fleece was already getting matted, though she doubted they were even two weeks old, rocking on their wobbly little legs. It had been tempting since first sighting the lambs to jump on the bike and race back to town to wake Alex, but she wasn't sure she could get back before they left, so she settled for making sure he came with her the next day.

And then they began to leave and she realized that this was not just a beginning, but also the end of something. She promised herself that after the prom and the lambs, she would find out what had become of the life she had left behind. She couldn't make a break and start over completely until she did that.

It was time to get that unfinished business in Florida taken care of.

The diner didn't start to get busy on the weekends until at least 8:00 a.m., so Buzz had no problem with her wandering in a little late. She was melancholy as she told them all about the lambs, but no one seemed to notice. She had also been concentrating on exactly how she was going to explain who she was and where she'd come from.

It appeared she was not going to have the chance to orchestrate the events in her own order. Before 9:00 a.m. a long black limo pulled up to the diner, and every head turned to look at it.

"Jesus Christ," Gloria said. "We don't usually get the high mucky-mucks here at the Can."

The driver got out and held the door open for his passenger, a short and thick bald guy. Well, this is it, Jennifer thought. Here he is. As Jennifer saw Nick stand there looking at the diner, she slowly removed her apron, hung it on the coatrack just inside the door and walked outside, resignation in every step. But at least she was no longer afraid he would kill her.

Just as she had long suspected he might, he knew her instantly. Recognition showed in his eyes. She might be able to fool a lot of people, but not Nick. Nor Alex. These two men could not be more different, yet neither was fooled for a second by her disguise.

"Hi, baby." He cocked his head, winked and smiled. "You look good."

Without the heels and teased hair she was shorter than him by a couple of inches. She stood patiently while he looked her over, amazed by how quickly it all came back to her—the way she wouldn't shrink under his gaze but rather let him take his fill. She wore jeans and a collared shirt—the usual diner attire. Her only makeup was some lip gloss, but with her rosy cheeks and dark sooty lashes, that was all she needed.

"You, too, Nick."

"Yeah," he said, nodding. "I like this version."

"What about the leggy blond version? I thought you were into that?"

"Aw," he scoffed. "You're one of those people who can look good no matter what. Got a minute?" He looked around, up and down the street, into the diner. Ten or more faces stared back at him from inside. "This is a little personal." He stepped aside so she had access to the open door of the limo.

"Sure," she said, getting inside. When Nick was in beside her and the door closed, she said, "I'll talk to you for a minute, but I'm not going anywhere with you."

"Hey, what's up with this? Huh? You run away from me and dump me like that? What's your deal? What'd I do? Huh?"

"I guess it turns out you didn't do what I thought you did," she said. "But that day your wife showed up at the MGM, I overheard your fight. It was awful, Nick. I went back later and saw the room. I'm sorry, but I couldn't deal with that. I can't be with a man who can have a violent fight with a woman—with his wife."

"What did *I* do?" he asked.

"I didn't just see the room, Nick. While you were taking a shower, I snuck in there. I saw Barbara on the bed. I thought you'd *killed* her!"

"I shoulda killed her," he said. "She made me so damn mad. You can't believe the threats she was making. She's gonna turn copies of my records over to the IRS, she says. Get me sent to prison for tax evasion. I'll tell you what, I wanted to kill her. But I just gave her a knockout drink. She'd already trashed the room, damn near broke my nose and didn't show any sign of settling down. So I said, 'Lou! Get Barbara a drink. She's got herself all worked up here.'"

"A mickey?" she asked.

"Well," he shrugged, "a roofie. Rohypnol."

"The date-rape drug?"

He laughed hollowly. "You can believe it had nothing to do with rape. I just wanted that broad to shut the hell up. Damn, she pissed me off."

"Hmm," she said. "That explains it."

"And you left me because of that? Jesus, Jennifer. Haven't I been good to you? I ever raise a hand? You ever have reason to be afraid of me?"

"I was never afraid of you. Not until that day. Not until—" She stopped for a moment, thinking. "You mean to say you didn't throw anything, or hit, or—"

"Hey, I was getting real damn close to decking her, you know? I don't pretend to be an angel. If she'd've been a guy, I would have clocked her. Him. But I don't hit girls, okay? There aren't very many places I draw a line, but—" He shrugged again. "You shoulda talked to me, baby." He reached over and gave her jeans-clad knee a pat. "I was worried sick, you know. I thought someone snatched you or something. I looked. I hired detectives. I posted a reward with the police."

"Worried?"

"Hell, Jennifer—why do you act like you don't know me? Huh? I was totally wrapped up in you! I thought I'd lost you!"

"I heard you tell Lou to go find that bimbo...."

"I don't always say the right thing, you know that. I'm not as good with women as I'd like to be—but I make up for it, don't I? Didn't I give you nice things? Jesus, baby, you scared me to death."

"I'm sorry, Nick. It was a huge misunderstanding."

"Tell me about it…"

"How'd you find me?"

"Get real! You don't think I have contacts all over the place?"

"But how?"

"I'm not going to kid you, Jennifer. It cost me. But it was worth it. I just had to see for myself that you were all right."

Maybe it was worth it, she thought. Because at least this will be over. Finally. "I'm really glad Barbara's all right and you're all right. Did she turn your records over to the IRS?"

"A lot of talk," he said with a dismissive wave of the hand. "I don't think she's going to threaten like that again, though. I think she knows she punched the right button that time." He laughed in spite of himself. "She's a pistol, all right. I always marry pistols. I just don't see 'em coming." He patted then grabbed her knee. "Now, you—I like your style. You got class. How about that— running off because you can't be with a guy who fights with his wife?" He laughed. "Who'd've known? Huh?"

"If I'd just gone to the police with what I'd seen, it would have been cleared up real fast," she said.

"Yeah, well, that's not my first choice, either. I guess if you felt you had to—but I have a feeling the cops would've locked me up for the roofies. I don't know what it is—but the cops have a case of the ass for me. You'd think I was some kind of crook or something."

"Well," she said, "what about the tax records?"

"Aw, that. It's nothing, really. I might owe a little here and there. Lotta people do. I could get fined. I'd *hate* to get fined. But there's no way I'm going to jail for taxes. Jesus."

"Then why did you knock out Barbara?"

"Baby, you know how much it costs to defend yourself in these deals? Holy Jesus, it's a fortune. My lawyers are busy enough with real estate deals—they're robbing me blind just to close those. A guy's *wife* goes to the feds and you know what happens? They like to never give up."

He looked out the left window and right window of the car. "So, baby, what are you doing in this place?"

She smiled her winning smile. "Waiting tables. Dog-sitting."

"Gimme a break."

"Serious as a heart attack."

"Well, let's go get your stuff, take you home…." He looked her up and down again. "You're cute as a button, baby, but this just isn't you."

"I told you, Nick. I can't go with you."

"What are you talking about? Of course you're going with me."

"I didn't do any of this on purpose," she said, "but this place suits me. I like the pace. I'm not trying to please anyone, and it turns out, I please a lot more people this way."

"So what? You like the short hair? The jeans? Fine— you can wear jeans anywhere…."

"I met someone."

The statement seemed to throw him back in his seat. "You're putting me on. Here?"

"It's a nice little town," she said.

"It isn't you," he said.

"The other girl wasn't me, Nick. Plastic boobs, puffed-up lips, capped teeth, dyed hair…"

"Dyed?" he asked almost painfully.

She couldn't help herself—she smiled at him. "You can build yourself another Barbie," she said. "I'm leaving that old life behind…."

"You're leaving me." It wasn't a question.

"I'm afraid so."

"Damn!" he said, and looked away as if he couldn't let her see the look in his eyes. And she thought, *Is it possible he really cared for me?* "What about all your things?"

She lifted a brow. "I still have things?"

"What did you think? I sold your stuff or something?"

She shrugged. "I thought it possible you put some other blonde in that condo. If you found one about my size, she'd have a nice wardrobe, too."

His eyes were sad as he reached a hand toward her face, cupping her cheek against his palm. "Hey, you're killing me here! I gave you the best I had and it turns out you never even trusted me! You telling me you're not even going back to Florida at all? You're going to leave the mail on the buffet table? The Jag in the garage? Your lacy underwear in the drawers?"

She frowned slightly.

"I'm over there every week. Me, personally. Just to

see if you've been back. If anything has been touched. Because, baby, I thought you felt about me like I felt about you."

"I'm sorry, Nick."

"You're just going to leave it all?"

"I'll go back there eventually. Soon, maybe. Get my mail, pack a bag—but I'm not stupid, Nick. It's not like you're giving me a Jag. And the condo is in your name. Like the furniture. I'm only going to take what's mine."

"Well, I am stupid," he said. "Because until five minutes ago, I was going to let you have anything you wanted. Right now I don't think I even want you to have the rings."

"I'll be happy to give them back. And the bracelet."

"Got 'em on you?" he asked. Gone was the brokenhearted expression, replaced by an angry smirk. "They at the little old lady's house?"

"Whose…?"

"The little old lady's house where you're staying with the dog?"

"You do know everything, don't you?"

"Let's go get 'em now—then you can have a real fresh start. Come on." He pressed a button on the dash and lowered the window that separated him from the driver. "Go up the street to 2902. Little brick number on the right."

The limo began to move immediately, slowly crawling down the street, past the park. She looked out the rear window and saw that Buzz and Gloria were standing on the sidewalk, watching. She wanted to yell to them not to worry—she'd be back in time to give the check to the couple in the back booth.

The limo stopped in front of Louise's brick house. "Make it quick, will you?" he said. "I'm not crazy about this dumpy little town. Gives me the creeps. Reminds me of my poor days in Philly."

"It'll only take a second," she said, getting out of the car.

This, she decided, was going to feel kind of good. To have this part of her old life over. She didn't delude herself that she'd done anything to deserve the jewelry, and she'd be happy to give him back what was left of the money, as well. Then she would ask Alex to go with her to Florida to collect the old mail and pack up her personal effects.

She gave Alice a cursory pat on the head. "Don't get excited," she told her. "I'm just stopping by."

The little Kate Spade bag was still in the backpack, still on the floor of the closet. She looked inside, assured herself that the bracelet and both rings were still there. She'd only dipped into a couple of hundred dollars and there must be three thousand or so left. She didn't count it, and didn't bother to remove any.

She gave Alice another pat on the way out, got into the limo and sat beside Nick, leaving the door open. She opened the purse to begin giving him the items he asked for, but he reached past her, pulled the door closed and the car immediately pulled away from the curb.

"I think this is where we left it," he said. "You're coming with me."

"You're going to get into big trouble for this. You can't think you can make me go with you. I'll tell—"

"You're not telling anyone anything," he said sternly.

"We're getting the hell out of here. You put up a fuss, I'll make trouble for your new friends. What's her name—Rose? The kid with the funky hair? The old guy with the diner?"

"Are you threatening to hurt them?" she demanded.

"Aw, I'll just screw with 'em a little. I wouldn't want to hurt anyone. But if I get pushed far enough…"

"Why would you do that?" she asked, sincerely perplexed. "It's not like you can hold me captive."

"Don't plan to. What we're going to do is take a little vacation. A week. Maybe two. And if you still want to call it quits, you go ahead. But I have this idea that once we have a little time together, you'll want to go back to your condo and all your nice stuff. You'll forget about that dump you just walked out of. Huh? That's what I think."

Tears came to her eyes. "You don't know anything."

"Good, you prove me wrong, then. But all I want is you back with me. *No one* walks out on me like that."

"I *can't*. The dog—she's old and it'll upset her."

"We're talking about a freaking *dog!*"

"I have to at least make a phone call—"

"I'll make the call. Who you want? Rose or the kid?"

She shook her head in confusion. "How do you know these things?"

"Don't worry about it, sweetheart. Rose it is," he said. He pulled his cell phone out of his shirt pocket and clicked off a couple of numbers. "Not a sound," he said to her. "Believe me, you don't want to cross me now."

"Nick, wait," she said. "You better let me. She'll never believe you. She'll call the police."

He seemed to think about that for a moment, then passed the phone to Jennifer. Rose answered and she said, "Rose? Hi, it's Doris. Listen, I need a favor—I need you to take care of Alice and watch out for Hedda. I'm leaving town." She listened as Rose responded in total disbelief. "I know it's sudden, but my ex showed up and surprised me. Yes, in the limo. I'm going to have to go with him." She pinched her eyes closed and fought tears. "I'm not planning to stay long—but if I don't go back where I came from and pack up some of my things, he's going to give everything away. Throw it away, maybe. Now, don't worry, I'll be fine. I'll explain when I get back…. I don't know how long…a couple of days, a week. I'm sorry I didn't tell you about all of this before, but, Rose, I have this whole life back in Florida and I have business to clear up." She listened again. "No, there's nothing to worry about. Tell Buzz and Adolfo for me, will you, Rose? Tell them I'll be back. And I'll give you a call when I get where I'm going."

She clicked off and handed him the phone.

"Nicely done," he said. He had a rather sinister smile on his face as he pocketed the cell.

How is it he can so easily fool me? she asked herself.

He made another quick call, asked that the plane be ready when he got to the executive airport and informed the agent there would be another passenger. One Jennifer Chaise. *Please, Rose, call Alex,* she thought with desperation.

"Here's what we're going to do, Jennifer. We're going to board the plane like it's been planned for months, and like you couldn't be happier about it. You behave yourself and don't make any kind of fuss—because if you do it'll just be one big headache. No one's ever going to believe I forced you to come along because, see, I don't have a gun or anything. And I'm just a nice rich guy who gets taken advantage of by bimbos all the time."

"And then what?"

"Then you think about things. If you still want to wait tables in a crappy little diner and sleep with a cop—"

She jumped in surprise, her eyes round as silver dollars. But why should she be surprised? He knew about Rose and Hedda, why wouldn't he know about Alex?

"But Jesus, Jennifer. A *cop?*"

She was all done talking. She was getting pretty nervous. *Rose, call Alex,* she prayed. *Before the plane can leave, please call Alex.*

"So when we get home you either shake off this cop or you don't, and if you don't, I guess you go back to that little dump and… What? Have a bunch of sweaty little kids, live in the desert, pinch pennies?" He laughed and shook his head, like the idea was very amusing. "Well. Whatever," he said.

He was lying, of course. She knew he had absolutely no intention of letting her leave him again. But she wasn't sure what he meant to do with her. Either keep her under lock and key or maybe he'd just use her for fish bait.

The important thing to remember is that if she didn't balk or make trouble, he had no reason on earth to bother or hurt Hedda, Rose or Buzz. It would make no sense for him to do so.

When the limo arrived at the airport, she could run screaming from the vehicle. There were always lots of security people around airports, even small executive airports. But she did not trust that her friends would remain safe—today or sometime down the road Jennifer knew Nick would make good on his threats.

She watched out the window as they drove through the desert, back to Las Vegas. She wished it could be a longer drive so that there would be time for Rose to call Alex. She watched the rough landscape slide past and could not help the tears that rose to her eyes and coursed down her cheeks. Poor Alice, she would be so distraught to think Jennifer would leave her. And how would Hedda cope? Rose was tough, Buzz was resilient, Alex was proud and strong, but what about poor Hedda?

"I don't know what you're crying about," Nick said. "It's not like life with me was hard or anything."

She turned back to him. "What would you know about it?"

"Hey! Watch it. You don't want to piss me off."

"Or what?" she challenged.

He pressed his face close to hers and the meanness she had always really known existed glittered in his eyes. "You wanna try me out, baby?"

She lifted her chin. "Stop it, Nick."

"I don't know what your problem is. Just suck it up. Be a big girl. I'm not such a bad guy."

"Sure Nick. What's not to love," she said, backing away from his face. "You're irresistible. Such a sexy little guy."

She looked back out the window. She was going to go along with this for now. There was simply no other choice.

He grabbed her arm and jerked her around to face him again. "Straighten up! And don't you ever...*ever* call me a sexy little guy!"

Rose was a little confused. Doris had never indicated that the ex she was fleeing was wealthy. And even so, Doris didn't seem the type to do this. She was so sincere in her care of Alice, her closeness to Hedda. And if she wasn't mistaken, she was falling in love with Alex.

And Rose had begun to think of her as the daughter she had never had.

She didn't call Alex to alert him, but to ask him. If anyone knew the details of Jennifer's life, she thought he might.

His phone was turned off. He might be in the middle of some big important police business. "Alex, it's Rose calling," she said to the voice mail. "I'm a little confused. Doris just called me to say she's leaving town. A limousine picked her up and took her away. She asked me to take care of Alice, look out for Hedda, and tell Buzz and Adolfo she had to leave. She said she'd call later. But I'm a little confused...." And then Rose hung up the phone.

It was forty-five minutes before he called her back, and he was clearly distraught. "Did she say who she was with? Where she was going? How she was getting there?"

"She said her ex came for her and that she had to go back to where she came from and take care of things. I think she said she had a life in Florida and she'd call when she got there, and that she would be back. But she gave absolutely no warning."

"Rose, listen—did she say how she would be traveling?"

"No. She just said she'd come back in a few days or a week, when she could. What was so strange, Alex, is she never mentioned you. Everyone else, but not you. Was I completely mistaken? I thought I saw the two of you falling for each other."

"You were not mistaken," he said. "And you need to know—she would not do this. She did not want to leave us."

"What should I do?" Rose asked, fear creeping into her voice.

"Do exactly as she asked. Take care of the dog and look out for Hedda. I'll be in touch."

It didn't take Alex long to learn that Nick Noble had boarded the MGM's Gulfstream with his party, bound for Fort Lauderdale. He alerted the FBI immediately that he didn't believe Jennifer Chaise had gone with him willingly. He was pacing back and forth in front of Sergeant Monroe's desk. "He snatched her. At the very least he tricked her. She would not have left."

"Because of you, Nichols? Is that what you believe?"

"Not just me, but I do believe that. She was completely hooked into this old, old dog that she's caring for and a kid, a teenager, who has a rough life at home.

Not to mention the little old retired stripper next door. I'm telling you, she would not do this!"

"I agree with him," Paula said. "I met her, I've seen her with these people."

"Turn the plane around," Alex suggested.

"Can't do it," the sergeant said. "You can go over to the airport yourself, but the word is that she was perfectly calm, polite, friendly—and left completely of her free will. Lots of witnesses."

"I don't believe it! She was totally committed to staying here! He scared her!"

"It appears she is no longer scared. But—we'll give this to the feds, make sure they're aware of the situation…."

"I need a leave. A few days. Family emergency," he said.

"You can't get involved."

"I won't go as a police officer. That's my *girlfriend*," he said desperately. "Regardless of what anyone else thinks, I think she's been abducted."

"Don't, Alex. Let the feds take care of this."

"I can't, boss. You don't get many chances like this and I can't let it go. Especially knowing what I know."

"I can give you four days. Maybe five, but it'll be tough."

"Thanks," he said, turning around and practically running out of the office.

"Boss," Paula said. "I'm going to need a leave. A few days. I have a ton of vacation and comp time."

"Aw, Jesus criminole, don't do this to me," he said, resting his forehead in his hand.

"Family emergency."

"My hairy ass!"

"Someone's gotta watch him. He's wacko for this girl. Who, by the way, I think wouldn't leave him—or her other friends. She happens to be a real nice person."

"Who thought it was cool to hook up with an underworld slimeball like Noble."

"Hey," she said, leaning forward, "they haven't been able to get him in all these years. If the feds can't nail him, how's Jennifer supposed to know?"

"They always know."

"Boss. Come on. I'll be useless here. You know he needs me. I have a clear head."

"All right, all right. But this is not official police business, this is clearly personal, and you are not licensed to carry in Florida."

"Right," she said. "Thanks, boss."

She left the sergeant's office and found Alex on the computer, his fingers racing along the keys as he tried to book a flight to Fort Lauderdale. She looked over his shoulder and saw an airline timetable on the screen.

"Book two. I'm going with you."

He looked back at her in surprise. "No," he said, going back to the computer.

"Sarge gave me the time to go with you."

"What about John?"

She laughed. "What? You think he'll be jealous?"

"Don't be stupid."

"Don't *you*. You're all hot. You need a partner."

He turned around in his chair and looked at her hard, right in the eyes. "Are you *sure?*"

"I am sure. Annoyed, but sure."

"We don't have time to pack a lot. You have to be fast."

"Just book two," she said again.

The sergeant's door opened. "Hey, you two. Thought you might want to know, they changed destinations. They're not going to Florida. They're going to St. Martin."

"Shit," the detectives said in unison.

Sixteen

Jennifer had a brief moment of satisfaction when she came face-to-face with Lou and his eyes widened in shock. Yes, she wanted to say, it's me. Fooled ya.

She was warned, very sternly, that if she made any trouble at the airport, she would deeply regret it. In fact, Nick said, "You'd better act like this was an answer to your prayers—that you're so happy to see me, you're beside yourself, or there's gonna be hell to pay."

So she laughed at his attempts at humor, smiled when he asked her if there was anything she needed, held his hand and hid the surprise from her face when she recognized the very suitcase and hang-up bag she had brought to Las Vegas three months earlier.

But the biggest shock of all waited on the jet. "Oh, my God," Barbara Noble shrieked. "You did *not* bring your chippy on this plane!"

"This is a nightmare," Jennifer said, rubbing her forehead between her thumb and forefinger.

"Tell me about it," said Nick.

"Only you, Nick," Jennifer said. Talk about major balls in a minor body.

"I swear to *God,* Nick, you're going to pay for this!" Barbara shouted.

He took long, hard strides with those short, thick little legs and whispered something in her ear that made her smile and say, "Ooh," with a great deal of satisfaction. And Jennifer thought, *Swell. He's going to push me out over New Mexico.*

She watched out the window in vain, hoping to see police cars or unmarked federal vehicles roaring up to the plane, though she didn't know what in the world she would do if they did. She'd have to pretend this was what she wanted, or her friends might pay the ultimate price. So she sat in her seat, put on her seat belt and did as she was told. Barbara Noble, with a superior smirk, just kept staring at her from the other side of the cabin.

As they taxied out and took off, Jennifer felt her eyes well with tears. She had been so close! She had almost believed there was a happy ending for her after all! She kept her eyes focused out the window; it was one thing to let Nick see her cry, she'd be damned if Barbara would.

She had no one to blame but herself. This is what happens when you get involved with someone like Nick Noble; when you get involved for all the wrong reasons. She looked at Barbara and wondered, what were her reasons? Had she loved him once? Was it affection or possessiveness that caused her jealous rages? Or just plain greed?

Barbara was a beautiful woman, just a few years older than Jennifer. She had dark ebony hair, pale skin and flashing green eyes. But unhappiness caused her to look hard. She took out her compact, flipped it open and ran her index finger over the rise of her cheek. She pressed her lips together, blotting them, then patted her dark, shiny hair, almost in affection, in a gesture that Jennifer recognized from her own very recent past.

Her glance moved to Nick. He was watching her.

Without asking her if she'd like anything to eat or drink, the flight attendant brought her a champagne cocktail. She looked across the cabin at Nick. "Lighten up, baby. It's a long flight."

She took the cocktail and thanked the attendant. She took a sip. Only the very best, but this gave her no pleasure now.

She could feel the plane level off at their cruising altitude and heard Nick's seat belt buckle open. He went to the front of the plane where Lou and Jesse were strapped into their seats. The cabin attendant, meanwhile, opened the closet and pulled out Jennifer's suitcase and hang-up. She brought them to her, lying the hang-up on the chaise longue beside her.

She didn't understand. Nick, from the front of the plane, called out to her. "Find something in there to put on. Something that makes you look like a girl."

"I'm… I'm fine," she said, declining.

He stomped toward her. "We gonna argue about this?"

"What do you care?" she asked.

"I care because you look like a boy and you smell like a pork chop. Now, find something to wear."

Resignedly, she got out of her seat. She opened the suitcase and knelt in front of it. She lifted the lid and the scent of her expensive perfume wafted upward. Everything was just as she had left it—neatly folded stacks of expensive, lacy thongs and bras, blouses, shells, slacks, thin silky sweaters, snugly fitting capris. She found her toiletries, makeup, jewelry case and her now perfectly useless mousse and hair dryer. She looked inside the hang-up for something comfortable and not terribly sexy and ended up with a lightweight black knit pantsuit. Under her neatly folded clothes were her shoes, all the heels much too high. One thing missing from her belongings—her cell phone. Naturally.

She took a stack of toiletries, makeup, belts, bracelets and clothes to the lavatory. At least in the private jet there was plenty of room for changing. This transformation would be impossible in a commercial jet.

As she traded her shirt and jeans for this expensive, soft and silky pantsuit, she remembered too clearly the last big change she'd made, and how it had made her cry. But then it was more out of fear than disappointment that she wept. The tears that threatened now were wrought of a breaking heart. She didn't want to be that woman again! She had grown so comfortable in her own skin.

Would Nick let her go? Would Alex be waiting? Would he believe what she'd told Rose—that she was just going home for a while, that she'd be back soon? If Alex believed that, maybe he'd just wait around. But for how long?

The top was low cut, but not the lowest she had in

the suitcase. She put on silver bangles, a silver pendant that hung from a black cord just above her breasts, and a black-and-silver belt that hung low on her hips and fastened with a big silver hook. She was in no mood for makeup, or the heels for that matter, but if there was one thing she had learned, it was best not to disappoint Nick. He was as tenacious as a bulldog at getting what he wanted.

When she exited the rest room, he was standing there with a drink in his hand and a smile on his lips. "Better," he said. "Much better."

She held the discarded jeans and polo. He took them from her and handed them to the cabin attendant. "Get rid of these," he told her. Then, taking Jennifer's hand, led her back to her seat. He looked between Barbara and Jennifer. "The two of youse is pretty damn good-looking," he said.

Barbara groaned and turned her face away, looking out the window. Jennifer just stared at him in awe. What was this? Did he think he was going to have a harem now?

The flight seemed longer than usual and they had flown over water for quite a while. They were obviously not going to Fort Lauderdale as the cabin attendant had originally announced. But this was typical of Nick, to change plans on a whim. He enjoyed watching people jump around to keep him happy.

Four hours into the flight, Nick finally went to the front of the cabin. He talked to his boys for a minute, then stood in the cockpit doorway to talk to the pilots.

Jennifer crossed the cabin to Barbara's side of the plane and sat on the end of the chaise beside her. Barbara was lazily filing a nail.

"Look, Barbara, I don't want to be here."

"Oh? And you think I do?"

She was a little surprised. "That's what I assumed."

"Shouldn't make assumptions, little girl."

"Then what are you doing here?"

"The same as you. Enjoying the pleasure of his company. Or that of one of his boys. Twenty-four-seven."

Jennifer sat back, frowning as she tried to comprehend this. "Since when?"

"Since March."

"So you *have* been out of the country. At spas, in Costa Rica, on a cruise..."

"How would you know that?" she asked.

"I was trying to find you. I thought he killed you and hid your body!"

A look of shock passed over Barbara's features just before melting into laughter. She laughed a little at first and then laughed harder until it verged on hysteria. "No kidding? You were trying to find out if I was *dead?*"

"Shh," she warned. "We don't need him back here."

"What made you think I was *dead?*"

"That day. That fight. I snuck back into the suite. Nick was in the shower and you were facedown on the bed. You looked dead to me."

"Oh, that," she said. "Let me give you some advice. Never take a drink Lou has fixed for you."

"I saw blood. I thought—"

"Bloody nose," she said.

"You hit him in the face?"

"No, I didn't hit him in the face," she replied, sarcasm dripping. "He just started gushing. It was disgusting. I think his blood pressure got so high, he sprang a leak."

"Oh. Pushed some buttons, did you?"

She laughed a little. "I'd say so."

"That tax record stuff?"

Now Barbara looked confused. "What are you talking about?"

"He said you threatened to turn his records over to the IRS to get him into trouble for tax evasion."

Her smile was slow and mocking. "God, he is such a liar."

"You didn't do that?"

"I threatened to turn him into the FBI for fraud and money laundering."

"You can prove that?"

Her eyes lifted to look over Jennifer's head. Nick stood behind her. "Isn't it nice," he said, "that my girls are getting along so good?"

When the plane landed, Jennifer recognized the airport. She'd been here with him before—the island of St. Martin. One of the most beautiful places on the planet. Under any other circumstances, she might have really enjoyed this. Nick had a big place on the beach, fully staffed and luxurious, and every bit as gorgeous as a resort. But it looked very much as if he was planning to keep her prisoner, along with Barbara. He handed her her passport and told her to behave herself. "Don't make any trouble for me." And after they cleared Customs, he took it back.

She didn't say anything. Barbara might have the goods on him, but she didn't. She had absolutely no idea what kind of illegal activities he'd been involved in, as she had already told the FBI.

They were taken to the house, a ten thousand square foot beach house surrounded on three sides by a ten-foot wall and on the remaining side by the sea. The sky was bright blue, the weather warm and balmy, and the house a big glittering gem with an enormous pool. It appeared as though a person could just walk away from this rich and lavish prison.

She went to her room, the same room she'd had on previous visits. The door remained unlocked and she sat on her balcony, staring at the sea. There was a knock at the door; a maid brought her a glass of lemonade and some fresh towels. It was surreal—that he should bring her here against her will and yet do nothing to try to keep her from leaving. She toyed with the idea of walking down the beach until she came to the road. But she had no shoes for walking.

She wandered around the house for a while, found the staff at work. There was meal preparation going on in the kitchen, the dining table was being laid, and to all appearances Mr. Noble was visiting for a little vacation.

She decided to walk right into the lion's den. She found him at a poolside table, wearing his terry robe, chewing on a cigar, his phone handy and briefcase open. She sat down. "Nick, you can keep me here against my will by threatening my friends, but things are not going to be the way they were between us."

He smiled. "What? No jewelry? No money for shopping? What?"

"I'm not your girlfriend anymore."

"Aw, baby, you'll come around."

"I don't know what you want from me."

His fist hit the glass tabletop. "I want you under wraps until my people get my business straightened out! Then you can do whatever the hell you want."

She never flinched. "I don't know what you're talking about."

"Maybe you do, maybe you don't."

"Nick! What do you *mean?*"

"Don't be cute. One of the things I like about you is that you're smart. Maybe too smart. So, we'll have a nice little vacation until the coast is clear."

She leaned forward. "Is that why you've kept Barbara with you for three months? Till you can tidy up your tax records? So if she talks, she'll be too late?"

He looked into his briefcase, shuffled some papers, stuck the cigar back in his mouth. "Something like that…"

She laughed. "Nick. Three months?"

He made eye contact with her again. Not happy eye contact. "Yeah. It's been a real picnic."

"I'll bet," she laughed. "So—how long you think this will take?"

"Not so long. And is this place so bad? You think you can stand this?" he asked, waving a hand.

"Let me call my friend Rose so I can tell her I'm all right and make sure she's all right."

The hand holding the cigar dropped to the tabletop and he looked at her curiously. "You're really into these people."

"They were awful good to me. I landed in that town with nothing but the clothes on my back."

He pointed the cigar at her. "What'd you do with the hair?"

"Left it in a crappy motel behind a railroad track."

He sucked on the cigar again. "I can't believe you were that scared of me. What ever made you think I could kill someone?" He reached across the table and gently stroked her arm. "You really think that of me? I know I'm a little rough around the edges, but baby…"

"I don't know. All of a sudden I was terrified. I really thought you'd done it."

He puffed some smoke. "Yeah? Well I shoulda. She's a giant pain in the ass."

"Three months?" she repeated. "Oh, Nick."

"Tell me about it."

She glanced over her shoulder and saw Barbara standing in the doorway. She was dressed in a lovely silver caftan, scowling blackly. She had seen her husband toying with his mistress, or so she thought. She whirled around and went back into the house.

"When this is behind you, what are you going to do about her?"

He didn't even have to think about it. "Shit-can her. Big D. Cut her off without a cent. She'll wish she was dead."

For a minute, Jennifer almost felt sorry for her.

It took Alex and Paula two days to get to St. Martin; flights were oversold all the way to Miami, and since they weren't on official business they couldn't pull rank of any kind. Neither could they take weapons. But the unavailability of flights did give Paula a chance to pack decently—and gave Alex a chance to speak with Rose before he left.

Rose was clearly disgruntled. He'd never seen her less than cool, less than totally poised. She was suddenly unsure of Doris, who she now knew was Jennifer, even if she didn't know the whole story yet. She obviously wanted to believe, as Alex did, that Jennifer did not leave because she wanted to. At the same time that implied she was being forced, and that terrified her.

"I know you think of me as a kinky yet hip little old lady, but I used to date rich men in limousines and I know, from experience, they're not the kind of guys you play around with. They're serious—and sometimes dangerous."

"That's why I'm going to get her," he said.

After they arrived at their hotel in the French section of town, Paula was overwhelmed by the quaint beauty of the place. She'd started oohing and aahing on the plane as they made their final descent over waters of clear blue bordered with white sand beaches. "Look at this place! This place is awesome! I'm going to make John bring me here," she was saying.

Alex was busy opening his suitcase. He pulled out his binoculars, camera and film. He dug around in it and finally produced a Taser, a nonlethal weapon that produced a five-second-long electric shock. It could render a person helpless for that long, and the shock could be reengaged for another five seconds, if necessary. He had hidden it in his checked baggage where, if it had been discovered, would only have been confiscated once he produced a badge. He could argue that it was part of his work gear and he forgot he even had it. It would go harder on a civilian, of course.

Having it and using it on this island would be a whole other story—one that a Nevada police officer's badge wouldn't easily solve.

"Oh, Alex, you are going to get us into such trouble."

"Only if I have to use it—and I won't use it unless I'm about to die."

"You know we're not supposed to—"

"The less you say out loud, the better."

So she pointed. *You. Me. The Finger.*

Then they went, posing as a couple on their honeymoon, to rent a boat. Finding the location of one of the richest estates on the island was no trouble at all. Nick Noble was anything but incognito. He was flamboyant and relished in being well known. He employed an entire staff of islanders.

Jennifer was bored senseless. How she had managed to lie around and soak up luxury with nothing to distract her but the occasional novel was now beyond her. No wonder she had spent so many hours primping and managing a near-perfect appearance—there had been little else to do! And she might have told herself that she always kept a job for the sake of her self-esteem and maybe medical benefits, but now she realized that without work to do, she would go crazy.

She napped, she swam, she walked the beach. She

read, she had a manicure and pedicure and a facial—all provided in the residence—and it soon became impossible for her to be still another second. Relaxing when one has earned a break, a rest, is one thing. Enforced relaxation, even in lavish comfort such as this, proved maddening.

Nick, she noticed, was not resting on his laurels. He was either at work in his study or on the phone—and when he was on the phone he was usually pacing. Now, with her mind turned toward self-preservation, she tried to pay attention to what he was saying, what he was doing—but he either closed the door or left the vicinity.

Barbara must certainly be equally bored because she seemed intent on playing lady of the manor and haranguing the staff. Nothing, it seemed, was folded quite right, prepared or served well enough, cleaned to her satisfaction, and no one was quick enough to carry out her demands. Jennifer stayed as far away as possible. If Barbara was at the pool, Jennifer went to the kitchen; if Barbara went to the kitchen, Jennifer went for a walk on the beach or to her room. They separated like oil and water.

If someone had suggested to her that she would suffer this feeling of listlessness and tedium a year ago or even two, Jennifer wouldn't have understood. She was always so busy just trying to hang on to some semblance of security, of order, that she hadn't realized it felt so much better to be *useful*. It had been such a wonderful accident, stumbling into that desert town, into the diner, where work was hard and steady. And then there were the acts of caring—taking a meal to a destitute elderly person, being a support to a young girl in need of a friend, walking an old dog. Doing something not for herself but for another somehow became more personally important than all the selfish indulgences of a lifetime.

She even began to envy the fishermen in the simple boats that she could see from the beach. She envied their industry, the fact that they had to work for the very food they fed their families.

As she looked back at the house from the water's edge, she saw that there was a man on the third-story veranda. Was someone always posted there? She had never noticed before. But the thing that really got her excited was a telescope, mounted on a tripod on the highest veranda. She went back to the house. At least there was something new to do.

It was Frank, one of Nick's employees from Florida, on the veranda. He was comfortable in his flowered shirt and silk shorts, enjoying the afternoon on his rattan chair, playing his Game Boy, his rifle and telescope nearby. Having an armed guard at the house was something completely new. Despite the fact that Nick always had at least two big guys at hand, there had always been an obvious absence of weapons. The Game Boy beeped as he played his game and he looked out from the veranda occasionally. "I certainly hope you're not planning to shoot anyone," she said.

He smiled and said, "Very doubtful."

"No one's going anyplace, you know," she said. "He has the passports."

"He's just being cautious." He went back to beeping on the Game Boy.

If Nick were hiding out, there were much better locations around the islands to do so. St. Martin was an island shared by the French and Dutch, known as the Friendly Island, a mere thirty-six square miles. This shared government was very American-friendly— American authorities would be treated with grave deference. This was not some shady little Caribbean Island where police or officials could be bought. Aside from the fact that he'd had this house here for ten years or more, Nick must be very confident that his affairs would soon be in order.

"Most people try to escape *to* places like this."

"I hear ya," he said.

"I saw the telescope from the beach. Can I look?"

"Help yourself."

She needed a little help to learn how to focus and sharpen the images, but she quickly found it easy to maneuver. It was amazing. She could not only see the little fishing boat offshore, she could almost count the bristles on the little old fisherman's chin. Over the wall of a neighboring house was a nude sunbather; a yacht slowly passed by and she zeroed in on the people on the deck, having a party. There were frequent speedboats roaring past. She could see the road over the wall on the far west side of the house, the continuation of that same road on the far east side. The old fisherman gathered up his net and started his motor to leave, while another fisherman was just coming around the bend.

"You have the best job in the house," she said.

"I do," he said. "Want to let me have a look for a minute?"

"Sure," she said, stepping back.

He took possession of the telescope, swerved left, then right, examined the water and various watercrafts, the neighbors, the side yards, the roads. "Looks good," he said, letting her look again.

"I'm assuming you have infrared lenses so this can be used at night."

"'Course."

"Have you looked at the stars?"

"Yep. And satellites."

She saw several different spots around the side of the property that were mostly out of sight. This place was not so secure, even with Frank up here. But then Jennifer was here because her friends had been threatened, and Barbara? Maybe Barbara was exactly where she wanted to be.

Then she saw them. A colorful speedboat out in the water with a couple lying on the front deck, making out. But not making out—pretending to make out while they also used cameras and binoculars to study the property. The woman lifted her head and the man turned his face toward the house. It was *them!* Alex and Paula! But what did they think they were going to do? A counter kidnapping? What good would that do? She couldn't take the chance that Nick would retaliate.

Then it came to her that if Nick were arrested, taken into custody, and it had nothing whatever to do with Jennifer, there would be nothing to fear.

She straightened slowly, arching her back as though

bending to the telescope had given her a backache. "If I come back up here tonight, will you let me try looking at some stars?"

"Sure. But I think tonight it might be Lou up here."

"He's a good guy," she said, taking her leave.

She tried to keep from scrambling down the stairs in excitement. She went looking for Barbara, but the house was big and madam was obviously busy with something. "Have you seen Mrs. Noble?" she asked a maid. Head-shaking answered her. "Have you seen Mrs. Noble?" she asked a houseboy, and again, head-shaking. From the looks on their faces, they didn't want to see her.

She knocked on Barbara's door.

"What is it?" she demanded sharply.

Jennifer slowly pushed open the door and found the woman reclining on the bed with a fashion magazine in her lap. "Barbara? Put on your sandals and come for a little walk on the beach with me."

"Hah. In your dreams. The beach is full of sand and bugs and *sun!*"

Jennifer would be disappointed in Nick if he didn't have at least a couple of listening devices in the house, if he was serious about keeping these women under watch twenty-four seven. So she made the expression on her face urgent and tilted her head several times toward the beach. But her voice she kept cajoling. "Come on, Barbara. You've been cooped up too long. You're going to get cabin fever!"

"Too bad," she said.

Jennifer pointed urgently at the beach. "Look, if

we're going to be kept in this place for an unknown length of time, let's at least try to get along."

She made a face, looking back at her magazine.

Jennifer jumped up and down, waved her arms, pointed to the beach and then said, as calmly as possible, "Come on. You'll love it. Five minutes, and if you don't love it, you can have me punished."

Finally, Barbara had a look on her face that she might be catching on. "Oh, that is too tempting to pass up. I love a good punishment."

"And you know how Nick loves it when his 'girls' are getting along," Jennifer said.

"Don't push your luck," said Barbara.

Jennifer tried to make small talk on the way out of the house and down the wooden stairs to the beach, but it was hard. And Barbara, wondering what was up, wasn't very responsive. Finally they reached the beach. "Come closer to the water," Jennifer urged. "In case these thugs who work for your husband have those long-distance listening devices."

"They probably do," she said. "Nick gives them free rein with their toys."

"Walk along the water's edge with me. So, you want to get out of here?"

"If I really wanted to go, I could go. It's not like we're locked in."

"Listen to me, Barbara, because this is your only chance. Whatever you know about his illegal dealings, he's having cleaned up as best he can while he's got you under lock and key. As soon as the coast is clear, he'll unlock the door and then you know what? He's going to drop you like a hot potato, take his prenup to court and cut you off without a dime. And it will be too late for you to leverage anything."

She turned in a huff, hands on hips, and stared at Jennifer. "And you know this *how?*"

Jennifer grabbed one of her arms at the elbow and pulled her along the waterline. "Well, for starters, he told me. You know, you're so damn busy fighting with him all the time, you've forgotten how to use your feminine wiles to get what you want. I can't believe you were a mistress!"

"So what are you saying?"

"You have to make a choice. Either you're going to give him up, or you're going to be given up. I'm only here because he threatened my friends. I don't know anything about his work."

Her mouth twisted in a wry smile. "Sometimes life just isn't fair," she said. "You know, one of the things he was always throwing in my face was that you *amused* him. You were *smart,* he said."

"Well, obviously not *that* smart."

"No kidding. You were doing the actual work, you know. It's the business property. The office space. He has five or six different property managers collecting rent for the same investment properties. You were just one of them."

As the facts became clear, so did Jennifer's eyes. Money laundering. Pouring money into those business accounts for business that wasn't actually taking place.

Barbara began to laugh. "That was just one of his schemes. I can't believe you never caught on. Smart. *Humph.*"

"Okay, look. You're obviously the smart one. The only one who knows where the bodies are buried. You have to decide. You going to give him up and salvage at least some of your lifestyle, or are you going to let him, as he so eloquently put it, shit-can you?"

Funny how that was the term that got Barbara's attention. She recognized it. From the look in her eyes, she now believed that Nick had told Jennifer that was his plan. She'd heard him use the term before and it never failed to bring the desired results.

"I can get you out of here," Jennifer said. "If you leave this house and get hooked up with the FBI, you can tell them what you know before he's done cleaning up his mess. And then he gets arrested, and instead of getting dumped with nothing, you can at least have whatever is left after they seize all of his ill-gotten gains."

"I don't have a *passport,* you dumb bunny!"

"Oh, Barbara, I'm pretty sure they'll come to you," she said with a smile.

"Well…"

She turned Barbara around, heading back toward the house. "It's your only chance."

"I have a feeling you just want him for yourself," Barbara said.

"Oh, Barbara, I wondered. You love him."

"No. No, I hate him. But I didn't want my marriage to be over."

"I don't want him," Jennifer said. And then came the lie that would send Barbara to the feds. "But he wants me. And he's not going to let me go."

They were at the water's edge, in front of the house. She faced the house and waved at Frank. Frank waved back.

"I'm going to go up there tonight, and whoever is on watch is going to let me use that telescope to see the stars. I'll distract him. You go around the house to the road out front. Someone will pick you up."

"Who?"

"Just trust me, they're watching. What's a good time? Eleven?"

"Sure. Fine. But how are you going to—"

"Now we're going to do some exercises. Okay? Watch me." She spread her legs out, bent at the waist and stretched her arm left, then right. She did this again and again, pointing at the sides of the house. "Come on," she told Barbara.

"Jesus, I think you're a nutcase," the woman said, but she complied.

After about ten of the right-left stretches, Jennifer straightened and said, "Okay, eleven jumping jacks. Exactly. Ready? One, two, three…"

They stopped, still facing the house, and did more right-left stretches. Then stopped and did exactly eleven jumping jacks. Jennifer looked up and saw that Frank was quite enjoying the exercises.

"Have you lost your mind?" Barbara asked her.

"If this doesn't work, I have given someone way too much credit," she said, finally determining that if they didn't get it by now, they weren't going to.

"Tonight, at eleven, I'll be on the veranda. Leave. Go

either left or right around the house and out to the road in front and start walking toward town. And good luck, Barbara."

"Yeah," she said, heading toward the house.

"Really. I mean it."

Barbara turned around, walking backward for a moment as she looked at Jennifer. There were tears in her eyes.

Jennifer did her part, going to the veranda and using a little of her flirtatious skills to get Lou to let her look through the telescope, but she wasn't up there long, and although she tried to look at the sides of the house as well, she never saw Barbara. It occurred to her that the woman could have gone straight to Nick and sold her out.

At eleven-thirty she went to bed, but it seemed like hours before she slept, and when she did, she dreamt of the bighorns and the lambs. She was up at dawn, but stayed in her room, where breakfast was brought to her. She ate on the veranda, watching the sea. There were the fishermen and the occasional pleasure boat, but no sign of the boat that had carried Paula and Alex the day before.

At nine-twenty all hell broke loose. There was shouting, running through the halls, doors slamming. Jennifer opened her bedroom door. It was the household staff and Nick's men doing the running and door slamming, but downstairs she could hear the booming, angry voice of Nick.

"Where the hell is she? You better find her or all youse asses is grass, you hear that? I mean it."

The voice was getting closer as he was coming up the stairs. He saw Jennifer standing in her opened door. "Where the hell is she?" he demanded.

"Who?"

"Your new best friend, Barbara? I wondered what the two of youse was up to, out there on the beach! I guess we know now!"

Years of being under complete control, knowing what to say and when to say it, didn't fail her now. She feigned confusion. "Nick, what are you talking about?"

"She's *gone!*" he shouted.

"Did you check the pool house? The beach?"

He grabbed the front of her peignoir and scrunched it up in his hands, bringing her nose to nose with him. "If this is your doing, you're gonna be so sorry, baby."

"Nick," she said, "if it were my doing, *I'd* be gone. Not Barbara."

He shook her off. "Pack your things," he demanded.

It was four hours before Nick had himself convinced that Barbara was not somewhere on the property, but really gone. He secured a private jet to take them off St. Martin and they were soon on their way to the airport. He handed Jennifer her passport and said, "You know how to act."

"I know," she said with a sinking heart. No way the FBI could act fast enough to turn Barbara's information into an arrest in a few hours. "Where are we going now?" she asked.

"The less you know, the less you have to worry about."

They got out of the car at L'Espérance Grand Case Airport, leaving Lou, Jesse and Frank to worry about their luggage. This wasn't the international airport, but a regional airport—for inter-island travel. The international airport was on the Dutch side of the island. So, either they weren't going far, or he had another transfer or change of destination on his mind. Who knew where she might end up?

He grabbed her hand to pull her into the airport. "Nick, don't," she said, resisting. "I'm not going. This doesn't have anything to do with me."

"Don't fool around with me—I'm in no mood."

"I'm no threat to you. I don't know anything."

"You're coming with me, and if you argue, I'm gonna—"

"Yeah, you're going to terrorize little old ladies and teenage girls. We're going to have to take our chances. I can't let you hide me on some isolated little island—one you might never leave!"

"You're coming with—"

"Nick!" They both turned to see Alex coming rapidly toward them. "Let her go! She doesn't want to go with you!"

"Alex," she cried, reaching toward him with her free hand. But Nick wouldn't let go. He was pulling her into the small building.

"Lou!" Nick called. "Frank!"

The big men left the luggage sitting on the curb and ran to their boss, arriving at about the same time Alex did. There were suddenly four men surrounding Jennifer.

Jennifer's wrists were in a lock—Lou had one and Nick the other. Alex took a swing at one of them, but he was grabbed in a bear hug. Paula was watching this

from just a few feet away, because she had convinced
Alex that she should carry the Taser, that she was the
more stable of the two of them. She was going to use it
on someone, she was just trying to decide who. If one
of the big guys went down, she could help Alex wres-
tle Jennifer away from the remaining two men. They
were past caring if Nick got away—let him be the FBI's
problem.

Jennifer screamed; a couple of island police officers
from inside the airport came jogging toward them.
Paula's moment of opportunity was passing. She fixed
the red dot from the Taser on Lou's back and pulled the
trigger. The darts attached to wires shot out of the Taser,
but Lou moved just as Frank flipped Alex around. The
Taser got Alex right in the butt. He went stiff and fell,
the jolt rendering him completely useless. In the five
seconds the electric shock lasted, Nick, Lou and Frank
dragged Jennifer into the terminal.

Alex rolled over with a groan. "Oh, jeez, Alex,"
Paula said, trying to get the darts disengaged. Before
she could complete that process, they were hoisted to
their feet by a couple of island cops.

"Don't let them get her on the plane," he said weakly.

Alex and Paula had their hands pulled behind their
backs like common criminals, and the Taser darts were
pulled none too gently from his behind and confiscated.
"They're not going anywhere," Paula said, looking inside the terminal to see the party of four detained by uniformed guards. Standing off to the side, wearing his
signature black pants, thick-soled shoes and thin tie,
was Dobbs. "Never thought I'd be happy to see him."

Alex looked at her. "You shot me in the *butt!*"

"Sorry," she said. "I'm going to have to practice up on that thing."

"You shot me in the *butt!*"

They were being roughly pulled toward a police vehicle. "What did I tell you, Alex. You. Me. Screwed."

The next twenty-four hours were filled with recriminations toward Alex and Paula. There were a lot of unhappy people around. The FBI was not happy with them, even though they had notified their local bureau office that they were going to try to bring Jennifer home. The island police were very unhappy that a weapon—even though it was a nonlethal weapon—had been discharged at the airport. Sergeant Monroe was rather looking forward to chewing their asses in person when they got home.

Although they didn't have to endure his recriminations, Nick was understandably upset. Dobbs had convinced the local constables to detain him until it could be determined that Barbara's evidence would indict him of federal crimes punishable in the United States, to which the kidnapping of Barbara and Jennifer could possibly be added. And given his ease with travel, bail was not a possibility. The law enforcement of St. Martin was most cooperative.

It turned out the only person genuinely happy with Alex and Paula was Jennifer, with whom they were reunited the next day.

Of course, Paula may as well have been invisible. They met outside the local courthouse; Jennifer flew

into Alex's arms and met his lips with overwhelming relief and hunger. He held her clear off the ground as he
devoured her mouth. Tears ran freely down her cheeks,
and his breath was ragged as he fought his own emotional urges. And this went on, and on, and on...

"Okay, yeah, ah, you're welcome," Paula said.

Yet they kissed. And kissed. They broke apart only long
enough for Jennifer to say tearfully, "You *came* for me!"

"You think I could let you go?"

"You believed in me!"

"I'm in love with you. It wasn't a temporary thing."

"I was so afraid I'd never see you again!"

"Okay, guys," Paula said. "That should do it, huh?"

Yet they kissed again and again.

Paula made a sound of impatience and turned away.
"I'm getting a cab," she yelled. "I'm going to the airport! You can stand there and eat each other alive or
come with me!"

They turned reluctantly in her direction, but their
eyes were still on each other, their arms around each
other's waist.

Paula hailed a cab and instructed the driver to take
them to Princess Juliana International Airport. Then
she said to Alex and Jennifer, "Do not sit with me on
the plane."

They both gave her brief, weak smiles and then went
right back to kissing in the back of the cab.

"Because that's why," Paula said.

The flight was long, but of course the reunited lov-
ers didn't care. Jennifer's welcome back to Boulder

City was heartwarming—Adolfo and Buzz threw a little last-minute party for her at the diner the first night she was back. Even though they weren't sure what was to become of Nick Noble until indictments were filed in court in Miami, it appeared that the only role Jennifer might have in his life would be that of witness for the prosecution. And with the way the court moved, that could be years away. But everyone was there to find out who she really was, and what dramatic story had brought her to them.

Someone was missing from the celebration, however.

"Why isn't Hedda here?" she asked Buzz.

"I thought she was coming. She just hasn't been herself since you left—but now you're back, I'm sure she'll be fine."

"Do you think maybe she went home to get Joey?"

"Probably," he said.

But another hour passed with no sign of Hedda. Jennifer could have asked someone to go check on her, but her house was close to the diner. She ducked out and walked quickly in the direction of Hedda's house. Daylight lasted a long time now and the temperature was barely dropping.

She found the girl sitting in the opened front door, her feet on the steps. She was crying.

"Hedda?"

"I'm so glad you're back," she said.

Jennifer went to her. "What's the matter, kiddo?"

"We had some trouble when you were gone. My mom—she got in an accident."

"Oh, no!"

"No one was hurt."

"Oh! Thank God!"

"But she was DUI." She shrugged. "I guess I always knew that was going to happen someday."

"Oh, honey," she said, realizing Hedda had told no one. She wasn't just out of sorts because Jennifer was gone—she had this huge trauma, and bore the weight of it alone. "Didn't you tell even Buzz? He would have helped you!"

"It's no fun always needing help."

"Oh, kiddo, I'm so sorry. Where is she now?"

"Well, that casino she worked for, they have real good benefits. She's in treatment. It's probably going to be a month. Maybe longer."

"And where's Joey?"

"They took him," she said, breaking down. "They're going to get his grandparents to come for him." She rested her head on her knees and just let it go.

"I know this hurts like mad right now—but this is going to work out for the best. Especially if your mom somehow gets better."

"I haven't even seen her. I talked to her, you know?"

"What did she say you were to do?"

Hedda chewed her lip and raised her watery eyes upward. "She said, 'Why don't you just go live with your precious *Doris!*'"

Jennifer smiled a small smile. She put the palm of her hand against Hedda's damp cheek and said, "I think that can be arranged. That can most definitely be arranged."

One Year Later

There was too much excitement in the air for anyone to sleep in. It was graduation day. Hedda was the first one up to let Jeb, the puppy, outside. The sun was barely rising. Jennifer couldn't just lie there quietly. Even though she made a few grumbling noises about early risers, she was grateful she could finally get out of bed. In less than five minutes they were dressed and banging on Alex's door, getting him up for a ride.

"Do you think he'll be mad?" Hedda asked.

"If he is, he'll get over it fast. Any day now, we'll have lambs."

"What if Jeb barks at them?"

"Then you have to take him around the block. We don't want a stampede."

"You won't bark, will you, buddy? That's a good boy."

Alex answered the door fully dressed, newspaper in hand. "I guess no one felt like sleeping in."

"Not today," Jennifer said. "Get your bike."

Within minutes they were off in the direction of the park where the bighorns grazed. They looked every bit the all-American family—but things hadn't been easy.

A year ago Hedda had moved in with Jennifer. The first hard pill to swallow had been Joey—his grandparents came from Tucson to fetch him from Child Protective Services and took him home without so much as a goodbye to Hedda. It devastated her. But a few letters and phone calls later, a plan for visits was established, and while difficult at first, everyone settled into the routine and enjoyed their time together. Most often, Hedda flew to Tucson, a quick and inexpensive trip, but occasionally Joey's grandparents brought him to Nevada for a visit. Today marked one of those times—they were coming to Hedda's high school graduation. Afterward, the seniors would have their all-night party, and on Sunday there would be a big open house at the Garcias'.

Then there was Sylvia—who put in an appearance now and then, sometimes sober, sometimes not. But even if the disappointment lingered, the danger was past—Joey's grandparents had filed for custody and Hedda, being almost eighteen, was not obligated to stay in the custody of her mother. Learning to cope sanely with the ups and downs of growing up with an alcoholic was growing easier for Hedda with the help of a support group known as Alateen.

And of course there was Alice—who had not waited long before following Louise. Saying goodbye to her took its toll on everyone, but no one grieved as hard as Jennifer. Everyone from Buzz to Rose thought she should get another dog right away, but she insisted she needed time to think about that, and time to miss her friend. So it was just recently that Alex and Hedda, taking matters into their own hands, brought Jeb to her. "I can't go away to school and leave you with just Alex and Rose," Hedda said.

But until Hedda left, Jeb was her baby. He clung to her, chewed her shoes and socks, slept in her bed when he got too fussy in the kennel, and wouldn't be still for anyone else.

"I'm going to be taking care of someone else's dog again," Jennifer said.

So they cried a lot that first year together, but laughed a lot, as well. Rose would pop over and find Jennifer and Hedda on the sofa holding each other, tears flowing over Joey or Alice or even Sylvia, and she would say, "Building an awful damn lot of character around here again." And the tears would melt into laughter.

Adjustment problems came and went, and all through that year they kept close tabs on the indictment and prosecution of Nick Noble. Numerous felony counts were leveled by the federal government and it looked as if he was going away for a long time. His allies vanished as his assets were frozen, likely to be seized with his convictions. And Barbara didn't make out too well; she had counted on a big settlement out of Nick's wealth, and it seemed she had very little she could call her own.

But Jennifer was fine. Besides some jewelry, nothing of her savings or investments could be linked to any ill-gotten gains. Her short-term plans for that money were to supplement her diner income and make sure that Hedda, already an academic-scholarship recipient, had no shortfall of money for college.

Jeb, three months old and already fourteen pounds, rode in the basket on Hedda's bike, and when they got to the park the bighorns were already there, complete with a new flock of lambs. Jeb made a puppyish gurgling growl and Hedda clamped a gentle hand over his snout and told him to be a gentleman.

"How many do you count?" Jennifer asked her.

"Five," she said. "No, six."

"Doesn't it make you feel brand new to see the lambs in spring? It's like life is starting today, and is just going to get better and better. God, I love my life!" Jennifer said.

Hedda made a strange sound and buried her face in Jeb's fur.

"Don't you dare start crying! We're not crying today! We have a million great surprises ready for you!"

She lifted her head, her eyes glistening. "You'd better give me one now," she said. "I'm feeling a little sentimental, not to mention freaked out about college."

"Okay. One. Just before you go to school, we're going to combine your going-away party with a wedding reception."

"Oh, really?" she said. "Am I getting married?"

"I don't think so," Alex said. "Not till you're twenty-seven. But we are. We thought we'd better make it legal since our chaperone is going to be away so much."

"Wow," she said, her eyes brightening. "Are you getting a big ring?"

"No, honey," she said. "I'm all done with big rings. I'm getting a big man."

Special 10th-Anniversary Edition

KATHERINE STONE

PEARL MOON

It's the year before Hong Kong's reversion to Chinese control—
a year of danger, betrayal...and romance. Allison Whitaker
and Maylene Kwan, two sisters who don't know of each other's
existence, meet there for the first time. They also meet two
extraordinary men: aristocratic and powerful James Drake,
developer of luxury hotels, with whom Allison falls in love, and
Sam Coulter, the Texan builder who captures Maylene's heart.

"A can't-miss combination of multigenerational romance and
international suspense, financial rivalry and family secrets."
—*Booklist*

Available the first week of May 2005
wherever paperbacks are sold!

www.MIRABooks.com

MKS2185

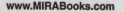

If you enjoyed what you just read,
then we've got an offer you can't resist!

Take 2 bestselling novels FREE!
Plus get a FREE surprise gift!

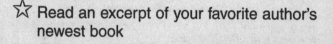

Robyn Carr

66940 JUST OVER THE MOUNTAIN	___ $6.50 U.S.	___ $7.99 CAN.
66704 DOWN BY THE RIVER	___ $6.50 U.S.	___ $7.99 CAN.
66609 DEEP IN THE VALLEY	___ $5.99 U.S.	___ $6.99 CAN.

(limited quantities available)

TOTAL AMOUNT	$_____
POSTAGE & HANDLING	$_____
($1.00 FOR 1 BOOK, 50¢ for each additional)	
APPLICABLE TAXES*	$_____
TOTAL PAYABLE	$_____

(check or money order—please do not send cash)

To order, complete this form and send it, along with a check or money order for the total above, payable to MIRA Books, to: **In the U.S.:** 3010 Walden Avenue, P.O. Box 9077, Buffalo, NY 14269-9077; **In Canada:** P.O. Box 636, Fort Erie, Ontario, L2A 5X3.

Name: _____
Address: _____ City: _____
State/Prov.: _____ Zip/Postal Code: _____
Account Number (if applicable): _____

075 CSAS

*New York residents remit applicable sales taxes.
*Canadian residents remit applicable GST and provincial taxes.

MIRA®

www.MIRABooks.com   MRC0505BL